PRAISE FOR PAUL FINCH

'Wonderfully dark and peppered with grim humour.
Finch is a born storyteller and writes with the authentic
voice of the ex-copper he is.'
PETER JAMES

'Edge-of-the-seat reading . . . formidable – a British
Alex Cross.'
SUN

'An ingenious and original plot. Compulsive reading.'
RACHEL ABBOTT

'As good as I expected from Paul Finch. Relentlessly
action-packed, breathless in its finale, Paul expertly weaves
a trail through the North's dark underbelly.'
NEIL WHITE

'A deliciously twisted and fiendish set of murders
and a great pairing of detectives.'
STAV SHEREZ

'Avon's big star . . . part edge-of-the-seat, part
hide-behind-the-sofa!'
THE BOOKSELLER

'An explosive thriller that will leave you
completely hooked.'
WE LOVE THIS BOOK

D0242576

Paul Finch is a former cop and journalist, now turned full-time writer. He cut his literary teeth penning episodes of the British TV crime drama, *The Bill*, and has written extensively in the field of children's animation. However, he is probably best known for his work in thrillers and crime. His first three novels in the Detective Sergeant Heckenburg series all attained 'bestseller' status, while *Strangers*, which introduced a new hero in Detective Constable Lucy Clayburn, became an official *Sunday Times* top 10 bestseller in its first month of publication.

Paul lives in Lancashire, UK, with his wife Cathy. His website can be found at www.paulfinchauthor.com, his blog at www.paulfinch-writer.blogspot.co.uk, and he can be followed on Twitter as @paulfinchauthor.

By the same author:

Stolen
PAUL FINCH

avon.

Published by AVON
A division of HarperCollins*Publishers* Ltd
1 London Bridge Street
London SE1 9GF

www.harpercollins.co.uk

A Paperback Original 2019

1

First published in Great Britain by HarperCollins*Publishers* 2019

A catalogue copy of this book is available from the British Library.

ISBN: 978-0-00-824401-9

Typeset in Sabon LT Std by Palimpsest Book Production Limited, Falkirk, Stirlingshire
Printed and bound in UK by CPI Group (UK) Ltd, Croydon CR0 4YY

MIX
Paper from
responsible sources
FSC **FSC™ C007454**
www.fsc.org

This book is produced from independently certified FSC™ paper
to ensure responsible forest management.

For more information visit: www.harpercollins.co.uk/green

For my wife, Catherine,
always my strong right arm.

Prologue

The Hollinbrook estate, in Crowley, was as suburban as they came.

Not rich, but the gardens were neat, tidy, their lawns smoothly mown if not expansive. The cars on the drives were mainly family affairs, some a little beaten-up, all implying middle-income rather than wealth. But if it wasn't hugely prosperous, at least the Hollinbrook had the air of safety. It might be part of Greater Manchester's sprawling conurbation, but Hollinbrook was peaceful and quiet, a sedate backwater, where children could play unsupervised, and where pensioners like Harry Hopkins could take their dogs out for a late evening stroll in full confidence that nothing bad would happen to them.

Not that this would normally have been an issue for Harry. A former collier, he'd been a burly bloke in his youth, and though seventy-seven now, he still had a bluff, rugged aura. In *his* day, 'graft' had been a word that meant something: hot sweat, aching muscles, hands cut and callused, a body shrouded black with coal-dust. And none of it a source of complaint – because that was your job, your life, that was what you did to put food on the table.

1

A quarter of a century had passed since Hollinbrook Pit had closed, but Harry wasn't the sole relic of those arduous days. He still lived at No. 8, Atkinson Row, the only line of dwellings that hadn't been bulldozed in the late 1990s, when they'd finally started developing the vast brownfield site. This was partly because Atkinson Row had never looked out of place in the proposed new townscape. Its houses were more than serviceable, a terraced row of traditional two-up-two-downs, but with solid roofs, secure foundations and no hint of subsidence. These days they were downright attractive, their brickwork repointed and whitewashed, new pipes and gutters fitted, each with its own little garden at the back instead of a tiny yard and outdoor privy. They were still referred to locally as the 'Pit Cottages', even though Harry was the only ex-pitman living there. He had lived alone for the last nine years, since Ada had passed, but his property was the smartest of the lot, with a box of flowers under the front window, and his front door painted canary-yellow.

It was just after ten o'clock when Harry closed this handsome door behind him, the lock catching. Milly, his small Pekingese, waited patiently. She was thirteen now, tubby, grey at the jowls and bandy-legged. But she was an affectionate little soul who liked nothing better than an idle wander with her master. Harry buttoned up his overcoat, tugged his trilby down at the front and drew on his fingerless gloves. It was September, and the searing heat of August had noticeably diminished. Nights were cool, and there was an edge to the breeze.

They set off up the road together, Milly snuffling at the base of every streetlight, lapping at the occasional puddle left over from the afternoon rain, despite Harry's gruff admonitions. They turned right at the top of the road, following their usual route.

Though it wasn't terribly late, it was midweek, so each

street they came to was bare of life: Candlemaker Avenue, Rotherwood Drive, Hornby Crescent, Billington Grove. They even *sounded* suburban, and they certainly looked the part: more of those manicured front gardens, rockeries, shrubbery. It was a far cry from the narrow terraced streets of Harry's day. But in general, he had to concede that things tended to change for the better. It was too easy to get dewy-eyed about the past, especially if you hadn't been part of it.

Most windows were now curtained, only soft lamplight filtering through, though now and then he passed an open bedroom window, and heard music playing or what sounded like a TV programme. That was something that had *not* changed for the better, in Harry's opinion: kids having all that kit in their bedrooms when they should be out, running around. Not that he would really have expected that at this late hour, of course.

And not when there was that other thing supposedly keeping them indoors.

The black van.

By instinct, Harry tightened his grip on the lead, drawing Milly closer. The old girl wasn't too worried. She didn't exactly scurry these days.

The black van, though . . .

Harry didn't know if it was one of these so-called urban legends. But if it was, he'd only heard about it recently. It had been down at the bookies a couple of weeks ago.

'Whenever you're walking your Milly, Harry . . . keep your eye out for this black transit van. It's touring the neighbourhoods late at night. I'm not sure what it's supposed to be up to . . . but you can guarantee it'll be no good.'

'Well, if you don't know what it's up to, how do you know it's no good?' Harry had responded, puzzled.

A helpless shrug. 'I dunno, pal. People are just saying it.'

'Oh . . . *must* be true then.'

But now that he was out here on the road alone, and it was past ten o'clock, Harry didn't feel quite so scathing. He was sure the black van thing was a myth. Good God, there were black vans all over. But though certain parts of Crowley, like this, had been prettified in recent years, he couldn't deny that life wasn't as tranquil overall as it once had seemed. Not even in the shopping district where you saw homeless folk everywhere. That was a sad story, but it was a nuisance too. Some of them had mental health problems, some of them were drug addicts, and nearly all of them were beggars. That had been almost unknown during his youth, even though everyone had been considerably poorer back then.

Equally unknown had been this new level of nasty criminality. Harry had always fancied himself a rough customer, but he wouldn't go anywhere near the town centre pubs on a Friday or Saturday night, not these days. He much preferred The Horsehoe at the top end of the estate, even if it did have a reputation for being an old fellas' pub. Harry didn't mind. Anything was better than someone smashing a bottle over your head because you'd looked at them the wrong way, and then kicking your face as you lay on the floor. And it wasn't just the town centre either. There were plenty of housing estates around Crowley that were just as bad; run-down neighbourhoods like Hatchwood Green for example. Nearly everyone in those miserable districts was unemployed, which didn't help of course, though to Harry's mind it didn't excuse the wife-battering, the drunks sitting on doorsteps, the needles and condoms left in playground sandpits.

Harry knew all this went on because he knew men and women of his own age who were unfortunate enough to live in these areas, and they reported it every time he met them. But even the Hollinbrook wasn't as safe as it might appear. Not these days. It had been idyllic once, but slowly and subtly things had been changing as the villains had started to notice it. There were burglaries here now and occasional vehicle thefts. Prowlers had been reported, even some pets had allegedly gone missing.

And then, as he pondered this, he heard the scuff of what sounded like boot leather.

He glanced up and caught someone stepping out of sight.

Just ahead of him, on the other side of the road.

Harry faltered in his stride.

He almost stopped – before pressing on, grumbling to himself.

Highly likely his imagination had been running wild thanks to those worrying reflections. But he was now approaching the crossroads between Billington Grove and Bucks Lane, and it really *had* looked as if someone had just scampered away around the left-hand corner.

Big deal, he told himself. Was it an offence to walk home?

But actually it hadn't looked as if he'd just glimpsed someone walking home. It had looked as if they'd been standing watching him, and then had ducked away to avoid being seen. When he came level with Bucks Lane, he glanced left, not sure what he expected. Perhaps unsurprisingly, he saw nothing and no one – though that didn't mean there was nobody there, as whoever it was could have gone to ground in any one of the front gardens.

'Bloody hell, lad,' he muttered. 'You're letting these daft stories get to you.'

He trudged on past the junction, and only after a hundred yards glanced back, to ensure that no one was behind him.

No one was. At least, no one who was close by. But was that dark, diminutive shape back at the crossroads a figure? Standing there motionless? Staring after him?

Harry squinted. Perhaps it was another dog-walker? That wouldn't be unusual. Or some other innocent resident standing outside their house having a smoke? But if so, why did they seem so interested in him?

Unless they weren't. Unless there was no one there at all.

Harry couldn't be certain. Most likely, he was seeing things. Fading eyesight and substandard streetlighting were the probable explanation. But, determined to show that he wasn't concerned either way, he ambled casually on, turning left down Tottington Road, Milly toddling at his side. Everything along here was as it should be: cars in driveways, front lawns scattered with children's toys and occasional bits of garden furniture; typical end-of-summer scenery.

He looked back over his shoulder. The road was deserted.

Daft, he chided himself. If that had been some idiot waiting to jump him, he'd have done it back at the crossroads. Why would he be following?

Harry turned right onto Langtree Brow, and then right again into a ginnel. Here he halted, tall hedges on either side, as Milly squatted to do her business. After she was finished, he got a poop bag from his pocket, scooped it all up and tied the bag in a knot. More by instinct than design, he again glanced behind him. He was halfway along the ginnel, which ran for about seventy yards before crossing a narrow footbridge over the Manchester-to-Southport railway. The gap where it opened into Langtree Brow was empty, though why he'd thought it might not be eluded him.

He strode on, turning up his overcoat collar against the chill, depositing the poop bag in the next bin. Milly seemed happy, sniffing under the hedges, nothing troubling her.

They crossed the footbridge together, the railway cutting a strip of blackness beneath them. They were now at the furthest point from home, and Harry was ready to head back, his legs getting tired. Walking south along Rampton Road, he crossed the railway line again and then followed alongside it. The only sound was Milly's gentle panting and the clicking of Harry's leather soles on the damp pavement. Occasional gusts of wind whispered through the leafage in the gardens or moaned among the electric cables down in the cutting.

It was easy to feel alone at moments like this. And vulnerable.

He passed another couple of street-entrances on his right. The first led into Hopwood Lane, the second into Delamere Avenue. Again, no one was around, though, as it happened, halfway down Delamere a black van was parked up on the right.

Harry forced a chuckle, reminding himself that there was nothing unusual about that. He hadn't seen the van before and he'd walked past here a dozen times this last month alone, but that meant nothing.

He turned left onto Rose Street, now well on his way home, though this was always the least comforting part of the journey, because though there were houses on the left, Hollister Park stood to the right. It was nothing really – a miniature green space provided by the estate's original builders so the local kids would have somewhere to hang out. It had a playground, and lots of grass for football. Even so, it probably occupied no more than a handful of acres – though at this time of night it was an unlit void. There'd been some problems here during the summer, with teenagers gathering late on, drinking and shouting. But the police had been called, and that had been it.

Of course, that didn't mean there wasn't somebody there now, maybe just beyond the outer fringe of trees, keeping a silent, steady pace with Harry. Not that Harry knew what any would-be mugger would have to gain. It wasn't like he carried money when he was walking the dog, or wore an expensive watch, or even had a mobile phone (despite his daughter Janet's endless badgering that he acquire one).

Again, he was vexed with himself for even thinking this way. This was his home neighbourhood, the place he'd lived all his life. He'd seen whole families come and go, he'd seen houses come and go, hell . . . he'd seen the pit come and go.

And he was frightened? Seriously?

Even so, he crossed to the other side of the road, so that the wet, leafy blackness of the park wasn't directly at his shoulder. That wasn't a sign that he was scared, he told himself; it was simple common sense. But he was still relieved to come to the end of the road and turn down Bradley Way. When a quick backward glance showed a clump of thickets on the edge of the park shuddering as though someone concealed among them was moving, Harry forced another chuckle.

'Bloody breeze,' he mumbled.

There *was* a breeze. He wasn't making that up.

On Bradley Way, there was a minor incident when Harry glanced back and saw the headlights of a slow-moving vehicle only twenty yards to his rear.

He stumbled to a startled halt, at which point the vehicle, a large estate car, swung into the kerb to park. Harry continued to watch it even as he lurched on, until he blundered into a lamp-post. To the accompaniment of a faint, broken, rasping sound – what might have been muffled snickering laughter, though in truth was probably another breeze rattling the wet bushes – he hurried on, turning right into Malvern Avenue and then right again into Deerwood Close, where he stopped to get his breath and dab his forehead with a handkerchief.

It was okay, he told himself. He'd be home in a couple of minutes. He was almost there.

He glanced down at Milly, who'd craned her neck up to regard him curiously.

Even the bloody dog was wondering what was up with him.

Grim-faced, he crossed the road and turned onto Lodge Lane, and a few minutes later entered Atkinson Row at its bottom end. Harry could only feel relief as he wheezed his way along the pavement to his yellow front door. He inserted the key, looked to either side one last time – no one was anywhere in sight – and turned it. The door opened, and he stepped inside, Milly jumping over the step next to him. He wasn't telling anyone down the bookies about *this*, that was for sure: how he'd become unaccountably afraid while walking the dog.

No . . . 'afraid' was the wrong word. He'd been nervous, that was all. A tad nervous. And why wouldn't he be? Like it or not, he wasn't a young bucko any more. And there *were* bad things going on. It might be a thought to take their evening stroll a little earlier from now on.

Harry closed the door, threw the bolt and applied the safety-chain. He unfastened the dog's lead, and she trotted down the hall, turning into the living room, where the lights were still on and the television playing to itself.

Harry pulled his gloves off and took off his hat and coat, draping them over the newel post at the bottom of the banister. Milly meanwhile re-emerged from the living room and went through to the kitchen, which lay in darkness.

'What's up, lass . . . need a drink?' Harry followed her in, switching the light on.

As always, the kitchen was impeccably clean, everything put away, the linoleum floor swept, the worktops sparkling. The mug Harry had left beside the kettle before he'd gone out still waited for him. It contained a teabag, one and a half spoonfuls of sugar and the spoon itself, and only required him to flip the kettle on, which he now did.

Then he noticed that Milly hadn't touched her water-bowl.

9

Instead, she stood with rigid spine, staring at the back door.

'Something bothering you, lass?' he asked.

He leaned over the sink and looked out through the kitchen window. He had a light in the back garden, but it was motion-sensitive, and at present was off. That was a positive thing, because it meant there was no one trespassing. But it also meant that he couldn't see anything. Milly whimpered and pawed at the door.

'Nothing out there, lass . . . what is it, a cat?'

It couldn't have been that. If it had been, the light would have come on.

Harry leaned closer to the window, straining his eyes.

Gradually, the streetlighting seeping over the tops of the houses revealed the garden's basic dimensions. It wasn't large, about fifteen yards by ten, and mostly turfed, with the exception of a crazy-paved path running down the middle. To the right, where the coal-bunker had once stood, there was a brick-built dais – all Harry's own work – with stone vases on top, containing plants. He could see that much. He could also see the potting shed standing to the left of his back gate, which, painted canary-yellow like the front door, was also clearly visible.

But now that he was looking hard, there was something else.

The top of a tall vehicle stood on the other side of his gate.

Harry felt a stab of confusion – that thing hadn't been here when he'd left.

And then he got annoyed.

The Backs, as they called it, was a straight passage running along the rear of the terraced houses on Atkinson Row. It was little more than an access road; though narrow and unevenly cobbled, it was barely wide enough for vehicles, which meant that whoever had left this one here would be causing a massive obstruction – and right on the other side of the gate to No. 8. Harry wasn't even sure if he'd be able to get out there. He had no clue who the vehicle might belong to, though he had a notion that the Rodwells, the young couple next door, were a bit rum. Okay, they weren't lowlifes – they were teachers, apparently – but they'd had more than a few noisy barbecues in their garden during the summer months, which had gone on until late, and which they'd never offered apologies for. Even when they weren't having barbecues, their friends tended to come and go loudly. A couple of times, he'd heard the Rodwells themselves squabbling through the dividing wall between his bedroom and theirs. So it wouldn't be unlike them, or someone they knew, to have thoughtlessly left a vehicle in such an inconvenient place.

Grumpily, all previous concerns forgotten – because one thing you could never do was challenge Harry Hopkins in his own home – he unlocked the back door and stepped out. The garden light came on, and there was no mistake: a large, dark vehicle was parked just the other side of his back wall. He stumped along the path, Milly trotting inquisitively behind him, undid the bolts and yanked the gate open – to find a vehicle there so large that it literally filled the alley. Though its rear end was close to his gate, perhaps a yard to his left, there was minimal room to manoeuvre; less than a foot's clearance separated its offside flank from his wall, which meant that he could only move along it if he slithered sideways.

But none of that mattered as much as the kind of vehicle it was.

A van.

A black transit van.

Fleeting pinpricks of sweat appeared on Harry's brow; it was several seconds before he could even engage his voice.

'Okay . . . okay,' he grunted to himself.

11

This was a challenge, and no mistake – but there was no need to get jumpy. He'd already worked out what the problem was here: the Rodwells and their inconsiderate friends.

Thankfully, he hadn't changed his shoes for slippers yet, so the fact there'd likely be lots of dirty puddles out there wasn't a problem. He stepped from his gate and, as the rear of the van was nearest, edged in that direction first. For some reason, Milly hung back in the gateway. But Harry barely noticed, his temper continuing to fray as he thought more and more about the Rodwells and their loutish, snot-nosed pals. He noticed that the van wasn't parked across *their* gate. When he reached the back of it, its rear doors were both closed, doubtless locked.

Moving to the vehicle's nearside and finding that the passage on that side was wider by several inches, he sidled along it more quickly, though his feet sloshed through inches of mucky water. When he got to the front, there was nobody inside the cab. Both the front doors were also probably locked, but when Harry put his hand down to the radiator grille, warmth exuded from it. As he'd suspected, the damn thing had only recently arrived.

The more he looked at it now, the more he thought it was dark-blue rather than black, which was a relief in a silly kind of way. But that didn't stop it being any less of a nuisance.

He was now well positioned to view the rear of the Rodwells' house. There were no lights on at the back, but there could be at the front. Harry would need to go back through his house to check.

His slid along the vehicle's nearside, circling its rear end towards his own gate – and there stopped in surprise. The left of the van's two rear doors now stood open.

Harry was stumped.

Could it have been the wind? No, that was preposterous. There was the odd gust tonight, but nothing like sufficient to open a vehicle door, even if that door had been left ajar, which he was damn sure this one hadn't.

So – had someone inside this van just climbed out?

He glanced over his shoulder, but the alley dwindled away in a straight line until it joined with the next street. There was no one there.

'What the bloody hell?' he muttered.

He leaned forward, poking his nose into the van's interior. It was too dark to see anything, but now he wondered if that was a faint rustle of cloth he was hearing.

'Is someone . . . someone in here . . .?'

Two hands in black leather gloves shot out of the darkness, gripping him by the cardigan collar.

He was yanked forward with tremendous force, smashing both kneecaps against the van's rear bumper. The material of his trouser legs hooked on jagged metal, briefly anchoring him in place, allowing him to splay his arms out and grab at the door-frame on one side and the closed door on the other, wedging himself. As his shock ebbed, he began resisting, pushing backward, but those gloved hands were strong, and they dragged at him all the harder. Harry travelled forward again, feet leaving the ground, the material of his trousers ripping, along with the flesh underneath.

As he shouted in pain, one of the hands released his collar and slapped palm-first across his mouth. Then there was a thundering impact on the back of Harry's head.

His world spun as his hands slipped loose and he slumped forward. Somewhere, there was a frantic yipping – was it Milly?

Whoever had hit Harry from behind now wrapped both arms around Harry's thighs, and lifted him bodily, feeding him forward into the van's interior. The person already in there continued to lug him.

The next thing Harry knew, though he was too groggy to

make sense of it, he was lying in oily darkness, face-down on corrugated metal. As if that wasn't enough, someone knelt on the middle of his back, pinning him with their full weight. And still that yipping went on, though it turned into a squeal of fright as a bundle of fur and paws was flung in alongside him. With an echoing *CLANG!*, the door slammed shut, and blackness descended.

The back of Harry's head throbbed appallingly; hot fluid leaked through his thinning hair. Milly grizzled and snarled alongside him. When he attempted to speak – absurdly, it was to try and calm the dog – it came out a spittle-clotted burble. His captor responded by shifting one of his knife-like knees from the middle of Harry's spine to the back of his head, pressing it down sideways, which intensified the raw, stinging pain. The old man yelped aloud, but it was lost as the vehicle rumbled to life and, with a shudder-inducing growl, accelerated away along the Backs.

Chapter 1

The men began arriving shortly after ten o'clock that night. At least, Lucy assumed they would all be men. The intelligence suggested that, and while she wasn't so naïve as to believe that casual cruelty was solely a male preserve, this particular business, as well as being totally disgusting, just seemed so childishly laddish that she couldn't picture any of the female offenders she'd arrested over the years participating willingly.

'All units, we're on,' she said into her radio. 'But sit tight . . . wait for the order.'

From where she was concealed in the woodland hide, just beyond the cover of the trees, Lucy had a clear view of the rutted track leading to the farm cottage. Over at the point where it joined Wellspring Lane, the gateman was busy admitting a succession of vans and cars, which now passed within seventy yards of her position, travelling slowly in cavalcade. Already she could hear the yipping and yelping of the dogs caged in their boots.

Geraldson, the RSPCA inspector, dabbed with a handkerchief at the sweat glinting on his brow. He was young and nervous.

'Is there a black van out there?' His voice was querulous.

'Even if there is, it won't necessarily be the one that's been abducting pets,' Lucy replied. 'These are all paying participants. They'll have their own animals.'

'So . . . when do we move?'

'Not until it gets going.' Lucy – Detective Constable Lucy Clayburn – continued to watch through her night-vision scope but reached out a hand and squeezed his shoulder with a firm, hopefully reassuring grip. 'Don't worry, we've got this.'

'There'll be some rough customers.'

'That's why we've got the Tactical Aid Unit with us. They're mostly ex-military. They like nothing better than a ruckus.'

Geraldson nodded and smiled, eyes gleaming wetly as more headlights rolled across the hide, shining fleetingly on his face.

By Lucy's estimation, about fourteen vehicles had now arrived at the cottage. Each one would likely be carrying more than one dog. So that would be twenty-eight animals at least, not counting any that were already being kept on site. The RSPCA were anticipating thirty-two in total, which would provide a straightforward knock-out contest. The members of this ring were clearly anticipating a long night.

As the vehicles pulled up haphazardly in the farmyard, a bulb sprang to life outside the ramshackle building to which it was attached, and a man slouched out. He was heavy-set and bearded, in a ragged green sweater and khaki pants. One by one, the parked vehicles opened, and men disgorged from them: generally at least two, sometimes as many as five. Like the guy from the cottage – whom Lucy had already identified as Les Mahoney – they mostly wore outdoor-type clothing: khaki, camouflage fatigues and such, though there were a few leather jackets among them, and a bit of oily denim.

16

'Christ,' Geraldson breathed. 'There's more than I expected.'

'We'll be fine,' Lucy replied.

As a rule, when you were facing big numbers, quite a few of them weren't looking for legal entanglements and would scarper at the first opportunity. That was when they were most vulnerable; all you had to do was pick them off. Though, looking at these guys – and she turned the super-zoom dial on her scope – there might be as many fighters as runners. She saw shaved heads, scarred faces, scuzzy tattoos. For once she was glad the sixty officers from the TAU were parked in a layby in their troop-carriers a little way down Wellspring Lane.

She continued to observe the men as they greeted each other with high fives and bear-hugs, before swaggering over to Mahoney and thrusting at him the wads of banknotes that made up their admission fees.

Another cop came into the hide behind her. It was PC Malcolm Peabody, once Lucy's probationer when she too had been in uniform. He was still only young, but a tall, rangy lad, with short red hair, a freckled face and jug-handle ears. Currently, he wore heavy-duty body-armour, plus a ballistics helmet with its visor raised and strap tight under his chin.

'Sergeant Frobisher says everyone's in position,' he said quietly.

'Everyone except you, Malcolm,' Lucy replied, thinking that if it suddenly kicked off, she didn't want handy lads like Peabody anywhere other than the front line. 'There's not enough space for all of us in here. Go back to your LUP and stay sharp.'

Peabody nodded and stooped back out through the low, narrow entrance.

None of them knew what the hide had originally been constructed for. It might indeed have been a wildlife observation point in the past. But it made a perfect OP for today: a flimsy, flat-roofed wooden hut, partly dug into the ground so it had an earthen floor, its exterior covered with vegetation, which, at the tail-end of summer, partly obscured the horizontal viewing port at the front – partly, but not completely.

Its interior was so restricted that it could only contain two with any comfort. But it gave an excellent view of the farm cottage, some fifty yards beyond the trees, and the open grassland to the east of it, where at this hour nothing stirred save a couple of tethered ponies munching the cud.

An increasingly excited canine yelping drew Lucy's attention back to the cottage, where the rear doors to vehicles were now being opened and muzzled dogs brought out on chain leashes. Even through the zoom-lens of her scope, and with the whole of the farmyard area lit up, many of them were already so horribly scarred from battles past that their breeds were unidentifiable, but by their lean, squat, muscular frames she reckoned they'd be fighting species of old: pit bulls, Staffies and the like, an impression enhanced by the thick muzzles they wore, and their steel-studded leather harnesses.

Lucy shook her head.

Mahoney now walked across the farmyard, his guests following, though they kept their four-footed charges well apart from each other. As most of these animals, if not all, had been trained through years of brutal abuse to despise other dogs on sight, they were already snarling and rearing, having to be forcibly restrained.

Geraldson watched through a pair of binoculars.

'Savages,' he whispered.

'Yeah, well, don't worry,' Lucy replied. 'Tonight, *they're* going to learn what it means to be chained and caged.'

At the other side of the farmyard, perhaps fifty yards from the cottage, there was another clutch of outbuildings, all in a similarly dilapidated condition to the main house. The largest had clearly once been a barn of some sort; it was an ugly brick and concrete structure, but its roof had evidently caved in some time ago, because while the rest of it was rotted and flimsy, that was relatively new, made from sturdy sheets of corrugated steel.

Mustn't have the guests getting wet if it rains, Lucy thought.

Mahoney went into the barn first, through a side-door. Lights came on within, and then he re-emerged on the east-facing side, pushing open a large pair of timber doors, through which the men and dogs now trooped. It was difficult to be sure what went on after that, because once the majority were in there, all Lucy could see through the open doors was a chaos of bodies milling about, the dogs still grizzling and snarling at each other.

She lifted the radio mic to her lips but refrained from issuing an order, relying on her ears to tell her what was going on. When the snarling and grizzling gave way to full-on barking, that would mean that muzzles had been removed, and when the men also began shouting, the first bout would be in progress.

A person Lucy hadn't seen before entered the farmyard, almost certainly Mahoney's wife, Mandy. She was a slatternly, overweight woman wearing sandals, jeans that were too tight for her, and a baggy, semi-transparent cheesecloth shirt that barely concealed her naked, pendulous breasts. Ratty grey hair hung past her shoulders, and she had a pudgy, porcine face, tinging red as she made cumbersome trips back and forth from the cottage to the barn, hefting crates of beer.

'Shouldn't we go now?' Geraldson asked quietly.

'No,' Lucy said firmly. 'Just wait.'

She leaned forward, almost pushing her head through the greenery curtaining the aperture. But it was pointless. She couldn't see the woods stretching away to the right of the hide and fringing the open pasture. She'd simply have to trust that Sergeant Frobisher, who was on secondment from Area, would have everyone adequately concealed but also primed for action, so they could jump up and move in the instant she gave the word. There were other lying-up points around the one-time farm: behind the stone walls bordering the eastern end of the pony paddock, sixty yards further away than Lucy's own position; and in the trees on the west side of the farm buildings, though the lads over there had needed to dig in further back because it was open woodland and there was a risk of their being seen. So Frobisher's team would be the first into action, and they'd need to make a very rapid approach.

An explosion of barking suddenly sounded from inside the barn. Geraldson gazed at Lucy, white-faced, a globule of fresh sweat trickling down his nose. She raised a hand for calm but leaned closer to her mic. 'Clayburn to TAU, over?'

Static crackled, before Inspector Rick Crawley, heading up the TAU, responded. '*Go ahead.*'

'Tine to move, sir. Can you block the gate on Wellspring Lane, over?'

'*Roger, received.*'

Lucy glanced at Geraldson, who nodded wordlessly, his mouth clamped shut. And then, inside the old barn, men began shouting, bellowing encouragement, but laughing too, with an angry, raucous delight. The barking took on a new, savage, monstrous overtone.

'All units,' Lucy said into the mic. 'Hit 'em!'

Sergeant Frobisher and Malcolm Peabody's eight-strong snatch squad broke cover and scampered across the grass, dark and stealthy in the night, the only sound a clack of visors being snapped down and a repeating metallic click as Autolock batons were flicked open.

She turned and stooped out through the small rear entrance

of the hide onto the access lane behind. Here, screened by late-summer undergrowth, several RSPCA vans were parked, their personnel standing around in taut silence. Lucy signalled to them and walked around to the front, pushing through the foliage and onto open ground. She wasn't fully armoured like the snatch squads, but she wore a stab-vest and basic Kevlar padding over her scruffs.

The RSPCA officers followed her out, wearing thick handling gloves, carrying deterrent sprays and poles with slip-leads attached. Well-equipped as they were, they kept a safe distance behind.

From this angle, the pony paddock lay in front of them. More police officers were scurrying across it from its eastern perimeter wall. As Lucy veered towards the farm, Mandy Mahoney had waddled back into view, heaving another crate of beer, apparently unperturbed by the terrible sounds emanating from the barn and seemingly oblivious to the advancing forces. Several pairs of moving headlights also caught Lucy's attention. Along Wellspring Lane, on the far side of the paddock, three large vehicles – the TAU troop-carriers – were slowing to a halt in front of the farm gate. The gateman was slow to respond, probably because he was stumped by the sight of them. However, half a second later, he was haring back down the farm track, shouting hoarsely and incoherently.

Lucy switched on her loudhailer and raised it to her lips.

'Leslie Mahoney!' she called, her voice projected across the darkened meadow. 'This is Detective Constable Lucy Clayburn of Crowley CID. You and your friends are all being arrested under Section 8 of the Animal Welfare Act. The entire plot is surrounded, Mahoney . . . so I want you all to come out of that barn right now. Bring your dogs with you and keep them in check. Make sure they're muzzled and leashed. Anyone resisting will also be arrested for assaulting police officers and assault with intent to resist arrest. Anyone using a dog to resist will be arrested for attempting to cause grievous bodily harm.'

Forty yards ahead, Mandy stood frozen in place as she listened to this message from the darkness. But only when Frobisher's snatch squad burst into the light, having advanced across the paddock in complete invisibility, did she respond, dropping the crate of beer and running comically towards the barn. Some of the men inside, presumably those closest to the main doors, had also heard. Heads were fleetingly stuck out, and then disappeared again. The wild shouting inside took on notes of panic and then hysteria. Several seconds later, a confused knot of bodies emerged, both human and canine, the animals leaping and whining in confusion, the men hauling on their chains. Those unencumbered by dogs ran every which way, but already there was no escape. The snatch squad from the woods on the west side of the farm surged into view from between the decayed buildings, shouting orders and warnings. Other uniformed cops emerged from around the back of the barn.

The men and dogs scrambled for their cars, and there were gut-thumping collisions as the officers piled into them. Despite this, several vehicles started up, but as they all sought to rev away up the track at the same time, they slid into each other, clunking and shunting, grinding to a chaotic halt. The couple that managed to get ahead of this tangle only made it a few dozen yards, before the sight of a police troop-carrier blocking the gate and a whole phalanx of TAU men, as well armed and armoured as the divisional lads and yet somehow looking more menacing, more military as they advanced down the dirt track, brought them to a halt. The next thing, doors were being yanked open and burly policemen dragging out the drivers and their passengers.

Lucy lowered her loudhailer as she entered the farmyard.

22

Arrests were being made on all sides. There was no serious violence, but there were struggles as brutish, swearing men were wrestled to the floor and clapped into cuffs. One was struck across the back of the knee with a baton to help him comply. The dogs would have been a problem, especially as several had got loose and were darting back and forth, but they were all still muzzled, and now, at Lucy's direction, the RSPCA handlers came forward to take charge of them.

'Prisoner transports move in,' Lucy told her radio. 'We've got a large number detained.'

One suspect, a younger guy with longish, fair hair, wearing what looked like a wolf-fur doublet, made a semi-successful break for it, shaking off a lone PC and racing onto the open ground of the pony paddock, veering towards Wellspring Lane – only to stop at the sight of several more police vans pulling up behind the troop-carriers. He didn't know they were divisional vans coming to take prisoners, and, thinking they were yet more police reinforcements, slowed to a trudging halt before dropping to his knees and raising his hands, allowing the pursuing officers to take him into custody.

Lucy was still in the thick of the action, though it was mostly over. On all sides, cautions were being issued, and the responses, mainly f-words and other more imaginative profanities, being recorded on dictaphone as the jostling, cuffed men were frogmarched to the farm cottage wall and held there, each by his individual arresting officer, while others commenced searching them. One resisted more than the rest, kicking out and spitting, and was given a backhander across the mouth for his trouble. Lucy wasn't worried. When the evidence was finally presented, she doubted there was a magistrate in the land who'd be swayed by farcical complaints about police brutality.

Quite a bit of that evidence was on display inside the barn itself, when she went in there. The centrepiece was a purpose-built pit, squarish in shape, about ten yards by ten, dug to a depth of five feet and lined with brick, with a steel ladder fixed in one corner and a camera mounted on a tripod overlooking it, alongside an upright chalkboard scribbled with betting information.

Two dogs still occupied the pit. One, an American pit bull, charged crazily back and forth, jumping up to snap and snarl at the officers, despite the excessive blood dabbling its jaws and jowls. The other one, whose breed was uncertain, lay in a quivering, panting heap, gashed and torn and spattered with gore.

'We need one of the vets in here,' Lucy said to a PC at her shoulder. 'And a handler . . . to control the other one, yeah?'

The PC moved away, just as acting DC Tessa Payne, a young black officer, formerly in uniform but currently on secondment to Crowley CID as a trainee, leaned in through a doorway connecting to another outbuilding. Like Lucy, she only wore light body-armour over her jumper and jeans and was in the process of pulling off her protective gloves and replacing them with latex.

'Lucy . . .' she said. 'You might want to look in here.'

'This going to make me throw up?' Lucy said.

'More likely make you dance a jig.'

Lucy went through into what was a basically a lean-to shed lit by a single electric bulb, its damp walls lined with shelves groaning beneath the grisly accoutrements of dog-fighting. She saw piles of spare muzzles and harnesses, stacks of grubby second-hand magazines with grotesque images on their covers, homemade DVDs, DIY veterinary kits, including staple-guns and tubes of superglue, and a number of 'breaking sticks', thick wooden bars impressed with toothmarks, which would normally be used to pry open a victorious animal's jaws when it had them locked into its latest victim.

'Perfect,' she said. 'Bloody perfect. All this needs bagging and tagging, Tessa.'

Payne nodded, at which point they were distracted by the sound of more canine whining. The outhouse had its own outer door – again just a frame with no actual door in it. On the other side they found an enclosed yard containing a set of weighing scales, a treadmill and a large glass tank, very grimy and filled to the brim with water so filthy and green that it was almost opaque. There was also a row of grillwork cages with crudely built kennels attached. Each was occupied by a dog, but these were animals of a different ilk to those they'd seen so far. They were highly subdued, lying still with ears flat, each one watching the humans beyond their cages with fearful intensity.

And it was clear why.

They were brutally scarred, in many cases so bitten and ragged that the fur was entirely missing from their faces. Several had lost so much flesh from their jowls that their teeth were exposed. At least a couple were missing an eye, the empty sockets crudely sutured shut. Lucy saw ears hanging in ribbons, paws chewed into lame, leathery stumps. The reason for that was evident in their breeds, for these were mostly mongrels, but those that weren't were recognisable as Labradors, spaniels and retrievers, suburban pets rather than fighting-dogs.

'Bait,' Lucy observed as she walked along the cages.

'Looks like this is where all the abductees we've been hearing about have finished up,' Payne said, following.

'Maybe.'

'No sign of the black van yet, though.'

'We need to keep looking.'

To Lucy's mind, the existence of 'bait dogs' was one of the most sickening aspects of the whole dog-fighting disgrace. That these trusting, innocent creatures could be thrown into the pit repeatedly as part of a callous training regime for the fighting-dogs, where they'd be attacked mercilessly, again and again, by savage beasts that wanted nothing more than to senselessly kill anything they were faced with, didn't bear thinking about. But that such a thing could happen to one-time pets, allegedly stolen from loving homes by this mysterious black van that had been reported several times when an animal had vanished, was somehow even more horrible.

'We need the vets again,' Lucy said, to which the younger detective nodded and hurried away.

'At least you're not going to need them in here,' a voice said.

She glanced around, and saw Malcolm Peabody leaning out through the entrance to an ugly breezeblock building with no glass in its windows and a sagging tarpaper roof. He'd removed his ballistics helmet and now carried it under one arm. His hair was damp and spiky, his freckled features greased with sweat. Normally an affable young bloke with a great enthusiasm for the job, his expression was grim and angry, his pallor waxen.

Deeply apprehensive, Lucy followed him inside.

Torchlight revealed that it was a basic shell of a room with bare walls and a rugged concrete floor. It was also stained with the blood of ages and strewn with dog carcasses. There were at least ten of them, all relatively recent; Lucy could tell that because flies buzzed everywhere, and a fetid odour thickened the air. She surveyed the heap of twisted forms with what a stranger might have called indifference, but in truth was cold professionalism. It wasn't that it didn't affect her, it was simply that, twelve years in, Lucy was a veteran of this kind of ghastliness, and she knew that to get emotional would only cloud her judgement.

Peabody, a relative newbie, was less in control.

'These are obviously the ones they couldn't use any more,' he said, looking nauseous as he indicated a heavy mallet hanging from a nail by a leather strap. 'And this is how they put them out of their misery.'

'Don't touch it,' Lucy replied. 'Don't touch anything. Not till we've had Photographic in here.'

They stepped back outside into the fresher air, and Lucy indicated to one of the other uniforms to come and stand by the door. Walking back through the barn, they came to the farmyard where the prisoners were lined up, their details and the details of the officers who'd detained them being tabulated by Sergeant Frobisher to ensure there'd be no confusion back at Custody. One by one, the prisoner transports were reversing into place, their back doors swinging along with the cage doors inside.

'Your cards are fucking marked!' the hefty figure of Mandy Mahoney squawked as two armoured policewomen frog-marched her to a waiting police car. As the only female detainee, she would travel separately from the others. 'All you pigs . . . you're all fucking marked!'

Not far behind her, the even more ponderous and dishevelled shape of Les Mahoney was also manhandled forward. He stank of sweat, and when he grinned at Lucy, showed a full set of rotten teeth.

'Sorry to disrupt your evening's entertainment, Mr Mahoney,' she said.

His grin never faltered. 'Fuck you, you slip of a tart.' Hawking a green one, he spat it on the floor at her feet. 'And tell your fucking clodhopping arse-bandit mates not to make too much of a mess, or I'll sue the fucking lot of you.'

'Some chance,' Peabody retorted. 'You're going to jail, pal.'

'Yeah?' Mahoney guffawed. 'Good. I could use a five-month holiday . . . you spotty-faced lump of dogshit.'

Peabody lurched forward, but Lucy physically restrained him.

'Get him out of my sight,' she said.

Mahoney laughed loudly and brashly as he was led away.

Lucy shook her head. 'Last of the old-school charmers, eh?'

Peabody scowled. 'It's right what he said though. We'll be lucky if he gets any more than a slapped wrist for this. We should drive the bastard around a corner somewhere and smack the living crap out of him . . . just in case he gets a free ride later.'

Lucy watched as they assisted the cuffed Mahoney into one of the vans. 'What've I told you about getting too involved, Malcolm? You won't go the distance if you let this job screw with your head. Those things back there . . . they're just animals.' She patted his cheek before walking away. 'Wait till you see it done to humans.'

Chapter 2

Though she'd worn a uniform for the first decade of her career, Lucy Clayburn had now been a detective constable for two years, but in all that time she had only ever worked her home patch of Crowley, Greater Manchester Police's legendary November Division.

The one-time industrial town – though these days it was more a post-industrial wasteland – had an infamous reputation for villainy, though it probably wasn't any more deserved than those bad reps attached to other northern English cities where full employment was a thing of the past and drugs and alcohol had flowed in to fill the gap.

The problem with being a police officer – anywhere really, not just in a place like Crowley – was that you knew what went on behind the sometimes paper-thin façade of the local community. So she wasn't entirely surprised that night of Wednesday, September 12, to look down the list of prisoners waiting in the traps at Robber's Row police station, November Division's HQ, and see that they included professional men with sedate family backgrounds: a senior civil servant, a local journalist, an estate agent, even a bank manager. There were louts and scallies among them too, all the usual suspects; but respectability was a keyword where several were concerned, or superficial respectability at least. Maybe, to an extent, she should have anticipated this, because dog-fighting wouldn't have existed at all, even as an illegal sport, without the hefty cashflow it generated. It was only ever about gambling, and if you didn't have the readies for that, you couldn't participate.

'Worrying, isn't it?' Lucy said, scrolling down the file on the screen belonging to Sergeant Joe Cullen, the Robber's Row custody officer. 'Lots of these guys come over as perfect citizens . . . so able to create the impression they're normal that they can function easily in everyday society. They do jobs efficiently and make them pay. They impress socially. They have friends, families. But deep down, they're so disturbed that they derive pleasure from watching innocent animals rip each other apart. Either that, or they're so indifferent to it that they don't care so long as they make a few quid.'

'I wouldn't be surprised if it was the thin end of the wedge, to be honest,' Cullen replied. He was a foursquare old-schooler, with a weathered hangdog face and a brush of thick grey bristles on his head. 'If they're prepared to do this, what else are they up to? Like you say . . . they're not normal.'

'Mahoney's solicitor here yet?' Lucy asked.

'Doesn't want one,' Cullen replied.

She arched an eyebrow.

Cullen shrugged. 'Asked him twice, but he insists he'll be fine. Confident little toe-rag, I'll say that for him.'

'So, Mr Mahoney,' Lucy said, 'you understand that you remain under caution?'

Mahoney nodded. Still in the scruffy, rancid clothes they'd arrested him in, still smelling of sweat and cigarettes, he slouched on the other side of the interview room table, grinning.

Lucy rolled back the sleeves of her sweater and got the ball rolling. 'For the benefit of the tape, we're in Interview Room 3, Robber's Row police station. I'm DC Lucy Clayburn, in company with acting DC Tessa Payne. This is the interview of Leslie Mahoney. Interview commencing –' she glanced at the clock on the wall '– 11.15pm.' She watched him carefully. 'So, Mr Mahoney . . . how was your day?'

Mahoney guffawed with laughter. 'That's a funny one, I must admit.'

'No more effing and blinding?'

He shrugged. 'Just caught me at a bad moment, that's all.'

'The moment you're referring to, of course, was the moment when you were arrested outside your home tonight, at 39, Wellspring Lane. Isn't that correct?'

'Yeah . . . that's correct.'

'I'm guessing you're also aware *why* you've been—?'

'Let's not fuck about, love. You've got me for running professional dog-fights.'

Lucy remained cool. 'You don't seem too concerned.'

'It's a bang-up job, isn't it? You caught us at it red-handed, so yes . . . before we have to go through all that boring question-and-answer shit, I *was* causing the dogs to fight, I *was* receiving admission fees from the attendees, I *was* accepting bets on the outcome, I *did* possess premises and equipment adapted for use in dog-fighting, I *was* in possession of videos . . . and so on and so on.'

He grinned again, showing brown, scummy teeth, his ragged beard dotted with saliva.

'Where'd you get the dogs from?' Lucy asked.

'Don't own any dogs,' Mahoney said. 'I just organise the fights.'

'I'm not talking about the thirty-plus fighting-dogs we recovered from your property,' Lucy said. 'We've yet to establish exactly who their owners are. I'm more interested in the

31

seventeen dogs we found in kennels at the back of your barn. And in the thirteen dead dogs we found in what looked like an improvised mortuary.'

'You're talking about the bait dogs.' Mahoney caught Payne's mingled look of contempt and bewilderment. He chuckled at her. 'Surprised, darling? I bet most of the poor sods you lock up are rarely this forthcoming, eh?'

'So where did you get them?' Lucy asked again.

'I bought them. Or got them from rescue centres.'

'So, they *are* yours?' Payne said. 'Even though you just said you don't own any dogs.'

Mahoney looked amused again. 'Fuck off, kid . . . they're not *real* dogs, are they? Strays, mutts. God knows what kind of parentage most of them had. Every one a fucking mess.'

'They were certainly a mess when *you'd* finished with them,' she retorted.

Lucy glanced sidelong at her. Tessa Payne was a recent recruit to Robber's Row CID, having done her initial uniform work out of Cotehill Crescent. She was sporty and fit – apparently a top athlete – but was also a college graduate, possessing the sort of sensitivity you rarely found in the police at one time. At present, she seemed calm, but Lucy could tell that she had no love for Les Mahoney.

'If you're talking about the dead ones, I was doing them a favour,' Mahoney said. 'You think ordinary vets don't do the same thing . . . put some creature that's beyond repair out of its misery?'

'Ordinary vets normally do it in a clinical environment,' Payne said. 'In a humane way.'

Mahoney looked puzzled. 'What could be more humane than a quick smack on the noggin?'

'So you're admitting killing the thirteen dogs in the shed,' Lucy said.

'Yeah, sure.'

'With this?' She placed the mallet on the table between them. It was now enclosed in a sealed plastic evidence bag.

'Yep.' Mahoney didn't even bother checking it. 'That's it.'

'So, as well as the gym – we saw your swim-tank and your training treadmill – you also provide a bait dog service? Is that what you're saying?'

'Correct.'

'Fighting-dog owners come and visit you, and presumably for more cash, you'll put one of your bait dogs in the pit . . . so the fighting-dog can get a lot of practice in?'

'That's about the gist of it, yeah.'

'The other dog doesn't stand a chance, does it?' Payne said. 'Don't bother answering that, by the way . . . we've seen the outcome for ourselves.'

'Look . . . why are you pretending you care?' Again, the prisoner looked amused. 'You're a fucking rozzer. Kicking the shit out of people is part of your job description. And that's *people* . . . not dumb fucking animals, brainless mongrels that no one fucking wants.'

'So, you took possession of them,' Lucy said, remaining focused. 'By buying them, or . . . excuse me if I smirk, *rescuing* them.'

'Correct.'

'All done officially?' Payne asked.

'Absolutely. Paperwork straight and everything.'

'There were certainly some dogs in your kennels that didn't look as if they'd ever seen the inside of a rescue centre,' Lucy said.

Mahoney tried to think. 'Suppose there were one or two pedigrees. Yeah.'

'Where'd you get those from?' she asked.

'Those were the ones I bought. Owners couldn't look after them any more, or they were moving away, or a family was splitting up or something. Sad, eh? Like it's not bad enough, the kids seeing their mum and dad separating, and then they get their pets taken off them too. But who cares, really? I mean, come on . . . *pets*. Soppy, poofy things. Fucking toys pretending to be dogs.'

'You *bought* them?' Lucy said, seeking confirmation.

'Again, I've got all the documents.'

Which they would no doubt soon find, Lucy reminded herself. In addition to the dog-fighting offences, she'd also arrested Mahoney on suspicion of theft – i.e. having stolen the missing dogs – which had empowered them to perform a thorough search of his premises. Right now, as Lucy and Mahoney spoke, Malcolm Peabody and one or two other uniforms were still down at Wellspring Lane, going through the property inch by inch.

'Do you want to know what's really funny, though?' Mahoney said.

'Funny?' Lucy replied.

He leaned forward conspiratorially. 'You've come in here thinking: "Gonna teach this bugger a lesson. He'll try and wriggle out of it, but we've got him. Gonna fucking wallop him." And yet . . . I've *not* tried to wriggle out, have I? I've coughed to it. Because you and me both know the worst I'm going to get for this is six months.' He grinned again, mouth filled with brown, shovel-like teeth. 'Like I said, I could use the holiday.'

He sat back again, his grin broadening.

'Done you like a pair of brain-dead kippers, haven't I?' he said. 'Because you now reckon you're going to lay a few theft charges on me. You're thinking, "The only chance we've got of sticking this bastard somewhere the sun doesn't shine is to prove that he's pinched some of these dogs, especially these pedigrees because they're worth a bob or two." I bet you've got a list in your back pocket of a load of missing dogs, haven't you? *I've* heard the stories too.

34

House pets getting lifted all over Crowley by this evil black van.'

He gave Lucy a long appraising stare.

'I wonder, DC Clayburn, if you've actually verified yet whether any of those missing pooches marry up with any of those in my kennels . . . or are you just guessing that's the case? Because if it's the latter, bad luck.' He laughed again. 'And to pre-empt your next dumbfuck question . . . no, I don't own a black transit van. I've got three vehicles, and I've got documents for all of them. But don't bother looking around my place for this mythical black van, because you'll just make bigger arses of yourselves than you already have.'

DI Stan Beardmore, Lucy's divisional supervisor, was an easy-going guy in his mid-fifties, short and squat, with a head of neat, snow-white hair, and a habit of wearing shabby tweed jackets over his smart shirts and ties. At present he looked nonplussed.

'I don't understand the problem,' he said. 'The bastard's coughed to everything.'

'Trouble is, he's right, isn't he?' Lucy replied from the other side of the connecting office between Custody and the front desk. She whipped a folded print-out from the back pocket of her jeans. 'I've got a whole raft of animals here that aren't accounted for.'

'Lucy, they're just dogs. We've got a longer list of missing *people* who we haven't even got time to look for.'

'That's not the point.' She shook her head. 'We've got enough to charge him with the dog-fighting stuff. But unless we can hit him with a decent theft charge too, he'll get a tap on the wrist and then go home laughing.'

'He had one or two pedigrees in his collection, didn't he?'

'Yes, but I've already checked and none of those marry up with anything registered as missing.' She spread her paperwork on the desk and indicated a section that she'd previously drawn a square around in biro. It contained printed details, and a poor-quality black-and-white photo of a fluffball dog. 'I was hoping to find this one, at least. Petra. A dyed-pink Toy Poodle, she disappeared two months ago from a back garden in Cotely Barn. Her owner reported a mysterious black van in the vicinity that evening.'

Beardmore rolled his eyes.

'The point is that Petra originally cost her owner £650 when first purchased,' Lucy said.

'She definitely wasn't in Mahoney's kennels?' Beardmore asked.

'I think we'd know if we'd found a dyed-pink poodle.'

'What about that shed where the dead ones were?'

Lucy shook her head, grim-faced. 'She wasn't there either. There's another thing though. When Petra went missing, she was wearing a pink leather collar with diamond studs in it . . . that alone was worth two thousand quid. Ridiculous expenditure on a dog, I know. But if we could do Mahoney for that, he'd get a few extra months, if nothing else.'

'And would it be worth it? For a few extra months?'

Lucy shook her head. 'Stan . . . if you'd been there. If you'd seen what we saw . . .'

'Okay, I know, I know.' He looked frustrated. 'I agree it's a bag of shit . . . a bastard like Mahoney deserves the book throwing at him. He'd go down for five years if it was up to me. But we don't make the law, Lucy. We just enforce it.'

'I need something else. That jewelled collar at least—'

'Excuse me, DC Clayburn,' a voice interrupted. 'There's someone to see you out front.'

It was Daisy Dobson, one of the civilian employees who worked the station's front desk. She was a tall, statuesque girl, with a mess of blonde hair and a permanently sour countenance. She might still have made a good impression in her smart shell-blue uniform, but she was also in the habit of chewing gum noisily. She stood impatiently awaiting a response.

'Is it important, Daisy?' Lucy asked. 'Only . . . I've got a whole raft of prisoners.'

Daisy chomped on but didn't move away. 'I don't know whether it's important or not.'

'In that case get rid of them,' Beardmore replied. 'We're busy.'

'It's a nun,' Daisy said.

'A nun . . .?' Fleetingly, Beardmore was lost for words.

'That's right, sir,' Daisy replied. 'A proper one. With all the gear on.'

Beardmore recovered himself. 'Get rid of her politely then. We're still busy.'

'It's all right,' Lucy said, knowing who this caller would be. She folded her paperwork and slid it back into her pocket. 'I'll go through. She's not a real nun. I mean, she *was* a real nun once. Well, a sister rather than a nun. Anyway, she's neither now, because . . . well, it's a long story.'

Beardmore was blank-faced. 'Are we talking some kind of crackpot?'

'That's the problem.' Lucy headed to the door. 'With Sister Cassiopeia, you're never quite sure.'

Chapter 3

Sister Cassiopeia, or Sister Cassie as she was better known, was seated on one of the benches in the waiting room. Given the lateness of the hour, she was there alone, but she'd have stood out even in a riotous crowd.

She wasn't particularly tall, perhaps five-foot-seven, and never wore makeup, but she possessed a natural elfin beauty, a shadow of which remained even now, in her forties and after much hardship. She was thin, these days, rather than slim, but who wouldn't be after living on the streets for a time, and yet her distinctive female shape remained visible, in fact was almost accentuated by her monastic clothing: the long black habit and brown scapular, the white wimple, black cloak and black veil. It was only when you were close to her, and the odour of her rank, unwashed clothes reached you, or when you noticed the patches, and the ragged hems of her skirts, and the mud spattered up them, that you realised there was a problem here. By then it probably wouldn't surprise you to learn that if her arms were ever exposed, you'd see patterns of needle tracks.

'Lucy, my child,' she said in her soft Irish accent. She got up and crossed the room, her ever-present satchel swinging by its shoulder strap. As usual, she seemed remarkably ener-gised for such a scarecrow of a person. 'My, my . . . you've all been very naughty, this time, haven't you?'

'Oh . . . have we?' Lucy replied.

Sister Cassie eyed Daisy Dobson with undisguised irrita-tion. The big blonde girl, still noisily chewing, stood behind the desk openly and unashamedly eavesdropping. 'May we speak somewhere a little more private, child?'

Lucy nodded. 'I think we'd better.'

She led the ex-nun to a side-door, tapped in the combi-nation and diverted her towards one of the station's non-custodial interview rooms. 'I have to tell you, though,' she said over her shoulder, 'I haven't got a lot of time.'

'Well, that's always the problem,' Sister Cassie replied, following her in, unhooking her cloak and seating herself rather primly in an armchair. 'We're all rushed off our feet these days.' Then she became stern. 'But I *do* think these disappearances are getting a little out of hand.'

Lucy sat in the facing chair, which thankfully was several feet away. Sister Cassie attended to her own hygiene as much as any homeless drug-addict could be expected to, regularly using the showers available in the shelters, but she also insisted on wearing this ancient religious garb of hers, which, by the look and stink of it, probably hadn't been laundered in two decades or more.

Lucy shrugged. 'Sister . . . we're looking into these pet abductions as part of a larger operation . . .'

'Pet abductions?' Sister Cassie seemed baffled. 'My child, if only it were pets I was talking about.'

Lucy could only shrug again, bemused. 'Okay, so . . . *what* disappearances?'

'My dear child . . . three of my regulars have recently dropped out of sight.'

'Dropped out of sight?'

'I believe that's the vernacular. They've vanished. They're no longer here.'

'Sister, I'm afraid I'm still not sure what you mean . . .'

'Oh, child.' A look of patient frustration briefly etched the ex-nun's face, a hint maybe of the teacher she'd once reputedly been. 'This is not difficult. You know Edna Davis, I take it?'

Lucy couldn't help thinking about the custody clock ticking next door. 'I'm afraid I don't.'

'They used to call her the Cat Lady.'

Lucy paused. This name rang a bell.

'Always sits at the junction between Stoker's Street and Kiln Lane,' Sister Cassie explained. 'Or she used to. I don't know where she is now.'

Lucy recollected the homeless woman in question. She was a lot older and in a far more decrepit state than Sister Cassie and was instantly recognisable for her beige mac and overlarge trainers, and for the crumpled, flower-covered hat she wore, but, most noticeably of all, for the three or four cats she always had with her.

'Stoker's Street and Kiln Lane?' she sought to confirm.

Sister Cassie nodded.

'And she's disappeared, you say?'

'One day, I was making my usual evening rounds – and she was no longer there. And she hasn't been there since. No one I know has seen her.'

'When was this?'

'I would say . . . five days ago.'

Lucy pondered. Five days wasn't that long, and some homeless people were transient and prone to wandering.

'But I'm afraid that isn't the worst of it,' the ex-nun added. 'Ronald Burke . . . you know him?'

Lucy regarded her quizzically. 'No, but he's also homeless, I'm guessing?'

40

'You, most likely, will have met him when he's been causing trouble in public houses.' The ex-nun sighed at such regrettable behaviour. 'He used to wear a brown overcoat and a grey balaclava. Whatever the weather.'

'Yes, now you mention it . . . I remember.'

'Well . . . he hasn't been seen for two or three weeks.'

'Sister . . . couldn't these people have simply moved on? They've no work to keep them here, no fixed abode.'

'Oh, my child . . .' Sister Cassie gave a sad smile. 'Let's not find reasons *not* to investigate, mmm? You are a police detective, after all.'

Ever the school-ma'am, Lucy thought. 'You said that *three* of your regulars have gone missing?'

Sister Cassie was thoughtful. 'The last one is a little more troubling. For a brief time, I was unsure whether to include him on the list, because he can really be rather naughty. Frederick Holborn . . . you know him?'

Lucy shook her head.

'Ah. Probably a good thing. No doubt he would attempt to impugn your honour.' The ex-nun arched a disapproving eyebrow. 'As he regularly does mine.'

'I'm sorry . . .' Lucy was puzzled. 'You're saying he's assaulted you?'

'Perhaps "assault" is too strong a word. Let's just say that he has several times sought sexual favours from me. I think he regards my religious calling as a challenge to be overcome.'

From what Lucy knew, it wouldn't have been much of a challenge. Sister Cassie might don the trappings of a nun and adopt the role of carer with her fellow vagrants, but she had a heroin habit all of her own, and she needed to earn the money for it.

'I almost stopped including him in my nightly rounds,' the ex-nun added, 'but though drink and other poisons have ravaged many of these poor creatures to a point where they

41

are closer, frankly, to God than they are to men, they still have needs and desires. I don't mind admitting, there've been times when I've almost complied—'

'Sister, please. If you're not actually making a complaint against Fred Holborn, can we get to the point?'

'Well, he's vanished too, child. Completely . . . as if he was never put on this Earth.'

The door opened, and Tessa Payne stuck her head in. 'Sorry, Lucy, but Sergeant Cullen's wondering what the delay is.'

Lucy signalled that she'd be out shortly.

'You're a very kind person, Sister,' Lucy said. 'And I know you genuinely care for those in want. The fact you make these nightly rounds at all is . . . well, it's going to win you a lot of brownie points with the Lord, even if it doesn't get you anything down here.'

The 'nightly rounds' she referred to were a real thing. Sister Cassie spent the best part of each day scavenging what scant supplies she could – food, drink, cigarettes, money – and despite holding some back in order to feed her own habit, was often able to make a nightly circuit of the doorways, sewers and underpasses where so many of Crowley's homeless bedded down, doling out whatever she could to the most needy, or sometimes simply offering company and comfort.

'But the first point I made still stands,' Lucy said. 'Edna Davis, Ronald Burke and Fred Holborn . . . they might just have wandered off.'

Sister Cassie shook her head.

'Look,' Lucy said, 'they may have been fixtures in Crowley for years, but there's nothing to keep them here.'

'I know these people well, child. None of them have anywhere else to go.'

'What do the others think?' Lucy asked. 'I mean, the rest of your community.'

'They're as worried and bemused as I am.'

'So why haven't they come forward? You say Ronald Burke vanished two or three weeks ago.'

'My child . . . they will not come into a police station.'

'Why not?'

'They don't trust you. And why should they? One young lady I see on my regular rounds . . . she was raped by a gang of men some nine months ago. Not just raped, sodomised too. It was a terrible attack and I know, because I'm the one who cared for her afterwards and persuaded her to go to the police station.'

'I don't remember this,' Lucy said.

'It wasn't here at Robber's Row, it was at Cotehill Crescent.'

'Okay, and . . .?'

'Well . . .' Sister Cassie sighed again. 'It's a sad tale already, but it gets sadder still. While the police ladies were helping her undress for examination by the nurse, they found certain *substances*. As such, this young lady herself was questioned. It made her feel very uncomfortable . . . as if she wasn't already uncomfortable enough.'

'I *do* remember that one, actually,' Lucy said. 'That young lady had quite a bit of heroin on her, and several uncapped needles, all of which she failed to mention. As a result, one of the policewomen assisting got her finger pricked and had to go through all kinds of health checks afterwards. Are you surprised they got cross with her?'

'It doesn't matter. They were searching for evidence that might have incriminated the young lady's attacker, and they ended up making a fuss about evidence which might well have incriminated the young lady herself . . . and for something completely unconnected with the original complaint. So, you see, child, my community, as you call it, is not very keen on your community.'

Unconnected with the original complaint . . .

Lucy thought about that, wondering why it seemed meaningful.

And then the penny dropped.

'Is everything all right?' Sister Cassie said, noting Lucy's gradual change of expression.

Lucy stood up stiffly. 'Sister . . . I have some rather pressing business, I'm afraid.'

The ex-nun nodded sagely, and she too made to stand. 'Of course.'

She smiled as she pulled on her cloak and picked up her satchel. She wasn't being sarcastic. This was one of the disarming things about her: despite everything, she still radiated charm and civility. Even with the occasional admonitions, her attitude throughout the short interview had mainly been one of gratitude that a police officer had found time for her.

Lucy showed her out into the front waiting room. 'I'll come and find you,' she said. 'It won't be tomorrow – I've got too much on, and I've got Friday off. Over the weekend, maybe?'

'Of course.'

'Where will you be? St Clement's Avenue, is it?'

'That's my usual haunt, child.' The ex-nun opened the front doors to leave.

'I'm serious, Sister,' Lucy said. 'I'll come down there and look you up.'

But the ex-nun was already walking away along Tarwood Lane, her robes flapping behind her. She waved one-handed, without looking back.

Briefly, Lucy was discomforted by the thought of the woman travelling all the way back to St Clement's Avenue alone and on foot. Even if she got there safely, St Clement's was one of the most dangerous neighbourhoods in the borough. But that was Sister Cassie's life all over: the streets,

44

the darkness, the isolation – she was no stranger to any of it. Besides, Lucy had more important things to do at present than offer rides to hobos.

Such as once and for all squashing a very nasty, very self-confident little bug.

Chapter 4

Lucy drove back to Wellspring Lane at speed. All the way, three sentences replayed themselves over and over through her head.

I wouldn't be surprised if it was the thin end of the wedge.
If they're prepared to do this, what else are they up to?
Those first two, courtesy of the laconic Joe Cullen.
Completely unconnected with the original complaint . . .
That latter the homespun street-wisdom of Sister Cassiopeia.

It was now very late, past midnight, so though Wellspring Lane was at the extreme southern end of the borough, away from most residential districts and edging onto the famous Chat Moss, there was almost no other traffic on the road. Lucy got her foot down nevertheless, concerned that the search of Mahoney's premises might be approaching its end.

She was only just in time, bouncing her Suzuki Jimny down the rutted track to the farm cottage, swerving at speed around the abandoned vehicles there, and seeing Malcolm Peabody and three other constables outside the building, next to what looked as if it was the last divisional van on site. They were still in protective clothing, but even as Lucy arrived, gloves were coming off and the press-studs down the fronts of overalls being plucked open.

Peabody advanced, grinning, as she screeched to a halt in the farmyard.

'We've bagged and boxed everything,' he said. He tapped the side of the van. 'We've got enough here to do such a number on this Mahoney wanker that he'll never forget it.'

'Did you find the jewelled collar?' she asked, jumping out.

'Erm, no.' Peabody pondered. 'But he's banged to rights. Photographic have only just gone, and they've got loads of stuff too.'

'Any other animals?'

'Only the ones we found before.'

'What about the black van?'

He shook his head, frowning as he sensed her displeasure. 'No sign of any van on these premises. We've been through all the outbuildings. But Luce, we've got him – we caught him at it.'

'We've got him for dog-fighting, Malcolm – not something that's going to see him do serious time.' She entered the cottage via its still open door. 'Everyone, come in here, please.'

The other officers trooped inside, joining her in a small, cluttered kitchen.

All kinds of revolting mess filled its central table and surrounding worktops. The dull lighting and low, beamed ceiling only added to the gloom and the cramped atmosphere. The door had been open for hours now, but there was still a staleness in the air, a vague odour of spoiled food.

'How thoroughly have you searched this house?' she asked, her gaze roving from one blank, tired face to the next.

'We've had a look around,' Peabody answered, 'but we gathered so much evidence from the barn and the outbuild-ings—'

47

'So you're saying you've not searched it at all?' she interrupted, visibly vexed.

'We've had a look around.'

'What does that mean, Malcolm? A cursory look? You've checked in a few drawers?'

No one spoke, but several shamefaced glances were exchanged.

'Come on, Lucy,' Peabody protested. 'We're looking for evidence of organised dog-fighting. And we've found it outside. Stacks of it. What exactly could he keep in here?'

'I found some paperwork,' a young policewoman called Laurie Darlington chipped in. 'It was in a cupboard in the dining room. So I put it in the van.'

'Show me,' Lucy said.

They went back outside and opened the van. PC Darlington rummaged among the boxes and various plastic bags before lifting a clear plastic envelope tagged LD1, containing a bundle of dirty documents stapled together. Lucy didn't unseal the paperwork but examined what she could of it through the plastic. Though the top sheet had been scribbled on almost unintelligibly, close analysis suggested that it was a customer log, detailing names and the services provided, plus payments and the like.

'This is good,' Lucy said. 'In fact, this is excellent. But just at present it's not what we're looking for. Inside again, everyone, please.'

Lucy held the same rank as the search officers, but they deferred to her naturally, not just because of her length of service, twelve years, but because she'd been point-man on this operation from the start, and because, even though a lowly divisional detective, she already had a rep for breaking tough cases.

'Here's the deal,' she said, when they were back in the kitchen. 'We're fully authorised to search this pad, so I want

48

every inch of it going over, yeah? If necessary, it needs physically ripping apart.'

There were thinly veiled groans. Most of these officers, including Peabody, had been on duty for several hours after their normal shifts had supposedly finished. They were being paid for it, but inevitably fatigue was setting in.

'Seriously, Lucy?' Peabody groaned. 'All this for a dog-collar?'

'Anything we can hit this bastard with, we have to do it,' she said.

'Won't he have sold it on by now?' another copper asked. 'I mean, if it's worth that much . . . why would he hang onto it?'

'We're not walking away from here without having a good look around,' she said simply. 'That dog-collar's too valuable.'

More irritated expressions; more shuffling feet.

'At least,' she said, 'that's going to be the *official* line.'

Immediately, their expressions changed. Feet stopped shuffling.

'Pricks like this guy Mahoney always have their fingers in more than one illegal pie,' Lucy said. 'So that's what we're *really* looking for. Anything else we might be able to use, but it's got to be good.'

'Aren't we only supposed to be looking for stuff relevant to the case?' someone queried.

'Section 19, PACE,' Lucy said. 'A constable engaged in a lawful search of a premises may seize anything if he or she has reasonable grounds for believing that it is evidence in relation to an offence he or she is investigating . . . *or any other offence.*'

They pondered this.

'Why do you think he's coughed to the dog-fighting so readily?' she asked them.

''Cause he's no choice,' Peabody said.

'Maybe, but maybe also because he wants us out of here quickly . . . before we find something else.'

With a greater degree of enthusiasm than previously, and now under Lucy's direction, the team went at it again, this time more robustly. First, they did the bedrooms, which were odious pits of filth and slovenliness, moving bookcases so they could look behind them, yanking out the contents of wardrobes and doors, checking under beds, lifting rugs and carpets, even dislodging loose floorboards and peering underneath. Downstairs, they investigated the under-stair closet, which was filled with what appeared to be rubbish, though there was a double-barrelled shotgun there. Knowing Mahoney, it was almost certainly unlicensed, but it was unloaded, and a vigorous search of the under-stair crawlspace provided no cartridges either, while the weapon itself looked so ancient that it might even be classifiable as an antique, which would exempt it.

In the cottage's living room, they lifted more carpets, checked under more sideboards, dug behind and underneath the upholstery on the couch, probing through welters of crumbs and tattered newspaper. They prodded thick tufts of fluff gathered behind radiators, and pried loose skirting boards away, only for mice and cockroaches to scamper free. Some shelves next to the television were stacked with unmarked DVDs. They played a few of these and found they were nothing more than pirate copies of recent movies. Peabody suggested that this was another charge they could add, but Lucy called it 'Mickey Mouse stuff'.

She was getting tired herself now, and deeply frustrated. The clock was ticking on her prisoners, and she couldn't keep these officers on duty for ever. When she glanced at her watch and saw that it was nearly three in the morning, she was ready to call it off. She was standing at the top of the cottage stairs contemplating this, when a voice came up to her from below. She went back down and found PC Darlington in the doorway to the ground-floor privy.

'Could this be what we're looking for?' Darlington wondered.

Curious, Lucy stuck her head into the cubicle, where another PC, a tall lad, had stood on the toilet lid to check inside the cistern, which was high on the wall, and in so doing had accidentally hit the ceiling with the top of his head, dislodging a concealed but loose panel, from behind which a bulky plastic sack had tumbled. He'd already opened the sack and discovered maybe a hundred sachets of white powder, which he offered to Lucy in two gloved hands.

For the first time in two or three hours, she smiled.

Forty minutes later, Lucy was back in the Custody Suite at Robber's Row police station. A few of the lesser miscreants, those who didn't own dogs themselves, were already lined at the counter, being charged with attending a dog-fight and making bets.

DI Beardmore, who ought to have gone home hours ago, stood to one side, arms folded, looking sallow-cheeked. He'd even removed his jacket and tie and unbuttoned his collar, which was not his normal form. When he saw Lucy, he frowned all the more.

'Can we get this show on the road, please?' he said grumpily. 'We're running out of space in here, Lucy. The night shift have started nicking real criminals and we've nowhere to put them.'

'Sir . . . Mahoney's a *real* criminal.' And she told him what they'd found at the cottage, and the phone-calls she'd made afterwards as she'd headed back here from Wellspring Lane.

A short time later, she walked down the cell corridor, produced a bunch of keys and unlocked one of the doors. Inside, Mahoney was lying on the narrow mattress, arms folded behind his head. He sat up and yawned. 'About fucking time.'

'Sorry about the delay, Mr Mahoney,' she said. 'We're almost finished here.'

'Don't know how lucky you are, love. If I was as bad at my job as you are at yours, I wouldn't make a penny. But you get paid anyway, don't you? There's the public sector, eh?'

'The situation's simple,' she said. 'You're shortly going to be charged with causing dogs to fight, receiving money for admission to these fights, publicising these fights, accepting bets on these fights, possessing materials in connection with these fights, allowing your premises to be used for these fights, possessing videos of other dog-fights, and, to top it all off, causing unnecessary suffering to protected animals.'

It was quite a laundry list of villainy, but Mahoney shrugged indifferently, as if this was only to be expected.

'But I wouldn't make any plans to go home just yet,' she said.

A man sidled into the doorway alongside her, wearing a sweater and jeans. He was tall and lean, with a shock of black hair and rugged, lived-in looks. He fixed Mahoney with a hard but unreadable expression.

'This is DCI Slater of the Drugs Squad,' Lucy said. 'Once we've charged you with those offences, he'll be re-arresting you on suspicion of possessing controlled drugs with intent to supply.'

The colour drained from Mahoney's brutish, bearded face. He leaped to his feet.

'If I were you, I'd think about getting lawyered up after all,' she added.

She closed the door with a clang, though the prisoner's voice all but punched its way through the heavy steel.

'You flatfoot bitch! You can't do that!'

Lucy walked back down the corridor, Slater, an old colleague, ambling alongside her.

'Got a lot of tired officers going off-duty now, sir,' she said, 'who'd thoroughly appreciate it if you nailed that bastard's bollocks to the wall.'

'No promises, Lucy,' Slater replied. 'But that tends to be what we do.'

Chapter 5

It was Cora Clayburn's fifty-fifth birthday, in honour of which she was done up even more impressively than usual, and she was rarely ever seen out of the house minus lippy or eye-liner.

In appearance alone, Lucy was very different to her mother, five-foot-eight tall and, thanks to years of sporting activity, possessed of a trim, athletic build. She was naturally tanned and had glossy, crow-black hair, which these days, as a plain-clothes officer, she wore well past her shoulders. Her green eyes and sharp features had a feline aspect, which men seemed to find both attractive and intimidating. In contrast, Cora was more of an English rose: she only stood five-foot-six, was more buxom than her daughter, and had silver/blonde hair currently styled in a short bob, blue eyes, pink lips and a soft, pale complexion. Age had caught up with her a little. She was 'no longer wrinkle-free', as she would frustratedly say while standing in front of the bathroom mirror, but, thanks to her exercise regime, plus the fact that she ate like a bird, she was still in terrific shape.

She also knew how to dress.

When they met at The Brasserie that evening, while Lucy

was in kitten heels and jeans, with a stonewashed denim jacket over her black sleeveless vest, her mother wore stiletto heels and a flowery, figure-hugging dress which instantly took ten years off her. The Brasserie was a small place just off the town centre. It had once been a stable block or saddlery, and it attempted even now to retain that aura, with intricately paved floors, period timber beams, and walls adorned with framed, sepia-toned photographs depicting the Bridgewater Canal during the horse-drawn era. But it provided good service and very good food, and was perfect for a quiet midweek celebration. Lucy and Cora were allocated a table alongside the huge stone fireplace, but it was a mild September so far, and though the hearth was stacked with logs and kindling, no flames had been lit.

'Late night?' Cora asked, after they'd ordered a couple of drinks.

Lucy flipped through the menu, only vaguely aware that she'd just stifled a yawn.

'Sort of.' In fact, she'd only hit the sack after ten that morning, and even then had only managed to grab a couple of hours in an armchair in the rec room at Robber's Row, as she'd needed to get back on duty in order to bottom the paperwork.

'You couldn't take today off?'

'Would've been nice, but no. Finishing off a big job.'

'Well . . . you still found time to send me a very thoughtful present. Thank you very much.'

'It was only a voucher,' Lucy said.

'A voucher is good. No point taking a wild guess, is there? And no point giving me money, either. Where's that going to go, if not on bills?'

Lucy picked up her glass of prosecco. 'Happy fifty-fifth.'

They clinked glasses, even if Cora pulled a face. 'Don't say *that*, please . . .'

'Hey, *I'm* no spring chicken,' Lucy replied.

'You're thirty-two. I wish I was.'

'Well . . . theoretically, I've got my best days ahead of me.'

'Not theoretically. You have, trust me. Just don't waste them.' Cora leaned forward, staring at her daughter meaningfully. 'Promise me *that* . . . you won't waste them.'

In reality this meant: *Please get yourself a fella.* So Lucy opted to change the subject. 'How's the shoulder?'

'Stiff, but I'll live.'

The previous year, Cora had accidentally become embroiled in one of Lucy's more extreme cases and had suffered a pistol shot to the left shoulder. The wound was relatively clean, the bullet passing through, and quick emergency surgery had prevented any life-changing damage, but it had still seen her spend several weeks in hospital, and even now she was on a course of recuperative physiotherapy. It was typical of Cora's courageous self-confidence, though, that despite the very obvious scar, she was still happy to wear a strappy summer dress, and to look good in it.

'Get anything nice?' Lucy asked. 'Apart from my voucher?'

'Well . . . I've been meaning to tell you this.' Suddenly, Cora looked cagey. 'On the basis that you were bound to find out anyway, you having such a nose for trouble . . .'

'Okay . . . go on.'

Cora sighed. 'Yesterday morning, a florist's van turned up at the house. And delivered . . . well, I don't know for sure . . . maybe a couple of thousand pounds' worth of summer blooms. Living room's currently like a greenhouse at Kew Gardens.'

'Two grand's worth of flowers?' Lucy said, astonished.

'At least.'

'So . . . what is it, a secret admirer?'

Cora took a sip of prosecco. 'Hardy secret, Lucy.'

'Ohhh, you're not telling me . . .?'

Their eyes met, and Lucy shook her head with angry bewilderment.

To say that her father, Frank McCracken, was estranged from her would have been the euphemism of all time; in truth, the mere mention of his name put Lucy on edge as almost nothing else could.

He was a gangster. It was that simple. But not just an ordinary gangster; he held high rank in the Crew, the most influential crime syndicate in the whole of Northwest England. It hadn't always been that way, of course. Thirty-two years ago, he'd been a small-time enforcer, one of whose duties was to mind the girls and watch the punters in a mob-owned strip-joint in central Manchester. It was there that he'd met a young Cora Clayburn, who, in a completely different life to the one she led now, had been one of the stars of the show. She'd taken to McCracken quickly; he was handsome, tough, intelligent, and he had the gift of the gab – his role at the club had been more 'cooler' than 'bouncer'. They'd embarked on a relationship, but when Cora fell pregnant, she'd quickly reappraised her life. First of all, she'd decided that she wanted to keep the baby. Secondly, it was obvious that a rowdy strip-club was a completely inappropriate environment in which to raise a child. Thirdly, urbane though Frank McCracken could be, he was a criminal – and a violent one – and so were all his friends, so it didn't take long for Cora to decide that she didn't want him in her youngster's life.

It still wasn't a spur-of-the-moment decision to leave. Cora was open and honest with McCracken, and he accepted it, partly because he wasn't ready for fatherhood but also because he could take his pick of the other strippers and was still at an age when playing the field was viewed as a male birthright. He'd offered Cora money to assist her, but she'd even turned that down, insisting that she wanted to make a complete break, advising her former beau that he would likely never see or even hear from her again.

And that was how it had remained. The child, a girl called Lucy, was born in Crowley, where Cora made her new life. She grew up never knowing who her father was but, ironically, joined the Greater Manchester Police. It was only two years ago, in the very dramatic circumstances of Operation Clearway, an undercover mission she and numerous other policewomen had undertaken in order to catch a killer called Jill the Ripper, that Lucy had finally come into contact with McCracken – now a major player, of course.

When they became aware of each other, there was immediate distrust on both parts, though the man had been more intrigued than the girl, almost feeling proud that his daughter had overcome the difficulties of having a lone parent in a rough part of the city. Lucy, in contrast, was overtly hostile to him, but, by necessity, a truce had eventually been reached, both parties understanding that if word ever got out that they were related to each other, their careers would both be damaged, if not ruined. Even now, only four people knew about it, as far as Lucy was aware: she and her mother, and McCracken and his second-in-command, a psychotic bruiser called Mick Shallicker.

The truce had held, even though they'd had dealings with each other several times since then, but increasingly, Lucy felt, her father was becoming lax in his efforts to keep things secret.

'There was even a signed card with it,' Cora added, interrupting her thoughts. 'Just so there couldn't be any mistake. The card was so big, it wouldn't have gone through the letterbox.' Her voice was almost wistful. 'He not only signed it, he put fifty-five kisses on it.' She glanced up, her expression suddenly hard. 'So, go on . . . if you're going to start shouting and bawling, let's do it now and get it over with.'

'What's the point shouting?' Lucy asked. 'You didn't give him any encouragement . . . I'm assuming?'

'Of course I didn't.' Cora whipped her napkin off the table, a bit too aggressively, and arranged it on her lap. 'But I've not needed to. It's not like he's come back into our lives through ordinary circumstances, is it?'

'Well . . . not exactly ordinary.'

'But through no fault of ours.'

Lucy shrugged. 'And what are you trying to tell me . . . he likes what he sees?'

'Why shouldn't he?'

'For Christ's sake, Mum!' Lucy leaned forward, lowering her voice. 'You're in fab shape for your age, but he's walking around with Supertramp on his arm. Or he was.'

Carlotta 'Charlie' Powell was Frank McCracken's current squeeze, a Pamela Anderson lookalike, who had once been the most expensive hooker in Manchester.

'I can't explain his motivation,' Cora said. 'All I'm telling you is what's happened.'

'I take it you haven't done anything daft in response . . . like sent him a thank-you note or something?'

'Not yet.'

'Not *yet*?'

'Lucy . . . will you stop behaving as if you're the mother and I'm the child?' Cora said heatedly. 'Or as if you have a monopoly on common sense?'

Lucy sat back again, feeling admonished.

'For all the reasons that you constantly warn me against him, I dumped that man thirty years ago. And in the process I condemned myself to a lifetime of anonymous single-motherhood. All this happened before you were even wearing nappies. Now, some might argue, given the pillar of right-eousness you've become, that my sacrifice was worth it . . . and that maybe I'm finally entitled to a little *me* time.'

59

'Mum . . . you're not actually thinking of getting back with him?'

'Lucy . . . just because *you* don't want a man in your life, that doesn't mean I don't.'

'But he's already with someone.'

Cora shrugged. 'You think that'll bother your father?'

'What?' Lucy was aghast. 'You'd be happy to be the other woman?'

'I . . .' Fleetingly, Cora struggled with this dollop of common sense. 'Of course not. It's just that I . . .' Again, she had trouble articulating. 'I really liked Frank. Back then, I mean.'

'You left him easily enough.'

'The decision was far from easy, trust me.'

'You've had loads of chances to get to know other guys. I know you've been asked out at least three—'

'None of them measure up, Lucy. That's the trouble.' Briefly, Cora was wistful again, lost in a dreamy past. Only to snap out of it suddenly. 'Anyway, it's easy for you to talk. You're young, you've got your looks, your health . . .'

'So have you.'

'But you've still got years ahead of you. The pages on my calendar are turning fast.'

Lucy didn't know what to say. The idea of her mother taking up with a notorious gangster was intolerable, of course, the antithesis of everything she stood for. But ultimately this was her mother's business, not hers. Did she really have a right to intervene?

'If you want the truth,' Cora said, 'I think Frank's feeling the years too. He might have that ex-porno queen, or whatever she is, in his bed, but she's not like a real wife, is she? She won't keep him a tidy home, she hasn't raised his children.'

'So now you're saying Frank McCracken's missing his

family?' Lucy scoffed. 'A family he hadn't even met until a couple of years ago?'

'God, you can be harsh when you want to.'

'I'm stating a fact. And I don't want you to get hurt.'

'You've a funny way of showing it.' Cora threw down her napkin and stood up, much to the surprise of the waitress, who had just arrived with their first courses.

'Mum . . . please!' Lucy tapped the tablecloth placatingly. 'Come on . . . don't be silly.'

Cora sat down again but looked grumpy. Rather nervously, the waitress served their dishes. The twosome ate in sulky silence.

'Obviously this means more to you than I thought,' Lucy said when she'd finished her starter. She dabbed at her mouth. 'But you know the situation with him and me. As soon as word gets out, we're both finished in our respective careers.'

'And do you really believe that, Lucy?' Cora scrutinised her in a firm, motherly way, as though trying to wheedle the truth out of a deceitful child. 'Do you? Honestly?'

Again, Lucy considered this. Coming clean to her bosses about who her father was would be a huge risk. How would they ever be able to take her seriously as a police officer again?

'Just say, for the sake of argument,' Cora ventured, 'that I *did* start seeing him –' Lucy suppressed a shudder '– do any of your lot even know I'm your mother? I can count on one hand all the times during your career when other police officers have been to my house.'

'It's not just that,' Lucy replied. 'Look – Frank McCracken's a hardened criminal. Oh, I get it, don't worry. That refined aura, that rough-diamond charm. He could win anyone over. But he's a murderer. He's surrounded by murderers. I can't stress that enough. The man he works for is one of the most feared gangsters in Britain. He's literally a homicidal maniac.'

61

Cora looked unimpressed.

'But you know all this already, don't you?' Lucy said, deflated.

'I'm not saying I'm about to tie the knot with him. I just don't think we can keep pretending that he isn't part of our lives. And quite clearly, neither does he.'

Again, Lucy didn't know how to respond. All this had come completely out of left field.

'If you insist on it, I won't thank him for the flowers,' Cora said. 'But this won't be the last time I hear from him. I can feel it in my bones.'

I'd love to know why, Lucy suddenly wondered. *What is he up to?*

Was it conceivable – was it even faintly possible – that Cora was right, and that McCracken was hankering after a proper family? If so, he surely couldn't imagine that she and her mother would provide that?

'How's work anyway?' Cora asked, trying to change the subject. 'Sounds like you had a busy day yesterday.'

'Yeah . . .' Lucy frowned as the waitress removed their plates. 'I had a bit of a score, but it was none of it very edifying. Think of the quietest, leafiest neighbourhood you can, and there'll be monsters there. Hiding behind the privets and the chintz curtains.'

'And yet some of the lowliest people in society are exactly the opposite.'

Lucy shrugged. 'Good and evil don't make class distinctions.'

Briefly, Cora stared at nothing. 'And no one looks out for them.'

'Well . . . *we* try to.'

'You think so? What happened to that bloke Walter Brown?'

'Walter who?'

Cora relapsed into thought. 'I didn't know him very well. Gardener . . . but he had a drink problem. Lost his job, lost his flat. For a time, he was selling the *Big Issue* at the top of Langley Street. Then he went missing.'

'I'm sorry, what?'

'Used to see him every Wednesday lunchtime, when I went shopping,' Cora said. 'He was a nice man, when he was sober.'

'What do you mean, "He went missing"?'

'One week he just wasn't there. A week later, there was a young girl selling it. I asked her what had happened to Walter. She said she didn't know. They thought he'd just moved on. But he wouldn't have moved on, I'll tell you. He was a Crowley man. Been here all his life.'

'And did no one report this disappearance?' Lucy asked.

'Like who? He didn't have a family, didn't have any friends.'

'So, there's no actual evidence that anything bad happened to him?'

'No, but let's be fair, Lucy . . . if I was to tell you this about a neighbour, someone who actually lived in a house and paid their taxes, I reckon the next thing you'd do as a police officer would be to knock on their door, to see what was what.'

Lucy mulled this over and was sad to admit that it was probably true.

Homelessness was a major story in Britain today, and rightly so given that it was a national disgrace. At one time, you'd only see those poor wretches in the forgotten backstreets of big cities, but now they were everywhere, right under society's nose. And yet so few people even noticed them.

'I'm sorry, love . . .' Cora reached out and patted her daughter's hand. 'You're a good police officer. It's not your fault.'

Lucy didn't reply. For a moment, all she could think about was Stan Beardmore's comment the previous day: *They're just dogs . . . we've got a longer list of missing people who we haven't got time to look for.*

That 'list' comprised dozens of missing persons posters, each one depicting a grainy photograph of some poor individual – and there were all ages there, all races, all classes – who had dropped out of sight, never to be seen again. In many cases, it was so long ago that their posters had yellowed and curled. And it was the same story in police station foyers all over the UK.

And now they had more people vanishing from Lucy's own streets, and yet it had taken a homeless heroin addict dressed as a nun, and an off-handed comment from her mother, to draw her attention to them.

'No, it's not our fault,' Lucy agreed. 'But maybe we can do a better job than we are doing.'

Chapter 6

Mick Shallicker lounged in the penthouse suite of the Astarte Hotel in central Manchester.

The Astarte was a bland structure, looking like a typical midweek stopover for travelling businessmen, which was exactly the impression that its owners, Ent-Tech Ltd, aka the Crew, liked to give. The top floor, which was nominally the penthouse suite, comprised bedrooms, an office, a boardroom and a lounge bar, none of it accessible by public stairway or lift, only by a private express elevator, which ascended straight to it from a subterranean car park to which normal customers were also denied entry.

In fact, the Astarte was the hub of Crew operations, though few people who passed it would have the first clue that this presentable but on the whole innocuous building housed a crime syndicate whose baleful influence was so far-reaching that even the police had to tread warily around them.

Mick Shallicker was as much a part of this as the immense granite building blocks from which the Astarte was constructed. His prime role was as personal minder and chief enforcer to Frank McCracken, the Crew underboss in charge of shaking down all those non-affiliated criminal groups in the Northwest who didn't voluntarily pay 'tax'. By its nature, this department had constantly to be ready to threaten or employ violence to get its way, and Mick Shallicker was right at the heart of that. It helped that he was six-foot-nine, with a build to match. He was broad and strong as an ox, an all-round giant whose rugged, brutal face bespoke no mercy for those falling into his grasp.

At present, he was in the lounge bar, next door to the boardroom, sipping a cold beer and snacking on an excellent buffet. Others like him, at least in terms of rank, were dotted around the spacious, comfortable room, some on couches, some in armchairs, some, like Shallicker, standing at the bar. There was some chit-chat, but nothing especially warm or friendly, though there was no tension in the air. None of these men trusted each other, though they didn't dislike each other, and even if there was some animosity, theirs wasn't a paygrade that permitted outward displays of it. Watched closely by several dark-suited members of Benny B's security team, who had already disarmed everyone on arrival, they spoke civilly to each other if it was necessary to speak – there were even a few quips, a few chuckles – but for the most part they simply nodded, smiled their enigmatic half-smiles and kept quiet.

All, though, were listening – mainly for any sign of increased volume from the boardroom next door. At present, it seemed calm, though this was a special meeting that had been called at short notice by Crew Chairman 'Wild Bill' Pentecost, and that didn't always bode well. In fact, Mick Shallicker was so intent on listening – he knew there'd been a certain amount of strain in recent times between Pentecost and Frank McCracken in particular – that he half-jumped when his mobile suddenly buzzed in his jacket. Fishing it out, he saw to his surprise that he'd received a text from Lucy Clayburn.

Need to speak to him. ASAP.

He put the phone away and continued to wait and listen.

In the boardroom, Bill Pentecost was holding court from his usual place, standing at the head of the long teak table. At sixty-one, he was a tall, lean, permanently besuited man, and yet his appearance was never less than curious and unsettling. He had frizzy grey hair, a thin pale face and narrow blue eyes, which he levelled like a pair of laser beams through the square-lensed, steel-rimmed spectacles he always wore.

'These are difficult times, gentlemen,' he said in that slow, emotionless monotone that friends and foes alike found so difficult to read, and therefore so unnerving. 'New challenges, it seems, are presenting themselves every day.'

The meeting had commenced at nine that evening, and only now, after ten, having dispensed with some routine matters, did Frank McCracken suspect the Chairman was at last getting down to his main business. By the concerted attention on everyone else's faces, the rest of the Crew's directorship felt the same. For his own part, McCracken was resolved to look calm and relaxed. Like all birds of prey, Wild Bill could sense fair game before it had even broken cover. Not that McCracken considered himself in those terms. Things were strange at present – there was something in the air he didn't like – but generally he was at home in this dangerous company. Though in his mid-fifties, he'd kept well. He was tanned and fit, with a silver-grey crewcut, dark eyes and lean, predatory features that did little to conceal the hawkish personality underneath. As the Crew's shakedown captain, his line wasn't always as profitable as some of the others, but he was a regular and reliable contributor to company funds and he'd been close to Pentecost since their earliest days.

He wasn't what you'd call Pentecost's right-hand man. That honour was bestowed on Lennie Trueman, the Crew's official deputy chief, and a guy who could turn half the criminal population of Northwest England against them at the drop of a hat. But because of their history together, Frank McCracken was one of Pentecost's inner cadre of specially trusted henchmen, though in the last couple of years there'd been a slight fraying of the relationship, McCracken concerned that the Chairman was becoming too suspicious, too paranoid, Pentecost reacting to McCracken's blunt viewpoints with undisguised hostility.

'Only last week in Stockport,' the Chairman said, 'the Manchester Robbery Squad arrested two characters called Vladimir Boyarksi and Oleg Mikhalkov for a security vault robbery in Wilmslow, which had netted them around £900,000 in cash and jewellery. These two clowns were captured after beating their inside man, a cokehead idiot who was so stoned on the lunchtime in question that he wasn't able to assist them in opening all the strongboxes they'd targeted. Afterwards, fearing further retribution, he went to the nearest cop shop, and ratted them out. They and the hoard of cash and jewels they stole are now in government hands. The latter is a particular loss, I fear –' he threw a glance at McCracken '– because it means that our resident taxman will not be able to get his hands on our share.'

'That's the status at present,' McCracken spoke up. 'But there are ways and means.'

Pentecost made no reply to that, not especially appeased.

'These fools will get big stretches,' he said. 'But despite this they remain unknown to the British police. They're refusing to talk, of course, or even behave as if they understand English. They have no criminal records in the UK, or anywhere else according to Interpol. But, dim as our pals in the Manchester fuzz are, I doubt it will be long before they finally put names to faces and deduce that this terrible twosome is in fact Yuri Lyadova and Dimitri Guseva, two mid-ranking soldiers from the Tatarstan Brigade, who operate out of St Petersburg.'

He paused for effect. Everyone remained rapt.

'You may argue,' Pentecost said, 'that anyone who'd put his trust in some brainless junkie fuck is scarcely worthy of the designation "soldier". And I'd be inclined to agree, except that what these Russkie knuckle-draggers usually lack in brain-power, they make up for in numbers and loyalty.'

The boardroom hung on his every word. He surveyed them one by one.

'I'm not saying we're facing a Russian invasion here. At least, not an imminent one. But these two were most likely skirmishers sent ahead to check out the lie of the land. No doubt there'll be others.'

'A Tatarstan lieutenant was killed in a shootout with National Crime Group officers in Bradburn up in Lancashire last year,' ventured Adam Gilcrist. As the Crew's chief importer and seller of illegal firearms, he always had an interest in illicit gun-play. 'The coppers think he was acting alone, but this new intel suggests different.'

'The Russians have a permanent presence in Liverpool,' Lennie Trueman said in his deceptively gentle West Indian accent. 'And it's not just them. We've got Mexicans interfering with some of our supply-lines.'

'Ah yes, the cartels,' Pentecost said thoughtfully. 'It was only a matter of time before those gentlemen found the whole of Mesoamerica too small for their liking.'

'They'll struggle to make an impact here,' Benny Bartholomew chirped up.

Benny B, the Crew's Head of Security, was a beefy character, with slab-like arms and shoulders and an equally massive neck, but much of it was running to flab these days;

his face was podgy, his curly hair receding, and, as he viewed the world by squinting at it through a small pair of circular lenses, the effect was often more comical than menacing.

'You think so, do you?' Pentecost said, intrigued to hear more.

Benny B leaned forward, his chair squeaking. 'There're no deserts here for them to dig pits in, which they can stuff full of headless corpses, are there?'

'I hate to rain on your parade, Mr B,' Toni Zambala interrupted.

Formerly a pirate and smuggler in the pay of the Mungiki crime syndicate in Kenya, Zambala, despite a machine-gun-toting youth in which he'd violently rejected all things western, had effortlessly adapted to the capitalist lifestyle of the UK. He was now in charge of narcotics, importation and distribution, and his annual contribution to company funds was greater by far than everyone else's, so, though still an underboss, when he spoke, people listened.

'Not three weeks ago, one of my sellers was fished out of a Fallowfield sewer.' He took a sip of mineral water. 'He hadn't had his head cut off, I'll grant you, but that was only because the guys responsible had wanted to put him down the sewer while he was still alive . . . minus his hands and feet, I should add. The cops reckon the chopping tool was a machete.' He turned his gaze on Benny B. 'Kind of a Mex thing, wouldn't you say?'

Pentecost pursed his thin grey lips. 'Not an ideal situation. When our own people are getting their hands and feet chopped off.'

Frank McCracken was the only one who didn't mutter his discontent. He was too busy wondering where all this was leading. He too had heard rumours that foreign powers were slowly muscling in on their action. Not so much his, maybe. He dealt mainly with those established British gangs

70

who even after all these years still failed to recognise the Crew's authority. But it was plain there was a foreign presence on the streets.

'You're very quiet, Frank,' Pentecost suddenly said.

McCracken shrugged. 'We might have to make deals, Bill.'

'Surrender?' Benny B said, sounding shocked.

'Not that exactly,' McCracken replied. 'Just talk to them, so we can buy them off for a while . . . give ourselves more time to plan.'

'Bollocks!' Nick Merryweather blurted. 'We're not losing so much ground that we're being forced into *that*, surely?'

Merryweather was the Crew's whoremaster-in-chief, and a depraved, violent pimp. But for all that he was good at brutality, he wasn't the sharpest tool in the box.

'Even if we were confronting them,' McCracken replied, 'which we're *not* because we never know where they are, all we'd really be doing is fighting fires. Like you say, Bill, they're scouting rather than invading.'

A silence followed, as the rest of them ingested this.

'Well, Frank,' Pentecost finally said, 'the latest batch of accounts appear to support your POV inasmuch as we certainly need to rebuild our powerbase.' He wafted a fistful of print-outs before slamming them down on the table. Even those seated farthest away could recognise the columns of financial data.

'And as you gentlemen no doubt can tell from my demeanour,' Pentecost said, 'they don't make for happy reading.' He snatched a sheet up and turned to Jon Killarny, the Irishman who ran their counterfeiting scams. 'August this year – down three per cent on July. July down two per cent on June. June down one per cent on May.'

'Now, Bill . . . I . . . ' Killarny, a one-time IRA sergeant-at-arms, struggled to explain himself, only for Pentecost to

71

switch his attention to Al Reed, whose role was the 'protection' of pubs, bars and nightclubs.

'August this year . . .' The Chairman shook his head. 'Down six per cent on July. *Six per cent,* gentlemen. July down three per cent on June . . . and then this, June down *eight per cent* – yes, I kid you not – on May. None of you need to look smug, by the way.' There was now a snap in his voice, his frosty eyes roving the room. 'It's the same across the board. When we reach November, we'll have a better picture of our earnings for this last financial year, but even the boldest estimate puts them down an average four per cent on last year, which was four per cent down on the year before . . .'

And so it went, the Chairman listing and describing each and every one of their underperformances. In the end, only Frank McCracken's department's monthly returns were more or less in alignment, August showing a reduction on the previous month of less than half a per cent, though even that, to Bill Pentecost, was less than tolerable.

'Of course,' he said, resuming a calmer tone, 'these are our net earnings, are they not? They're not gross.'

There were visible stirrings of discomfort. Suddenly, they all knew what he was driving at, and it was exactly what Frank McCracken had feared.

The Crew was born of bloodshed. Back in those distant days of the twentieth century, numerous criminal firms had dotted the post-industrial wilderness that was Northwest England, each with its own territory, each with its own speciality, though they'd shared many overlapping interests, which for decades meant they'd existed in a state of semi-permanent warfare, ensuring that no one was earning to their full potential. The Crew had been the remedy, Wild Bill Pentecost, whose stronghold at the time was in East and South Manchester, and whose field was loan-sharking and general racketeering, eventually luring the bosses of his rival firms into a new kind of unity which promised peace and prosperity for all. Many of those original men still sat in the room, equal partners in the overarching enterprise that was the Crew, deferring only to their acknowledged Chairman, their various departments still reflecting the particular expertise they'd each brought to the table.

But all along Pentecost had known that he couldn't expect this rapacious band to work solely for him, each week feeding the entirety of their ill-gotten gains into central funds via an elaborate money-laundering operation, from which they would all be paid an equal monthly share. That would have been totally unacceptable because it would have been unfair. Toni Zambala, for example, outsold all the others, while at the other end of the scale Benny B added nothing to company cashflow, a discrepancy exacerbated by the fact that his role as Head of Security was largely nominal these days, most of the underbosses preferring to resolve security issues them-selves. McCracken alone had at least as many bent coppers, solicitors, local government officials and journalists on his payroll as Benny did, while Lennie and Toni held both the region's major cities in thrall to their innumerable dealers, street gangs and general-purpose thugs. Benny B couldn't be underestimated, of course. Having spent much of his time recruiting mercenaries and other ex-military personnel, he could put a considerable force of well-trained killers into the field – but still, he didn't *produce* anything. Appreciating the dangers of this imbalance, Pentecost had authorised at an early stage what he called 'the skim', which allowed each underboss to keep 25 per cent of each week's earnings. It remained dirty, of course, and it didn't always amount to a massive sum, but it allowed his individual captains to pay additional staff, soldiers, runners, lookouts and the like, and to lavish a little extra wealth on themselves from time to time. It kept them happy, and encouraged them to work their people ever harder, because the larger each department's official income, the larger its skim.

Little wonder it was now regarded as a sacrosanct perk.

But of course, what a man could make, he could also unmake.

'Alas, we may have to pick up some of this slack ourselves,' Pentecost said, walking around the room with that slow, heavy tread of his. 'So . . . as a temporary measure, I propose that we cut the skim from twenty-five per cent to fifteen.'

There were audible murmurs of discontent. Chair legs scraped, narrowed eyes exchanged surly glances.

'It's a proposal at present,' Pentecost added, no tension in his voice. 'But I want you to consider it very seriously, gentlemen. These are difficult times, as we've already discussed. Even now, it may not seem necessary that we prepare a war-chest, but wars often happen when you're least expecting them.'

'Yo, Bill,' Merryweather protested, 'if you're talking about cancelling the skim . . .'

'I'm not talking about cancelling it, I'm talking about trimming it.'

'A ten per cent cut is some trim,' Toni Zambala pointed out.

'Slashing it then. Never fear, there'll be *something* left.'

More mutters of irritation.

'Gentlemen, you surprise me.' Pentecost strolled back to his own end of the table. 'Are we not the ruling elite? Do you seriously expect the burden of these losses to fall elsewhere when we ourselves –' he tossed the paperwork down the table '– are directly responsible for them?'

'If there are losses across the board, Bill,' Al Reed ventured, 'couldn't it just be the effect of austerity?'

'Austerity is something that impacts on the ordinary,'

74

Pentecost replied. 'On those who lack the means and the will to resist it. *We* are immune to austerity, because we are the extraordinary.'

'Don't we get to vote on this?' Trueman wondered.

Pentecost met him eye-to-eye. This was the potential crisis point. Trueman's body-language suggested they had not okayed this beforehand. That would be typical Wild Bill these days. Increasingly, he reacted to developments in knee-jerk fashion. Previously, he would never have made a potentially controversial move without discussing it with his number two first. It would have been difficult for any of them to tackle Wild Bill on his own, but to tackle him and Lennie Trueman together would be suicide.

Billy Boy is riding his luck, McCracken thought.

But perhaps, on further consideration, Trueman, a cooler head who saw the bigger picture quickly, had decided that the very least they could do in these trying circumstances was put business before pleasure. So, though he remained taut, he awaited his Chairman's response politely.

'Of course,' Pentecost said, walking again. 'We're all equals in here.' He paused at the other end of the table. 'Any objectors raise their right hands.'

He swept them with his gaze as they each struggled with the matter.

One by one, with many a truculent stare directed downward, they folded their hands on the table in front of them, until it was unanimous.

'I think the motion is carried,' Pentecost said. 'Which concludes our business for today.'

The meeting didn't break up as amicably as usual.

The Chairman saw them out in his usual fashion, accompanying them into the penthouse lobby, where Benny B and his men restored their guns to them.

Pentecost spoke fake fond words as they departed. But when he went back into the boardroom, he found that they hadn't all left. Frank McCracken stood by the main window, taking in its panoramic view of the city.

'Still here, Frank?' Pentecost approached. 'I thought after that pep talk, we'd all consider we had rather a lot of business to attend to.'

'Just wondering if I could have a little private chat?' McCracken replied. 'For old times' sake, if nothing else.'

Pentecost mulled it over. 'Suppose I can spare a minute for one of my oldest muckers.'

'If a minute's all I've got, I'll get straight to it,' McCracken said. 'I wonder if you'd consider reversing that decision about slashing the skim?'

Pentecost looked sad. 'How disappointingly predictable of you.'

'Bill, come on . . .' McCracken allowed a conspiratorial note to creep into his voice. 'Look, these guys are on your side. Since you put the Crew together, they've never made as much dosh. Okay, they have to pay three quarters of it into central funds, but they're well rewarded for that, plus they recognise it's working. That's why they're happy to go along with it.'

'Go along with it, Frank? You make it sound like they have a choice.'

'Bill, you put this outfit together on the understanding everyone would have a certain degree of autonomy. We all sit at the same boardroom table, we all have the same ambition, but it's always been the case that each one of these guys is a gaffer in his own right, too.'

Pentecost affected a puzzled expression. 'Are you lecturing me about something I invented?'

'What I'm trying to say is they're loyal. But that we can't take that loyalty for granted.'

Pentecost headed for the door in the frosted glass wall partitioning the boardroom from his own office. He went through, leaving the door open for McCracken to follow.

The Chairman's office, or the Head Office as it was usually referred to, wasn't used a great deal, hence it existed in a permanent near-pristine state, its blocks of shelving lined with books, mostly legal and business tomes (which, from time to time, Pentecost actually read), but everything else hinting more at luxury: it had a plush carpet, expensive artwork on its wood-panelled walls, a seventy-inch hi-def television, a row of carved Italian chairs and, in the very centre, dominating everything, a huge, leather-topped desk with a neat stack of phoney paperwork at one end and a desktop computer at the other.

Pentecost strode to the drinks cabinet in the corner, where he filled two large tumblers with ice cubes and poured malt whisky from a crystal decanter.

'You know what I'm talking about, Bill,' McCracken said from the doorway. 'Lennie could close the entire Port of Liverpool to us. So how would Terry Underwood bring in his knock-off Italian dresses and shoes? You think the Camorra would be happy to put business on hold for as long as it takes us to buy another port? What about the Triads when it comes to knock-off tech from China? Aside from that, we get a cut of *everything* that comes through the docks. The merchants are happy to pay, the shipping lines are happy to pay – anything for a smooth operation. And when we don't get it, we steal it. What happens if all that dries up? And how would it impact on the narcotraffic? Toni would need to find a completely new way to import his product. Most likely, he'd go off and do his own thing. That'd be half our most lucrative operations down the toilet at the same time. Plus, if Lennie and Toni walk, it'll cost us the streets . . . we'll lose our eyes, our ears, our noses.

77

Meanwhile, Nicky and his vice girls are worth ten million to us each year alone. What if that cashflow dries up too?'

'And when will all this happen, do you think?' The Chairman offered McCracken his drink.

'I'm not saying it will.' McCracken took the glass. 'I've not heard a sniff of rebel talk. But it *could* happen. That's just common sense, isn't it? And look, Bill . . . I wouldn't be saying all this if me and you didn't go right back. You've got my firm promise, my solemn guarantee that whatever happens, I'll stand with you. You know you can always rely on me. But if it was two of us against the rest . . .'

Pentecost regarded him coolly. 'You seriously think I haven't considered this possibility, Frank? You think I haven't got contingency plans?'

On reflection, McCracken didn't think that for one minute, and had a fairly good idea what any such plans would entail. Bill Pentecost was nothing if not a forward thinker, especially where supporters whose loyalty might be suspect were concerned. For all the Crew's underbosses knew, any one of them could be sleeping in a house that might, at the touch of a match, become an escape-proof crematorium, or driving cars that could blow themselves to smithereens at the flick of a switch.

'We just don't want a civil war,' McCracken said, trying to sound as reasonable as possible. 'Not with everything else that's happening. Let the lads keep the skim. It helps them to pay their soldiers and runners in cash. And it gives them a bit extra to play with.'

'I think *that's* the real issue, don't you, Frank?' The Chairman sipped his malt. 'A bit of *personal* belt-tightening never goes down well.'

'Why should they do that? They've earned these extras.'

'They'll be earning nothing if these foreign nuisances continue to encroach on our territory.'

78

'I'm not pretending that isn't an issue, Bill. But why take it out on the lads?'

'Because the lads, as you call them, are not pulling their weight.'

McCracken pointed at the window. 'The enemy's out there, not in here.'

'The enemy won't meet us in open battle. Instead, he strikes us here, there, everywhere . . . whenever we aren't looking. But we *need* to be looking, Frank. That's my point. We *need* to be. *All* of us. If my own captains can't do that, the men who take a fortune out of this company every year for their own private pleasures, what fucking use are they?'

'Bill, come on . . . you know as well as I do that this is no straightforward war. Like you say, it's slow encroachment . . . and it's happening everywhere. It's the way things are, it's a new age of crime . . .'

'And we don't have a role any more. Is that what you're saying?'

McCracken placed his whisky on the desk; he hadn't touched a drop so far.

'We need to negotiate,' he said. 'It won't be difficult. Look . . . the Russians, the Mexicans, whoever it happens to be, they don't want a major scrap any more than we do.'

'So we should accept slavery?'

'No . . . but how about an equal partnership? Look, Frank . . . this is happening the world over. Yeah, there are occasional flare-ups, but most firms are finding out that if they're prepared to sit down at the table and talk with these guys, deals can be done.'

'There's a problem, though, Frank.' Pentecost seated himself behind his desk. 'You see, the Crew only exists as an entity if we're considered to be rule-makers, not rule-takers. And to be honest, I'm surprised I have to remind you of this.'

'How can we maintain that if we fall out among ourselves?'

'We won't be falling out among ourselves.'

'Maybe not.'

'*Definitely* not.'

'How can you be sure?'

'Because we took a vote on it.'

'That vote was coerced.'

Pentecost's eyebrows lifted. 'Really?'

'Okay, maybe not coerced. But the lads are all going home now, where they'll sit and have a good think about it . . . and in a short while they'll be steaming.'

Pentecost pondered this.

'Come on, Bill,' McCracken coaxed him. 'You *know* this. You don't need me to say it.'

'If that's the case, the only conclusion can be that even *more* stick is required.'

'Bill . . . are you not listening to me?'

'Frank . . . I think it's you who's not really listening to me. The way I see things, the *lads* have already had plenty carrot. A bit of stick too, I'll admit. But evidently not nearly enough.'

McCracken couldn't say anything else, and he didn't really need to. His disbelieving expression said it all.

'Your concern is noted.' The Chairman sat back in his swivel-chair, fingers steepled. 'And I've absolutely no doubt that should any of our . . . *lads* come to you with any kind of complaint, much less a scheme of any sort, you'll report it to me forthwith.'

'Yeah.' McCracken gave a small shrug. 'Sure.'

'I'm so glad.' Pentecost smiled, and because it was something he did rarely and was so unpractised at, it looked more than a little deranged. 'Your loyalty to the company is most welcome . . . even if it's only to be expected.'

Chapter 7

Raimunda was the ultimate platinum blonde.

Her glorious mane hung to the small of her back, her 38-24-38 figure accentuated by her body-hugging, electro-pink minidress, while her matching pink six-inch platform-heel sandals, which elevated her five-foot-ten inches to an intimidating six-foot-two, added what seemed like miles of luscious, shapely leg. As always, her sultry looks were daubed in makeup: blusher on the cheeks, thick kohl rimming her sapphire eyes, cherry gloss on the lips.

Clarissa had something even more exotic about her.

Her locks were shiny and tar-black. She was olive-skinned, her enchanting golden eyes almond-shaped, her cheekbones delicate, her mouth small but sensual, though ripened tonight with purple lip-glow. She was a similar shape to Raimunda: tall, almost unfeasibly so for a woman, but equally curvaceous. An archetypal Amazon warrior, her outfit comprised a green zip-sided miniskirt, a green camisole top and strappy shoes with six-inch clear heels.

The pair of them walked with an elegant sway even as they tiptoed through the grotty yard at the back of the terraced inner-Manchester residence. They kept it sexy – that was their stock-in-trade – but it was dark, so they also had to be wary of tripping over stacks of bricks, or sacks crammed with broken masonry.

'I'll see you next Monday,' Dean Chesham said from the open back door behind them. He was a muscular young black guy, film-star handsome, clad only in a pair of red silk undershorts. Despite the evening chill, his strong, stocky physique was slick with sweat.

They replied with lazy waves as they vanished through the back gate. Grinning to himself, Dean went back into the house.

The air indoors was cooling fast, because there was no central heating installed yet. He'd only recently had the electrics turned back on, because the darker nights were drawing in. For the most part, the house was a shell, its interior stripped to the bare bricks and boards. Only the back bedroom had any semblance of habitability. Dean padded back upstairs and walked down the landing towards it, towelling off with a stained and scruffy T-shirt. In normal circumstances, he'd have preferred a shower, but there were two good reasons why that wasn't in tonight's programme. Firstly, it would suit him to look sweaty when he finally got home; secondly, there was no running water.

The back bedroom was still bereft of wallpaper, plus it wasn't very large. Dean had just about managed to get a three-quarter-size double bed into it, and this was currently a mess, its mattress askew, its sheets tangled, clothes draped all over it. He pulled on a T-shirt and climbed into a pair of torn jeans with dried paint on them. Equally paint-stained was the dusty old sweat-top he put on over his T-shirt. He sat on the bed to knot the laces on his workboots, then he hit the light switch and headed along the landing, grabbing his L-Quad leather jacket from the newel post at the top of the stairs. Before going outside, he made sure to pull his hood up. Though cooler now that it was autumn, it wasn't cold. But he still had to get to the car without being recognised.

Exiting by the back door, he made his careful way across the cluttered yard. Out in the alley, a beaten-up Honda Civic waited for him. It had been around the mileage clock at least twice, but Dean didn't mind being seen in such a heap. It wouldn't stand out, and still had sufficient life left under its bonnet to get him quietly and unobtrusively back to the lock-up garage he rented in Styal, where he'd swap it for his black-and-red Range Rover Evoque.

Seventy-five big ones, that beauty had cost him. Even if he hadn't thought it would attract undue attention, he couldn't have risked bringing it to this neighbourhood. And perhaps it was ironic he was thinking this, because he now turned left through the gate into the alley, and the first thing he saw was a man loitering in the narrow space between the wall and the Honda's front nearside door.

Dean halted, but more through puzzlement than fear.

Lights shone from the windows of some of the surrounding houses with just enough strength to show that, whoever this guy was, he didn't look threatening. He was about average height, average build, with neatly combed silver hair over a thin, pinched face, and a trim silver-grey moustache. He wore a buttoned-up Burberry trenchcoat, and underneath that a shirt and tie. Dean glanced down, spying well-pressed trousers with proper creases in them, and leather shoes.

He ventured forward, fishing the car keys from his jacket pocket, but then he spied a second man standing behind the first. This second guy was about the same height as the other, but twice the width. He too wore a jacket and tie, but it bulged around a massive body, while his collar hung open on a neck the girth of a tree-trunk. He had cauliflower ears, a dented nose and small eyes beneath heavy bone brows. He was younger than the first guy, probably somewhere in his mid-forties, with a dense, matted beard and moustache.

'If it isn't Black Lightning,' the guy in the trenchcoat said. By his accent, he was a Manchester man, but it was modified, refined.

'Do I know you?' Dean replied.

Trenchcoat looked worried. 'Sorry, that isn't racist, is it – Black Lightning? Isn't that what they call you on the Stretford End?'

'That's what they call me, yeah.'

'Good. Thought so.'

'If you don't mind . . .' Dean pointed his key at the Honda, but Trenchcoat stayed where he was.

'Your footwork's seriously amazing,' he said. 'I've seen you dance through defences like . . . well, like no one did since the days of Georgie Best.'

Dean glanced again at the Neanderthal visage of the bearded guy behind him. Then he became aware that a third character had circled into view around the other side of the car. This one too was in his forties; he also wore a suit and tie, but was rangy of frame, with a hatchet nose and a messy thatch of dirty blond hair. He now stood directly behind the footballer, blocking any possible retreat.

'Okay, listen . . .' Dean backed into the brick wall. 'You fellas surely realise I don't carry money round with me? I mean, I've got a few quid.' He dug into his jeans pocket. 'You can take *that*.'

'I'm surprised you've got any left after tonight,' Trenchcoat said.

Dean offered him a tightly wound roll of twenties. 'Just take it, yeah?'

'Relax, Lightning. We're not here to rob you.'

'Yeah?' Dean's nervous gaze flicked back and forth between

them. 'Well, I'm sure this isn't a welcome-to-the-neighbour-hood party.'

'More like welcome-to-the-jungle round here,' the bearded one said. He was Mancunian too, though much more obviously. 'Ideal for the kinds of tricks *you* get up to, eh?'

'Look,' Dean said. 'I don't know what you fellas think you know.' He thumbed at the house on the other side of the wall. 'I'm just doing this place up.'

'Yeah, we've heard,' Trenchcoat said. 'Your little retirement plan, isn't it? You've been buying run-down houses all over the Northwest, doing them up till they're spanking new and selling them on at considerable profit.'

'Nothing illegal about that,' Dean ventured.

'Course not,' Trenchcoat agreed. 'But I'd like to bet that none of the houses you've *officially* bought so far are quite as run-down as this one, eh?'

'I've *officially* bought this one.'

Trenchcoat half-smiled. 'When I say "officially" . . . I mean, as in your lovely wife, Lydia, knowing about it. Oh, I'm sure she's well aware and totally approves of this safety net you're putting together for when your playing days are over. But the problem is, Lightning . . . she thinks it means houses round Knutsford, Didsbury and Altrincham, doesn't she? I bet she'd be stunned to know you've got a new pad in the backstreets of Withington.'

'Okay, it's a shed.' Dean shrugged. 'But we'll still make money when we've done it up.'

'You're a great footballer, Dean,' the blond guy said, speaking for the first time; his accent was more Cheshire than Manchester. 'But you're not too smart if you seriously think we don't know what's going on here.'

'You believe in quality, I'll say that for you,' Beard added. 'That Clarissa bird. Bloody hell . . . you'd never know she was a bloke. And Raimunda! Some dong, that. John fucking Holmes in drag.'

'John Holmes, Lightning,' Trenchcoat said. 'Remember him? No, course you don't. Too young. There are similarities between you and him, nevertheless. For example . . .' He drew a leather-gloved hand from his pocket; it contained an iPhone. 'You've both been immortalised in naughty films.'

An MPEG began running. It had been shot from several different angles, all of which were most likely covert, but it was in full colour and painfully clear. It was also full of action, a 'highlights reel', snippets of different sessions involving either Dean and Raimunda, Dean and Clarissa, or more usually Dean and both of them, each sequence trimmed to the bare essentials and then edited together.

Fleetingly, the footballer was too numb to respond.

'All right . . .' he finally said. 'All right, you've caught me. But I'm not sure this'll be quite as damaging as you fellas seem to think. Raimunda and Clarissa are trans women. Yeah . . . so what? It's not so shocking these days.'

'That's true.' Trenchcoat pocketed his iPhone. 'We live in a very inclusive age. But the problem is, Lightning . . . you're a married man. And your wife, Lydia, well . . . she's been wondering for some time where you've been disappearing to for two or three nights a week. So she asked us to find out.'

'You're saying you're private detectives?' Dean wasn't sure whether to be relieved or even more horrified.

'Good job it doesn't take you that long to get to the back of the net,' Beard chipped in. 'Otherwise, no one'd give a shit what you get up to in this secret nookie nest of yours.'

'She doesn't trust you, pal,' Hatchet Nose said. 'She never has.'

Trenchcoat smiled again. 'When Lydia married you, Lightning, she knew she'd landed on her feet . . . and she

Chapter 8

The woman was called Janet Dawson, and she was het up. Lucy met her at her father's house just after ten that morning. She was in early middle age and tubby, with curly fair hair running to grey, and a pale, worried face.

The address was 8, Atkinson Row, and it belonged to an OAP called Harry Hopkins.

'I've been ringing Dad for the last three days,' she said, ushering Lucy down a short hall into the interior of a terraced house so neat and tidy it could have passed for a show home. 've been asking around too. His friends and the locals down e pub. No one's seen him.'

'He keeps a tidy home,' Lucy said, looking around the unge and then heading upstairs.

'Oh, yes.' The woman followed. 'He's always been very use-proud.'

There's absolutely nothing out of place?' Lucy asked, king into the two bedrooms.

Nothing obvious. Oh . . . apart from out at the back. Do know about that already?'

eah, I was told about that before I got here.'

hat had really panicked Janet Dawson, on calling to see

was in it for the long haul. She was going to milk it for everything she could . . . even if it ended up in the divorce court—'

'Wait a minute,' Dean interrupted, glimpsing hope. 'Just wait . . . you're saying she doesn't suspect anything specific? She's just watching me?'

'She half suspects,' Trenchcoat said.

'You must admit, you've been away from home a lot recently,' Hatchet Nose added.

'And if she's not getting it in the bedroom, which she presumably isn't,' Beard said, 'she's going to wonder.'

'On top of that, she's never been entirely convinced that you're doing these houses up yourself,' Trenchcoat said. 'She doesn't believe you know the first thing about DIY. Isn't that why you spent a million quid getting someone else to fit that new bathroom in your mansion down Alderley Edge?'

'So you've been watching me for a few weeks,' Dean said. 'But you haven't reported back to Lydia yet? Is that what you're saying?'

'That's the sum of it,' Trenchcoat replied. 'Want to know why?'

'I'm guessing it's not because you like football.'

'You guess right where I'm concerned,' Beard replied. 'I fucking hate it.'

'I, on the other hand, *do* like it,' Hatchet Nose said. 'I'm even a Man U fan. But the Reds were great before you, Dean, and they'll be great again after.'

Dean's eyes flitted from one to the other. 'So . . .?'

'So we want to get paid twice,' Beard said.

'What do you mean?'

'Your wife's giving us two hundred grand to tail you for four months,' Trenchcoat explained. 'To find out exactly what's been going on, and whether or not it's dodgy . . . and if it is, to provide indisputable evidence. Now, we've got that evidence, as you've seen. But, you see, here's the thing . . . we don't *like* to ruin people's lives. We only do it if we absolutely have to. So, our normal method, once we've collected said evidence, is to give the guilty party an opportunity to buy it back.'

'I think I understand,' Dean said, with a dull, sinking feeling.

'Course you understand,' Trenchcoat replied. 'But do it our way, and it all works out beautifully. We go back to your missus, tell her you're clean as a whistle. You then go home and get hugs and kisses instead of a solicitor's letter. Everyone's happy. And we get paid twice.'

'And how much is this going to cost me?' Dean asked.

'Well, your wife's paying us two hundred. We thought the very least it'd be worth to you, given that your kids won't see Mummy and Daddy split up, and the Chelsea boot-boys won't suddenly have a whole new generation of nasty names to call you . . . maybe four times that.'

'Eight hundred grand?' Dean was stung, but he could easily afford it.

'Makes it a round million.' Hatchet Nose grinned. 'And we only get taxed on a fifth of it.'

'You look surprised, Lightning,' Trenchcoat said. 'No doubt you thought, as someone who earns two hundred grand a week just for showing up, the cost would be a lot more. Well . . . the sad fact is there's always a danger that something could slip out to the press at a later date. Not straight away, obviously. But we'll still have your best interests at heart, so every so often it'll be worth us checking in with you . . . just to ensure that it's a false alarm.'

Dean nodded. It was unbearable of course, but he had no choice.

'Okay.' Trenchcoat's tone lightened, almost became friendly. 'Well, that's it. There's nothing else to discuss. We'll

be in touch shortly, about how and when this needs happen.'

He turned and walked away, Hatchet Nose going w him. But the larger, bearded individual remained, hoveri like an ape in the half-darkness – before lurching forwa coming close to Dean, nose to nose.

'You got off easy,' he grunted. 'No one on this fuck planet thinks you and those other prima donnas are w the fortune you earn. You may reckon they love you, su star, but don't be fooled. Away from the footy groun half of them saw you lying in a gutter burning, they'd r your wallet before even thinking about calling the Brigade.'

Then he turned and lumbered away too, vanishin the gloom.

her father this morning and discovering the house empty, had been the back door and back gate, which were both wide open. She'd quickly called the police. Uniform had arrived first and, not liking it either, had passed the info to CID.

'We'll look down at the back in a sec,' Lucy said, still checking around upstairs.

She noticed a large, circular cushion on the carpet next to Harry's bed. A well-chewed rubber bone sat in the middle of it.

'Your dad has a dog?'

'Yes. Milly . . . she's a Pekingese.'

'Does he take her out a lot?'

'Yeah. She gets at least two walks a day. But he leaves her in when he's off to the pub or the bookies, or something like that.' The woman's voice trembled as she spoke.

Lucy pondered. She didn't say it aloud, because she simply wasn't sure, but the absence of the dog made foul play a little less likely. If you were going to abduct someone, would you really go to the trouble of abducting their pet too? It seemed more possible that something had happened to the old guy while he was out walking the dog, but if there'd been an accident, or he'd dropped dead from a heart attack, someone ought to have found him by now. And then there was the mystery surrounding the back door and the back gate.

'Could your father have left her here, forgotten to lock up at the back, and she's just run away?' she asked.

'I honestly don't think she'd run away,' the woman replied. 'And I've never known Dad make a mistake like that before. Plus, why would he go out without his hat and coat?'

They went downstairs and through into the lounge, where the television was playing away to itself, a range of Saturday-morning chefs producing a selection of mouth-watering dishes.

'And that's not like Dad either,' Janet Dawson said. 'The telly being on.'

'It was on when you arrived here this morning?' Lucy asked.

'Yes.'

'Could he not just have left it on as a security measure while he was going out . . . you know, to make thieves think he was in?'

'Yes, but he only does that at night.'

The implication was evident.

'What time did you arrive this morning?' Lucy asked.

'Just after eight.'

'So you're worried the television might have been left on all night?'

The woman looked even paler than before. 'I can hardly bear to think what that might mean if it's true.'

'Your father doesn't own any other property that we might look around?' Lucy asked. 'An allotment with a shed perhaps? A garage?'

'No, I'm sorry.'

'Okay.' Lucy walked back through the house to the kitchen, where she halted next to one of the spotless worktops. A mug containing a dry teabag and an unused spoon sat alongside the kettle. This was more suggestive than anything she had seen at the house so far.

Most telling of all, though, was the open back door.

Lucy pulled on a pair of disposable latex gloves.

'Oh, my God,' Janet Dawson moaned.

'It's just a precaution.' Lucy checked along the door's edge and down the edge of the door-jamb. 'There's no sign of any damage here.'

'I don't think anyone forced entry. I mean, there's no damage anywhere. And it's not like there's any sign of a scuffle. Nothing's broken, there're no blood spots or anything.'

'So, if someone came into the house this way,' Lucy said, 'your father must have let them in willingly.'

'I suppose so.' Janet Dawson gave a weak, forced smile. 'That's good, isn't it?'

Lucy didn't mention that most of the violence in modern society was inflicted by persons known to the victim. Instead, she said, 'How many of your father's house-callers are in the habit of coming to the back door?'

'I must admit . . . I can't think of any who would do that, or why.'

They crossed the garden together. It was smoothly turfed aside from a crazy-paved path, with a brick platform on the right covered in potted plants. At odds with all this neatness, the back gate hung ajar.

'The gate was like this, this morning?' Lucy asked, again noting an absence of damage, which meant that this hadn't been forced open either.

'Exactly like it is now.'

'We shouldn't necessarily read something bad into this,' Lucy said. 'There are lots of possibilities here at present.'

Internally, however, she'd closed in on three main ones: a) an intruder had approached the house from the rear and had got inside that way, because Harry Hopkins had forgotten to lock up; or b) Harry Hopkins had gone outside himself, leaving the property by the back door and the back gate, and for some unknown reason had still not returned; or c) neither of those unpleasant alternatives had happened, and he was simply going about his everyday business, absent from home at this moment, again having neglected to lock up (and having left his hat and coat behind), and by pure coincidence had also been absent every time in the last three days when his daughter had phoned the house.

You wouldn't earn a police commendation for working out which of those options seemed least likely.

Lucy stepped through into the back alley. 'How often have you tried to contact your father in the last few days, Janet?'

The woman followed her out. 'First it was every few hours, but then . . . I mean yesterday and last night, it was once every ten minutes.'

'Is your father hard of hearing, by any chance?'

'He wears a hearing aid, but no . . . he can hear when the phone's ringing. He normally answers straight away.'

Lucy surveyed the alley. It was narrow, cobbled, and little more than a service passage running behind the row of houses. At present, it was clear of vehicles, or bins, or sacks of rubbish. On the other side, a high red-brick wall rose about ten feet, screening off the rest of the estate.

Lucy wasn't comforted by this. A narrow backstreet hidden from view on one side.

She turned back to the gate – and stopped in her tracks. Like the house's front door, the back gate had been painted a bright canary-yellow, but on the outside it had been spattered top to bottom with dried black trickle stains.

'This is a bit of a mess, isn't it?' she said.

'Oh.' Janet Dawson looked genuinely surprised. 'Dad'll go mad if he sees that. He hates scruffiness.'

'He'd scrub it off, would he? Even though it's on the outside?'

'Certainly. As soon as he saw it.'

Which likely means this has happened since he went missing, Lucy thought to herself. *Or did it happen at the time he went missing?*

She wondered what might have caused it. A vehicle travelling at speed would have kicked up ground water, spraying the gate, though not today of course; it was sunny today, unusually warm for mid-September. She glanced around. The cobblestones were bone-dry. Thinking about it, the last time they'd had proper rain – the sort that would leave proper puddles – was on Tuesday afternoon.

Three days ago.

Alan Rodwell was somewhere in his late twenties, bald, bespectacled and bearded. He stood barefoot on his front doorstep, wearing mismatched shorts and a T-shirt, blinking at Lucy's warrant card as she explained who she was and why she was here. A few seconds later, his wife, Sam, came down the hall from the kitchen. She was about the same age, a petite woman, also wearing shorts and a T-shirt, but with flipflops on her feet. She had shoulder-length brown hair, and plain, pale features still marked with makeup from the previous night.

'We haven't seen Harry for a couple of days,' Alan Rodwell said, shaking his head.

'When do you think you last saw him?' Lucy asked.

'Oh, I don't know. Could be a week ago, easily. I don't keep a record.'

'So definitely not since last Tuesday?'

'Nah, no way.'

'Do you ever hear him?' Lucy asked. 'I mean through the dividing wall between the houses?'

'Oh, yeah.' This time it was the woman who answered. 'In fact, you can hear his TV now. It's been on for ages. It was on all night last night, and . . . *oh*?'

Only belatedly did this seem to strike her as strange.

'It was on all night?' Lucy asked.

'And the night before, I think. And . . . maybe . . . hell, I don't know . . . maybe the night before that, as well.'

For the last three days in fact, Lucy thought.

'It never occurred to you, maybe, to go and knock on his door?'

Oddly, the couple glanced at each other with half-smiles, as if they were harbouring some mischievous secret.

'We don't really like to complain,' Alan Rodwell said. 'I'll be honest, Harry does that quite a bit with us.'

'I'm sorry?' Lucy said.

'Whenever we've got friends round,' Sam Rodwell explained. 'During the summer holidays usually. He gets upset if our barbecues go on too late and comes around, making a fuss. We don't want to do that back to him . . . he'd just think it was retaliation.'

'And, you know . . .' Alan Rodwell shrugged. 'Complaining's not really our thing.'

Lucy looked at them askance. 'I didn't mean knock on his door to complain, I mean to check if everything was all right.'

'Oh . . .' Their impish smiles faded.

They shuffled their feet awkwardly but didn't look guilty or afraid. Hardened criminals often had the ability to brazen things out when they were under suspicion; they could put on a front that even a seasoned detective might find it difficult to penetrate. But when ordinary people like these two had done something wrong, there were usually clear signs. Not so on this occasion. It was as though it hadn't even struck them yet that they might be in the frame.

'You've been hearing his television play continuously since – when?' Lucy said. 'Could it have been as far back as last Tuesday?'

'Around then, I suppose,' Sam Rodwell replied. 'Tuesday night was probably the first night we heard when it hadn't been turned off.'

'That's right,' her husband agreed. 'We were in bed and I could hear gunfire – like movie gunfire, you know. And cowboy film music. I said to Sam, "Christ, Harry's pulling a late one."'

Lucy nodded, and scrawled some notes in her pocket-book, one of which was to check if there'd been a western on TV late on Tuesday night.

'Is this going to take long?' Sam Rodwell asked. 'You see, we were just going to—'

'It'll take as long as it needs to, I'm afraid, Mrs Rodwell. We have a pensioner missing, and we'd like to get to the bottom of whatever's happened to him. So, I'd like you both to throw your minds back to Tuesday. Not just the night, but during the daytime as well. Did anything unusual happen? Doesn't have to be serious, but anything that seemed like a break from the norm, apart from the telly being left on?'

Their faces turned blank as they tried to think it through.

'You didn't hear any raised voices, perhaps?' Lucy prompted them. 'Any shouting or even laughing?'

They still looked blank.

'Any vehicles coming and going? Maybe at the back of the house?'

'Oh yes, wait . . .' Sam Rodwell said. 'There *was* something like that. Hell, I think this was on Tuesday night too. We heard like a screeching of tyres along the Backs.'

Lucy watched her carefully. 'Definitely along the Backs?'

The young woman nodded. 'Like a vehicle was tearing away, you know. It was quite unusual, because it's very narrow back there.'

'Yeah, I remember that now,' her husband said. 'Only lasted a second and then it was gone.'

'What time would this have been?' Lucy asked.

'I don't know.' Sam thought about it again. 'We weren't in bed at that stage, so not too late. Half-past ten, something like that.'

'You don't really think something bad could have happened to Harry, do you?' Alan asked, finally sounding concerned.

'That, sir,' Lucy replied, 'is what I'm trying to discover.'

'What do we think about the daughter?' Stan Beardmore asked from Lucy's laptop screen.

Lucy sat back in her office chair. 'I think she's genuine. She took a long time coming around to check, but she lives in Blackburn, plus she's a radiographer at the hospital there, so she works shifts. Sounds like this morning was the first chance she had to visit.'

'And the neighbours?'

'There's no one in No. 6. An old lady owns it, but she's in long-term care. The Rodwells, the couple who reported the speeding vehicle, live at No. 10. I don't get any particularly bad vibes about them. Typical young suburbanites. Bit self-centred maybe, but who wasn't at that age?'

'These were the ones Hopkins didn't get on with?'

'I don't think it was a case of him not getting on with them. Sounds more like the odd disagreement. Plus, if they *were* involved, wouldn't they just have turned his telly off, locked the house up, tried to make it look like he'd gone away?'

'Not if they wanted to make it look like he'd been attacked by an intruder,' Beardmore suggested.

'Outside his house at the back?' Lucy said. 'Late at night? If you were making a story up, would you seriously expect someone to buy that?'

Detective Sergeant Kirsty Banks, who was sitting on the desk behind Lucy, now cut in. She was a hefty woman, with an unruly mop of blonde hair and a penchant for wearing big cardigans over her T-shirts and jeans, though as it was warm today and electric fans whirred in the otherwise empty CID office, the cardigan at least had come off.

'I must be honest, Stan,' she said, 'if the Rodwells had done something to Harry Hopkins, and were trying to make it look like an intruder, surely they'd have wrecked the interior of his house . . . tried to make it look like a burglar had broken in?'

'That's your gut instinct, is it, Kirst?'

'I think Lucy's on the money. This needs further investigation.'

Beardmore thought about it. From his open-neck polo shirt, the garden chair he reclined in, the kids running around the lawn in the background and the muted conversation of friends and neighbours, he too was spending his Saturday at a barbecue.

'Lucy,' he eventually said. 'What other work have you got on?'

'Just bottoming off the paper from the dog-fighting arrests,' she replied.

'Get that done ASAP. Then you're on this exclusively till we get some kind of result.'

'No probs.'

'Kirsty . . . how buried is Tessa Payne?'

Banks flicked through the crime log. 'Not very. Plus, she's on call today.'

'Okay. Lucy . . . you've got Tessa.'

Lucy nodded. That would suit Tessa, she thought. The youngster had come into CID excitedly, and even more so on learning she'd be working with Lucy, whose recent results had caught the imagination of many young women in the job. Whether having an adoring student along for the ride was ideal for *her*, Lucy was less sure, but help was help.

'Right . . . you all know what you're doing.' Beardmore reached forward to switch off his laptop. 'If you need me, get on the blower.'

'Oh, boss . . .?' Lucy said.

'Yeah?'

'Can we copy Serious Crimes Division in?'

Beardmore sat back, looking suspicious. 'Why?'

'I don't know . . .' She shrugged. 'But I'm hearing second-hand that some homeless people have dropped out of sight recently.'

Beardmore pondered this. 'Pensioner age?'

'They're older people, certainly. And two different sources have now drawn my attention to it.'

'Any suggestion these mis-pers have been abducted?'

'I don't know about that. I've not looked into it yet.'

There was a long pause while he considered it.

Lucy had already mentioned the vehicle at the back of Harry Hopkins's house, but she'd purposely said nothing about a black van. In truth, the thought had occurred to her immediately on hearing about the screeching tyres, but, on reflection, it was a real stretch. Firstly, no evidence had been found that any such vehicle existed. From the outset, the black van had been more legend than fact. They'd gone after Les Mahoney through intel received by the RSPCA. It had seemed possible at the time that there was a connection with this rumoured black van, but it wasn't the van, or any vehicle in particular, that had led them to his farm. Secondly, even if the black van was real, dog-napping didn't easily equate to kidnapping. Where was the actual link between the two?

'Copy Serious in if you want to,' Beardmore said, interrupting her thoughts. 'But be careful how you word it. Tell them this whole thing is open-ended as yet, and we're only marking their card. Underline that we've observed nothing thus far to make us suspect that a series of abductions is under way.'

Lucy nodded and Beardmore leaned forward again and cut the call.

Banks stood up. 'Big difference in MO, that, Luce. Grabbing someone from off the streets and grabbing someone from their own back door.'

'I know . . .' Lucy was equally uncomfortable with it. 'Hunch, sixth sense, whatever you want to call it.'

'Well, don't beat yourself up too much.' Banks headed back to her own desk. 'Hunch and sixth sense have caught killers in the past.'

Killers, Lucy thought.

She wouldn't have used that word herself. Not yet. But there was something disconcerting about all this, and the weirdness didn't reduce it to merely silly. Despite the arrests at Wellspring Lane, over twenty dog-napping cases were still wide open, along with rumours that a late-night vehicle had been prowling the housing estates where they'd disappeared. And now they had people disappearing as well, and yet another late-night vehicle was possibly involved in that.

It was like an urban myth coming slowly to life right on their doorstep.

But no, *no* . . . she resisted that idea strenuously.

They only had fragments of information, none of which necessarily married up. This whole thing could still turn out to be nothing. And the only way they could make firm judgements on that was if they started gathering and collating some real evidence.

No. 8, Atkinson Row and the backstreet behind it were now officially designated crime scenes. The first CSIs would be there later today. That could only help. In addition, there were witness statements to be taken. As soon as Tessa Payne checked in, Lucy would send her to speak to the Rodwells – because she herself had someone else she needed to speak to, and that would be far from straightforward. If she wanted to learn more about these alleged missing homeless, to try and work out whether they actually had disappeared, rather than left the area of their own volition, the only thing to do was go and talk to the homeless themselves.

Or at least to their spokesperson.

'Sister Cassie,' she muttered, taking a *Greater Manchester A-Z* from the drawer in her desk and flipping to the page on which a street map of Crowley, and the St Clement's ward especially, were displayed. 'Where on earth do I find you today?'

Chapter 9

It was quarter to ten on a Saturday night, and like every night Lorna Cunningham hit the pavements running in her hi-tech Ultraboost trainers and pink and green running vest and tights.

Her friends, even fellow exercise freaks, were always amazed when they learned that she went out for a run on Saturdays too.

'Seriously, babes?'

'You owe yourself some downtime.'

'You need to live a little bit, at least.'

Lorna smiled to herself as she lolloped across the housing estate. It wasn't a graceful running style, but she had long, lean limbs and she covered the ground quickly and effortlessly. Fitness was a big thing these days, but so many people played at it. Not Lorna. She was the real deal, getting herself into shape so that she could compete, denying herself chocolate, cakes and nights on the town so that she could bring her best game to the running track and the volleyball court. So that she could win. But that required mental strength as well as physical, which was exactly what she was demonstrating now: sticking rigidly to her routine, coming outside and putting herself through it on club night.

Even Alex, her boyfriend of several years and a three-times Ironman competitor, was fascinated by the discipline this required. Not that he was hugely supportive, though that was more out of concern about the lateness of the hour and the quietness of the streets.

Lorna simply told him not to worry. It was true: unless you were in the very centre of town, Crowley was usually quiet on a Saturday evening. The few cars on the roads were taxis and minicabs and there were almost no pedestrians. In his eyes that made it dangerous for her to be out alone, but Lorna always argued the opposite. Anyone of a thuggish inclination would probably be down in the bar and nightclub district, where they would find more than enough violent action.

However, Alex's unease had transferred itself to Lorna a little. He wasn't being overly protective; she knew there was some sense in his words of caution. A woman jogging solo after dark . . . well, you couldn't be too careful, could you, whatever night it was? Which was why, over the previous year, she'd devised this particular route and now followed it religiously. The first part, which she'd almost completed, led mainly through middle-class housing estates, where it seemed unlikely there'd be anyone hanging around looking for trouble. After that, she'd be out of sight completely, so there'd be no one at all to bother her – and she was almost at that point now.

Her breathing steadied, her pace increasing, as she circled around the top end of Queen Alexandra Park and joined Leatherton Lane. This was one of the busier roads in Lorna's part of town, but even here only a single vehicle flitted past, a blue transit van, its two occupants paying noticeable attention to her, though that was no surprise. Lorna had a tall, coltish figure but was freckled and pretty, her copper-red hair cut in a fetching pageboy bob.

It didn't matter anyway, because she now diverted from the pavement, vanishing into a passage between two maisonettes. It was an unlit cut-through, which, once it passed the back of the maisonettes and their rear gardens, sloped downward for fifty yards before joining the towpath on the north side of the Bridgewater Canal. Still sticking to her normal route, Lorna followed the towpath east, lengthening her stride alongside the night-black water, her feet thudding on the dry cinders. It was quite dark along here, the only light filtering down from streetlamps on bridges or over the tops of factory walls, but she had come this way so often in the last few months that she felt she could have run it blindfolded.

Some of her friends thought that she was extra-brave for coming this way. This was possibly the quietest stretch of the canal, with no residences, no houses or narrowboats. If pressed on the matter, Lorna supposed that, yes, it would be an ideal place for some weirdo to launch an ambush. But firstly, why would some predatory individual hang about down here, where he wouldn't expect to find anyone? And secondly, she had faith in her physical abilities. She was now two miles into the run and still travelling at a pace well above jogging speed. She might be hot and sweaty, moisture pooling on her brow, but she had plenty of energy left. Her lungs were going like the clappers, her hamstrings and the backs of her calves steadily tightening, but she was fit, and actual fatigue was still far away – she could keep going for hours yet and was certain that she could easily outrun the average person.

She'd just reached the Navigation Lock, however, where the gaunt shell of a pub stood on the other side of the water, its windows boarded, when she suddenly sensed that there was someone else on the towpath. She glanced behind her and was just able to distinguish a diminutive shape some fifty yards away. Disconcerted, she glanced back again, this time for longer, trying to get a proper view of whoever it was.

The shape passed through a patch of streetlighting, and Lorna glimpsed a slim, girlish figure in a pale-grey tracksuit, wearing what looked like white trainers, with a mop of light blonde hair.

She ran on, uncertain why she still wasn't happy. Almost unconsciously, she increased her speed a little, legs now pumping, lungs working furiously, until she was moving at what felt like a half-sprint. That wasn't really a good idea. She still had about three miles to go, and if she kept this up she'd be exhausted long before she reached that target. She decelerated again, glancing over her shoulder a third time.

Inevitably, the figure had fallen behind a few yards and was in dimness again, so it was difficult to identify anything about her aside from her sex. That alone should have made her presence less threatening, but Lorna still couldn't help thinking it odd that the other runner had come upon her seemingly from nowhere. Of course, that made it sound more sinister than it possibly was. The girl or woman might have been jogging along the canalside anyway, Lorna coming down the cut-through from Leatherton Lane just ahead of her. There was no reason why it couldn't be as innocent as that. But again, at the risk of thinking like Alex, it was late, the towpath was dark and that other runner was a lone female.

Lorna had assumed that only she was bold enough to take a route like this so late at night.

She glanced behind one final time. The other runner had fallen a significant distance behind. It wouldn't be long before she was out of sight altogether.

Now, several hundred yards past the pub, the wall on Lorna's left gave way to rusted wrought-iron fencing and, on the other side of that, flat open ground. She knew from having run this way earlier in the year, when the evenings were lighter, that it was mostly allotments over that way; the terraced houses to which they belonged were still visible about three hundred yards distant, but only in outline. A little past the allotments, the fencing ended and the garages began. There were six of them, a terraced row, all backing onto the towpath, all disused. They were decades old and built from cheap wood: flimsy, teetering structures, their sagging tarpaper roofs ready to fall in.

Lorna passed them by without a second glance, driving relentlessly forward, her breathing more ragged now, but her feet still pounding the cinders. Further iron fencing appeared on her left. Whatever lay behind that was lost in total darkness. Then, from somewhere not too far behind, there came a sharp cry of pain.

Lorna glanced backward again, once and then twice, the second time looking for longer, trying to focus through the dimness.

The second runner, the woman or girl, appeared to have fallen, and now rolled about on the path alongside the fourth of the garages, both hands gripping her left knee.

Lorna continued forward, determined not to be distracted from her schedule, though already her heart was sinking because almost immediately she'd realised that she was going to have to go back. She was a civilised being, after all; you couldn't just ignore it when someone had an accident. She tromped on along the towpath for a dozen or so yards, glancing backward again and again, hoping against hope that the diminishing figure would be getting back to its feet. But increasingly difficult though it was to see, it looked as if the woman, whoever she was, was still on the ground.

With no other option, Lorna slowed to a halt, turned and, with shoulders heaving, trudged back along the path.

'You all right?' she asked, as she approached the fallen shape.

'I'm so sorry,' the girl whimpered, sitting upright on the path but still clutching her knee. In the half-dark, it was difficult to be sure, but she sounded young, no more than a teenager. 'I don't know what I've done.'

'What happened?'

'I don't know . . . I'm just glad you came back. I didn't want to be stuck here on my own.'

'Let's have a look.' Still breathing hard, fresh sweat glinting off her arms and shoulders, Lorna knelt down to make a quick examination. 'If you can just roll up your—'

The girl stuck her in the bicep with a syringe.

'Hey!' Lorna jerked backward. 'What the hell do you . . .?'

Instantly, she lost focus, the towpath seeming to tilt, her words slurring. When the girl reached up and grabbed her by the wrists, she resisted as much as she could, struggling as they grappled with each other, trying to roll back onto her heels and push herself away – but suddenly Lorna couldn't maintain even that minor effort. Within moments, all strength and coordination had left her. She slumped sideways onto the cinders, while the girl got hurriedly to her feet, panting. A deep, sluggish cold now surged the length of the athlete's body. She was only vaguely aware of the rough ground against her cheek, her blurring vision fixed across the water on the towering brick structure of a mill, which overlooked the scene of her defeat with broken, empty windows.

Then a thunderous impact sounded on the other side of the back wall of the fourth garage. Lorna watched from the corner of her eye, unable to make sense of it as the rotted timbers broke apart, a sledgehammer's head appearing, and then a heavy-booted foot kicking savagely and repeatedly at the lower planks until they too were smashed. By the time a dark-clad shape had fought its way through, Lorna's eyes

107

were fluttering closed. As her vision faded completely, two pairs of hands gripped her and turned her roughly onto her face. The last thing she knew, her wrists were folded across each other in the small of her back, and a tight plastic cord bit into them.

Chapter 10

Crowley, like so many parts of Greater Manchester, had once been heavily industrialised. In its heyday, it boasted coal mines, textile mills, rail sidings for heavy goods, and endless traffic on its canals. But those days had passed. The flywheels on its pit-heads were gone, and though its skyline was studded with tall chimneys, none of them smoked any more. Most of its factories had stood empty for years: towering red-brick edifices filled with dirt, dust and silence, decayed symbols of a formerly proud heritage, totemic reminders that municipal prosperity could come and go in the blink of an eye.

One part of Crowley where many of these defunct landmarks could still be found was the St Clement's ward. Here, ten or twelve former industrial premises stood close together, forming a miniature ghost-town within the overall fabric of the real town. All were long disused, separated from each other by narrow, rubble-strewn lanes that no longer led anywhere, and mostly fenced off to prevent public access, though in many cases the fences themselves were so old that they too had collapsed. They now provided an unofficial refuge for the homeless, especially as a concerted effort was due in the next month to start clearing the town centre's doorways and side passages of vagrants.

When Lucy drove over to St Clement's, it was later than she'd intended, just after ten o'clock at night, mainly because completing the paperwork on the sixty-plus arrests made at Wellspring Lane had severely tested both her and her keyboard's durability. But she didn't think the lateness would be much of a problem. St Clement's could be scary at night but going into dark and threatening places was the police officer's lot.

She parked on a cul-de-sac just off St Clement's Avenue, in front of a row of six terraced houses now boarded up and marked for demolition. Walking to the end of the short road, which no longer had a name of its own, she stopped and listened. Hearing nothing, she headed south along St Clement's Avenue, following a rickety fence of corrugated metal. Some two hundred yards later, the fencing gave out, entire sections having fallen and been trampled. On the other side, two monoliths of rotted brick reared, vast and ghostly, into the night sky: Penrose Mill and its sister carbuncle, the old Griggs Warehouse. The ground in front of them was open and littered with every kind of refuse, and normally at night would be pockmarked by small fires burning with greasy reddish flames, the dark, tattered shapes of homeless folk clustered around them. Lucy especially expected this in the current warm, dry spell: the town's forgotten people enjoying the balmy night rather than huddling beneath broken stoops or crammed into sewer pipes and burned-out cellars.

But at present there was no one. Not a soul in sight. Which was strange and not a little eerie. It was also inconvenient, as the only way to find the ex-nun would be by asking someone where she was.

Lucy walked forward warily. She'd consciously dressed

110

down for this, putting on jeans, training shoes, an old hoodie and a denim jacket. This wasn't simply so that she could blend in with the crowd, but to make it look as if she wouldn't be worth robbing. There'd be many unfortunates here, men and women who through no fault of their own had fallen through the cracks of society, but there'd be addicts too, alcoholics and mentally unstable characters who could turn violent in an instant. That was also why she had an expandable Autolock baton in a special scabbard sewn inside her jacket, a small can of CS spray in one back pocket, and her handcuffs in the other.

At the moment, though, it looked as if she wouldn't need any of them.

The place was deserted.

She walked on, increasingly puzzled, coming to a derelict railway line so tangled in thorns that she half tripped over it. She followed this into a canyon between the soaring outlines of the two main structures. Concrete platforms now stood on either side, and Lucy climbed onto the one on her left. It was scattered with bottles, cans, food cartons and wastepaper – yet more indications that folk had been living here and probably still were. She glanced behind continually as she ventured along it, still seeing no one, though when she looked left through the various apertures into the warehouse proper – tall, glassless window frames, or even larger gaps where loading-bay doors stood partly open – it was easy to imagine furtive movement in the darkness. She was tempted to shout, to simply call Sister Cassie by her name, but Lucy didn't think she'd like the way her voice would echo through the labyrinthine concrete.

She pressed on, holding back from switching on her Maglite, as that would indicate that she might be worth attacking after all. Besides, dim but adequate starlight from the narrow strip of sky above showed that she was

111

approaching the end of the platform. A crumbling mass of half-collapsed brickwork was all that remained of the wall in front of her. On her right, down in the pit, she saw railway buffers peeking through the dense, rancid foliage. On her left, an entrance gaped, a corridor of sorts, which appeared to lead into the very guts of the warehouse. She glanced back along the platform to her rear, just to ensure that hostile forces weren't encroaching from behind.

It wasn't easy to be sure. Beyond a couple of dozen yards, the dimness obscured much, allowing for optical illusions. What appeared to be someone crawling towards her on all fours, and freezing on the spot when she looked, gradually resolved itself into a crumpled heap of cardboard.

She glanced back into the passage on her left. If it had ever had a door, it was long gone, but it seemed to offer a direct thoroughfare from one side of the building to the other. That was the obvious way to go next, though Lucy wasn't convinced that it would be sensible. It wasn't as if she was anticipating trouble – if so, she'd have called for support. The problem here seemed to be that the place was empty. For all that this dark, decayed environment was menacing, she was sure that no one back at the nick would think any less of her if she delayed this thing until daylight tomorrow.

But that was assuming she'd be able to find the time tomorrow, which she wasn't certain about. Also, she wanted to make progress quickly. Lucy didn't like knocking things on the head before she'd even tried, and the suspicion that she might be onto something with these so-called disappearances would not go away. She needed answers of some sort, and she needed them promptly.

She stepped forward into the passage and found herself stumbling over broken planks and littered, tattered newspapers, her nostrils filling with a stench like stagnant urine. She became aware that she was passing more entrances, both left and right. It was now so dark that she was forced to switch on her Maglite and shine it through every doorway. In the first she thought she saw a pale face peeking over the top of a mouldy old quilt, only to realise that it was a roundish patch of malodorous fungus on the wall behind. In all the rooms after that, she saw only rusted pipework and bare, moss-covered bricks.

She glanced repeatedly over her shoulder as she proceeded, the rectangle of dimness that was the entry to this passage steadily receding. Another twenty yards further on, she came to a point where the roof and left side of the corridor had collapsed, forming a landslip of rubble on one side. She was shocked – gut-punch shocked – to see a featureless figure perched on top in an apelike crouch.

'I'm . . . I'm looking for Sister Cassiopeia,' she said, thinking it wise not to shine her light up there.

'Good luck,' came a whispered response.

Still watching the figure, Lucy pressed on, clambering over fallen bricks and masonry, and now seeing a glint of moonlight ahead. Relieved, she came to a hanging steel door. It was already partly open and screeched the rest of the way when she pushed. It brought her out into another passage, transverse to the one she'd just come through, and much broader. It had a slanted ceiling made from glass panels, though all of these had collapsed, leaving flaking metal frames and jagged fragments. This side of the warehouse caught the moonlight squarely, leaving it bathed in a spectral luminescence, which at least meant that she could switch her torch off and conserve the battery. The wooden wall on the right no longer existed, having been burned, leaving only a charred framework, which made the passage feel more like an arcade. She walked along it a good sixty yards or so, but there was never much to see: more moonlit ruins, more roads to nowhere, more weedy plots of ground.

Then she thought she heard something; the screech of a metal door being forced. She glanced back along the arcade, thinking that she would easily see someone approaching her from behind. The passage had curved, however, so that the last noisy door she had come through was out of sight. Of course, if someone *was* following her – she couldn't help thinking about that crouching, apelike figure – it wasn't necessarily the best idea to hang around and meet them.

She decided to head back now. This had clearly been a futile errand. She had other work to attend to anyway and would simply put out a BOLO, or 'Be on the Lookout', for Sister Cassiopeia. A steel-framed doorway a few yards away looked most promising. When she glanced through it, she saw another brick corridor, but with light at the far end. However, she was no more than five yards inside when she realised that a dark figure was coming down it towards her. It came quickly but awkwardly, moving with a horrible seesawing gait; the closer it got, the more of the light at the end it blotted out.

Lucy backed stiffly into the moonlight, thinking that if someone was behind her as well, she might be cut off. Her hands slid under her jacket, fingers caressing the hilt of the baton. She could now hear whoever this was; feet clumping, damp material whisking over bricks and concrete. Before she knew it, she'd retreated to the other side of the arcade. Where once there'd been a timber wall, now there was a drop of seven or eight feet onto heaps of burned, mangled rubbish. Her heels were right on the edge, and she was tottering.

She stopped, risked a glance behind, and then looked back across the arcade – just as a voluminous shape, cowled and cloaked in black, ballooned into sight.

Lucy half-sagged with relief.

Sister Cassie briefly managed to look even more ghostlike

than usual, hobbling forward through the moonlight rather than gliding gracefully as she usually did. Consternation was written on her face.

'Lucy, Lucy,' she said admonishingly. 'I'd heard you'd come here looking for me. For Heaven's sake, child, whatever possessed you to come into this place on your own?'

Lucy released the baton back into its pouch. 'I told you I'd come and find you.'

'Yes, but this dreadful place isn't safe for a girl like you. Not at night.'

'Sister . . . I'm a police officer.'

'And that's something else that worries me.' The ex-nun tut-tutted, eyeing her up and down. 'A child like you . . . in a job like this.'

'Sister . . .' Lucy suppressed her irritation. 'Your concern is appreciated. But if it's safe enough for *you* . . .'

'Ahhh, no.' Sister Cassie wagged a finger. 'I have an advantage you lack. I commune with the Lord daily. Matins at midnight, Lauds at dawn, Prime at breakfast, Terce in the morning, Sext at Midday, None at mid-afternoon, Vespers in the evening . . . Compline before bed. I enjoy His full protection.'

'And what does He feel about your heroin habit? Or the tricks you turn?'

Sister Cassie shook her head with an air of disappointment. 'You try to express concern for your fellow creatures . . .' She turned and limped haughtily along the arcade. 'It's our Christian duty to survive, Lucy. Any way we can.'

Lucy fell into step alongside her. 'Survive? On heroin?'

'At present, I can't shake the need. But at least I can suppress it.'

'Or feed it.'

'Call it what you will. My medicine enables me to look after my regulars.'

'What about Fred Holborn? Was he one of your regulars?'

'Poor Fred.' Sister Cassie sounded sad but kept on walking, or rather limping. 'He had an appetite for the carnal pleasures, but at heart he was decent. A ship's mate in his youth, I believe. Past seventy now. How fallen are the mighty?'

'Sister, I know you've reported Fred Holborn missing. But are you quite sure something bad has happened to him?'

'It certainly looked bad.'

'*Looked* bad?' Lucy turned, grabbing her shoulder, stopping her in her tracks. 'Sister, did you *see* something?'

'Why yes.' The ex-nun seemed surprised. 'Did I neglect to mention it?'

'I'm not sure . . . I had my mind on other things. But tell me now.'

'It was here. This very place.' She veered to the left and a jagged portion of outer wall that hadn't burned away. At its base, sheets of brown-stained newspaper covered an old mattress. 'This was where Fred preferred to sleep.'

'So tell me what happened,' Lucy said.

'Well, I was making my nightly rounds.' Fleetingly, Sister Cassie sounded disapproving. 'I *had* considered cutting Fred off my roster because of his lewd behaviour. But . . .' She sighed. 'One mustn't exaggerate. They were suggestions, not actions. In short, well, to be frank, on one occasion he asked me to—'

'Sister, I'm not worried about that . . . just tell me what happened to him. And when.'

'It was . . . I'd say a week and a half ago.'

'As recently as that?'

'Well, yes. That's why I remember it so well. It was nine o'clock in the evening. I'd come along to tuck him in, keep him company for a while. I'd managed to scavenge half a pizza which some lout had left on a wall outside an Italian takeaway. A whole half-pizza. I'd already distributed some

116

of it, and there were only a couple of pieces left. I'd made an effort to save one for Fred, though. He's skin and bone, these days, the poor man. Not that this has tamed his lusty conversation. Oh, dear me, no . . . some of his comments would even shock a police officer—'

'I'm sure,' Lucy cut in. 'Just tell me what happened.'

The ex-nun pursed her lips. 'On this occasion, it was a little too much. Especially after I'd saved him a whole slice of pizza. I told him that I was offended. I gave him the whole flask of tea I'd intended to share with him but said that I wasn't staying with him a moment longer. I was halfway down this path here . . .'

She moved further along the arcade, coming to a point where a hole had been kicked in the remaining scorched planking. On the other side, rough ground sloped up to the edge of the concrete. A well-trodden footpath snaked down it, cutting through dense weeds near the bottom, before joining another derelict cobbled access road.

'That's Canning Crescent down there, I believe,' the ex-nun said. 'Or it used to be. Such a shame. When I was teaching—'

'What happened to Fred?' Lucy interrupted.

'Why, he became remorseful. Very much so. He followed me down, limping of course. His poor feet are terribly infected and inflamed. I often change the bandages for him. Sometimes, I can acquire clean ones at the needle exchange on Saddler's Row.'

'Sister, please . . .'

'Well . . . when we got down to the bottom here –' she descended the path, Lucy in her wake '– when he caught up with me, which was just about *here*, this spot, he told me he was sorry. That he hadn't meant to insult me, and that if it made any difference, the next time I came he would have tried to scrape some money together.' She tutted again. 'That was his idea of an apology. He thought that if he offered to buy my favours, I'd somehow be placated. The sad state of these men . . .'

'Okay, and . . .?'

'I told him I would think about it, but that at present there were other, needier souls I must attend to. So I left him here and walked up this narrow lane.' She pointed left, to where a ginnel cut away from the cobbled road, curving out of sight between outbuildings. 'I'd gone maybe forty yards when I heard a motor vehicle engine revving, and a shouting – a loud shouting, as if there was a fight. I hurried back but all I saw when I got here was a vehicle pulling away along Canning Crescent. And no sign of Fred.'

'A vehicle?' Lucy said. 'Had it been parked here when you came down the path?'

'I didn't notice it. But as you can see, there's a shadowy area over there.' The ex-nun pointed right, and about fifty yards away, a cement ramp tilted down through a square, garage-type aperture into what looked like a subterranean parking zone beneath the warehouse. At this time of night, what little light there was petered out at the entrance, so a vehicle could easily loiter there, just out of sight.

'Did you see what kind of vehicle it was?' Lucy asked.

'Of course. It was a transit van.'

'A transit van?' A shiver scurried down Lucy's spine. 'What colour?'

Sister Cassie thought this over. 'Dark. It was dusk, of course, but I've always been blessed with good eyesight. I'd say . . . purple maybe. Or blue. Yes, that's it. Darkish blue.'

'I don't suppose you remember any part of its registration number?'

'I never remember minor details, I'm afraid.'

'Okay, fair enough. Look—'

'Which is why I wrote it down.'

Lucy's hair prickled. 'You did?'

'Well, the first part of it at least.' The ex-nun rooted in her satchel. 'I know I put it here somewhere.'

When she finally located it, she'd written five characters down on a condom wrapper, which she apologised for, but said was the only thing she'd found when she'd scrabbled around for something to write on. Lucy could only shake her head, fascinated by Sister Cassie's resourcefulness. She gloved up and slipped the wrapper into a transparent plastic envelope, saying that it didn't matter about the missing characters – this was more than enough for them to work with.

They headed back through the building together, the ex-nun guiding the police officer along open passageways, clear of rubble, which would have been far less frightening had she discovered these avenues for herself earlier. All the way, Lucy tried to get through to the PNC on her radio, though the signal broke repeatedly.

On the other side of the great edifice, rather bewilderingly, they entered open ground where now there seemed to be ragged people everywhere, raddled and wizened beyond their years, standing alone and contemplating the darkness, or huddled around small fires. It was almost as if Sister Cassie's friendly welcome had thrown some kind of 'she's okay' switch, and they'd all come scrambling out from wherever it was they'd been hiding.

One young man seemed to be especially unhappy. In fact, he looked out of place here, with his longish hair, tight stonewashed jeans, tasselled leather jacket and leather trilby. He strode quickly away, swerving between the campfires as he glanced repeatedly back at Lucy, or rather at her police radio. In the lurid light of the fires, she saw what looked like a shark tattoo on the side of his neck, and a spotty pizza-face twisted with dislike – and fear.

She let him go. She wasn't interested in dealers at present.

'DC Clayburn to PNC, over?' she told her radio for the umpteenth time, now weary.

Static crunched, and a male voice suddenly replied. *'PNC receiving. Go ahead, Lucy?'*

Lucy sighed with relief. 'Vehicle check, please.'

'Go ahead.'

'Full index unknown, but I have the first five characters, which are as follows: Oscar-two-two-zero-Mike, over.'

'Stand by, over.'

Lucy slipped the evidence bag into her pocket and glanced at Sister Cassie as they walked back towards St Clement's Avenue. 'What will you do with the rest of your night?'

'What I always do, child. Tend to those less fortunate than myself.'

'There's a fish and chip van parked on Ellis Lane. If I give you some money, do you solemnly promise you'll go and buy a few portions, one for yourself and several for the hungriest of your regulars . . . and that you won't spend it on smack?'

Sister Cassie gave a conspiratorial half-smile; a hint of how pretty she'd once been briefly flickered there. 'I've already purchased adequate medicine for tonight. You may notice I'm walking uncomfortably. He was a young man, very dirty and . . . I'm sorry to say, rather rough.'

Lucy shook her head as she opened her purse and handed over a couple of twenties. Her radio crackled to life again.

'DC Clayburn from PNC?'

'Go ahead.'

'Index Oscar-two-two-zero-Mike . . . unknown. No such number listed. Nothing even similar, over.'

'Roger, received.' Lucy was thoughtful. 'Thanks for that.'

'I assure you I was not mistaken,' Sister Cassie said.

'No, I believe you.'

'So, maybe your computer is wrong?'

'Trust me, Sister – the Police National Computer is never wrong. But that van *is*.' She thought about it. 'Whether it's purple, blue or black, it's running under dummy plates.'

Chapter 11

Miles O'Grady deliberately ran his private investigations business as if it was a small non-lucrative thing. He always turned himself out well: hair coloured silver to hide the grey, moustache clipped, and wearing his best suit and his £1,800 trenchcoat in all but the hottest and most sultry weather. A thorough professional, first appearances were vital to Miles O'Grady. It had certainly paved the way to immediate success with that braindead footballer Dean Chesham. But when it came to his company, it was a different story. Most of O'Grady's and his men's earnings were illicit and therefore non-taxable. So it only made sense that the firm itself, Walderstone Enquiries Ltd, kept a low profile. Hence the shabby little office at the top of the creaking back staircase in Dashwood House, the tired old building in Long Acre, a little-used cul-de-sac off Crowley bus station. It was such an unprepossessing place that no one was likely to visit it on spec, and even if they had an appointment with the firm, most of the time they were suspicious spouses who put great stock in their personal dignity, and so would opt to meet their investigators in neutral venues like coffee shops and wine bars. Almost none would be prepared to call at an address like this.

In fact, it was unusual for O'Grady to be in the office, especially on a Sunday lunchtime. It didn't contain much – a desk, a landline and a clunky filing cabinet filled with dummy paperwork. But after their recent approach to Dean Chesham, a tactical meeting was now in the offing. And that wasn't the sort of thing O'Grady wanted to do over the phone. However, the other guys weren't due for another hour at least, so the last thing he was expecting while eating his takeaway lunch was someone knocking on the door.

He glanced curiously up at the frosted glass panel. An indiscernible shadow stood on the other side.

'It's open,' he yelled, laying down his plastic fork, dabbing his lips with a napkin.

The door opened and a man stood there. 'Mr O'Grady, is it?'

'I'm sure you already know that, else you wouldn't be here.'

The man's half-smile broke into a chuckle. 'Wow . . . do private eyes' cubbyholes like this really exist, then? Fantastic. Mind you, *you're* a bit disappointing. I was expecting to find Humphrey Bogart or a young Robert Mitchum. You've got the trenchcoat, though, I see.'

O'Grady's narrowed eyes flitted to the coat on the hook in the corner, and then back to the man in the doorway. There was something instantly unsettling about him. He was probably in his fifties, but lean and fit-looking, with steel-grey hair, dark eyes and sharp, diamond-hard features. He wore an Armani suit and a Marwood tie, and advanced from the office door with a lithe, easy grace.

'Who are you?' O'Grady said, yanking loose his paper bib and scrunching it.

'Oh . . . didn't I say?'

'Well, whoever you are, as common courtesy seems to be something that eludes you, I suggest you take a walk back

123

down the stairs, closing the door behind you as you go, and come back at a more suitable time. Like never.'

The newcomer responded by closing the office door, pulling up a chair and sitting down at the desk. When his gaze met O'Grady's, it was long, hard and seemingly amused.

'Is this some kind of joke?' O'Grady growled. 'I mean, do you know who I am?'

'I know who you *were*. Detective Chief Inspector O'Grady of the Greater Manchester Police's Fraud Investigation Team. You had a glittering career until you very mysteriously failed to shred a batch of highly sensitive intelligence reports relating to various organised crime enquiries, and then, or so the scandal-mongers outrageously claimed, offered them to the highest bidder. Hardly a smart career move, Miles. Saw you drummed out of the job minus one very fat pension. But it's a good thing they couldn't actually *prove* anything, eh? That would've been a lot worse. Still . . . the word is you've done all right for yourself since.'

O'Grady turned slowly scarlet. 'Who the fuck *are* you?'

'Well . . .' The newcomer feigned uncertainty about how much he should reveal. 'I've not got as illustrious a background as you. But I *do* have a similar talent for turning over big sums annually.'

'Do you indeed?' O'Grady leaped to his feet, pulled out his iPhone and banged it on the desk. 'You know that all I have to do is make a single phone-call.'

'You've got quite a thin face, haven't you?' the newcomer noted. 'Ordinarily it looks okay, but when you get angry . . . kind of makes you look peevish. Not impressive.'

'I call that number, and someone'll be in here in less than three minutes with a fucking baseball bat! . . . You little shit!'

The newcomer chuckled. 'Who? That fat bastard with the beard?'

The redness in O'Grady's cheeks lessened. His mouth twitched as he struggled not to register surprise and concern that his unwanted guest was so well informed.

'Look, Miles –' the newcomer wafted the air, indicating that he should sit again '– I've no doubt you can do as you say. But it won't gain you much. I mean, you can bash my skull in. But all that'll mean is someone else has to come. And then your bill will be even bigger.'

'What fucking bill?'

The newcomer looked even more amused. 'It's quite funny, if a bit predictable, the way you've shown your "angry man" colours so quickly, when usually you like to play it calm and sophisticated. I think that's a major thing for you, isn't it? Appearances? I mean, currently it's the other way around. You like to make it seem as if this private eye firm is a backstreet affair. But really, that other business of yours, the blackmailing gig . . . that pays a lot more, eh?'

O'Grady couldn't initially respond. All he could think, incredible though it seemed, was that either Stone or Roper had blabbed to the wrong person – not that there was ever a *right* person in this line of work. For the moment, though, keeping his cool and brazening it out suddenly seemed like the most important thing in the world.

'Something wrong, Miles?' the guy asked. 'No more threats? No more promises to bring an apeman here with a bat?' He paused, but O'Grady simply glared at him, the breath hissing through his clenched teeth. 'You must have a few questions, at least?'

Slowly, carefully, O'Grady sat down again. 'I've already asked you twice. *Who* are you? And what *bill*?'

The newcomer pursed his lips as though these were entirely reasonable enquiries.

'Well, first of all . . . I'm an admirer. I *admire* your audacity. The guy who made such an inroad into Manchester's white-collar criminals and yet the same guy who's now made white-collar crime pay better than any of those poor, blundering saps he sent to jail. I *admire* the frugal way you run things. Granted, this shithole's a façade, but it also means you're barely spending a penny on your overheads. And as you're not paying significant tax either, it's nearly all going into you and your two buddies' pockets. I *admire* the way you're sticking it to those GMP bastards who kicked your arse out. I bet you get satisfaction from that every single day. Fucking straight men, eh? Spit and polish types, everything by the book. And yet it's all to make them look good, isn't it? Meanwhile, real detectives like you, crafty old-schoolers who were every kind of embarrassment and yet still had more luck getting into the guts of evil bastards like me than this lot would ever know . . . *you're* out on your ear—'

'Hey!' O'Grady pointed a finger. 'Stop pretending you know what motivates me. You're not an ally of mine, and clearly you're not my fucking mate.'

'No, but I *do* want to be your partner.'

'What . . . what's that?'

'This is the second question you asked me. "What bill?" you said. In other words, who are you going to be paying? It's a fair question . . . it's gonna be at least half your annual income, after all. It's only fair that you know where it's going.'

O'Grady rocked in his chair. He'd laugh if anything about this was even remotely funny. 'You've got to be kidding. You are seriously screwed in the head.'

'Steady on, Milesey.' The newcomer's smile hardened. 'This is a sliding scale. The tougher you are to deal with, the more expensive it's going to get.'

O'Grady smiled too, though it was hard and humourless. 'You seriously think I haven't dealt with cheap gangsters before? With chancers and wannabes? You think I can't sniff out some cocky spiv who's got all the blarney, all the gab, but who'd run a country mile if it ever cut up for real?'

'No, I *know* you have. Which is why I'm confident you're going to be sensible.'

'Just get out of here, pal. Right now, and we'll forget this ever happened.'

'Thought you were going to make a phone-call?'

O'Grady lugged open a drawer and grabbed out a short-barrelled Taurus .357 Magnum revolver. It was fully loaded, and he pointed it at the newcomer's face.

'You seriously don't know what you're getting into,' he warned.

'Okay . . . enough pissing around.' The guy straightened in his seat, seemingly unfazed by the proximity of the gun. 'I'm sure you know who I represent. It's a no-brainer, isn't it? You must always have known that at some point, as your star rose, we'd get interested.'

'You're getting nothing else,' O'Grady said tightly.

'Here's the deal. At the mo it's fifty per cent. Payable monthly, not annually. For which purpose we'll obviously need full access to your books . . . your real ones, that is. Not the Mickey Mouse ones you keep for the Inland Revenue.'

'I said, get out of here, you stinking piece of trash!'

'That pushes it to sixty-forty. In our favour, of course.'

O'Grady shoved his chair back and jumped up. Now he was aiming with both hands, squinting along the barrel. 'You little fuck!'

'Seventy-thirty.'

'Get out!'

'We like what you do, Miles. I told you I was an admirer. We all are. But it'd be a lot easier for everyone if you were to play nice.'

'Get the fuck out!'

127

'Oh dear.' For the first time, the newcomer looked disappointed. 'This can be put back on a more even keel, but I'm worried that you've already lost too much ground.'

'*I said get the fuck out!*' It was all but a shriek.

'Tell you what . . .' The newcomer remained seated, unconcerned that O'Grady was edging around the desk towards him, still staring down the barrel of his stubby but powerful pistol. 'Instead of going to eighty-twenty, which obviously would be ridiculous – wouldn't be worth you and your two boys getting out of bed, would it? – I'm going to give you a couple of days to clear your head of all this "I'm still the big man" nonsense.'

Only now did he stand up, apparently more interested in brushing bits of dust from his jacket than he was in the firearm trained on his head from less than four feet away. 'Just remember, this deal is non-negotiable. And it's going to happen.' He moved to the door, where he stopped and half-turned. 'All you've got to think about are the terms. But think about them properly, Miles, because so far you've done a hell of a job skewing them against you.'

When the man was halfway down the shabby staircase, O'Grady stumbled into the doorway at the top, his pistol still drawn but pointed at the floor.

'I'm not frightened of you, McCracken!'

Frank McCracken looked back up at him. 'There you are . . . told you you knew us.'

'I've met people like you all my career.'

'Uh-uh.' McCracken shook his head. 'You know why, pal? You're still here.'

As McCracken emerged from the building, the phone began chirping in his pocket. He took it out as he strolled towards his waiting Bentley Continental, smiling to himself when he saw who the caller was. He slowed to a halt next to the car.

'Cora . . .?'

'Frank!' Cora sounded surprised that he'd answered. 'I've called you a few times since you sent me those flowers. Why can I never get you?'

He stuck a hand into his suit pocket, affecting a nonchalant pose in case O'Grady happened to peek down from a window. 'It's not always convenient, I'm afraid.'

'Yeah, well . . . it wasn't exactly convenient for me when those flowers arrived. As you can imagine, our Lucy's played hell over it.'

'Yeah, I *can* imagine. I'm sorry, love . . . I'm a busy man. I sometimes have to screen calls.'

Cora didn't comment on that, no doubt because she knew what his businesses involved and didn't want to hear any more about them than was necessary.

'What was the reason for it?' she asked, still sounding stern. 'What are you up to, Frank?'

'What do you mean what am I up to?'

'Well . . . I wish I could believe that you'd remembered my birthday because you're a thoughtful guy who likes to stay in contact with his old friends, but it's thirty-odd years since you last gave any indication of that.'

McCracken was unsure how to reply. It was true that he and Cora had barely had contact since she'd left him and the SugaBabes club. In the last two years, though, he'd seen her much more regularly, though that was mainly due to their both becoming embroiled in Lucy's investigations. But even then, it was difficult pretending that renewing his acquaintance with her hadn't made an impact on him.

He remembered Cora vividly from her youth, a twenty-something dancer, whose flowing flaxen hair and sinuous, exotic routine had struck even the rowdiest clientele dumb with amazement. Okay, the alluring outfits had all come off piece by piece, in the sexiest way imaginable, and any

129

red-blooded male would have been stirred. But it wasn't just that. Cora had been the only stripper in the club to use a microphone, talking to the crowd, teasing them, taunting them. Even when fully dressed, she'd known exactly how to rock a man's world.

But needless to say, there'd been a lot more to her than that.

Whether it was her determined nature or adversarial spirit, McCracken wasn't sure – he'd always found those things appealing in a woman, because they were such a challenge to his own alpha-male status. But Cora had been morally upright too, in her own way, as if deep down inside there'd always been a model citizen trying to get out. On reflection it was no surprise that, when she'd learned she was pregnant, she'd extricated herself and her unborn child completely from the lowlife environment that had become her world.

'The least you can do is give me an answer,' she said into his ear.

'I'm working on one,' he replied.

'Oh, charming . . .'

Though that was the most genuine reply he could have given. He felt he knew what the real answer was, or at least he had a vague idea – but he couldn't articulate it. There'd been savagery all his life. He'd only ever known violent criminals, had only ever lived off the proceeds of violent crime – and so often his women had been part of those proceeds.

With the sole exception of Cora Clayburn.

When only a few things in your life were actually good – when everything else was wrong or bent or corrupt – didn't you sometimes cling to those few things? Didn't you go looking for them when you thought they were lost because so often they felt like your final hope?

Okay, he shouldn't get carried away. He couldn't put Cora

on too much of a pedestal – she'd been a stripper, after all – but, having hooked up with her again all these years later, he'd found that she'd indeed become that upstanding citizen, that conscientious working mum who paid her taxes, who had friends that weren't delinquents, who added genuine value to her community. She still looked terrific as well. She'd aged, obviously, but Cora clearly looked after herself, a habit she evidently shared with her daughter. And she still possessed that indomitable, rebellious spirit.

'There must be some reason why you'd send me a pile of flowers,' she persisted, refusing to be fobbed off. 'From most blokes it would be a loving gesture, but I know you, Frank . . . and so does Lucy, and neither of us think it can be anything of the sort. So, I ask you again: what are you up to?'

'Cora, I . . .'

For the first time in as long as he could remember, Frank McCracken was tongue-tied.

It was a staggering possibility, but could he actually be falling for this woman? All over again? It was difficult to imagine, with Charlie at home, the ultimate temptress, 'Sex on Legs' as the other lads called her. But Charlie was simply the best of a long line of hot ladies who'd warmed his sheets over the years and hadn't served much other purpose. Cora had been a lot more to him than that.

'That's it?' she said. 'That's all the answer I get? You finally deign to take my call, and then you've got nothing to say.'

'Cora, listen . . . just accept it for what it is. A birthday gift, yeah?'

'But what does it actually *mean*, Frank?' Her voice had changed slightly, the tone softening; there was almost a plea there. And now he couldn't help wondering how she felt about him. 'Give me something, Frank. Anything. So, I'm not left confused and worried by this.'

Perhaps she'd been lonely too these last thirty years.

Fuck. There it was. He'd just admitted it to himself. For all the drinking and gambling, for all the women who'd jump into bed at a click of his fingers, he was lonely.

'Frank, talk to me!'

'Cora, listen. We *are* old friends, you're right. More than that, in truth. Now, I'd like us to be new friends. But you know that can't happen under the current circumstances.'

'So, the flowers were . . . what?'

'Like I say, accept them as a gift.'

'Lucy wants me to throw them away.'

He snorted. 'The Cora I knew and lov—' He corrected himself. 'The Cora I knew so well would have made her own decision about that.'

There was a breathless pause at the other end of the line.

'Okay,' she finally said in a small voice. 'Thanks for the gift. It was very kind of you.'

'Happy birthday, Cora,' he replied, but she'd already hung up.

He opened the door of his Bentley and slid into the front passenger seat. Mick Shallicker, who was behind the wheel, regarded him curiously, perhaps wondering why he'd turned a little pale.

'Everything go all right up there?' the big guy finally asked.

'Up there? Yeah.' McCracken stared dead ahead. 'Perfect.'

Shallicker nodded and put the car in gear, detecting that no further questions would be welcome.

'Shit,' McCracken said to himself, as they pulled a U-turn in Long Acre. 'Like my life isn't complicated enough.'

Chapter 12

Lorna Cunningham was not the kind of woman who'd ever thought that she'd panic in a crisis. But then, she wasn't the kind of woman who'd ever thought that she could simply be snatched off the streets.

When she'd first woken up in this small, windowless room, her initial plan had been to jump to her feet and dash to the door, which, even though she expected it to be locked, she would attack with all her might, throwing her shoulder against it again and again, kicking it as hard as she could with those long, hard-muscled legs of hers until it collapsed. But in reality, the first thing that happened was that the drug she'd been given, which hadn't yet worn off, knocked her sideways as she scrambled up from the narrow, dingy bed, sending her reeling into one of the whitewashed brick walls. She slid down until she was sitting on the floor, legs splayed in front of her.

She was still in that inelegant position several minutes later.

In retrospect, though her thought processes were as sluggish as her coordination, she decided that failure to attack the door had probably been a good thing. Though she'd been wrong to assume that she wouldn't panic in a tight corner, it remained the case that she *shouldn't* panic. Even through eyes dimmed by stupor, and in the poor light of the dull, brownish bulb overhead, she could see that the door was made from heavy sheet-steel, and that it had no handle. How ridiculous if she was simply to pound at it, using up what few energy reserves she could muster, maybe injuring herself and rendering herself an even easier victim when whoever had abducted her finally came in here.

No, she had to keep a cool head and try to think this through, while staying still and relaxing, allowing herself as much recovery time as possible, so that she'd be in the best condition she could muster for the next fight. And all the while learning as much as she could about the opposition.

Though that wasn't easy in this blank page of a prison cell.

It was about ten feet in length and six in width, and, aside from the bed and the simple light fitting, it was almost bare. She guessed that she was underground somewhere, because what looked like a small steel-framed air vent was visible in the top left-hand corner facing her. In the corner opposite that, there was another tiny fixture: a glass bauble in the middle of a metal plate. Most likely some sort of camera.

None of these things should surprise her, she supposed. Whatever your warped reasoning, you didn't go to the trouble of taking someone prisoner unless you intended to keep them alive, at least for a short time. So, if you were going to hold them underground, they would need air. Likewise, you didn't just abandon them to their own devices once they were confined; if you had any sense, you'd keep checking on them – hence the camera.

'Okay . . .' she mumbled to herself. 'So . . . what . . . what does that tell me . . .?'

What do you think it tells you? an inner voice replied.

134

They're not keeping you alive because they like you, for God's sake! It's because they're going to use you for something!

Abruptly, Lorna threw her attempted rationalisations aside, wanting to shriek and rip out her hair instead. The plain fact was that someone had kidnapped her, dragging her away and unlawfully imprisoning her. God alone knew for what purpose! All kinds of nightmare images flitted before her eyes.

'Oh, God . . . please no!' she moaned, strength and awareness restoring themselves sufficiently for her to make coherent sound. She felt a scream building in her chest. Again, she wanted to rage at the door, to try and kick her way to freedom.

But no, no . . . she had to resist the panic impulse.

Firstly, it would prevent her thinking clearly. Secondly, it would show whoever was watching that she was now coming around, waking up, and that wouldn't do at all. Whatever trial lay ahead, she needed much more recovery time than this. It was vital to continue feigning semi-consciousness for as long as possible.

But who were they? How had this happened? And what was the reason for it?

She had some vague memory of an incident on the canal bank and a girl hurting herself, but she couldn't picture any faces or recall any conversation or violence. Another question was: if they really meant her harm, why wasn't it happening already? Was that a good sign? Probably not, because an answer suggested itself with indecent speed.

Sex slavery. Transportation overseas to some ghastly harem.

No one would pay top dollar for damaged goods.

'Oh, God . . . please . . .'

But before she could ruminate more, she heard a muffled

clatter of metal from somewhere beyond the confines of her cell. Silence followed, but it wasn't the silence of nothing. Lorna could easily imagine, in fact she could virtually sense, the approach of stealthy footfalls. But even then, she almost jumped out of her skin when, with a hefty *clunk*, a key turned in the lock. She slumped lifelessly down, as the door, which was clearly well oiled, opened silently and someone came in. With another *clunk*, it closed behind them.

Thanks to the angle of her head and her half-closed eyes, all Lorna could initially see was a pair of legs wearing some kind of heavy-duty, black canvas trousers, with what looked like combat boots on the feet. The legs came and stood directly in front of her.

The intense horror of that moment was almost over-whelming, the seconds seeming to telescope out, so pregnant were they with tension, so thoroughly did Lorna feel that she was being scrutinised. She was attempting to feign uncon-sciousness, but how would they fall for that? Surely, she was visibly trembling? Surely, she was breathing with frantic, desperate speed?

A boot prodded her left foot.

Lorna didn't respond.

The boot prodded her again, harder, less patiently.

Still, she didn't move. The blurriness and dizziness had left her, but simply by playing dead she'd managed to learn a little about the opposition. Perhaps there'd be more.

Suddenly, the boot kicked her. Sharply, and not on the foot this time, but on the ankle, causing her to flinch with shock and pain, to yank her leg back. But still Lorna resisted a strong response. Instead, she murmured slightly, burbling a bit of nonsense – who knew, it might convince her captors that the movement they had witnessed through the camera was nothing, and that their prisoner was still out for the count.

The legs remained in front of her, the booted feet now spread apart. There was a dull, muffled breathing. Which suddenly sounded angry.

Lorna felt a pang of fear. Had she miscalculated? Through half-closed eyes, she was shaken to see one of the boots slowly draw back. Clearly, it was about to land a kick on her unprotected face.

When it swung forward, she had no option but to throw herself aside, rolling across the cell until she reached its corner, her shoulder jarring on the wall. She slid up it, trying to assume a standing position. Her legs were still rubbery, her vision tilted, but gradually everything stabilised again, and she was able to turn around. Only to find that it was impossible to identify the person she now faced.

Whoever it was, they were slightly shorter than she was, and trim, though it was difficult to assess their physical shape because of the heavy black combat fatigues they wore. Likewise, the face was unrecognisable beneath a black knitted balaclava, though a couple of slots for vision allowed a pair of blue eyes to fix on Lorna with electric intensity. At the same time, the prisoner was jolted to see that the masked figure had drawn a knife: a large one, a hunting-knife maybe, with a cross-guard hilt and a partially serrated cutting edge.

In a moment of head-spinning realisation, Lorna understood the true depths of her peril. She was going abroad as an unwilling export? No such luck.

The newcomer drove the knife forward, full on as though to impale her through the midriff.

For all her sport, Lorna had only done basic martial arts, but it was sufficient for her to sweep her left arm down and parry the blow open-handed. What she wasn't expecting was for the newcomer's other hand to flash forward at the same time, clench into a fist and club her on the jaw. Dazed, Lorna was flung back against the wall, the impact knocking the wind out of her. The newcomer pulled the knife back, clenching its hilt tightly, as though to inflict a proper, downward stab-wound. Lorna threw herself forward, grappling with her assailant chest-to-chest. They tottered into the middle of the room, where the newcomer pivoted at the waist and flung Lorna to the floor.

Winded again, panting hard, she crab-crawled away, glancing over her shoulder. The newcomer's eyes blazed with anger. Clearly, Lorna's resistance had come as a surprise.

This gave her new heart, and she sprang to her feet as her opponent advanced, spinning on one leg, attempting a roundhouse kick. Alas, she wasn't expert enough in this field; her leg was caught and slashed across the shin with a single, brutal stroke of the blade. Lorna squealed like an animal, but as much in fear as pain. She danced on one foot as the knife came at her midriff again, before dropping onto her back, twisting over and scuttling forward, yanking her trapped foot loose, and planting both hands on the bed to lever herself upright.

She turned just in time, as the blade swept at her chest. Again, she parried the blow, following with a forearm smash, catching her opponent in the throat. Grunting in shock, the masked figure toppled backward, sliding in the blood spattering the tiled floor.

Lorna's only hope lay in going on the offensive. A stripe of burning pain crossed her left leg just below the knee-cap, indicating an open wound. She guessed it would hurt even more to put weight on that limb – and it did, severely, so much that the leg almost buckled – but she still catapulted herself forward off it, bypassing the flailing knife, trapping the hand that held it in her left armpit, and slamming her right fist into the newcomer's left eye socket.

The balaclava-covered head hinged backward, though it was a miracle that, whoever this was, they stayed upright, given that Lorna routinely trained with twenty-pound weights. It was even more of a miracle that the newcomer had enough fight left to retaliate in kind, landing a punch on the side of Lorna's head that sounded like an explosion in her skull. As Lorna staggered, her opponent fly-kicked her, catching her hip, sending her tottering. Lorna slithered through the gory smears covering the tiled floor, rebounded from the bed – a blow that itself accounted for a rib or two – and landed on her front, the air bursting from her lungs.

The mingled stenches of sweat and blood now befouled the air of the enclosed space.

'You bitch,' came a strained, hissing voice.

Wheezing, Lorna lurched over. The newcomer was less than a yard away, still wielding the knife but struggling with a left eye that had already swollen closed.

'You fucking bitch!' The knife soared upward in both hands, the intent clearly to plunge it into Lorna's throat and rip her open to the groin.

Lorna moved like lightning, and the blade struck the tiled floor with such force that a tile exploded, and the knife skipped loose. Back on her feet, Lorna attempted another kick. The newcomer again caught her ankle, lifting it. Lorna fell onto her tailbone, the juddering impact of which sliced through her. The newcomer swung a kick at Lorna's face. Lorna dodged, and the boot sailed past, a shinbone cracking on the edged steel of the bed-frame. The newcomer hopped away in disbelieving agony.

Scrambling to the nearest wall and using it to lever herself up again, Lorna was now dabbled all over in blood and hurting in half a dozen places. She'd been hit more times today than in the whole rest of her life. And it wasn't over yet. Tireless and determined, the masked figure came at her again, firing in another ferocious punch. Lorna ducked away, and with a meaty *smack* the flying fist struck the brick wall.

But Lorna knew that constantly running was of no value when there was nowhere to run to. As her agonised foe jerked around to face her, she did something she'd only ever seen drunken hooligans do: she launched herself forward, headbutting her opponent clean on the bridge of the nose.

It was surprisingly effective.

She felt nothing herself, but there was a *crunch* of cartilage, and the newcomer's head, eyes rolling and blood oozing through the sweat-damp fabric covering the nostrils, slumped down onto Lorna's chest, legs sagging. Lorna locked a tight-muscled arm around the exposed neck and throat, clamping it in a chokehold. All she had to do now was squeeze and keep on squeezing, perhaps throwing herself around a little bit, to affect a breakage of the spine.

The athlete was amazed by how lucidly she was contemplating this, considering that she'd almost never committed an act of wrongdoing before. Of course, having just needed to fight hard for her own life might have something to do with that.

The question was, could she carry it through?

The battle was over, and her opponent was at least semi-unconscious if not fully so. Was anything to be gained by killing? This lunatic would come around eventually, but would hardly be in a state to counterattack . . .

But while Lorna was dilly-dallying inside her own head about how best to resolve this, she hadn't been paying attention to anything else, including the door, which had now opened quietly on those well-oiled hinges, admitting a second assailant. When she realised, she dropped the groaning figure to the floor and twirled around, but it was too late. Some kind of super-tensile, metallic cord had already been looped over her head, cinched closed at her neck and was now tightening across her throat.

Lorna gasped, squawked, gagged.

the hard way rather than conferred upon her through any sort of positive discrimination. She was admired widely, but feared too, because, as one of the senior investigating officers in the Serious Crimes Division, she demanded hard, conscientious work and would crack the whip like a devil if she didn't get it.

'Morning, ma'am,' Lucy said.

'Sit down, Lucy,' Nehwal replied, not bothering with niceties. They'd worked together before, and they'd worked well – but the super didn't really do friendship.

Lucy took a chair in the corner, while Beardmore settled back behind his desk. Nehwal, who was perched on the edge of it, her feet not reaching the floor, didn't move.

'I understand you've been working on an abduction case?' she said.

Lucy shrugged. 'A possible abduction case.'

Nehwal picked up some of the preliminary paperwork Lucy had forwarded to Beardmore the previous day. 'This pensioner . . . Harry Hopkins?'

'That's right,' Lucy said. 'He's vanished and there's some evidence that he was taken by force. Possibly from the back gate of his house.'

Nehwal read the report again, her expression inscrutable. 'How're you getting on with it?'

'No real progress yet, I'm sorry to say. I'm working on a couple of theories.'

Nehwal continued to check details. For the first time, Lucy noticed the three tea-stained mugs on Beardmore's desk. His tie was loose and his shirt collar open. He looked sallow-cheeked and had clearly been up and on duty for quite some time. Whatever the reason for that, at some point during the night Serious Crimes had also become involved.

'We've had no contact from anyone claiming to be the kidnapper?' Nehwal asked.

'No, ma'am.'

'You've checked that with the local newspapers, online news sites, and the like?'

'Yes.'

'Because, you see –' the super laid the paperwork down '– we may have another one.'

Lucy was surprised. 'Another abduction?'

'Yes. And it's not a pensioner this time. It's a thirty-year-old fitness fanatic called Lorna Cunningham, who dropped out of sight late on Saturday night.'

'A fitness fanatic?' Lucy couldn't help but frown. 'That victimology would be very different.'

'Agreed. I said we *may* have another one. The jury's still out.' Nehwal eyed her. 'You think Hopkins may have been taken away in a vehicle . . . and that's because there was fresh mud splashed all over his back gate?'

'Well . . .' Lucy mused. 'The mud could have happened any time during the second half of the Tuesday in question. It rained that afternoon, creating puddles. Any car could have driven past and caused it, but Hopkins's daughter said he was a fastidious, house-proud man, and the interior of the property was like a new pin, which kind of backs that up. She reckons it's not the kind of thing he'd have left unattended to.'

'Couldn't it just be that he hadn't noticed some innocent person had made a mess of his back gate?' Beardmore asked.

'Could be that,' Lucy said. 'But then we have the neighbours, the Rodwells. Around half-ten that night they thought they heard the sound of a vehicle speeding off along the back alley, which would have been quite unusual. It's a fairly narrow passage, and they don't get vehicles along there very often.'

'But no one saw anything?' Nehwal asked.

'No one we've spoken to yet.'

'Any CCTV in the area?'

'Again, nothing yet, ma'am. I've got Tessa Payne, one of our acting DCs, trawling through footage, but I'm not hopeful. Hollinbrook's a quiet residential district. I mean, there's a Neighbourhood Watch thing going and there are *some* cameras, but so far zilch. If the abductor came in a vehicle – like, say a van – that kind of suggests that he or they are organised. And if they're organised, they might have scoped out the cameras first, and taken pains to avoid them.'

'The new one,' Nehwal said, 'the Lorna Cunningham incident. That one occurred about eight miles from Hollinbrook, on the canal towpath in central Crowley.'

Lucy was impressed they were able to be so specific so quickly. 'We know this for sure?'

'Oh yes.' Nehwal handed Lucy some paperwork of her own: it was a print-out containing a colour photograph of a woman somewhere in her late twenties, clearly taken at a sports meeting, as she was red-faced and wore a sweaty vest with a number pinned on the front. Her longish, copper-red hair flew as she vaulted over a large, timber hurdle. 'As I say, she's a fitness fanatic. She goes for a run every night at around 9.45, usually following the same route, which takes her along the Bridgewater Canal.'

'And she was definitely attacked on the towpath?'

'We're fairly certain. Her boyfriend, Alex Calderwood, reported her missing at around ten last night. Because her exercise gear was missing from the wardrobe and the wash-basket, the officers attending accompanied him along the running route she normally took.' Nehwal slid from the desk and crossed the office to a street-map of Crowley on the wall. She pointed to a specific section of the blue ribbon that marked the canal. 'They found her Fitbit *here*. It was damaged, it had literally snapped off her wrist, so there'd obviously been a struggle. Before you ask, the Fitbit is already down at the lab, priority request.'

'She went missing on Saturday, and her boyfriend only reported it late on Sunday night?' Lucy said.

'Well spotted,' Nehwal replied. 'However, he was in Wales all weekend, participating in a charity decathlon. We've already checked that out, and it's kosher. He claims that he'd had no contact from Lorna from Saturday evening onwards. He didn't think that particularly strange until he got home late yesterday, found that she wasn't there, rang around and learned from her friend Stella that she hadn't turned up for a Saturday-night sleepover with the girls that she'd been planning.'

'So why didn't the girls report it?' Lucy asked. 'On Saturday, I mean?'

'Sounds like it was only half an arrangement,' Beardmore said. 'Lorna had told them she might go around after her evening run, but not to expect her because she could be too tired. So they didn't think it strange when she failed to show.'

'She could have gone for a run on the Sunday and been attacked then,' Lucy said.

'She doesn't run on Sundays, apparently. It's her only day off.'

'Okay . . . so she's been gone one day and two nights.' Lucy pondered. 'Well, if she had her mobile with her, we can track her that way.'

'Apparently, she never takes her mobile when she goes running,' Nehwal replied. 'Because if she gets a work call, she'd have to deal with it, and that would disrupt her exercise regime.'

'More relevant,' Beardmore put in, 'a row of derelict garages backs onto the canal towpath at the point where the Fitbit was found. When the scene was examined earlier this morning, the rotted wooden panelling at the back of one of them had been smashed through.'

'Smashed through from the inside?' Lucy said.

He nodded.

'And are we sure that happened on Saturday night, and not some time in the past?'

'It looks recent,' Nehwal said. 'More importantly, the garage itself had a door at the front, which could be opened and closed, but had no lock on it. We're thinking that would have been a good place to conceal a vehicle.'

Lucy stood up and moved to the map. Up close, she could see that someone had already marked the point of attack on the canalside with red biro.

'Perfect place for an ambush,' she said, thinking aloud.

'Could be,' Nehwal agreed. 'If Cunningham used this route regularly, which she apparently did, someone could have observed her, probably over several nights, and then specifically chosen this spot . . . because they needed a vehicle to make it happen.'

Lucy nodded. 'The garage is part of a row, but all they had to do was go through the flimsy back wall to grab her. No one would have seen anything. Have we had dogs at the scene?'

'Of course. But they could only follow Cunningham's trail as far as the garage interior, which is further evidence.'

'We're not saying the cases are definitely connected,' Beardmore put in. 'But there *is* a similarity.'

Again, Lucy thought aloud. 'I suppose if your gig is abducting people in public, the most important thing, once you've overpowered them, is to get them out of sight as quickly as possible.' She glanced round. 'And a van is the obvious means by which to do that.'

'But even in this Harry Hopkins case, that would suggest there was more than one assailant,' Nehwal said. 'It's not that easy getting someone into a vehicle if they don't want to go. It would *certainly* have required more than one in Lorna Cunningham's case.'

Lucy nodded again. This thing was getting uglier by the minute.

'Something on your mind, Lucy?' Beardmore asked.

'It may be nothing,' she said. 'But . . . well, we may not have two abductions, we may have three. In fact, we may have more than that.'

The two senior detectives remained blank-faced.

'I think you'd better explain,' Nehwal said.

'The other day, my attention was drawn to the fact that several homeless people have disappeared in recent weeks,' Lucy said.

Nehwal frowned. 'Under what circumstances?'

Lucy shrugged. 'No clue as yet, ma'am. One day they were around, the next they weren't. No one seems to know any more about it than that.'

'Who reported them missing? Their families?'

'No one. Not officially. It's mainly Skid Row gossip.'

'Lucy, homeless people are often transient,' Beardmore said, shrugging. 'And they're usually in poor health. Sometimes they just crawl away and die, and no one even notices. I know that's awful, but we shouldn't let it muddy the waters of real investigations.'

'Stan, one of them was a chap called Fred Holborn,' Lucy said. 'And about a week and a half ago, he may well have been abducted by the occupants of a dark-blue transit van.'

Beardmore looked surprised. 'I haven't heard about this.'

'Again, it's based on unreliable intel,' Lucy explained. 'The only witness is a drug-abusing part-time prostitute called Sister Cassiopeia.'

'*Sister* Cassiopeia?' Nehwal said.

'She was a nun, ma'am, but she got kicked out. She still wears the habit, though.'

'A druggie sex worker who dresses as a nun . . .'

'She's homeless too,' Lucy said, 'so when you get close to her it's all a bit scuzzy.'

'A scuzzy druggie sex worker who dresses like a nun.'

Nehwal glanced at Beardmore. 'Be a laugh trying to get a jury to take *her* seriously.'

'What happened?' Beardmore asked sternly, clearly thinking that he should have been copied in on this by now.

Lucy told them everything Sister Cassie had told her, adding that sometimes it was difficult separating fact from fantasy with such a flaky character, and that she'd been mulling over its potential value as evidence.

'So, she didn't actually see anyone grab this guy Holborn?' Nehwal said.

'No,' Lucy admitted.

'Which would make her testimony next to completely useless.'

'That's another reason why I haven't reported it yet. But, ma'am, there's something else.'

'Go on . . .'

'Sister Cassie said this was a dark-blue transit van.'

'And?'

Lucy blushed a little. 'There's been a kind of urban myth in Crowley in recent months . . . that a black van's been prowling the neighbourhoods at night, looking to snatch pets.'

'Pets?'

'Dogs, for the most part.'

Beardmore frowned. 'I thought you'd wrapped up the dog-fighting enquiry?'

'We have,' Lucy said. 'At least, we've charged everyone involved. But there was a whole list of missing dogs given to us, twenty-six in total . . . and the dog-fighting enquiry hardly accounted for any of them, including a dyed-pink Toy Poodle, which, when it disappeared from its owner's garden in Cotely Barn, was wearing a gem-studded collar worth two grand – that one's still missing.'

Nehwal folded her arms. 'And I thought *I* was talking tenuous when I tried to link Harry Hopkins to Lorna Cunningham.'

149

'I know this is a wild shot, ma'am,' Lucy said. 'But initially, I assumed that all the dog-nappings would be connected to this dog-fighting ring . . . you know, snatched from their owners for use as bait dogs. But most of the dogs we recovered from the dog-fighting farm, even the ones that were dead, had either been bought by the organisers or, in one or two cases, stolen. But as I say, there were lots of others reported missing that just weren't there. And this black van that's supposedly been used to snatch them . . . that wasn't there either.'

Beardmore looked bemused. 'You're saying you think there've been two different parties nabbing dogs in Crowley? You've now shut one of them down, and the other one, which is still at large, has moved on to nabbing humans?'

Lucy shrugged. 'I know it seems daft. But it's the black van factor.'

'Your van is supposed to be dark-blue.'

'It could've been resprayed since. Plus, a lot of these dog-nappings were allegedly at night. Black, dark-blue . . . easy mistake to make.'

'Lucy, there are dark-coloured vans everywhere,' Nehwal said.

'I know, ma'am, I know.'

'But some gut instinct is telling you these cases are connected?'

'It's suggesting they *might* be. Look . . . one week you're on the prowl, looking for dogs – God alone knows for what reason – and a week later, you've upped your game, and you're now looking for humans. I know it's a massive leap. But there is a kind of pattern emerging. The missing dogs were mostly reported during early summer, May, June and July. We've had next to none since the beginning of August – except for Milly, Harry Hopkins's dog, but she probably wasn't the main target.'

'And let me guess,' Nehwal said, 'it's during August when these disappearances of homeless people seemed to start occurring.'

Lucy nodded. 'Quite a coincidence, eh? It's not just that, though, ma'am. It's the similar nature of the disappearances. It's the way the victims are there one minute and gone the next. I mean, according to reports, quite a few of these dogs were taken from their own front or back gardens. Their owners had let them out before bedtime, and left the door open, expecting them to come back in when they'd done their duty. The dogs didn't come back in, the owners went to look – the dogs had gone without trace. From their own gardens. Isn't that a little bit similar to Harry Hopkins?'

Neither of the two supervisors replied.

'And it suggests planning,' Lucy added. 'Stan, this wasn't just opportunism. These were incidents where someone had targeted families who owned dogs and had waited for their moment to strike. To a degree, it's the same with these missing persons.' She looked at Nehwal. 'And your conviction, ma'am, that there would need to be more than one assailant ties in with this very neatly. Even if your target's homeless, drunk, a drug-addict, whatever . . . you can't just drive up to him in the street and snatch him. You have to watch him, follow him, wait till he's most vulnerable.'

Lucy paused. Nehwal glanced at Beardmore. Neither of them seemed instantly dismissive, but she knew what they were thinking.

Why?

Grabbing a shed-load of pet dogs to use them as bait in fighting pits, while reprehensible, was at least logical. But what other reason could there be for such abductions? And why suddenly extend that to grabbing human beings? What was the pay-off in either case?

But then, second-guessing the motives of violent criminals

151

was often a fruitless quest. In all her police career to date, Lucy had never known an investigator's hypothesis regarding a crime be dismissed simply because the motivation behind it seemed unfathomable.

Psychopaths tended to have motivations entirely of their own.

'You really consider this a viable lead?' Nehwal said, watching Lucy carefully.

'Ma'am . . . I'm not trying to pretend it's anything other than a hunch at present, but the more I think about it, the more I believe it warrants further investigation.'

The detective superintendent nodded slowly. 'Well, it's your bed, so *you'll* be the one who has to lie in it.'

Lucy was puzzled. 'Ma'am?'

'Me and Priya have been chatting this morning,' Beardmore said. 'We're genuinely concerned by this case – that's the Hopkins and Cunningham abductions, not the missing dogs. We think it needs some, shall we say, *special* attention.'

'Okay . . .' Lucy said.

'So what we propose is to set up a small special-investigation unit dedicated to this incident. Only small, mind. A kind of miniature taskforce . . . to work solely on these two possible abductions, and either establish beyond any doubt that they're unconnected, in which case we're back as we were, or to establish that they *are* – at which point we kick it up the food chain for Serious Crimes' full and undivided attention.' He sat back. 'Do you want to take point?'

Lucy nodded immediately. 'Yeah . . . thanks.'

'Good God, don't thank us, Lucy.' Nehwal spoke almost pityingly. 'It's got all the makings of a classic ball-acher.'

Chapter 14

Miles O'Grady drove a brand-new silver-grey Jaguar XJ, which he hadn't just acquired for its elegance and power. He wanted people to know he was a success, though he didn't want to draw undue attention to himself by being overly showy. In that regard, the Jag was just right.

But O'Grady didn't feel especially empowered that Monday morning, as he circled the bus station and veered right onto the broken, weed-filled paving stones of Long Acre. Just across it from Dashwood House, he pulled up in front of the door to the subterranean garage he rented, climbed out, opened it manually, drove through, got out again and closed and bolted the door behind him. As he eased the Jag down the ramp, the motion-sensitive light flickered to life, exposing a dank concrete cellar large enough to accommodate about three vehicles, though O'Grady's was the only one that parked here. He paid for this place out of his own pocket, and so kept it exclusively for his own use. Roper and Stone didn't even know about it, and so whenever they came to the office, they had to use one of the pay car parks in the town centre.

But at present, neither the Jag nor his underground

153

concrete kingdom did anything to soothe O'Grady's anger. He parked, and then sat behind the steering wheel, seething. When the light switched itself off again, he barely noticed.

The only real thing to do, he finally told himself, was to go along with this.

At least for the moment.

Until such time as an opportunity arose to break it off permanently.

But when would that be, if ever? How much money would he lose?

The Crew. *The fucking Crew!*

How the hell did you fight them?

It only made sense to cooperate. If you didn't, the cost could be shocking. He'd heard enough bloodcurdling tales – drive-by shootings, firebombed properties, limbs broken by hammers and axes – to know what might await him if he didn't.

But as O'Grady walked stiffly up the steps to the garage's side-door, his fists were clenched at his sides like bone mallets, his incisors bared between lips drawn tight and grey.

It just wasn't in his nature to give in to toe-rag criminals. Because ultimately that was all they were. For all their swanky cars and hand-made suits, they were low-level filth from the bad side of town, bullying, immoral scum.

All that previous night, he'd been tormented by thoughts like these, tossing and turning under his sweat-soaked bedsheets, only just avoiding giving Megan a slap when she'd snapped at him to stop keeping her awake. When he entered the office and sat behind his desk, he glared at the open doorway in front of him, as if it was somehow the fault of the wooden frame that Frank McCracken had come in through it. However much he mulled it over, the essential problem remained – that attempting to double-cross the Crew, in any shape or form, was likely to be lethal. And it

154

wasn't as if they hadn't offered carrot as well as stick. It was a simple equation: you joined them or you died. But no . . .

'*No!*' he snarled.

This gig was *his* creation, *his* game. He hadn't gone to all this trouble teaching the law-abiding world that it had been a grave mistake kicking him out, just to see it immediately absorbed into some vast, shapeless underworld conglomerate.

He glanced at his watch, which jerked him back to the present and to his feet.

It was almost ten, and there was a job to do this morning; in the angst of the last twenty-four hours he'd almost forgotten.

A short side-passage led off the office, connecting with a toilet and a small tea-making area. O'Grady hurried down there, grabbed a plastic bag from the draining board, and took several items of clothing out of it: a sweatshirt, a pair of jeans, a baseball cap and some trainers. Hurriedly, he put it all on, taking care to hang his suit in its correct creases. There were four other items in the bag: a notebook and pen, a Tupperware lunchbox and a camera with a neck strap and extendable lens. O'Grady checked they were all present and correct and took the bag with him as he headed out of the office, stopping to pull a knee-length waterproof over his casuals and to take two mobile phones from his desk, his own and a throwaway device that he'd purchased the previous day.

A shabby green Volkswagen Golf awaited him on the other side of Long Acre, the decade-old rust-bucket registered to a fantasy owner, that he used for tootling around in when he was actually on the job. As he drove, he glanced at his watch again, the clock on the dash having ceased to work some time ago. It was 10.10am. Time was running out, but if he kept his foot down, he'd be okay.

As he hit Pearlman Road, he dug his mobile out and made a call.

'Yeah?' Roper said.

'Where are you?' O'Grady asked.

'Where I'm supposed to be. On the 10.05 to Southport.'

'Any problems?'

'Nope. Chesham got on at Salford Central, as instructed.'

'Any sign he's got a tail?'

'None whatsoever.'

That was reassuring, because if there was one thing Jon Roper was good at, it was sniffing out undercover cops.

'He's not seen *you*?' O'Grady asked.

'He's in the carriage in front of me. And he's not looked round once.'

'Anything with him?'

'Yeah. He's got a sports bag.'

'Good. Where are you now . . . what's your next stop?'

'Swinton.'

'Right.' O'Grady was pleased. He'd been a little behind his time, but that meant the train still had four stops to make before the handover. 'I'm on Manchester Road, heading west. We'll make the switch, as planned, at Hag Fold. Call me when you leave Atherton.'

'No problem.'

It was mid-morning, so the traffic was minimal. And quite soon, ahead of schedule, O'Grady had parked on a side-street near Hag Fold railway station. As he applied the handbrake, the phone buzzed in his pocket.

'We're leaving Atherton,' Roper said.

'Okay,' O'Grady replied. 'Sit tight.'

Ordinarily, when they were working a target, precautions like these wouldn't be necessary. But it was Dean Chesham's first payment, which made him a potential risk. You hadn't learned how to read them at this early stage, and you couldn't

156

afford to take chances. Not that half-arsed countermeasures like these would be effective against a full-scale police obbo, but O'Grady didn't anticipate that. Chesham had too much to lose. He put on a pair of sunglasses, grabbed his camera and his lunchbox, and, as he strolled towards the station entrance, took out the throwaway mobile. There was only one number listed on it.

'Yeah?' came the footballer's nervous voice.

O'Grady descended the steps, tugging the baseball cap down, so that it hid his face from any security cameras, and idled along the flimsy wooden platform, which, as he'd hoped at this time of day, was deserted.

'Get off at the next stop,' he said. 'Sit on the bench at the farthest end of the platform from the station steps. There'll be another train coming in from the other direction in a few minutes. Get on it, and it'll take you back into Manchester. Obviously, leave the bag on the bench.' He could have cut the call there, but his mood got the better of him. 'Let me tell you something, my lad . . . today is the very last day to fuck me around. Any sign of the police, any sign at all, you'll be all over the internet by tea-time. In fact, it might be fucking worse, okay? I know a certain disturbed character who's very good at video editing. I only need to click my fingers, and you're not just shagging trannies, you're doing goats and pigs as well, and you're the star turn at kiddie-porn parties. You get my fucking drift, Lightning?'

It went like clockwork.

The Southport train pulled in on time, O'Grady awaiting it at the farthest end of the platform, but now seated on the floor next to the 'No Members of the Public Past this Point' signpost, with his lunchbox alongside him, his camera on his chest, and his notebook in hand, every inch the convincing trainspotter. Dean Chesham wasn't the only person who got out, but the other two who did walked immediately to the stairway. The footballer was also in disguise, though somewhat more ridiculously than O'Grady, wearing an afro wig and shades, and a big fur-collared parka.

He was also carrying a zip-up sports bag, which bulged at the seams.

As instructed, he dumped it on the bench at the farthest end of the platform, paying no attention to the trainspotter only thirty yards away. A train bound in the opposite direction immediately came rumbling in. Chesham dashed over to it, climbed aboard and headed back into the city. No one had got off this train, so the platform was empty again.

As nonchalantly as he was able, O'Grady stood up, ambled to the bench, sat down alongside the abandoned sports bag and took sandwiches and a bottle of orange juice from the lunchbox. For five minutes he consumed his early lunch, all the time watching the stairs and the fences around the station's perimeter. He'd specifically chosen Hag Fold for the handover because it was only staffed on a part-time basis.

Half an hour passed while he munched contentedly, occasionally showing interest whenever a train passed, scribbling down its details. At the end of half an hour, still in casual mode, he gathered everything together, including Chesham's bag, strolled to the stairs, ascended and left the station.

Their rendezvous point that day was a derelict boatshed on wasteland just off the River Irwell, on the border between Salford and Bolton.

Roper arrived with O'Grady, having got off the train at the next stop after Hag Fold, which was Daisy Hill, catching the next service the other way, and being collected by O'Grady at Swinton. Bernie Stone, meanwhile – 'that fat bastard with the beard,' as McCracken had called him – who'd been working that morning on another target, had arrived five minutes earlier, and was waiting for them in nondescript, paint-stained overalls.

O'Grady said nothing, but unzipped the bag in stern, humourless fashion, one by one laying the elastic-banded blocks of twenties on the bonnet of his Golf. It was all there, two hundred Gs, as agreed for a first payment. He divided the take three ways, but still didn't speak.

'Something wrong?' Roper asked. 'You didn't say a dicky-bird all the way over here. You seemed a bit off yesterday as well, at the meeting.'

O'Grady gave him a look that could have cut glass. 'Nothing's fucking wrong, okay?'

'Okay.' Roper shrugged. 'But you can smile, you know. This is looking good.'

'Hey!' O'Grady pointed at his face. 'I choose when and where I'm happy, okay? If I decide the world's a fucked-up place, with fucked-up idiots on every side of me, I reserve the right to reflect it, yeah?'

After he was done with Roper and Stone, O'Grady drove back to Long Acre. It was now mid-afternoon, so the working day wasn't officially done, but he still found it hard to concentrate. He went back into the office, changed into his suit and tie, and then sat there and stewed for another two hours. His share of the cash, £66,000, sat on the desk in front of him in Dean Chesham's sports bag. He didn't bother putting it into the company's hidden safe or entering the details into the encrypted ledger on his laptop. He didn't even bother counting it again, which was his usual habit.

At around five o'clock, he left the office with money in hand, crossed the Acre, unlocked the side-door and went down the steps into the garage below. Ordinarily tonight they'd celebrate. Megan, adopting her usual 'ask no questions and I'll be told no lies' approach, would repay him three times over when they got back from the slap-up meal at whichever expensive restaurant he took her to. But this evening everything was inverted. That money might as well have been burning a hole in the bag and spilling out. Because it wasn't his any more. At least, half of it wasn't . . . maybe considerably more than half.

'Bastards!' he said under his breath, so infuriated that he didn't immediately notice when the motion-sensitive light didn't come on.

That only struck him when he was halfway across the open space to his car.

He halted, skin suddenly prickling.

With amazing speed, O'Grady's anger drained away, his back and shoulders stiffening as he turned his head, wondering about the lack of light. There was just enough of a grimy glow filtering down the ramp from the frosted glass panels in the garage door to show him the outline of his Jaguar. But even in that half-glimpsed state, he could tell that something was wrong.

He stood rigid, his eyes adjusting more and more to the gloom, the damage swimming more and more into view. Within seconds it was plain that the entire front of his beautiful sixty-grand motor had been brutally mangled, the bodywork crumpled as if from a head-on impact, what remained of the number plate hanging loose, the radiator grille bashed in, the nearside and offside light clusters shattered.

Even to Miles O'Grady's inexpert eye, there was thousands of pounds' worth of repair work needed here. When he spied the pool of semi-fluorescent liquid expanding underneath the engine, he realised that it would actually be tens of thousands of pounds.

At first, he'd thought a sledgehammer, or even a couple of sledgehammers. But surely even that . . .

Of course, none of this really mattered.

All that actually mattered was getting the hell out of this unlit hole in the ground before his car wasn't the only thing left ripped apart. And he did just that, turning and running for his life, loping back up the steps, three treads at a time.

It was probably the least dignified thing that Miles O'Grady had done in as long as he could remember, crashing in a sweaty heap through the side-door of the garage out onto Long Acre, slamming it behind him and frantically locking it. He backed away a couple of yards before glancing right, to where the main garage door still stood closed and seemingly locked.

How in hell had they got in?

It didn't matter.

A skeleton key, or something . . . they always found a way. He backed away further. The question was, were they still down there? Or were they now out here?

He looked around, spinning in a frightened circle. But there was no sign of anyone else on the Acre. Around and overhead, the windows looked to be empty. Less than a hundred yards away, beyond the entrance, traffic rumbled past as usual. Normality. That was what he needed right now. Normality was the only sure place to find safety.

He almost ran that way, slipping and stumbling over the broken, mossy flagstones in his leather lace-up shoes, but at the last second veering across the Acre to his beaten-up Golf. He expected that to be in pieces too, tyres shredded, the guts of its engine hanging out. But no – as far as he could see, this one was intact. They either hadn't known this car was his – he dug his keys out – or they'd wanted him to get in it and drive.

O'Grady hovered there, fresh sweat swamping the inside of his shirt. He dropped to a crouch, to check the undercarriage, only to realise that he wouldn't recognise a car-bomb if he saw one. When he stood up again, he still hesitated, key in hand, trying to work things out logically. What would be the point in wiring up such a device?

Because this is the car they intend to kill me in. After forcing me to drive it by smashing up the other one.

But it still seemed unnecessarily elaborate.

Why not just plant the bomb under the Jag?

But no, you couldn't rationalise the actions of maniacs like these. They always had their reasons, even if the average citizen would find them too twisted for words. And dallying wasn't helping. O'Grady had to get away from here.

Trapping the breath in his chest, he inserted the key and opened the Golf. Nothing happened. He climbed behind the wheel, dropped his bag of money into the passenger-side footwell, jammed his key into the ignition and turned it. The car came to life. And that was all. He got his foot down; the car rumbled forward – still nothing happened.

'Okay, okay . . .' he gasped.

When he hit the road network, it was slow and smooth, O'Grady doing his level best to behave normally. But all the time now, he felt that people were watching him. A fat man waiting at a bus stop with a tan jacket over his left arm seemed inordinately interested as the Golf rumbled by in the slow-moving traffic. When O'Grady got away from the town centre, and the log-jams of cars and lorries began to break up, he slowly tensed as two men in what appeared to be a fishmonger's van followed him around several corners, left, right, left again, left again, only to branch off at the next set of lights. Even then, there was no relief. He approached a footbridge spanning Halpin Road, in the middle of which a black guy, leaning on the railing, watched the traffic passing by underneath. On the other side, O'Grady craned his neck around to stare through the back window: the black guy was still there, only now speaking on his mobile phone.

'Oh, Christ . . .'

162

He headed for home nevertheless, because he had no option. He was sodden with sweat, and completely unsure what to expect, but quickly managed to concoct some half-arsed plan about cruising slowly up to the end of his drive on Astley Close in Broadgate Green, and if he saw anything untoward, hitting the gas and speeding away again.

And then what, arsehole?

What the fuck do you do after that?

You stupid fuck! This is what happens when you threaten the Crew.

But when he arrived on their quiet suburban street, there was no one waiting there. Megan, a sales rep in medical supplies, wasn't even home. The driveway was empty, the street deserted. Even so, he parked on the road in case he'd need a quick getaway.

As he walked warily up his drive, he was numb, intensely aware how vulnerable he was, how vulnerable he'd always been since that foul-mouthed exchange with Frank McCracken. Nothing happened, though – until he reached the front door, where a tiny square of paper had been fastened across the peephole with a glob of Blu Tack.

Fresh sweat running down his spine, O'Grady saw that it was a snippet of newspaper. No ordinary, everyday citizen would have touched it of course; they'd have read it once and then immediately called the police. Not Miles O'Grady. He didn't have the luxury of being an everyday citizen. He took it down, and after he'd read it once, he read it a second time, and a third, and a fourth. Only then did he turn and walk slowly and heavily back down the drive to his Golf, climb in behind the wheel and drive away, taking the long, meandering route back towards Long Acre.

When he parked, he did so shakily, leaving the vehicle askew against the kerb, fleetingly unconcerned for the first time ever that someone might notice this car and wonder what the heck it was doing here. He crossed the Acre to the garage, opened its side-door and went back down. The light still didn't come on. But that no longer mattered. And Miles O'Grady was no longer scared of the darkness. If anything, he felt too sick to worry about that.

He shone his phone-light on the wrecked front end of his Jag. He didn't need to focus hard to see speckles of what looked like clotted blood dotted across the scrunched bodywork, or the threads of torn material dangling from the knots of metal.

'Good God,' he breathed.

The slip of newspaper fell from his grasp. It was only a small thing, a clipping from the *Breaking* column of the *Manchester Evening News*:

OAP dies in hit and run horror

Greater Manchester Police are appealing for witnesses regarding a fatal hit-and-run accident in Crowley, which occurred just before lunchtime today. Gerald Ormisher (88), of 13 Riverbank View, was knocked down and killed by a speeding vehicle on Oxley Lane, Crowley, at around 10.55am this morning. The vehicle, which has not yet been identified, failed to stop, but Crowley Traffic officers say they are looking for a large silver-grey car, possibly a Jaguar XJ . . .

Chapter 15

It was indescribably filthy. A one-time boiler room, now with the boilers removed, it was little more than a brick-lined hole under the ground, the rusted, broken piping suspended along its ceiling dangling with cobwebs and stuffed with rats' nests, the walls caked with a black, greasy clag, a residue of the unimaginably disgusting process now employed there.

The air was so rank, so thick with fumes that it was toxic, so much so that the two people down there needed to wear full biohazard masks complete with panoramic visors and dual filters on their respirators, plus heavy-duty, plastic-based protective gauntlets and coveralls, just to be able to stand it for a few minutes.

One of the pair, whose suit was white, was seated on an old school-chair near the door, focusing through the mask's polycarbonate visor on an iPad, where a game of *Bejeweled* was in progress.

The other, whose suit was yellow, stumped around the room with what a casual observer might consider a surly attitude, heading first to the corner, where a human form was slumped against the wall, swathed in brown paper and bound with long strips of duct tape. Such secure packaging didn't offer much of a handhold, of course, so Yellow Suit had to crouch, wrap the figure in a kind of bear-hug and lug it across the room with back bent.

Who would have thought that a woman as trim and fit as Lorna Cunningham could be so heavy? When they'd first started watching her, it hadn't looked as if there was an inch of fat on her. But then Yellow Suit remembered from studying human physiology that body-fat was lighter than muscle and bone. With many a grunt and gasp, the inert form was dragged across the cellar room in just under three minutes. But from here, it would get really difficult.

Two four-foot-tall plastic drums stood against the wall, both open to the air, but black and crusty with soot, and streaked down their sides with vile stains. The one on the left was filled almost to its brim with an odious brownish stew, but the other was only half-full, a transparent greenish liquid sloshing when Yellow Suit nudged it. The corpse was left lying while a plan was devised. Eventually, Yellow Suit squatted, reached underneath the parcelled figure, secured it around the hips and then, pushing upward from the thigh, levered the former athlete upright until she was half-standing but had flopped forward over one yellow-clad shoulder. With another grunt, Yellow Suit then raised the lifeless form in a classic fireman's lift. White Suit glanced up from the iPad to watch as, slowly and warily, Lorna Cunningham was lowered feet first into the greenish fluid.

Immediately, it began fizzling and bubbling, which was only natural given that it was pure fluorosulfuric acid, the surface of which ascended rapidly as flesh and bone was fed downward into it. But they'd made the necessary calculations when filling the drum in the first place, and the girl was fully submerged before the acid reached its rim. Yellow Suit stepped back as the fumes began to thicken.

Satisfied, White Suit returned to the game.

Yellow Suit collected a thick plastic rod leaning against the brickwork in the opposite corner, and then turned back to the foetal figure in the drum. Though already unrecognisable as human, there must be air trapped inside it, because it was proving buoyant, semi-melted parts of it having broken back through the frothing surface. Yellow Suit applied the rod, shoving everything back out of sight into the hellish, seething soup.

A couple of minutes later, the rod was dipped into the first of three buckets of cold water, swished about and then replaced in the corner.

Yellow Suit stood back, hands on hips, seemingly pleased.

'Haven't you got more work to do?' White Suit wondered through the microphone link connecting their two masks.

Yellow Suit glanced around, puzzled. 'Nothing else I can do now.'

'Mr Hopkins, idiot.'

'What?' Yellow Suit sounded outraged. 'I've got to do that on my own too?'

'That's what he said.'

'I've already had to do the respray on my own.'

White Suit went back to the game. 'It's the price of stupidity.'

'There was nothing stupid about what happened back there. My foot slipped, that's all. That's why she was able to get the better of me.'

'I seem to remember we've already had this conversation.'

Grumbling bitterly, Yellow Suit moved three paces to the right of the two drums, tested one of the flagstones with a cautious foot and, when it rocked, squatted down, fitted gloved fingertips into the crack and, with muscles straining, lifted. The flag was heavy but had been chosen deliberately because it was slightly too small for the square hole they'd originally slotted it into, so it didn't need to be worked loose.

When it was upright, Yellow Suit walked it away on its corners and rested it against the wall. Underneath, there was a circular grid made of chunky steel. It was badly corroded, but it still felt as though it weighed a tonne as Yellow Suit crouched again, reached between the bars and, with teeth gritted, lifted it free. This, at least, could be rolled out of the way.

Below that, a cylindrical rock shaft fell four feet into rushing water. Sidling around the edge of it, Yellow Suit moved back to the second drum. 'Come on . . . at least give me a hand with *this*. It's dangerous.'

White Suit didn't move, other than to throw a nod at the small video camera mounted on the dusty stone shelf nearby, between a set of false teeth and an old military medal, a tiny point of green light indicated that it was active. 'He said you have to do it on your own. And he's filming us. Just to make sure you do as you're told.'

Yellow Suit turned back to the drum. 'If I get burned, it's your fault.'

'Nope. It's *your* fault.'

Being more careful now than at any stage so far, checking first the seals between gauntlets and sleeves, Yellow Suit slid around to the back of the drum on the left, and gingerly reached out to the facing edges of its rim, taking a firm grip, and then slowly rotating it and shuffling it forward. It was hugely heavy, and its dark contents, slopping from side to side, constantly threatened to overbalance it. Thankfully, the distance to the sewer shaft was no more than a yard. And Yellow Suit didn't even have to go that far, before halting, with both hands now tight on the closest section of rim. As cautiously as possible, body braced backward to ensure that it didn't get away, the drum was gradually allowed to tilt forward.

With heavy glops, gurgles and thick, steamy emissions, the

sludgy brown contents began disgorging, dripping slowly but steadily down the hole. When the drum had lightened sufficiently, Yellow Suit brought it back upright and drew it backward a foot, then tilted it forward again, this time to the horizontal. A vomit-like stream spilled downward. It contained various shapeless solids, and whenever globules of it spattered the rock at the rim of the pipe or down the inside, it hissed violently, issuing oily, greasy smoke – but the vast bulk of it vanished into the subterranean stream, all that remained of the late Harry Hopkins fastidiously flushed away.

'You know, this stuff doesn't get rid of everything,' Yellow Suit said, when the job was done, shoving the empty drum back into place. 'If they ever decide they want to use this building—'

'We block that sewer with cement before we scarper,' White Suit cut in. 'As planned.'

Yellow Suit brought the first bucket of water over and sloshed it down the pipe. Then grabbed the second and doused the one or two smouldering spots on the flagstones surrounding the aperture. 'You don't think they'd find that a bit unusual?'

'Probably no more unusual than the fact this place has stood empty for as long as it has,' White Suit said. 'Anyway, it'll just be some bunch of navvies . . . so it's possible you're overestimating both their curiosity and their intellect. They'll do what they usually do. Smash through the ground with diggers and JCBs. All they'll ever see is clumps of soil and rubble, and when they find the underground stream . . . so what, it's a stream?'

Yellow Suit considered this. 'I'm pissed off, you know. That plan for Cunningham . . . it should have worked. It *could* have worked.'

'Well, he said he thought it was complex,' White Suit replied. 'And now he'll be able to say he told us so.'

'He still gave us the go-ahead.'

'He said he thought it was complex. Not *too* complex. Anyway, we pulled it off.' White Suit closed the iPad down. 'The bit we fucked up . . . or rather, the bit *you* fucked up . . . that should've been the easy part.'

Yellow Suit stood over the first drum and peered down. It already looked like boiling stew, though sections of a vaguely humanoid outline were occasionally, fleetingly visible. 'I reckon they'll *really* start looking for this one.'

'That's the name of the game.' White Suit came forward. 'But, being professionals, we shouldn't have to worry about that, should we? That's why you got bollocked. That's why even the slightest fuck-up, even a fuck-up that occurs in private, where no one else knows about it, is unacceptable.'

Yellow Suit nodded, acknowledging the situation.

It wasn't like there was a point in arguing.

There was never any arguing with *him*.

Chapter 16

Perhaps unsurprisingly, Lucy found herself busy in the nick until quite late that Monday night. One day in, and the workload was mountainous.

In addition to Tessa Payne, she had three other officers working with her: DC Tim Lawless from Serious Crimes (who wasn't impressed to be under the tactical command of a divisional detective); DC Judy Stryker, who was on loan from Crowley Robbery (and who also didn't want to be there); and PC Malcolm Peabody, who was quite a bit happier with the gig, no doubt seeing it as his first real taste of CID, though his inspector had only agreed to see him put into plain clothes for one week, at which point they would review it.

'One week,' Lucy chuckled, as she drove. 'Hope it's bloody sorted by then.'

But it didn't feel as if it would be. Already they were pulled out. Payne had spent most of that day flogging through endless reams of CCTV footage, not just from the Hollinbrook area but from the various housing estates along the canal. Peabody, meanwhile, had been an actual presence in Hollinbrook, going door-to-door, after which his brief was to prowl the town's homeless shelters, making enquiries about other potential missing persons. Lawless was midway through chasing all known black or blue transit vans sold in the Greater Manchester area in the last ten years, while Stryker, having interviewed Alex Calderwood at length to see if Lorna Cunningham had made any noteworthy comments recently, perhaps regarding a suspicion that she was being watched or followed, or maybe having trouble with someone, would tomorrow move on to ask similar questions of Cunningham's other friends and associates (and in their case, to also ask about Calderwood himself).

Later on in the week, Lucy would do the same with the friends and relatives of Harry Hopkins, but that was after she'd personally perused Lorna Cunningham's phone records, examined the crime scene on the canal bank and liaised with DI Beardmore and the N Division's official press officer about how the public could best be brought in to assist.

But her last port of call today, now that she'd finally managed to get outside, was to speak again with Sister Cassie, and obtain an actual statement regarding the van she'd seen and the alleged abduction of Fred Holborn. She'd already double-checked the partial VRM written on the condom wrapper, and it had come up again as non-existent. This meant that number-plate recognition software would be next to useless, as the perp would likely have more than one such fake plate and would change them regularly.

As she slowed down to accommodate the late evening traffic on Adolphus Road, Lucy pondered the weirdness of a kidnapper who would start out by snatching vagrants off the streets, then would move on to an OAP outside his home, and finally would pick on a much younger person, an athlete no less. It was weirder still if you considered that this might be the same person, or persons, who'd begun their reign of terror by snatching dogs.

When you voiced it in those terms, it was too nutty for words. But so often with unusual cases, when you finally uncovered a viable explanation it left you kicking yourself at how obvious it had been, at how it had been right under your nose and you'd never once spotted it.

As she pulled off onto Greenway Lane, however, Lucy became distracted. She wondered if she was being tailed. It was a metallic blue Subaru Legacy, and she'd first noticed it about a mile back along Adolphus Road, never more than a couple of cars behind. When she turned into St Clement's Avenue, a much lesser used route, it copied the manoeuvre. She cut a sharp left onto Woodland Way, which, now that she was on the edge of the warehouse district, led only to a minor lorry park and a scrapyard. The Subaru also turned left.

Lucy wasn't particularly concerned. He was making no effort to conceal himself, so his intentions were unlikely to be totally villainous. When she pulled into a layby, the sole other occupant of which was a hotdog vendor now packing in for the day, the Subaru slid smoothly in behind her, braked and switched its interior light on. She glanced into her rear-view mirror and recognised the hulking form of Mick Shallicker behind the Subaru's wheel.

She climbed out and strolled back, more than a little irritated.

He remained in his seat but powered down his driver's window. He was wearing his usual outfit of specially made black suit and black turtleneck sweater.

'You followed me all the way from Robber's Row?' Lucy said.

'Seemed the best way to get you on your own,' he replied. 'Frank can see you now if you're free.'

'I'm not free.'

'It's up to you. But *you're* the one who asked for the meet.'

Twisted with frustration, Lucy hovered alongside his car. 'I'd rather you'd just texted.'

'Yeah, but you don't get to call the shots.'

'No, but I have to put up with your ugly face.' She backed towards her Jimny. 'Next time, text me.'

Lucy followed Shallicker's Subaru along Tarwood Lane and into Salford, but first of all had to pass Robber's Row, which was no fun. She doubted that anyone in the divisional HQ would notice her, much less notice that she was being guided to whatever destination she was bound for by a vehicle traceable to a man with a serious criminal record.

But it was the guilt factor.

Ever since two years ago, when Lucy had first discovered that her estranged father was a senior lieutenant in the Crew, and especially since she'd made a deal with him that for both their sakes they would keep it secret, she'd been tormented by the idea that she now had one foot in the other camp. Throughout her ten years of committed policework prior to that, she'd prided herself on being an honest cop, on obeying the rules and doing the job to the best of her ability. But from the moment Frank McCracken had returned to her and her mother's lives, she'd found herself withholding information from colleagues, getting into clandestine meetings and even turning a blind eye to certain criminal activities.

McCracken had told her that she should treat her fight against crime not as a job but as a war, in which all measures were acceptable. This was the way other, more senior and successful police officers had always behaved, he'd said . . . so why hesitate?

But that was her father all over: an amoral scoundrel.

Lucy had a different take on life.

Or at least she'd once had.

She tried to shut such ruminations out of her mind as she focused on the business at hand, following Shallicker along the A6 through Salford until it became Chapel Street and led into central Manchester. Five minutes later, just off Corporation Street, they came to the foot of a multi-storey car park, where, rather to Lucy's surprise, Shallicker swung in. She followed him, collected a ticket and sat a few yards behind him as they ascended ramp after ramp, passing one largely empty level after another, until they were on the last floor before the top. Here, the upward ramp had been bollarded off with orange traffic cones. Shallicker's Subaru slowed to a halt, and almost from nowhere, a car park attendant appeared. Without looking at the waiting vehicles, he moved several of the cones aside. The Subaru passed through. The attendant waited expectantly. Lucy eased her Jimny forward, also passing through. As she ascended the last ramp, she glanced into her rear-view mirror and saw that the line of cones had already been replaced. She shook her head, amazed by the sheer gall of the high-level under-world. Even as a serving police officer investigating serious crime, she couldn't call on privileges like this.

The top deck of the car park, which was open to the night sky, was completely empty apart from a gleaming black vehicle at its farthest corner. Lucy recognised it as her father's Bentley Continental. The man himself was standing alongside it, gazing over the top of the concrete barrier at the flat neon pattern of the city.

A few yards from the ramp, Shallicker pulled to a halt and braked. Lucy drew up alongside him. He pointed the way she needed to go. She drove the remaining sixty yards to the car park's far end, veering into one of the empty bays on the Bentley's nearside.

McCracken turned as she climbed out and approached.

As always, he wore a tailored suit, a pristine shirt and tie and what looked like a Rolex watch. It was now past nine o'clock on a September evening, and the temperature was falling fast, but he looked unaffected by the chill.

'Well,' he said, 'I didn't think it would be long before you wanted to hook up again.'

'Oh, really . . .?'

'Sure.' He cracked a half-smile. 'You talk like you hate me, Lucy, but last time we were in league, I seem to remember you were the main beneficiary.'

'We weren't in league,' she retorted. 'We just had a mutual enemy. And I'd say the benefits were about equally shared. But that case is closed and is now irrelevant.'

'Okay . . . so to what do I owe *this* pleasure?'

'What do you think?' She folded her arms. 'Last week you sent Mum a mountain of flowers and a lovey-dovey birthday card.'

McCracken furrowed his brow. 'You've called this meeting about *that*?'

'I consider it a serious breach of our truce.'

'Our truce . . . as far as I'm aware, does not extend to you telling me who I may and may not send birthday greetings to.'

'Except when it's Mum, I reckon.'

'I *don't* reckon.' There was a sudden snap to his voice. 'If she was eighty-five, maybe. But she's fifty-five, and she doesn't need your permission to get on with her life.'

'It's this "getting on with life" thing that worries me.' Lucy couldn't contain a mild concern that he wasn't responding to this in his usual airy, casual way. 'I mean, what's your game? She may think she's a toughie, she may act like one. But she's actually quite vulnerable. She lives on her own, and she earns just about enough to get by.'

McCracken shrugged. 'I can help her out there—'

'No, you can't,' Lucy interrupted. 'That would send exactly

176

the wrong message. Look . . . Mum's lonely. She's got a couple of mates, but no one she really cares about and no one who cares about her . . . apart from me. There's been no bloke in her life since she moved to Crowley.' She registered his surprise. 'Yeah, that's right. A belter like Mum, and she's been a singleton her whole life. She threw her best years away on raising her only child.'

McCracken contemplated this. 'Or alternatively . . . it's just that I'm a tough act to follow.'

'Hey, maybe,' Lucy said with sarcasm. 'Look – perhaps it genuinely wasn't your fault that you totally screwed her up the first time. But it *is* going to be your fault if you do it again. I might as well be honest . . . these flowers, this birthday card. She thinks you want a reconciliation.'

McCracken didn't respond but appeared to give it more and even deeper thought.

'I must admit,' Lucy said, 'I wondered it myself. What happened to Goldilocks?'

He glanced up. 'Charlie? She's still around.'

'Does she know you've been sending presents to other women?'

'Probably.'

'And she accepts it?'

He shrugged. 'Me and Charlie have frank discussions about these things.'

'This is bollocks. I want to know what you're up to and I want it to stop.'

'What I'm up to is showing affection to one of the most important women in my life. Come *your* birthday, maybe you'll get a card and kisses too.'

In your dreams, pal, she told herself, but his attitude was deeply disconcerting.

'Whatever the truth is,' Lucy said, 'you're out of line pulling stunts like this!'

McCracken looked disappointed. 'Sorry you think so.'

It was the first time she'd ever seen him vague or distracted. Could it actually be that he'd acted this way towards her mother from some minor but genuine affection, which perhaps was confusing even to him?

'Can I at least get a promise that you won't do it again?' Lucy said.

'No, you can't.'

'For Christ's sake! Look, I came here intending to tell you not just to back off, but to call her up and let her know there's been a misunderstanding. To tell her that it's best if you guys keep going your separate ways. Now all I want is that you don't send her any more presents. Surely that's not too much to ask?'

But it was as though he hadn't been listening. 'Does your mother *want* this reconciliation she thinks I'm looking for?'

'Of course she doesn't!'

'You sure, Lucy? You speaking for Cora now, or just yourself?'

'Look, I've asked you nicely. But I'll play hardball if I have to.'

McCracken looked amused. 'Really?'

'I've been toying with this idea anyway. Next time I'm in the office, I might just go and see my DI . . . and tell him exactly what my and your relationship is.'

'What . . . just like that?'

'I'll tell him I only found out recently. That I didn't believe it at first, but that once it was obviously kosher, I decided to come clean. And I'll take whatever shitstorm results from it.'

McCracken appraised her, perhaps wondering whether she was deadly serious or simply a good actress. 'You sure you want to do that, Lucy? You're a hero at the moment. Why throw it away?'

'I'm a divisional detective constable. We don't have heroes at my level.'

'And this'll keep you down there for ever.'

'And how will that stack against the outcome *you'll* face? Because the moment my lot learn the truth, your lot will too. You think Wild Bill will settle for denying you promotion?'

'It'll be bad, there's no question,' he agreed. 'It won't be pleasurable for either of us . . . but I think I'll be able to handle things at my end.'

'You don't sound too certain.'

'We'll only know when it happens, won't we? But I'm not just going to run.'

Fleetingly, that statement sobered her. The man in front of her had exerted life-and-death power many times. He was respected and feared across the underworld of the Northwest. Even the cops considered him untouchable because he had so many attack-dog lawyers at his beck and call, so many judges and jurors on his payroll, and so many fall-guys around him to take the rap, that he was almost impossible to prosecute. While if his reputation alone wasn't enough to protect him from gangland rivals, his army of enforcers and gunmen would. And yet here she was – 'a slip of a tart,' as Les Mahoney had called her – an everyday detective constable with a blemished record, and yet she was so positioned that with a single sentence she could place him in serious jeopardy. She literally had him on a cliff edge. It almost made her queasy. And not in a good way.

'Why don't you make it easy on both of us?' she said. 'Promise not to contact Mum again.'

His expression hardened. 'And I don't respond well to threats.'

She shook her head. 'This has got to be a wind-up.'

'Why? Because I've found something in life I actually

value? You think there's no heart at all beneath this steely exterior?'

She backed away but pointed a finger. 'This is the last warning. You are *not* inveigling your way back into our lives. You'd better believe that's more important to me even than my job.'

'We'll see.'

'Don't test me, *Dad*.'

He leaned against his Bentley, nonchalant again, the casual, confident achiever.

She turned and stumbled back to her Jimny, fiddling clumsily with the keys, numbed at how badly that had gone and how little she'd obtained from him.

'Rarefied atmosphere up on that moral high ground?' he called after her.

She didn't look back, just hit the fob and opened her car.

'Just remember, Lucy,' he said, 'when you tell them all about *us* . . . quite a few things have happened in your investigations of late which, shall we say, don't exactly figure in the Greater Manchester Police rulebook. And *they'll* come up too. Inevitably they will. But hey . . . if you don't mind that, if you're quite happy that you can just bullshit all that controversy away, in a career that's hardly been controversy-free as it is, then good on you. I was only thinking yesterday . . . you get more like me than your mum every time I meet you.'

She still didn't look back. Just got into the Jimny and drove.

Good God. She thought she'd had *him* on a cliff edge.

Chapter 17

He wouldn't admit it, but Nathan always felt challenged by men who'd done something with their lives. It was amazing the kinds of people who turned up at *FitnessFanatix*. Individuals who'd known serious self-discipline in their time, who'd done physically demanding jobs, or had regularly courted danger – ex-soldiers, ex-cops and the like – and yet for some reason had let it all slip away, their sculpted physiques now dwindled into unimpressive shadows of what they'd once been, their reactions turned sluggish, their outlook on life morose, tired.

Deep down, Nathan scorned such losers. But that wasn't why he avoided working with these one-time alpha males. Mostly it was because, for all his contempt of them, he still felt challenged.

That Monday evening, like all evenings, he walked the gym floor on the balls of his feet, in his regulation red tracksuit trousers, white tennis shoes and slashed crimson vest, the one that hid nothing from the world of his muscular, sunbed-bronzed physique with its multiple menacing tattoos. The vest was non-regulation, of course; as one of the permanent staff here, Nathan was supposed to wear a non-threatening white

T-shirt, but no one really cared. First of all, because he was a good personal training instructor; he didn't just talk the talk, he walked it too (or swaggered it). But also because he looked the part. A tad brutish maybe, with his shaven head and his constant menacing frown – it was all nonsensically macho, but wasn't that what this place was all about? Most of the blokes who came here did it because they yearned for big muscles and flat bellies, because they dreamed of being tough guys who would turn all the ladies' heads when they lumbered past on the beach, or while walking their pet pit-bulls in the park. Whether that sort of thing really worked for the sophisticated twenty-first-century woman was a moot point, of course, but this was still the way most men thought. So, in that regard, Nathan was a great advert for the place.

Even if, deep down, he was increasingly frustrated that this was all he'd ever be.

He was twenty-four now, and personal trainer was the only job he'd ever held. It was great on one hand, because it was something he was good at, and he wasn't too badly paid. Plus, it allowed him to run one or two other lines of private business, which were also pretty lucrative. But when he was putting some wimp through his paces on the rowing machine or the grappler, or watching him sweat and cringe as he pumped out the miles on the static bike, and then suddenly learned that the wimp had once worked in a field hospital in Afghanistan, or had flown fighter jets, or had climbed Everest or been to the South Pole, *he* was the one who felt inferior, *he* was the one who was intimidated – and that wasn't great for Nathan.

How could he prowl the gym as he was now, gruffly correcting poor technique, or telling people to put their phones away, or ordering them off the weights if they were going at it solo, when, inside, he didn't feel like a real man?

How could he smarm his way around the girls when the lies he told them about his undercover operations in Russia and Iraq, or his days as a submariner or paratrooper, were paper-thin, based on nothing more than his own imagination?

Of course, at the end of the day, that didn't stop Nathan looking for girls. When you were as red-blooded as he was, it was impossible to do anything else in a place like *FitnessFanatix*. They came in by the bucket-load. After the old ladies in the morning and the stressed-out mothers in mid-to-late afternoon, came the late teens and twenty-somethings in the evening, the lookers, the gorgeous babes who fitted their Lycra to perfection, whose skin soon glowed with perspiration. Those were the ones Nathan was really interested in, and the reason he always requested the late shift if he was allowed to choose. Of course, you had to be careful these days, in the age of the #MeToo movement.

Frankly, that rankled with Nathan.

You had to be especially careful in the workplace, where simply hitting on a girl could be seen as exploiting your position and might well be deemed a sacking offence. Looking was still free, of course – that was something, at least. Not that Nathan was content with that. He was bursting to get up close and personal with several of the regular girls here. But even so, for his own protection, he knew that he must win their confidence gradually, over a protracted period. Until then he'd have to restrict himself to feasting his hungry eyes. And right now, there were plenty such meals to choose from. From the blonde on the treadmill to the brunette on the power rack to the raven-haired darling on the dip bars. Above all, though, as always, his predatory gaze was drawn most to the redhead on the cross-trainer.

Mainly that was because, tonight, unusually, she was here alone, but also because she was an absolute knockout. He'd been watching her for at least a couple of months now. She

183

was a frequent attendee at the gym, and she worked hard when she was here, often pushing herself close to the limit, and fuck, did it show.

She was about nineteen, he reckoned, and though, up close, there was something vaguely wintry about her, she was still an absolute beaut, with a porcelain-pale complexion, a pink, cherubic mouth and piercing blue eyes. Her hair wasn't red as such but fair with reddish tints; it was also short, spiky and shaved at the back and sides, a near-punk look, which, along with her trim but terrific physique, and her little shorts and sweat-damp vest, only added to the 'action girl' lustre.

Truth be told, Nathan was no keener on being challenged by athletic women than he was by rugged men, but in their case, it was a different kind of challenge – it was a taunt, a tease, it virtually invited him to meet it, and Nathan would never turn down any invitation with such a honeyed promise at the end.

'See you're on your own today,' he said, idling past.

She threw him a quick, incurious glance. 'Very . . .' She was breathing hard, almost too hard to speak. 'Very . . . observant of you.'

He nodded and smiled, and then realised that he'd already been dismissed. Mildly vexed, he turned away.

'Sorry,' she added. 'Don't . . . don't mean to be rude. It's just that –' she forced a breathless laugh '– I'm totally . . . wiped out.'

He turned back. 'I'm not surprised.' The digital reading on the cross-trainer's VDU was ample evidence of just how hard she'd been at it. 'Four hundred calories! And this isn't the only machine you've been on tonight, is it? You're really putting yourself through it.'

She focused on the VDU herself. 'I like to keep . . . fit.'

'Well, you're . . .' He paused. He'd been about to say that

184

she was in great shape as a result, but that could have been construed as overstepping the mark. 'You're . . . certainly doing that.' He edged away, not wanting to press his opening too much. 'If you need anything, you know where I am.'

'Oh!' she suddenly said sharply. And then, more loudly, 'Oh! . . . oh! . . . *OH!*'

She came stumbling down off the machine on her right leg, all but carrying the left.

Nathan jerked towards her with a look of concern.

Her face etched itself with panicky pain as she hopped around in a half-circle. 'Think it's my hamstring . . . think it's just gone.'

'Okay, erm . . .' He glanced around. 'Here, quick!' He dragged a bench over, so that she could sit on it and extend her injured limb to full length. He dropped to his knees but didn't get any closer than was permissible. 'Unusual for a hamstring to go when you've been working out all night. Normally happens when you've not warmed up properly.'

The girl felt warily down the back of her left thigh, as she panted for breath. 'I don't think it's actually *gone*. It just . . . well, it suddenly really tightened.'

Nathan watched her carefully. She cringed again, in genuine pain, and he understood why. He'd torn a hamstring, himself, once, and he knew how horrible it could be. In his case, he'd literally felt and even *heard* it snap. Not that the naked, sensually muscled leg in front of him seemed in any way imperfect. He offered a spread hand.

'I can . . . erm . . . have a feel for you, if you don't mind? Or I can get one of the girls?'

'No, it's okay . . . you go for it,' she said quickly. 'See what you think, please.'

Very tenderly, determined to enjoy it as much as possible, he ran his hand up the back of her thigh. The muscle was smooth and firm, the soft skin still damp. Good Christ, it was just as he'd always imagined. More importantly from the girl's POV, though, there was no obvious damage there – no bump or ridge.

'Does that hurt?' he asked. 'I'm not pressing hard, but . . .'

'It's a bit uncomfortable,' she said. 'But not too bad, I suppose.'

'I can't feel any swelling or tear. It might just be a strain.' He moved his hand away and knelt back. 'Probably best not to continue, though. Not tonight.'

She nodded in full agreement. 'I may have overdone it.' She glanced at the clock on the wall. 'It's nearly knocking-off time, anyway. Do you think a sauna would help? Or a swim?'

'Well . . . a swim's always good for recovery. But we close in about five minutes.'

'Yeah, it's just that . . .' She extended an arm towards him, and he realised that she wanted him to help her stand up. He hurriedly obliged. Upright, she tried to balance again, pressing down gingerly with her left foot, and grimacing. 'It's just that . . . Hell, I don't think I'm going to be able to drive home.'

Nathan shrugged. 'If you want to call a taxi, your car'll be okay here overnight.'

He didn't actually know if that was true. *FitnessFanatix* was part of the Forton Country Club complex, located on the southwest fringe of Crowley, quite close to the M62 motorway, in a largely rural area, and thus encircled by woodlands and pasture. The only other building within half a mile was the small country church of St Barnabas, which stood a hundred or so yards to the south. There wasn't much daily villainy in this district, but though the Country Club had a hotel section, there'd only be a sleepy night-manager on Reception later on, and he couldn't be expected to keep his attention fixed on every corner of the car park. It wasn't impossible that a bunch of thieves could make an opportunist drive-by to see if there was anything worth pinching. But why scare her with that? The idea was to try and give the impression that he was being helpful.

Even so, the girl didn't seem keen on the idea. He wasn't quite sure why. Because she didn't have enough cash in her purse? Or could she be one of these women who didn't like the idea of travelling in a taxi alone after dark, with a male driver she'd never met before?

Either way, it was another opportunity for Nathan, one which, if he'd given himself two or three minutes longer to think about, he probably wouldn't have taken.

'The alternative is . . .' he said, all innocent. 'I mean, I don't want you to get the wrong impression or anything . . . but I can give you a ride home. Like I say, I'm going in ten or fifteen minutes.'

She regarded him thoughtfully, with no apparent emotion – which made him nervous, though there was no disdain in that coolly pretty face. With a jolt, he realised that she was appraising him, looking him over properly, maybe for the very first time; checking out his well-defined pecs, his moody features, his mean but stylish tats.

'Whereabouts are you going?' she asked.

Nothing she'd seen had put her off, he realised with a thrill.

'Just into central Crowley. If you're not too far from there, I'm happy to drop you off at home.'

She pondered it again, and as before, he saw no evident distaste.

'Okay,' she said. 'That might be a plan. Save me waiting out there on the car park for half an hour for a taxi, won't it?'

'Yeah, I suppose.' He noted that she hadn't yet told him where she lived. He wasn't sure what that meant. Either she didn't trust him to know her actual address, or she lived way, way across the borough and didn't want to dissuade him from his act of generosity before they'd even started. Either way, it worked for Nathan. The whole point of it was to get her into his car with him.

'I'll go and get showered,' she said, hobbling stiffly away. 'I'll see you at the bar in . . . shall we say fifteen minutes?'

Nathan glanced at the clock. It was 21.57. The gym officially closed at ten, which was why, when he looked around, there was almost no one left on the exercise floor. The cleaners would be in first thing tomorrow, so it would simply be a matter of switching everything off, hitting the lights and locking up.

'Yeah, that's great,' he said. 'Sure.'

She smiled and nodded, before limping away. Even moving clumsily, she looked amazingly sexy, the shorts and vest only enhancing her supple, shapely form. It was all Nathan could do not to lick his lips.

He spent the next few minutes in a flurry of activity, closing everything down, saying goodnight to his fellow instructors, none of whom appeared to have noticed his brief flirtation with the redhead, and then dashed to the staff locker room to get his stuff. He wasn't supposed to leave the premises in 'uniform', and so changed into a spare pair of joggers and a hoodie top and trainers, grabbed his bag and hurried through into the bar.

Though the gym was now closed, this part of the building was also for the use of hotel guests, and so it usually stayed open until midnight at least. It was fairly basic: low-key lighting, stripped-down décor, a tiled floor, but it was clean and tidy, and one or two patrons were in there.

Rather to Nathan's surprise, because girls always seemed to take an age to get ready, the object of his interest was already here, seated on a bar-stool in a beige tracksuit and blue anorak, a glass of what looked like sparkling water on the counter in front of her, and a bulging sports bag on the floor. She was chatting on her phone when he came in, but now cut the call and shoved the device into her pocket.

'Sorry,' she said. 'Hope you don't mind, but I've just rung home and they're coming to pick me up. I told them I had a lift, but they weren't happy. I'm grateful for the offer though, so I bought you this.' She pushed a half-pint glass of what looked like cola with ice along the counter towards him. 'The barman said you usually have Diet.'

'Uh . . . yeah, thanks,' Nathan said, struggling to conceal how disappointed he felt. In truth, it was more than disappointment. It was outright anger. He'd been stood up, slighted. When he took the glass of coke, he grabbed it forcefully as though he was about to throw it across the room. Thankfully, the girl didn't notice. She reached down, pulled her bag onto her knee and tried to work the zip up. Pissed off though he was, Nathan reminded himself, it was vital not to lose his temper. Not if he wanted to get another chance at a later date.

'Boyfriend coming for you, then, is it?' he said.

She glanced up at him and pulled a face. 'Boyfriend?'

She chuckled, and for an ugly moment Nathan wondered if she might be a lesbo. Usually, when she was training here, she had another girl with her. That was a more than unpleasant possibility; it had the potential to ruin *all* his plans. Despite common sense telling him to rein it in a little, to avoid being cheeky or forward, he needed to know more, so he had to probe further. It probably wouldn't seem too out of order now that they were in a social situation.

'I'm amazed by that,' he said, deliberately sounding unamazed, as if it was only of mild interest. 'I'd have thought they'd be lining up . . .'

'I get approached a lot, I suppose,' she said. 'I haven't met one that suits me yet, that's all.'

189

'Ah.' He nodded his understanding, feeling more relaxed. Nathan didn't have an issue with people's sexual preferences. As far as he was concerned, it was live and let live, a free world. If some lass got her rocks off with other lasses, that was fine. So long as it didn't get in the way of *his* ambitions.

The girl checked her phone, having heard a text arrive. She straightened on her stool. 'My ride's here.'

Nathan glanced from the window, puzzled. They had a good view of the main car park entrance, and no headlights had speared their way in in the last few minutes.

'Don't see anyone,' he said.

'No . . . the little idiot's parked at the church.' The girl shook her head. 'Don't know why, but it's not untypical.'

She clambered from the stool, again wincing with pain, carrying her left leg as if it was a dead weight. Nathan took a big swallow of coke, slung his own bag over his shoulder and made as if to collect hers. 'Want me to carry this for you?'

'Uh-uh.' She was quite decided about that, at least, though she smiled apologetically. 'Sorry again. Not being rude, but . . . well, don't want to give anyone the wrong idea, do we?'

'Erm, no . . . suppose not.' Nathan could have kicked himself for acting like an over-eager puppy. He leaned on the bar again, while she slipped her phone into her anorak pocket. 'Nice meeting you, anyway.' He offered a hand. 'I mean, I meet you every day, obviously . . . but . . . I'm Nathan.'

'Janice.' She shook hands with him, very demurely and platonically, before turning and limping away, struggling a little with her bag. 'And thanks for your help,' she called from the doorway, before disappearing outside.

Nathan nodded, sipping his coke again as he watched her go. She clearly *could* have used a hand with the bag but would have found that embarrassing. Or was it *him* that she'd have found embarrassing? He scowled to himself as he finished the drink. He shouldn't have fawned over her, that was for sure. But then again, she'd told him that she didn't have a boyfriend when there'd actually been no need to. Maybe that had simply been to assert her independence, to reinforce that *she* was always the one in the driving seat – or then again, perhaps it had been to let him know that he was in with a chance.

Cheered by that thought, Nathan finished his drink and headed outside, his own bag hanging down his brawny back.

Somewhat coincidentally, he himself was feeling untypically stiff tonight, mainly in his neck and shoulders. It was odd. He'd done his usual forty-minute workout before coming on duty, but he hadn't pushed himself harder than he normally did, and anyway, that had been hours and hours ago. The September night wasn't especially cold, but it was chillier than it had been, and it struck him harder than he'd expected. He loitered at the top of the steps, fleetingly feeling groggy, wondering if he might be coming down with something.

But Nathan didn't exactly feel ill. Even if he did, he would fight it. He wasn't the sort who called in sick easily. That was for layabouts and wusses.

He trotted down the steps and adjusted the bag at his shoulder as he set off across the car park towards his beaten-up second-hand Micra. As he did, he passed the entrance to the footway that led through to the car park at St Barnabas's – and a pair of flashing headlights caught his attention.

He glanced sideways, and found himself looking directly along the narrow, paved path that connected with the church car park. The shadowy shape of a vehicle was parked at the other side of it. Even as Nathan stared, it flashed its beams again.

He stopped and watched, and very briefly felt light-headed, even dizzy. It occurred to him that this might have been

191

caused by the half-hour he usually spent in the swimming pool at the end of each workout. He'd once been told that water in the ears could cause sensory imbalance.

The car flashed its beams again.

Were they signalling to *him*?

It didn't seem likely, but then Nathan wondered if it might be the girl.

He couldn't understand why she'd be trying to attract his attention, unless . . . perhaps her leg was giving her real problems. There was supposed to be someone else with her, but if they'd had no physio training, they'd likely be no use. And hadn't the girl called whoever it was an idiot, anyway?

Picturing some gormless younger brother sitting behind the steering wheel, or maybe a doddery old parent, he started along the path. As before, his vision tilted slightly, and he felt dizzy. Definitely fluid in the ears, he decided. He'd been doing lots of underwater lengths recently. But then why was he feeling sluggish too, and even sleepy?

Someone on his left gave what sounded like a choked scream.

Nathan turned sharply, and almost toppled over.

More than water in the ears, maybe. Now, he was really feeling tired, unnaturally so, his eyelids drooping . . . but first things first. Was someone in trouble?

He was maybe thirty yards along the path. The wall behind him had a dense rank of rhododendrons on the other side, but beyond the wall in front stood the church, a vast, gothic silhouette on the starlit fields. Just to the left of it, cluttered together somewhat, many of them old and leaning, stood the cruciform outlines of gravestones. Nathan tried to focus on these, because suddenly he thought he'd spied movement over there, as if someone had just flitted out of sight around the back of the main building.

As though in a dream, the edges of his vision blurring, he

192

spied the lychgate in front of him, pushed it open and stepped through into the churchyard.

'Everything all right over there?' he shouted, trying to get his vision straight, wondering why his voice sounded hoarse and weak.

Not water . . . flu. It could only be flu.

He dropped his bag before blundering forward, following the gravel path along the side of the church, the jumbled headstones drifting foggily past. When he reached the far corner, he wasn't sure what he expected to see. The girl from the gym maybe, whatever her name was – Janice? – being dragged through the long, straggling grass by some masked assailant. That he could have handled, rough and exhausted though he now felt.

But all he saw was a few more graves, a dry-stone wall and, behind that, open fields.

Nathan was bewildered. He knew what he'd seen. He tottered forward a few steps, his feet stumbling off the gravel and into the lengthy grass.

A reverberating *clunk* sounded behind him.

He spun around and again almost fell over, staggering sideways, only just managing to keep his feet. When he finally looked up, he realised that someone had emerged from the nearest church door, and now was standing with back turned, in the process of locking it. It probably should have struck Nathan harder than it did that, even though this was a church, it was odd at this late hour to see what appeared to be a cowled monk.

'Sorry . . . father,' he burbled, reality swimming. 'I just . . . I thought I heard . . .'

The monk turned around to face him, and for an amazed second, Nathan, intoxicated as he felt, was transfixed.

'Wha' . . . wha' the fuck . . . fuck happened to . . . you?' he stammered.

The monk didn't reply, because at that moment, three steel points were driven forcefully into Nathan's back. His senses were so dulled now that his reaction to the sudden, astonishing pain was sluggish. It didn't help, of course, that the middle prong of the pitchfork pierced his upper spine, causing his head to jerk back, his torso to stiffen, his hands to claw into talons.

It made it easy for the monk, who produced a large, heavy-bladed knife, complete with a cross-guard, and swept it once across Nathan's exposed throat, opening it clean to the back of the windpipe.

As the paralysed trainer sagged to his knees, his lifeblood boiling away in a raging crimson torrent, the monk with the mangled face lowered the knife, leaned down close and, phone in hand, commenced taking photographs.

Chapter 18

'Yo, Lucy?' the voice on the hands-free said. It was the next morning, and Lucy was driving in to work. The caller was PC Nina Pettigrew, the family liaison who'd been assigned to Alex Calderwell. 'Can you talk?'

'It's fine,' Lucy replied. 'What've you got?'

'Sorry it's taken me so long to report. First chance I've had.'

'It's okay.' Lucy felt secretly guilty that, with everything else in her head, she'd actually forgotten that she was waiting on this. 'Shoot.'

'This boyfriend of Lorna Cunningham's . . . he seems genuinely upset.'

'Does he seem worried?'

'Oh, yeah . . . jumps every time the phone rings. Pacing the house like a cat.'

'You've been with him a couple of days now, Nina, and you've had a chance to get a proper look at him. No fresh injuries that he might have been able to conceal during his interview with Judy Stryker? No marks on his knuckles, no facial scratches . . .?'

'Nothing.'

'Okay, thanks, love. Stick with it for the time being, yeah?'

They cut the call and Lucy drove on sourly, furious with herself that even in the midst of what was turning into a major criminal enquiry, her thoughts were still ranging over domestic issues. But they had to. The fact that she'd been brooding on it all night, barely sleeping, was hardly a surprise, because what was going on at home was not routine stuff; it had the potential to plunge her life and career into a crisis from which there might be no escape.

And then there was the emotional context.

On the few occasions she'd met with her father previously, he'd been a mischievous, patronising presence, comfy in the knowledge that he could toy with her while she couldn't ever risk calling his bluff because she shouldn't have been conferring with him in the first place. Doubtless, that was always the way of it when coppers and underworld bigwigs were involved in shady dealing. But with Frank McCracken, it was aggravated by the father and daughter thing, McCracken often assuming a teacherly role, as if she needed to know how things were *really* done in this business and he was the ideal man for it. It was also true that he'd helped her out when she'd been in over her head. Lucy repeatedly told herself that this had mainly been to help himself, because, a couple of times at least, their aims had been the same. But it was hard to deny that there'd been something else there too.

McCracken had never been a dad to her. She'd met him just two years ago and before then had known him only as a gangster. And even though he'd known about her, he'd made no effort to get acquainted until it had become unavoidable. But now that they *did* know each other, he'd related to her increasingly differently, expressing guarded interest in her career, showing admiration at the things she'd got right, even offering advice when it came to the things he thought she was getting wrong.

She couldn't bloody believe it, to be honest.

The closer she felt he was to her, the more frightened she was that the whole thing was suddenly going to go pear-shaped. Because it was impossible to overstate just how high in the criminal hierarchy Frank McCracken was, and, for all his civilised airs, just how dangerous. She couldn't even guess how many people he'd killed or beaten, or ordered to be killed or beaten. And just because they were his fellow villains, that didn't make it okay.

And now there was *this*.

It was a subtle change in his demeanour, but it was a change nevertheless, his connection to the Clayburn family suddenly taking a turn for the personal, as if they were no longer just a fact of life for him, but something he was starting to care about.

As Lucy drove along Tarwood Lane, everything her mother had said, even though it had been said heatedly and in a wishful way rather than a thoughtful one, seemed to be coming true. Perhaps he *was* getting tired in his middle age, perhaps the pleasures of the glamorous but high-risk world he inhabited *were* palling. Perhaps he *did* miss the everyday affection he'd draw from a genuine, caring wife. And it wasn't as if he and Cora hadn't been close once. He'd only stayed out of Lucy's early life because Cora had asked him to, not because he'd sought that.

Strange behaviour for a brute who'd supposedly never cared.

'God almighty!' she said, proceeding past Robber's Row, bound for Penrose Mill, because she still had to get a statement from Sister Cassie (in truth, the last thing she needed now was to have to go searching for the ex-nun among the backstreets and fleapits again).

But no. Most likely, he was rekindling his interest in Cora because he wanted someone to look after him in his dotage.

Where Carlotta Powell was concerned, once a high-class hooker, always a high-class hooker. But Cora would clean for him, cook for him, toast his slippers on the fire on cold winter nights, all that ridiculous, old-fashioned Northern bullshit.

'He'll still go and see Carlotta whenever he feels like it,' she said aloud, not for the first time in the last few hours.

It was a simple equation. Bad people were bad people because they were bad. It was part of their DNA, it was hardwired into them. You couldn't change it just by wishing they were different.

At which point, Lucy hit her brakes, going into a screeching skid.

Halfway down Adolphus Road, a figure had hurried across it ahead of her. But it wasn't that she'd nearly hit him – he was still a good forty yards in front – it was because she'd recognised him. He was a young, thin guy with long, greasy red hair, wearing grey drainpipe jeans, black cowboy boots and a black leather jacket with biker tassels. The only difference since the last time she'd seen him was that he hadn't bothered today with his stylish leather trilby. As he hit the pavement, he continued walking in the same direction she was driving, but when he realised she was following him, she expected him to bolt. So she stayed behind the wheel, slowing to walking pace and powering down her front passenger window as she drew up at his shoulder. At first, he didn't react, and she soon saw that this was because he was wearing earbuds.

Lucy's Suzuki Jimny was her own car but, since she'd been cleared to drive it on police duty, she'd had blue flashers incorporated into her standard external light system, and a discreet siren fitted. She hit the button for both, giving them a fleeting whirl. The guy with the tassels jumped and spun to look at her. It was definitely the same young bloke she'd

198

seen last Saturday night, the one with the shark tattoo on his neck and the rampant acne, the little bastard who'd been selling drugs to the homeless occupants of Penrose Mill.

'Hold up, mate,' she shouted. 'I need to speak to you.'

As expected, he darted away, dashing along the pavement in long, lanky strides, the heels of his cowboy boots clopping like hooves.

Lucy accelerated slowly as she pursued, glancing into her rear-view mirror in case he suddenly turned around and she needed to make a U-turn. After a few dozen yards, he veered left, vaulted a chain-link fence and ran over a grassy forecourt towards the first of several blocks of medium-rise flats, vanishing around the first corner. Lucy didn't activate the lights and siren again but took the first left she came to, which was about fifty yards further on, and found herself on a slip-road leading into the very heart of the project.

This was the King's Hill estate. It wasn't a particularly bad area, most of the units having been refurbished and privately sold, so she didn't anticipate trouble. The apartment blocks had been constructed in two parallel lines and stood facing each other across a succession of interconnected car parks. There was nobody in sight, save for a couple of builders just ahead of her on the left, who sipped tea as they leaned on the barrier of a balcony.

Then the idiot came into view again, his loping, lanky figure emerging from a ground-floor passage and cutting diagonally across the car park in front of her. He wasn't moving quickly – in a leather jacket, tight jeans and heeled boots, he was hardly dressed for sprinting – and she caught up to him without needing to speed. He diverted left as she swerved the Jimny around and in front, hit the brake and jumped out.

'Hey!' Lucy shouted, racing after him. 'Just wait up! You're not in trouble . . .'

He ignored her, making for the foot of a staircase, but he hadn't even got to it when a burly, dusty figure came heavily down. It was one of the two builders, a tall but overweight guy, clad in the usual dirty jeans and ragged jumper, steel toecaps glinting through the rotted ends of his wizened leather boots. The runner slowed to a halt as the builder stood there immovably, arms folded across his barrel chest, a stern look on his bristling face.

'Where *you* going, lad?' the builder demanded.

The runner, who looked as if he couldn't believe that someone had had the audacity to bar his path, was too breathless and reddened in his sweaty, pock-marked features to answer. In fact, all he could do now was lean over and cough up a load of phlegm. The builder, whom Lucy recognised as Jimmy Ogden, a native of the next street to theirs in Saltbridge, and a bloke who'd been sweet on her mother for many years, shook his head and pointed back across the car park.

'You're going nowhere, pal, but back there. The officer wants to speak to you. I heard her, so I'm damn sure *you* did. Now you be a good law-abiding citizen, like what you're supposed to. Then I won't have to rip your neck out.'

The lad didn't need to wait long. Lucy was there in less than a second, grabbing him by the collar of his leather jacket. She mouthed a 'thanks' at Ogden.

He winked in return and gave her a thumbs-up.

It wasn't always the case that Lucy could physically overpower a male suspect, despite her athletic physique, and most of the time she didn't even try. But it soon became clear that this guy was all skin and bone. She considered the possibility that he might have a concealed weapon, but at present he was too busy struggling for breath after his brief exertion to do anything other than turn limp in her grasp as she marched him down a narrow passage and, when she found space between two wheelie-bins, slam him back against the wall.

'Okay . . . who are you?'

'You, you . . .?' The guy was still sweaty and pink, but now he looked surprised as well. 'You don't know who I am, and you chased me?'

'I didn't chase you . . . you ran. And anyway, I might not know who you are, but I do know *what* you are.'

'I've not done nothing.'

'Maybe not today. Not yet. What about last Saturday night? Hang around the homeless crowd for their company, do you?'

He shook his head, rank sweat dripping off his unwashed mane. 'I've not done nothing.'

'You realise I'm fully entitled to search you?' Lucy said. 'That's because I suspect you to be carrying illegal drugs. That why you were heading back to St Clement's . . . to make a bit more money out of people who've got nothing as it is?'

He was recovering now, breathing heavily rather than panting. 'You've got to show me your ID, you have to tell me who you are, what nick you come from.'

'So, you've been stopped and searched before?'

'I know my rights, that's all.'

'Well . . . I *do* have to do all that, you're correct.' She released his collar. '*If* I decide to proceed with the search.'

He didn't reply to that but looked bewildered.

'Thing is, I'm busy,' she said. 'Especially . . . if you're willing to share a bit of info.'

'What do you want to know?' he asked warily.

'Tell me where I can find Sister Cassie?'

'Sister Cassie?'

'Fine, you want to do this the hard way . . .' Lucy pulled a wallet out and flashed her warrant card. 'I'm DC Clayburn from Robber's Row CID, and I'm officially requiring—'

'Okay . . . wait.' He raised his hands. 'Sister Cassie? All this just for *her*?'

'Like I say, *you're* the one who ran.'

'She's just a numb-nut. A mental case.'

'A mental case you're happy to sell heroin to . . . along with all the other lost souls. Bit of a captive market you've got, isn't it?'

'Does 'em more good than you lot do.'

'You cheeky bastard!'

'Hey, at least I leave 'em happy.'

'Who are you, anyway?'

'They call me Newt.'

She appraised him; his greasy, spotty face, his lank hair. 'Let me guess . . . because you're always getting pissed on the profits?'

'Because that's my name. Kyle Newton.'

'Okay, Kyle Newton . . . I'll ask you one more time. Where can I find Sister Cassie? And I mean, where can I find her *now*? I don't want to spend hours looking through that rabbit warren of misery again.'

'I've not seen her today. Not yet. If she's shooting up, she'll be in the women's toilets on that row of boarded-up shops. On the other side of Penrose Mill.'

Lucy nodded. 'I know it.'

'But I don't think she'll be there. Yesterday, she was saying something about going to services.'

'Services?'

'I don't know exactly what it means, but . . . she said it once before when she was going to someone's funeral.'

'A funeral?'

'I think so.' He tried to remember more. 'She said she wouldn't be around till this evening because this afternoon she was attending services out on Fairview.'

202

'Fairview?' Lucy was bemused. 'A funeral . . . on a land-fill site?'

Newton shrugged again. 'That's all I can tell you. I didn't ask, did I? Told you, she's a nutcase. Christ knows what she gets up to most of the time.'

'This is all I bloody need,' Lucy said, thinking about Fairview, that hideous, decayed wilderness, with its foul stenches and its drifting toxic smoke and its gangs of weirdo scavengers scrambling across it like beetles. 'If this is a wind-up, Newt, I'll make your life a misery from here on. It'll be stops-and-searches every time I see you. I've got good contacts in the Drug Squad, and I'll make sure you go right to the top of their list.'

'On my honour,' he protested. 'She's taking a few others to attend services on Fairview.'

'On your honour?' Lucy shook her head. 'Your *honour*. Are you serious?' She grabbed him by the collar, lugged him from the wall and threw him along the corridor with such force that he staggered and almost fell. 'Get out of my sight, soft lad!'

He hurried off, walking stiffly without looking back.

'I ever see you again,' she shouted, 'I'll pop those zits with the dirtiest needle I can find!'

She was halfway back across the car park when her phone rang.

'Lucy, it's Malcolm' came Peabody's voice.

'What've you got?' she asked.

'Naff all. I've door-to-doored all along Latham Street, Burton Avenue and Tulip Drive.'

Lucy was so distracted by events that, fleetingly, she had trouble placing those addresses.

'Housing estate alongside the canal . . . *remember*?' It would have been more helpful had he not sounded irritated with her. 'Near the garages where Lorna Cunningham got nabbed.'

'Okay, yeah.'

'It's the same as on the Hollinbrook. No one saw or heard anything.'

'Good.'

'Good?'

'Yes, good. Because now I've got another job for you. You got wheels?'

'I'm in my car, obviously.'

'Meet me at the entrance to the Fairview landfill site.'

'The landfill?' She heard both surprise and disgust in his voice.

'Yes.' She climbed into her Jimny.

'That's half an hour from here. When do you want me?'

'Now.'

Chapter 19

The Dead Man's Hand was a pub on Halpin Road, a nine-mile section of dual carriageway running between Crowley and Urmston and comprising little more than petrol stations, car dealerships and container parks.

In many ways, the pub's name and its sign – an Ace of Spades with a bullet hole in the middle – were the most interesting things about it. Aside from that, it was a plain, square, pebble-dashed structure, exuding zero charm. Inside, it was more like a working men's club than a traditional pub, but a club that had seen better days. Aside from the entry corridor, where the toilets and fruit machines were, it was a single room, big but cluttered with tables and chairs, and with one long bar on the left-hand side. It had a small stage, complete with the obligatory strips of shiny material hanging down the back, but these were tawdry and dingy now, and no one could remember how long it was since anyone had performed there. It was a spacious enough interior, the big row of windows on the right allowing in lots of light, though they only looked down on the concrete steps leading up from the car park, which was almost always empty.

Hardly anyone patronised the Dead Man's Hand any more, which is why it suited Miles O'Grady, almost guaranteeing privacy, even now at lunchtime. There were no other punters in, and even the obese barmaid, who had been disagreeably surprised to see him and his two cronies enter, had served them a round and promptly disappeared from view, as though to ensure that she wouldn't be called on to do any more work. Just to be certain, though, O'Grady chose the table farthest from the bar, around which to have his conflab with Stone and Roper.

'They didn't just take my Jag for a joy-ride,' O'Grady said, keeping his voice very low. 'They smashed it into some innocent bystander and then dumped it back in my garage. That means I can't even take it to be repaired. Sixty grand's worth of motor gone, written off, for ever.'

Stone's eyes bulged over the rim of his beer glass. 'Christ! Who was the poor sod?'

O'Grady stared at him as if he was an imbecile. 'What does that matter? Some old bloke past his sell-by date. The main thing is they're playing for keeps. This is the shit they'll stoop to, to get what they want.'

Roper hadn't touched his own drink yet. He listened grimly.

O'Grady leaned forward. 'So, the situation's simple. We either up sticks and move . . . as in relocate to somewhere where we don't know anyone and would have to start from scratch. Or we resist.'

'Resist?' Roper said, baffled.

'Something wrong with that, Jon?' O'Grady asked.

'You said this was the Crew.'

'Who else? Only Frank McCracken would be capable of that. Walking into the belly of the beast and making fucking ridiculous demands, at the same time as looking suave and managing to sound conciliatory.'

Roper shook his head. 'Miles . . . we know McCracken

of old. He's hardcore. A devil in a three-piece suit. And he's got about twenty other devils on his payroll, if not more.'

'And what are we . . . a bunch of pussies who don't count?'

'Miles, we can't fight the Crew. We shouldn't be fighting anyone. This routine of ours only works if we're discreet about it.'

'I went to bed on Sunday night thinking the same thing,' O'Grady said. 'That we're basically screwed. We pay up or we die. Talk about a no-win situation. Except . . . I've been straining the old grey matter since then, and maybe I don't accept no-win situations.'

'Why is it no-win?' Stone asked. 'I mean paying up?'

The other two looked round at their burly, bearded companion.

'Would it really be so bad?' he said.

'Are you serious?' O'Grady replied.

Stone shrugged. 'How much do they want?'

'It doesn't matter. They're not getting a fucking penny. If nothing else, it's the principle.'

'That principle's going to get us killed, Miles,' Roper said.

O'Grady held his jacket open, exposing a shoulder-holster and the grip of his Taurus. 'Not if we pop that bastard McCracken first.'

Roper shook his head again. 'You call that straining the grey matter? For fuck's sake, put the damn thing away. I mean for good. You never even carried when you were in the job. I doubt you've fired more than two or three shots in your entire life, let alone fired them into other people.'

'So what do you want to do, Jon?' O'Grady scowled. 'Surrender? After all that work, after finally getting ourselves an income stream that knows no limits? You want to give it all away to a bunch of scumbag gangsters?'

'It's not all of it,' Stone chipped in.

207

'It's too much,' O'Grady snapped back. 'And shut up, Bern. You're here as muscle, not to give fucking opinions.'

'You said we can't move locations,' Roper said. 'Why not?'

'For Christ's sake. We've got half a dozen gigs in motion right here, right now. Including Dean Chesham. He's going to pay us royally for years to come, and likely won't even notice the loss.'

'Can't we manage that from the other end of the country?'

'The Crew are not stupid. We'd have to cut all ties, we'd have to go abroad.'

'That's not a bad shout,' Stone said, no doubt thinking about the island paradise he'd always envisaged himself retiring to.

'Damn it!' O'Grady said heatedly. 'I'm not just cutting and running. And you two shouldn't want to either.'

'It's about how much you want to live,' Roper said.

'And will your life after this really be living?' O'Grady's voice became sneery. 'Remind me what they kicked you out for, Jon? Wasn't it something inconsequential? Something that wouldn't matter to anyone outside the job? Oh yeah, I remember . . . downloading child pornography from a site you were supposed to be monitoring. I mean, *you'll* be top of everyone's list for a job after we pack this racket in, won't you!'

He lurched around to face Stone. 'And how about you, Bernie? Battered any suspects recently? Kicked anyone in the nads so hard you've induced a hernia? On no . . . that doesn't happen any more, does it? Well, not so often . . . not as often as it used to when you were in uniform, eh?' O'Grady snorted. 'You're another one who'll easily secure a nice new career, aren't you?' He pushed his chair back. 'Don't you two cretins get it? Unless we're prepared to emigrate, which wouldn't be easy given our track records, we have no choice but to stand up to these animals.'

'Miles . . .' Roper's voice was almost a plea. 'The Crew are out of our league. You must accept that.'

'We'll see.' Suddenly, O'Grady seemed calmer. His expression turned crafty. 'I told you I don't accept no-win situations. So, instead of them cutting in on our action, how about we cut in on theirs?'

'What are you talking about?'

'McCracken's their shakedown merchant, right? Their taxman? He's the one who collects from those who won't willingly pay up.' O'Grady shrugged. '*We* could do that.'

There was a lengthy, uncomprehending silence.

'Don't look so bloody gobsmacked,' he said. 'We collect already, handsomely.'

'We pick soft targets,' Roper said. 'Daft, spoiled rich men who don't want it to get out about their secret lives. McCracken goes after the worst of the worst. A team pulls a blag, leaves security men all over the road, walks off with five hundred grand . . . are you gonna be the one who confronts them in a warehouse somewhere, demanding a fifty per cent share?'

'We can do that if we're official,' O'Grady argued. 'Look, the Crew don't give a shit who works for them as long as it pays. There's no loyalty among these thieving bastards.' He still sensed that they weren't on board. 'Look . . . we take McCracken out of the frame, and I'll make a pitch. I'll go to their top dogs and I'll say, "I can do that for you. If I can deal with Captain Shakedown, I can deal with anyone . . . so long as you lot back me up." Why would they say no?'

Stone gave it some thought, but again Roper shook his head. His long, thin hatchet-face now looked longer and thinner than ever.

'Miles, you're *not* going to take McCracken out. And even if you do, what about his outfit? For God's sake . . . he's

209

only a subdivision of the Crew, but that subdivision's fifty times bigger than anything we can muster. I'm sorry, mate, but –' he stood up '– you've lost it.'

'Where do you think you're going?' O'Grady demanded.

'I'm out. I've had it.'

'Wait!' O'Grady growled. 'Stay where you fucking are!'

Roper backed from the table. 'I always knew you were a narcissist, Milesey. Always knew you believed this "I should be king of the world, but other people keep cheating me out of it" malarkey. And I don't know, maybe that makes you just right for the Crew. But the problem is you've got to be able to back it up. And . . . you can't.'

He turned and walked across the room. O'Grady jumped up and followed, catching up with him in the passage where the fruit machines stood.

'You just going to walk out on us, Jon? You've got money coming in weekly. Good amounts too.'

Roper retreated to the pub's front door. He looked strangely sad. 'That's right, Miles. But I always knew it was too good to last.'

'You walk out now, you don't get another ha'penny.'

'I've done all right in the brief time we've been active. I'll live.'

'I'll tell the world what a nonce you are.'

'What? A disgraced ex-copper . . . living on his own . . . in a crappy backstreet flat . . . with no job and a wife and kids that won't talk to him? You think the world'll care?'

'You fucking pathetic specimen,' O'Grady snarled. 'You'd give it up just like that, at the first sign of trouble.'

'Not easily. I want it to go on for ever. But I want to live more.'

Jon Roper didn't wait for another scathing response. He turned and left the pub.

Churning with suppressed anger, O'Grady stomped back

down the passage. Stone was waiting for him in the doorway connecting with the tap-room.

'Looks like it's just me and you, Bern,' he said. 'But that's all right. Means there's more to go around.'

'More of what?' Stone grunted. 'The goodies that should rightly be going to Frank McCracken. We can't take *him* down, Miles. Even *I* can see that. Besides, I'm more interested in getting a proper answer to that question I asked you earlier. How much are the Crew into us for? If it's fifty per cent, why don't we just say yes? The two of us can live on that cosily.'

'Jesus, Bernie!' O'Grady all but threw his arms into the air. 'Fifty! In your fucking dreams, fifty! The best deal we're going to get is thirty.'

'Thirty?' Stone looked bewildered. 'They seriously thought you'd go for that?'

'Who knows what they thought . . .'

'But it doesn't make sense. We stop operating and they get nothing. Surely if we went back to them and tried to negotiate . . .'

'The negotiations are over!' O'Grady didn't want to admit it, but now felt as if he had no choice. 'They came in at fifty but ended up knocking me down.'

Stone's bemused expression slowly changed, became scornful. 'You mean you tried to play tough with them?'

'Wouldn't you have done?'

'And you're the bloke who reckons he's going to go and fight McCracken in the jungle like some wildcat?'

'Listen, you fucking idiotic gorilla . . . even if we do get a deal, there's only two of us now. You think we'll be able to track bastards like Dean Chesham down and put the knuckle on them? Even if they *are* spoiled, rich dickheads, two of us alone can't handle it!'

But Stone's face was now as blank as the substance he

211

was named after. 'How much have I got coming to me from the Chesham gig? Now that Roper's out.'

'We split it evenly . . . five hundred large in total.'

Stone pushed past. 'Just make sure I get it.'

'Whoa!' O'Grady tottered out of his way. 'Where are *you* going?'

'Not decided yet. But if you don't need me any more, what's the point me hanging round?'

'Bernie, we have to think this thing through.'

Stone turned in the doorway. 'You need a gorilla for that?'

'Come on . . .'

'Nah, you've got it sorted, Miles. You're the man with the plan, as you never cease to remind us. Just think on . . .' He lumbered back a few yards, squaring up close to his former colleague. 'I want my money from the Chesham gig. And if I don't get it, the next pair of nads I'll be kicking are yours.'

'Yeah?' O'Grady reached under his jacket. 'Any time . . .'

Stone snorted. 'You and that fucking toy gun. You're *nobody*, mate. When you were back in the job, you spent most of your time pawing the secretaries. When you weren't doing that, you were investigating white-collar crime. You barely mixed it with the heavy mob. Pull it out if you want. Just make sure you don't shoot your fucking toes off while you're doing it.'

Then he too left the building, leaving O'Grady alone amid the ruins of his firm.

'Nobody, eh?' the ex-DCI said with cold, tight-mouthed fury. '*Nobody?* We'll see about that.'

Chapter 20

Officially, cars belonging to members of the public weren't allowed anywhere near the Fairview Waste Management Site, but Lucy got past the barrier by showing her warrant card to the watchman. Such security wouldn't have made any difference to the likes of Sister Cassie, of course. Neither the ex-nun nor any of her acolytes had access to a vehicle, and so they would enter the desert of compacted refuse by any one of several dozen footpaths penetrating its flimsy perimeters.

When Lucy got down to the edge of the landfill, Malcolm Peabody was waiting for her alongside his red Ford Fiesta, a somewhat incongruous figure in his suit and tie, given that the parking area was nothing but dust and the only staff quarters a few prefab shacks standing alongside several massive pieces of static machinery so encrusted with dirt that their purpose was unidentifiable.

Lucy parked and got out, but there was no sign of any staff. She was in a rush to get this thing sorted; other calls had come in, other things needed attending to, and it was already mid-afternoon. And now there were no site personnel to offer assistance. She swore under her breath.

'What are we doing *here*, for Christ's sake?' Peabody asked.

As on the phone, his tone was unusually truculent. He'd have a raft of paperwork to do following the door-to-door, of course, and after that Lucy wanted him to trawl the homeless shelters. He'd been here a while already, and no doubt envisioned yet another nine-till-five becoming another nine-till-nine, or maybe worse. She didn't comment on that, because she understood his weariness at the prospect.

'I need a wingman' was all she said, walking past him through a gate in the steel-slatted fence, and taking the path on the other side.

He followed, hands in pockets, shoulders hunched. 'I don't get you.'

By rights, if they wanted to proceed from here they should have helmets on and protective clothing, but there was nobody around, and there was no time for that anyway.

'We're looking for a nun,' she said over her shoulder.

'A what?'

'You heard me, Malcolm. A nun. A holy woman. Long black cassock, wimple, veil . . .'

'I know what a nun is. I was raised a Catholic.'

'Excellent . . . probably means you've got more chance of getting to Heaven than me.'

'I just don't know why I'd be looking for a nun out here.'

Lucy told him why as they walked, giving him the whole story. About how, despite her status as an inspirational teacher and mentor, Sister Cassiopeia had suffered a severe crisis of faith, which had led to an affair with a young priest and subsequent dismissal from her order. And about how her response to such disgrace had been to get into drugs, which in due course had conspired to transform the once beautiful nun into a homeless, smack-addicted prostitute.

'Course, helping coppers is not a popular hobby among the downtrodden,' Lucy said as they picked their way along a rutted track, the stink of the place already bunging up her nostrils. 'But Cassie's pretty much on our side. And in her case, it comes from the heart. It's ironic, but since she's been destitute, she's rediscovered her belief. She's adamant that right and wrong exist, she believes that hurting your neighbour is hurting God. Somehow, the rest of them respect that . . . they see her as an honest person. So they give her a pass.'

Lucy glanced at the encircling trash heaps. They were crisscrossed with caterpillar tracks, compressed into an undulant, colourless moonscape stretching as far as the eye could see, much of it pulverised to unrecognisable mulch. They were only a few hundred yards in, but it was already swarming with flies. Aggressive gulls swooped overhead.

Lucy also mentioned the van and what Sister Cassie thought she had seen and knew, including the other possible abductions. 'We need to get it written down, Malcolm.'

'You mean before Sister Cassie disappears too?' He almost sounded hopeful that they'd already be too late.

Lucy ignored his attitude but gave thought to what he'd said. 'Yes, because anything can happen on the streets. So it's imperative we find out exactly what she knows as soon as possible and make a record.'

'Maybe we should think about locking her up?' Again, Peabody sounded pleased with the idea. 'You say she's attending a funeral. Whose funeral? Even if one of these poor fuckers has gone belly-up legitimately, disposing of the body out here . . . isn't that preventing a lawful burial? Attempting to obstruct the Coroner?'

'Let's just crack on.' She didn't even want to contemplate getting into a whole slew of new, different and complex offences like that. 'We'll have to split up in a minute. We've

215

got a lot of ground to cover. If we've got nowhere in an hour, I'm calling the chopper in.'

'Christ, they'll be happy.'

'They'll do their job,' she retorted, her patience finally snapping, rounding on him. 'And so will *you*! Listen . . . this may be something or nothing. But it may also be that Sister Cassie is the only witness we've got to a whole bunch of abductions and God knows what else! Now, are you with me on this, or not?'

'Yeah, sure . . .' The sudden show of force had taken him by surprise. 'I mean, what I mean is . . . sure, I am.'

'Right, good. We're all feeling it, Malcolm. We've all got stacks to do. Welcome to CID. Perhaps now you know why no one wants to be a detective any more.'

She turned and trudged on. He followed her sheepishly.

Lucy had been in uniform when Peabody had first joined up, and had served as his tutor-constable, personally guiding him through the trials of his probation. During that time, they'd got to know each other well, and had become friends, though the teacher-and-pupil relationship remained. But her mind was already on other things.

This landfill site was huge, covering several square miles at least. She couldn't even picture it geographically. She had some vague idea that it rose to a kind of plateau in the centre, from where they might be able to see what was happening farther afield. But it was difficult to pick anything out at present. It all looked exactly the same: a desolate, hummocky wilderness of rubbish. Occasionally, they'd see a distant tractor or JCB, a yellow light spinning on its cabin roof as it prowled the skyline, but such vehicles might as well have been toys, they were so far away.

After about ten minutes, they reached a part of the path where it divided into three. The divergence was marked by a tree, though what species was impossible to tell: it was

216

twisted, its branches spindly and with only rags and tags of leaves hanging off it, though in the very middle, suspended with arms outstretched, as though crucified, was a dirty, eyeless doll.

Peabody was fleetingly fascinated, regarding the horrible totem as if it had been left there specifically for him.

Lucy pondered their next move. It was much hotter here than it was back in town, and the air was harder to breathe as well. Fires burned nearby, veils of brackish smoke drifting across the heaps of ruin. The chances of finding anyone in the middle of this blight had to be zero. That was assuming the story about the so-called 'services' was even true, which Lucy increasingly doubted. Perhaps, if she hadn't been so preoccupied with everything else, she'd have sensed that Kyle Newton was pulling a fast one.

'Hey!' Peabody suddenly said. 'You hear that?'

Lucy turned, but wasn't sure what she was supposed to be listening to.

The rumble of a tractor was somewhere close at hand. As they stood there, it swung into view over a hilltop some fifty yards off, but was headed away from them, the grinding of its engine gradually fading as it rolled out of sight again.

Then Lucy heard it too.

A wavering, semi-ethereal sound. A voice, she realised, holding a tune – rather sweetly. Someone was singing. A religious song, by the sound of it, though she couldn't make out the words. She looked back at Peabody.

'Where's it coming from?' she asked.

He shook his head. Lucy ventured along the right-hand path. The words became clearer, though they were being sung in Latin.

'. . . *Et Jesum, benedictum fructum ventris tui,*
Nobis post hoc exsilium ostende.

217

> *O clemens! O pia!*
> *O dulcis Virgo Maria!'*

'Sounds like something a nun would sing, don't you think?' Peabody said.

Lucy didn't wait to hear more. She ran up the path, Peabody following.

It took them along a gully, which clove through a virtual mountain of cardboard boxes squashed on top of each other. The singing ceased but was replaced by a female voice – almost certainly the same female voice – speaking aloud.

'I am the resurrection and the life, saith the Lord: he that believeth in me, though he were dead, yet shall he live: and whosoever liveth and believeth in me shall never die . . .'

There was a mumbled response from several other voices.

'We must remember, brothers and sisters, that we come not here to commend the soul of a mortal man, one made in the Lord's own image. . .'

'That's her,' Lucy said haring ahead.

'. . . but we can still offer prayers for the lives here extinguished, for the souls, if souls they have, of these innocent creatures of God . . .'

The path veered left, before cresting a small rise. From the top, they saw an astonishing sight. A small section of landfill had sunk into a kind of depression; perhaps it had collapsed partway down an old mine-shaft before blocking it, leaving what looked like the interior of an inverted cone, though it wasn't steep. At the bottom, some thirty yards down, it flattened out a little, but centred around a pit, where twists of splintered furniture, broken planks and piles of mouldering newspapers had sagged into the earth. On the far side stood the figure of Sister Cassie, hands clasped in prayer, and on the near side a small group of about eight of her bent, tattered followers either standing or seated on broken chairs. There was a terrible reek in the air, while plague-like clouds of flies swirled around them.

The ex-nun interrupted her service, eyeing the cops sternly as they descended.

'And why are you here, detectives?' she called out. 'We are doing nothing illegal.'

Lucy stumbled downhill towards her. 'What exactly *are* you doing, Sister?'

The ex-nun still looked vexed. 'Performing a holy ritual, of course. Burying these poor, harmless creatures that were so viciously treated.'

Lucy already had half an idea that she hadn't interrupted a human funeral, but on reaching the bottom of the depression, she scrambled over anyway to look. The stench of decay thickened, becoming almost intolerable. Flies swarmed aggressively. In truth, it was a nightmarish scene, almost demonic: the figure of the nun, cadaverous, degraded, draped in her dirty, ragged raiment, yet hands joined in prayer as she stood upright on a hillside of waste and filth, a storm of winged horrors buzzing around her.

The contents of the pit were the crowning, hellish glory.

Lucy gazed down on a tangle of butchered, half-burned, half-rotted forms crammed on top of each other. Maybe ten or eleven, maybe more. But trampled down hard, with brute force, until they'd almost coagulated into a single mass. Even then, occasional body parts were visible: a canine snout, complete with whiskers and nose; a tongue lolling over exposed fangs; a twisted, shrivelled paw.

'Good Christ.' Peabody gagged.

In only two and a half years he'd already attended more death scenes than anyone in normal life could imagine. But still this was almost too much for him. He'd gone green in the cheeks; one heavy-knuckled hand clamped across his nose and mouth.

'The poor dears,' Sister Cassie said, hands still joined, smiling benignly down. 'Several days ago, one of my regulars came across them during his wanderings. He too was horror-stricken.'

Lucy glanced at the small group of Sister Cassie's followers. All were thin, raddled, clad in layers of dirty, mismatched clothes. All had the matted hair, sunken faces and dull, glazed eyes of the long-term alcoholic or drug-addict. Lucy wasn't sure which one of these was supposed to have found the dogs, not that it would make much difference. She'd have had more luck getting info out of corpses.

'Sister Cassie,' she said, turning back. 'When you say "viciously treated", what do you mean?'

'Look for yourself, child. One won't need to get too close to recognise the blow of the axe, the rip and tear of the knife.' Very sadly, she ran a finger across her own throat. 'Even the bite of the ligature. Certainly in the case of that poor creature on top.'

Lucy tried to focus on the object of interest. It was so caked in blood and grime, at least three quarters of it charred like an old carpet, that it was difficult to identify it as canine. She'd initially assumed that these would be the missing dogs that were still outstanding, probably more bait dogs that had died in the fighting-pit at Mahoney's farm. But if they *hadn't* been bitten to death, and if they hadn't been clubbed by Mahoney's hammer . . . what did that mean?

'A particularly heinous cord was used in that case,' Sister Cassie said. 'Something like a wire. A neck-wire. Can you imagine that, for a poor innocent creature like this?'

Lucy's eyes were drawn to what she supposed was the creature's neck. And some minor detail of it now, finally, caught her attention. So much so that she hunkered down to look more closely, but the stench was truly sickening.

When she straightened up again, she was white-cheeked, her mouth set like a trap.

'God's sake,' Peabody mumbled, holding his jacket to the lower part of his face. 'Can we get out of here?'

Lucy glanced at him, and then at Sister Cassie again. A freshly gathered pile of cardboard sheeting was stacked alongside her, next to her satchel.

'What do you propose to do here, Sister?' she asked. 'I mean when you've said your prayers.'

'Why, bury them.'

'They're already half-buried.'

'Of course. We need only cover them, but it's the very least we can do.'

'They need to be covered, all right.' Lucy turned back to Peabody. 'For preservation.'

He lowered his jacket. 'What?'

'Have a gander, Malcolm. Specifically, that one on the top. Difficult to tell from here, but what's left of its fur is actually pink.'

'Pink?'

'Yeah. And it's wearing a collar. A jewel-studded collar . . . which ought to be worth at least a couple of grand.'

Chapter 21

'Look, Lucy,' Beardmore said tiredly. 'Someone's killed a bunch of dogs. Apparently in a cruel and heartless way. I agree, it's terrible. Very upsetting. But I don't see how it's connected to the case you're supposed to be investigating.'

'Stan, come on,' Lucy said into her mobile.

She stood alongside the pit of carcasses, still in the midst of the stench and the droning flies. Of human beings, only Peabody remained nearby, and he was halfway up the slope, still with the material of his jacket spread over his nose and mouth.

'We've found the dyed-pink poodle with the jewelled collar. And that collar . . .' She held the object up in its clear plastic evidence sack; it was so coated in blood and gunk that it was barely discernible as something precious. 'I mean, it's a bit of a mess, but it's been priced at two grand minimum. Now, why would any hoodlum kill a dog and dump it . . . along with something so valuable?'

'Perhaps he was too stupid to realise what he had,' Beardmore suggested.

'Stan, come on . . . there's something weird about this.

These aren't bait dogs. I'm pretty sure they've all died by human hand.'

'Didn't I hear from you that when Mahoney's bait dogs got badly injured in the fighting-pit, he put them out of their misery himself?'

'Yeah, but this poodle . . .' She stepped back to the pit and glanced down. 'While it's partly burned, most of its head and upper body is intact. And there's no sign of any scarring there. And that's usually where bait dogs get hurt the most. Someone killed this dog just for the sake of it. Garrotted it with a wire, or something similar.'

'Like I say, how terrible.'

'Stan, please . . .'

'Lucy . . . it's not even the same colour of van. Those so-called dog-nappers were driving a black van. The abductors of this hobo down in St Clement's were driving a blue van. There's no certainty that abduction even happened.'

'So that means we don't look into it? How's that going to play in the press, Stan? That we had a possible lead on a bunch of missing homeless people, but we couldn't be bothered following it through because we weren't certain?'

'We don't actually know that any homeless have gone missing at all.'

'We've got a fairly good idea. And like it or not, there *is* a link to the missing dogs. And now we've found the dogs butchered. So, what do we think's happened to those missing people?' Lucy was being as forceful with her boss as she'd ever dared. But after some wariness at the commencement of this enquiry, she now felt increasingly as if things were adding up, and the picture they were creating was horrific. 'Look, all I'm asking for—'

'All you're asking for is a full forensics team,' he snapped. 'To examine a pile of dead dogs. Seriously, Lucy?'

'We won't need the whole show. Can't they just spare us a couple of CSIs? And it's not just for these dogs, Stan. It's not even for the missing homeless, if that's also a concern . . . those ragged non-persons who most folk don't even notice, never mind care about!'

'Easy, Lucy,' he cautioned.

'Ultimately, it's for Harry Hopkins and Lorna Cunningham.' She paused, breathless.

Beardmore sighed long and hard. 'A couple of CSIs . . .?'

Finally, it sounded as if he was considering it, though he clearly wasn't happy. She understood why. He'd signed off on a reasonably large operation of hers quite recently, and though they'd got results, it had mainly concerned dog-fighting. Someone would ask questions about that at some point. Spend a few quid in the twenty-first-century police, and you had to give a good explanation why.

'Maybe if Serious can pick up the tab . . .?' he said.

'But they're not even officially attached to the case yet,' Lucy replied. 'And you know how difficult Priya can be.'

'Yes, I do,' he said. 'Which is why this'll be one phone-call I'm *not* looking forward to.'

'Perhaps just tell her what this is. That whoever killed these animals might now be killing people. But also, if it's like some kind of graduation process, where they start with animals but then move on up to a higher challenge . . . well, maybe they won't have been too careful at the early stage. So we could have an absolute treasure trove of evidence here. But not unless we get this crime scene cordoned off and secured, and we get Scientific Support at the first opportunity.'

'I'll see what I can do,' he said, after another long sigh. 'As I say, I'll make a phone-call. In the meantime, you do what you can.' He cut the call.

Lucy hurried across the bottom of the depression, heading

back up the slope, passing Peabody in the process. 'Come on,' she said.

He looked massively relieved. 'Where we going?'

'Back to the car park.' She descended the other side of the rise to the footpath. 'I've got some incident tape in my boot. You can bring it back here and close the scene off.'

'The scene?'

'Gimme a break, Malcolm. I'm sure you overheard most of that conversation.'

'You mean we've got to go and get stuff from your car, and then I've got to come all the way back here on my own?'

'Not only that –' they passed through the defile between the mountains of boxes '– you've then got to stand guard.'

'So where are *you* going?'

'First, I'm going to try and get a vet, to officially examine the remains in situ. Then . . . I've got a spare forensics tent in my garage at home. It's seen better days, but it'll do till we get the real thing.' She glanced at the sky, where heavy yellowish clouds were gathering. 'Last thing we need now is more rain.'

'How you going to get a forensics tent all the way out here?' he asked, as they passed the tree with the hanging doll. 'Must be three quarters of a mile from that car park.'

Lucy pondered this as they stumped along. 'I'll get my Ducati. It's in the shed at Mum's. Should be able to carry the tent on the back of that.'

'You can get your bike out here?' He sounded sceptical.

'More easily than I can get a car, wouldn't you say?'

Peabody shook his head, evidently not liking the sound of it, but liking even less the idea that he was going to be stuck in this desolation for a bit of time yet.

'How long before the CSIs get here?' he asked.

'How long's a piece of string?'

'Will it be tonight?' It was a fatalistic kind of question, as if he already knew the answer.

'I hope so,' she said. 'But I wouldn't count on it.'

'So, if it's tomorrow . . . who's going to stand guard all night?' He sounded as if he knew the answer to that one as well.

'Don't sound so upset, Malcolm. This'll be the easiest overtime you've ever had.'

Chapter 22

'So,' Charlie said over her glass of rosé. 'Am I just supposed to be okay that you're sending birthday greetings and bouquets of flowers to women I don't know?'

Frank McCracken, who'd been distracted and preoccupied all through dinner, sipped his cognac. 'Thought me and you had a kind of open relationship?'

'Well, we do . . . but we have to draw the line somewhere. And you suddenly getting interested in old girlfriends again is a bit of a concern for me.'

To look at Charlie, one would never have expected any man in her company to have his head turned by another woman. Tonight, out for the evening, she was the ultimate blonde bombshell, platinum locks falling in snakelike curls down her back and shoulders, looks to die for, an hourglass physique wrapped to perfection in a strappy, flower-patterned, figure-hugging Versace dress, yellow Jimmy Choos with five-inch heels, which added even more lustre to her bronze, athletically toned legs.

She'd been cool with McCracken all evening, mainly because back in his spacious pad in Didsbury his housekeeper had let it slip that she'd recently arranged the delivery of flowers, balloons and a birthday card to a former flame of his in Saltbridge, Crowley. More fascinating to Charlie, though, was McCracken's own reaction. He'd seemed unconcerned that she knew, refusing to get into one of those edgy tit-for-tat games she liked to play when trying to wheedle out some truth about his latest infidelity. In fact, throughout the evening, despite the delicious and very expensive meal they'd just eaten, his conversation had been muted, as if his thoughts were somewhere else.

'I mean, surely it's only a coincidence that you've brought me *here*?' Charlie said, fixing him with that cornflower-blue gaze.

'Uh?' He glanced up. 'Charlie, you've known for yonks that Redwood's is my favourite eaterie. No one does steaks like they do here. And I thought you liked it too.'

'But we're in Crowley,' she replied. 'And so is Saltbridge. Is she perhaps at one of these other tables as we speak, this mysterious lady from your past? Did you bring me here so that she could check out the opposition?'

'Christ's sake, Charlie . . . grow up.'

'I'm not angry, Frank.' She leaned back in her chair, adjusting her eye-catching décolletage. 'I'm just interested to know.'

'Cora's not here,' he said. 'And she couldn't hold a candle to you in the glamour stakes, so stop worrying. Look . . . she was a great lass, but she's fallen on hard times. Don't see any harm in helping her out a little.'

'If that was all it was, I'd agree. But flowers, balloons, a birthday card?'

'Charlie, it doesn't mean anything, okay? Me and Cora . . . we were an item thirty years ago. These days, it's just platonic.'

'Oh, so you have been *speaking* to her then?'

'My love, just content yourself with the knowledge that

228

it's a small world, yeah? None of us have any clue what or *who* is waiting round the next corner.'

'Very profound.' She fanned herself with the dessert menu. 'But my petty jealousies aside, you, Frank McCracken, ought to know better than anyone how unwise it is to get involved with a woman who's not in the life.'

'Oh, she's in the life. Or rather, she used to be. But she got out of it.'

'She got out of it?' This was the first thing Charlie had heard about this other woman that genuinely intrigued her. 'And how did she do that?'

McCracken shrugged. 'One day she just upped and walked.'

It seemed politic *not* to mention the fact that this was because Cora had just found out that she was pregnant. Charlie didn't know that Frank had a daughter, and as far as he was concerned, it was best if she never did.

Even so, the blonde beauty at the other side of the table was now regarding him with a doubtful expression. 'She just upped and walked?'

'I know,' he said. 'I didn't think it would last, either. But it has.'

'Except that now she's fallen on hard times?'

'Well . . . I wouldn't say hard times as such. But maybe her life isn't all it could be.'

'And you want to do the right thing by her . . . by dragging her back into this one?'

McCracken regarded her thoughtfully. Charlie was by no means dumb.

'That's actually a good point,' he said. He signalled to a waiter for the bill. 'That's a very good point indeed.'

It was late evening now and around them the restaurant was gradually emptying.

Redwood's was part of Crowley Old Hall, a Tudor manor

229

house and Grade I listed building on the border between Crowley and Salford. It had gone to ruin until ten years ago, when its transformation into a cordon bleu restaurant had brought the whole site back to life.

Even here in the dining room, it epitomised olde-worlde charm, with its low, gnarly beams, its dark oil portraits and its suits of Cromwellian armour standing sentry-like along the walls. But it was going on for 9.30 now, and, this being a Tuesday, most of the tables were being draped with fresh linen and arranged with cutlery and accoutrements for the lunchtime crowd tomorrow. It was time to go.

'Well, Frankie,' Charlie said, as they strolled arm in arm into the car park. 'You've really shown a girl a good time tonight.'

'You enjoyed the meal, didn't you?'

'The meal was great. The revelations . . . not so much.'

McCracken couldn't disagree with that. Sometimes, passing fancies could prove expensive for all concerned. They crossed the tarmac to where Mick Shallicker leaned against the Bentley playing on his iPad, McCracken so lost in these thoughts that he didn't notice the shadowy form lurking in the shrubbery on the car park's right edge.

'Hey, Frank!' it called, stepping out behind them.

Everything then happened in a rush. McCracken heard the voice but was distracted by the sight of Shallicker snapping upright and dashing towards them, reaching under his jacket. He spun around, seeing a figure he recognised: moustached, with mussed grey hair over a sweat-damp face, its Burberry trenchcoat flapping open on a crumpled shirt and loosely knotted tie.

Then he realised that the figure was pointing a pistol at him, and firing.

The first shot hit McCracken high in the upper left of his body, the thudding impact spinning him like a top. The

230

second hit Charlie in the middle of the back, knocking the wind out of her. They struck the tarmac together, dead weights. As Shallicker drew up alongside them, he'd already drawn his Colt Cobra, and now took aim at the fleeing shape, which had only managed two shots before turning and haring back into the shrubbery.

Shallicker squeezed one round off but knew that he'd missed; the figure was already out of sight. He dashed in pursuit, his huge feet pounding the floor. It was a thin belt of undergrowth, and on the other side lay a subsidiary car park, where the shooter's vehicle, a Volkswagen Golf, waited close by. Neither the colour of the Golf nor its registration mark was clear in the dim light, and when Shallicker got there the shooter was already behind the wheel and spinning the car in a tyre-screeching semicircle. Before he could let off another round, it veered through the car park exit and vanished, its engine roar fading as it sped into the night. Shallicker sprinted back along the passage he'd torn through the shrubbery. No one had come out from the restaurant yet. The old building's thick stone walls might have absorbed the sound of the shots, while the kitchen, where the windows were likely to be open, would be clattering with crockery.

Not that it made a lot of difference to Frank McCracken and Carlotta Powell, both of whom lay face-down in widening pools of blood.

Chapter 23

Malcolm Peabody waited glumly about thirty yards from the dog-pit, halfway up one of the encircling slopes, though even there he wasn't out of range of the choke-inducing stench. He still wore the same civvies he'd been wearing earlier, though when Lucy had popped back on her motor-bike, bringing the forensics tent, she'd also, at his request, brought him a black police-issue waterproof jacket. In the end the rain hadn't come, but Peabody was still wearing it, because, as the night drew on, the breeze stiffened.

They'd managed to erect the tent over the pit, but clum-sily. It would normally be a square, boxy structure, but here it was lopsided, leaning precariously, partly because of the unstable ground surrounding the hole. To compensate, they'd deployed an extra barrier of incident-scene tape around the outside. Not that anyone was likely to come snooping out here.

Lucy had departed again on her bike a while back, in an effort to get face-time with the brass in order to beg for a full forensics team. But Peabody wasn't quite alone. A light still bobbed inside the forensics tent, where an RSPCA vet was looking over the charred remains. She'd been in there a good hour, and even though she was clad neck-to-toe in biohazard overalls and wearing breathing apparatus with a small oxygen cylinder slung at her hip, the PC was beginning to wonder how she could stand it.

Of course, it was no more fun outside. Down here in the depression, it was difficult to see the rest of the landfill, but on the few occasions during the evening when he'd trekked up to the rim to check things out, he'd seen progressively less and less of it as dusk became twilight and twilight became night. Now, there was nothing out there but darkness, though occasional lurid glows issued from the one or two fires still burning, with skeins of greasy smoke drifting ghostlike across the shapeless terrain.

'Fucking Mordor,' he muttered.

Thanks to the silence that otherwise embraced this lifeless land, Peabody heard the approach of Lucy's returning motor-bike some time before she arrived. It was a red Ducati M900, an excellent road-bike but not ideal for scrambling, hence she was taking her time as she followed the rugged track. The grinding rev of the engine sounded for several minutes before her headlight speared into view and she braked on the ridge, applying the kick-stand and climbing off. Peabody scrambled uphill as she removed her helmet. She'd pulled a leather jacket over her sweatshirt and replaced her trainers with lace-up boots. Now she pulled her gloves off and jammed them into her helmet, before producing a Maglite and switching it on.

'Anything?' she asked.

'Vet's not finished yet.'

She nodded, as they plodded down the slope together.

'Did you find a petrol can or anything?' she asked, refer-ring to the last order she'd given him before setting off earlier.

'Nothing in the vicinity that might have been used to transport or deliver any kind of accelerant.'

233

She made no reply.

'So . . . is the show on the road?' he asked.

'Not yet. I managed to speak to DSU Nehwal. Like Stan, she wasn't impressed. Says she'll see what the vet says before she can even think about sparing us a couple of examiners.'

'She shouldn't be long now.' Peabody nodded at the tent. 'Been in there ages.'

'Yeah, but she's not going to write her report up immediately as she comes out, is she?'

'Probably not,' Peabody sighed. 'She'll want her shower and her tea, and then to snuggle up in bed and get a full night's sleep.'

'Which reminds me – before I go, there's a torch for you in the storage locker under my seat. I also went to the canteen. There's a packet of sandwiches and a flask of coffee too.'

'Very kind,' he grunted. 'But I prefer tea.'

'Tough. We can't have you falling asleep.'

'I'm not bloody likely to out here.'

'I dunno . . .' They'd now waded through trash until reaching the crime-scene tape, where they halted. Lucy nodded at one of the old chairs the vagrants had been using. By the look of it, Peabody had set it up for himself a little closer to the pit, until the reek had overpowered him. 'Looks like you were already getting comfy.'

He didn't even dignify that with a response. 'And what are you going to be doing all night while I'm suffocating in the stink of this place?'

'You're not going to be here all night,' she said. 'I've spoken to the duty officer. You've got uniform relief at three.'

'Oh.' He was genuinely and pleasantly surprised. 'Okay, cheers.'

'And to answer your question, I'll probably be on the move till three as well. To start with, I've got to interview

234

Sister Cassie, who told me she'd spend tonight in "Old Fred's crib". I think I know where that is.'

'You really think there's a connection?' he said. 'I mean, just because of a van?'

'One part of me hopes there is, Malcolm. Because that would mean we're closer to getting an answer. The other part of me hopes there isn't.'

'Why?'

Before she could reply, the vet emerged from the forensics tent. As Lucy's light was already on, she turned her own torch off and removed her mask. She was a youngish woman with collar-length brown hair, rather pretty, though at present her face was set in a scowl.

'That's just about the most disgusting thing I've ever seen!' Her accent was cut-glass, her tone almost accusing, as though the officers themselves were to blame. 'Who on earth is responsible for a horror show like that?'

'Trust me,' Lucy said, 'we're as eager to find out as you are.'

'Is this some kind of ritual, or something?'

'Do you see anything to indicate that?' Lucy asked.

'I don't know . . . all these animals have been brutally killed, and in various ways.'

'So they weren't killed by other dogs?' Peabody asked.

The vet glanced disdainfully at him. 'I've never heard of canines committing strangulation before, or cutting throats . . .'

'What my colleague means is: could these animals have been badly injured in dog-fighting?' Lucy cut in. 'And maybe put to death afterwards?'

'None of those poor creatures were fighting-dogs. I couldn't establish all the breeds, but there are thirteen bodies down there in total, all ages, and most of them, if not all, were once probably household pets. They *could* have been used as bait, I suppose, but I didn't see any obvious indication. No, I'm sorry to say that the perpetrators of these crimes are very human.'

'You said some of them were despatched by strangulation?' Lucy said.

'Four of them, yes. I'd hazard a guess that the ligature in each case was the same, or at least the same type of implement. A thin cord . . . something like a wire.' She grimaced. 'One of them, a French bulldog, had had its spine severed with a heavy, sharp-bladed instrument. An axe or cleaver, or a big knife. I'll be honest, I can't for the life of me work out what was going on here.'

'I assume they were all burned afterwards?' Lucy said.

'Yes.' The vet glanced back at the tent. 'This is a deposition site. I imagine they were cluttering up someone's garage or outside shed for a while, until the decision was made to get rid of them altogether. The smell probably became a problem. By the looks of it, whoever's responsible used insufficient petrol. Most likely it was rain that put the fire out again. In addition, of course, flames don't eat their way downward. Instead of throwing these remains into a hole, whoever did it should have built them into a bonfire.'

'How recently do you think this happened?' Lucy asked.

'I'm not an expert, but none of these animals died more recently than a couple of weeks ago, I'd say. You'll want something on paper, I'm assuming?'

'And as soon as possible, if that's okay.'

'Tomorrow morning?'

'That'd be great. Just email it through, if you don't mind.' Lucy handed over her card.

The vet pocketed it before squatting down and packing the rest of her equipment into a hold-all. Having done her job, she now seemed eager to be off. She zipped the bag closed and trudged away, nodding once, curtly, as she passed them.

'You'll be okay out here?' Lucy asked, at they stared again at the darkened tent.

'Gonna have to be,' Peabody replied.

'Got juice in your radio?'

'Should have enough to get me through till three, yeah.'

'Any real problems, call me? Doesn't matter what time it is.'

Peabody still looked disgruntled. 'I'll be fine. Like you say . . . I can use the overtime.'

'One thing, officers,' a voice behind them called. They turned. The vet was halfway up the slope but had clearly had an afterthought. She walked back down a few yards. 'I'm not sure when it was that CID began investigating animal deaths. But I'm glad the police are taking this seriously.'

Lucy shrugged. 'Animal cruelty's an issue we always take seriously.'

The vet smiled politely. 'I'm sure, yes . . . but the main thing is, I'm an animal-lover, as you'd probably expect. But even *I'm* in a position where I must express hope that this thing, whatever it is, ends with the animals.'

'I'm not following,' Lucy said.

'DC Clayburn . . . whoever's responsible for this, I think it's a safe bet that they're not even close to being in their right mind.'

237

Chapter 24

Even by her usual standards, Sister Cassie realised that she'd walked some significant distances today, but thankfully she'd been able to acquire her medicine and take it just before sunset, adequately rejuvenating herself for the nightly round.

After that, she could sleep. Though she still had that policewoman to speak to.

She abruptly checked herself as she bypassed the row of taxis on Bakerfield Lane.

She ought not to think of Lucy Clayburn as 'that policewoman'. She was a hard-working young woman, who maybe was a little intense, but was also personable and pleasant, and much less officious than the norm, and seemed to be completely at home in a job which, in Cassie's youth, had been exclusively occupied by rough, gruff men.

Of course, that didn't make it any the less inconvenient that Lucy wanted to speak to her; it would mean that she'd be disturbed late on, probably woken up from that deep, dreamless slumber her medicine eventually dropped her into.

Some thirty yards on, she halted beside a figure huddled under newspapers in a shop doorway. She crouched and began conversing with him, digging into her satchel to bring out her tatty, dog-eared prayerbook. His name was Albert, and he was a rail-thin young Irishman. The first time she'd encountered him, it had been later than this and quieter, and he'd jerked upward in fright, only smiling through his sores and his fuzz of beard when she'd come right up alongside him. He'd told her that she'd made an 'eerie spectacle for an unprepared fellow', her cloaked, cowled form 'gliding like a spirit'. She'd assured him she was no such thing as she'd squatted down and tried to make him comfortable, and he'd believed her, asking only that she pray with him. She'd been happy to oblige then, and every night since. She did so now, saying with him first the *Hail Mary*, which both of them knew by heart, and then leaning close with prayerbook open, so they could read together and aloud that part of the *Liber Hymnorum* known as *St Patrick's Breastplate*.

Content that both of them were now protected against the wickedness of others, she perambulated on, eighty yards or so, before stopping at another recess, where two more shapes sat under blankets amid a detritus of beercans and other trash. They were grizzled, brutish-looking older men, neither of whom she knew, though she had met them several times before. Despite this, they were glad to see her, going through their usual routine of asking for whisky and cigarettes, but gratefully accepting her gifts of biscuits and bottles of clean water, and allowing her to tuck them in.

'Stupid fucking bitch!' a shrill voice called from a passing vehicle. 'Givin' 'em all a crafty wank? Making life easier for parasites!'

She ignored the abuse, as she always did, refastening her satchel as she cut across the road and took a side-passage. This brought her through to Hildegard Way, normally a quieter thoroughfare, though on this occasion she was almost run down by a green transit van, which came screeching around the corner as though in a frantic chase and had to swerve to avoid her. It pulled up some twenty yards further along, as if the driver was about to leap out and berate her. Sister Cassie girded herself for yet more nastiness. But that didn't happen. The van simply pulled away again, now much more slowly.

She crossed to the other side of the road and headed down a side-street.

This was Laidlaw Green, a much narrower avenue running behind the backs of shops. Yet more dark, huddled shapes, blurred under rags and filthy, improvised sheets, were dotted along it. One by one, the ex-nun interacted with them all, sometimes crouching and doling out from her satchel, sometimes kneeling as though to pray or at least offer what gentle words she could.

It was late, and, feeling the first hints of drowsiness from her medicine, she knew that the need for rest and sleep would soon become overpowering. So she pressed on down the length of the Green, the farthest end of which was dominated by the derelict outlines of the mills and warehouses of St Clement's.

She crossed Adolphus Road, diverting left onto an avenue lined with boarded-up terraced houses, and at the end entering a mini-labyrinth of streets which no longer led anywhere, their properties long demolished, leaving a mosaic of interconnected, weed-covered lots. One of these long-forgotten byways was Canning Crescent, which was still cobbled, as if it hadn't been used since the days of clog irons and cartwheels.

Directly ahead now stood the colossal double blot on the skyline that was the twin outlines of Griggs Warehouse and Penrose Mill. The closer Sister Cassie drew, the more immense the aged structures seemed, and the more broken and desolate the occasional smaller buildings on either side of her.

The only light now came from the upright patterns of windows denoting distant tower blocks.

Any normal person might be frightened in this district, especially at night, but the ex-nun was a familiar fixture here. The denizens of this wretched place didn't just know her personally, they knew that she carried nothing of value.

And of course, even if that wasn't the case, she'd said her protection prayer.

Just ahead, the road curved past a section of warehouse wall whose upper portion, having burned and collapsed, had created a slope of thorn-covered rubble. A footpath had been beaten through this, allowing access to the skeletally moonlit interior, and to Old Fred's crib.

For all that she was confident in her safety, thoughts about Fred stirred a momentary unease in Sister Cassie. This was the place where he'd been abducted.

Forty yards on, just before Canning Crescent curved, there were two other thoroughfares. The one on the right was no more than a ginnel, a footway veering off between gutted outbuildings. That was the route she had taken the night he'd been attacked. On the left, some fifty yards from the sloped footpath to the warehouse's interior, was the concrete ramp leading down into the subterranean section of the building, from which the dark-blue van must have emerged. That said, there was nothing down there now. Nothing she could see, except shadow.

At which moment a cat-like whimpering caught her attention.

Sister Cassie halted, surprised, but knowing instinctively that it wasn't a cat.

She pivoted around, scanning the moonlit ruins. And immediately spotted the source of the sound.

A figure sat against the wall midway between the underground entrance and the sloping path up to Fred's crib. It was huddled underneath a carpet, which had been folded into a cone, so that it covered everything except the face.

The ex-nun was thirty or so yards away but could already make out that it was a young girl, perhaps no more than a teenager. Her blonde head lolled as if she was half-insensible, but she was crying loudly. Sister Cassie started hurriedly towards her, already unfastening her satchel. She thought she had a few bits of plasters in there, and maybe even a squeeze of antiseptic ointment left in that old tube she'd found. And she'd need them, because even from two dozen yards off, the youngster's features were visibly puffy and blotched.

She'd been badly beaten.

'My dear child,' the ex-nun said, shrugging her satchel from her shoulder and hunkering down.

When she tore the old carpet away, it was stiff with dirt and age, and hordes of woodlice cascaded off it. Used as she was to these woebegone backstreets, Sister Cassie shuddered with revulsion at that and threw it away gingerly, making as little contact with it as she could. As she did, she failed to notice the look of pain and misery on the battered face beneath split into a grin that was more like a feral scowl.

242

Chapter 25

Lucy heard the scream loud and clear.

She was less than a hundred yards away. Not overly familiar with the road layout in what remained of the St Clement's ward, she'd stopped at a junction of unmarked lanes and sat astride her parked bike as she used the sat-nav on her mobile to locate Canning Crescent.

Now she no longer needed it.

She rode the derelict roadway slowly, standing on her footpegs, visor raised as she scanned the verges.

A scream at night could mean anything, from someone being attacked to kids engaged in horseplay. But in this district the latter seemed unlikely. It demanded an immediate but cautious response. She was alert and ready, therefore, when, not far ahead, a pair of headlamps sprang to life and came rocketing towards her.

As she veered out of the way, skidding on the mossy cobblestones, a green transit van flickered by. She swung around, almost turning sideways as she slid to a thirty-yard halt, bewildered by the sight of one of its two back doors swinging open. It swerved out of view, not giving her a chance to clock its registration mark. But if this was who she thought it was, the VRM would likely be useless – just another fake plate. With its rear doors unsecured, it seemed unlikely the vehicle would be carrying a prisoner, or any other illicit cargo, but even so, the only thing to do now was pursue it, flag it down and perform a stop-and-search – if she hadn't already lost track of it, because it had had a hell of a start.

At which point Lucy heard a second scream.

Not as shrill or as shocking as the first, but muffled, as if it had come from indoors. What was more, it had sounded from somewhere nearby.

Her gaze roved up the dilapidated frontage of the massive building lowering over her. Griggs Warehouse. Given the state of its current occupants, that sound didn't necessarily mean that someone was being attacked. Of course, she wouldn't be any kind of police officer if she didn't investigate it.

She rode on towards the foot of the slope where the path beat its way up to what she'd thought of previously as 'the arcade'. At which point, she heard another scream, this one even more muffled, but distinctly the sound of someone in grave distress.

Lucy braked and looked left, and saw again that entrance to the warehouse's undercroft, or whatever it was, where the suspect van had apparently emerged when Fred Holborn was abducted. She veered towards it, accelerating as a fourth scream sounded, slowing down again as she spied a couple of items on the floor that she recognised: a brown leather satchel with a shoulder-strap that had snapped, its contents scattered, and a heap of ragged black material, which looked suspiciously like a nun's cloak.

Lucy throttled forward, hitting the top of the ramp at 35mph and hurtling down it forty yards or so, her headlamp spearing through the darkness, flooding over a mound of white, dusty rubble lying across her path. At some point in the past, a concrete pillar had toppled across the foot of the ramp, bringing down a mass of masonry, which now formed a barrier impassable to a four-wheeled vehicle.

But not to a bike.

She slowed again, but the rubble wasn't steep and was loosely compacted, which gave her an easier tread. She wove her way up it, arriving on the top and braking hard.

The glare of her light now revealed a much larger cellar than she'd expected, an unloading area of some sort. It was fifty by sixty yards, and almost entirely concrete, much of it cracked or water-stained, the many pillars holding up its ceiling scrawled with incomprehensible graffiti. There was plenty more evidence that folk had been sleeping down here; she saw blackened braziers, stained mattresses, food cartons, but the only two people present were in the very centre of the underground space, engaged in what looked at first like a violent dance.

One of them, by her spinning, tattered skirts and the fact that her veil had come off, allowing a mop of damp red-grey hair to billow free, was Sister Cassie. The other, her assailant, was younger, leaner and wearing what looked like black combat fatigues complete with boots and gloves, and a harness to which weapons were visibly attached.

To Lucy's incredulity, this second person, who'd snatched the ex-nun by her front collar with one hand and was aiming punches at her with the other, looked female. That was the only impression that could be gleaned from the blonde, sweat-slick hair flying around her head, though it was difficult to be absolutely sure, as she ducked and weaved in her efforts to avoid retaliatory blows from Sister Cassie.

Lucy cut her engine. 'Police officer!' she bellowed. 'What's going on here?'

The blonde girl responded quickly, jumping ramrod-

245

straight, glaring in Lucy's direction. She'd clearly noticed when the glow of the headlamp had appeared over the pile of rubble, but perhaps, in the midst of combat, had mistaken it for her confederate's vehicle. Now the light caught her full-on, revealing what looked like extensive facial injuries. At the same time, it distracted her, and she caught a left-hand swing from Sister Cassie hard on her left cheek, which drew a squawk of rage and pain. She replied with a vicious punch, hacking it into Sister Cassie's ribs, doubling her down to her knees, and then, after kicking her in the side and sending her sprawling, running towards a distant doorway.

Lucy slammed her visor shut and screeched down the other side of the rubble on her rear wheel. Masonry and grit showered behind her as she raced across the cellar, skidding to a halt alongside the ex-nun, who was looking up again, and indicated with a limp, bloodstained hand that she was okay.

Lucy sped on, passing through the narrow doorway and entering a long, concrete passage that had never been intended for vehicles. Again, it was cluttered with debris, as though part of the ceiling had collapsed, which made it difficult going. A dark shape bobbing ahead of her revealed her fleeing prey, but before she could catch up with it, she reached a junction of passages obstructed by a wheeled cart that was loaded with wooden pallets.

Lucy braked sharply. She heard feet hammering away ahead as she leaped from her seat to shove it all aside. What this place had once been, she couldn't fathom. Whatever it was, if the rest of the structure was anything to go by, it was likely to be labyrinthine, which was all she needed when her quarry had a head-start like this.

She clambered back onto her bike and accelerated forward at reckless speed. At the next intersection of corridors, she had to slow down to listen. Hearing an echoing clatter of rubble on her right, she swung her machine after it, accelerating again. It was the same at the next junction. Even with her headlamp on full beam, she now saw nothing but endless concrete tunnels telescoping ahead, black elongated nightmares along which her Ducati hopped and skipped as it cleared mound after mound of masonry. Some were so narrow that at times her handlebars all but carved their way along the walls and turned the reverberation of her engine into a barrage of gunfire; it was thunderous even to Lucy, whose ears were padded by the helmet. Though it probably explained why the fugitive, who suddenly came into view some sixty yards ahead, streaked forward with athletic prowess, no doubt galvanised by the racket behind her, and gained ground with every corner she turned because they were too tight for the bike to take quickly.

Lucy swore. She could have overhauled this suspect in any normal circumstances, but it was typical that she'd wound up chasing her in what had to be the only place in Crowley where the speed and power of her Ducati were nullified. At the same time, she found herself having to duck, as missiles came flying back from the fleeing form: bricks, discarded bottles, wooden laths heavy with cement. At least her adrenalin was up, dulling the thudding impacts on her body, the blows of bricks and cans, the crunch of smashing glass on her visor. But Lucy knew that she wasn't immune to this punishment. If her headlight was taken out, that was it; she'd be marooned in this unlit maze, at the mercy of whoever this maniac was, and with a mountain of mouldering brickwork overhead, there was almost no chance that she'd be able to get a phone or radio signal out.

That didn't happen, but she was constantly impeded in other ways, the twosome emerging into rooms at such speeds and angles that the bike would lose traction, slewing sideways through tangles of trash and filth, always allowing the

247

fugitive to stay ahead, turning corner after corner, again swooping down to grab more projectiles that she could pitch over her shoulder. Lucy followed stoically, her headlamp reflecting kaleidoscopically from cracked walls, rotted ceilings and stretches of opaque, ankle-deep water that exploded from her tyres as she blasted through.

She'd now lost all sense of direction, but it felt as if she ought to have passed through the entire undercroft of the industrial complex. And as this occurred to her, she sped out into a much larger space, the floor changing from rubble-strewn cement to well-worn timber. There was light in here too, that milky combination of moonlight and streetlight filtering through a row of square apertures high up on a distant wall; some looked like the openings to outdoor chutes, though a taller, broader one was clearly a doorway, possibly for the use of small vehicles like forklift trucks. Lucy wasn't immediately able to focus on this because she had to evade all kinds of immediate obstacles: boxes, crates, the blackened hulks of skips filled with refuse. She twisted and turned deftly to avoid headlong smashes, and so never even saw the heavy hanging chain with the huge rusty hook at the end come rushing at her head.

It struck the side of her helmet with a *BANG!* like a hand grenade.

The impact was so forceful that not only did it half dislodge her helmet, the visor breaking loose at one side, it sent her skidding out of control. The shock and concussion were terrific, but she clung to consciousness just sufficiently to attempt a controlled crash, sliding on her side through rivers of rank, desiccated newspaper.

No sooner had she come to a halt than a weird, whinnying laugh filled the dusty air above her. Lucy turned groggily from where she lay and saw the figure of the girl on a high point some twenty yards off. Possibly it was a loading platform of some sort. She'd clearly been crouching there, lying in wait, but now she stood up and was silhouetted against the rays of light penetrating the chute apertures.

Lucy disentangled herself from the fallen bike and scrambled to her feet, only to turn woozy when she stood up. Disoriented, she struggled to rip aside the broken visor but made sure to keep her helmet on. When she glanced up again, she saw that the girl had drawn something from her webbing; Lucy spied the outline of a heavy-bladed knife complete with a medieval-style cross-guard. The girl squatted again, as though to leap down from her perch, and perhaps come gambolling forward through the shadows.

Before she could do this, a car horn blared angrily from a distant corner of the depot. Lucy and her opponent turned to see that a vehicle with green bodywork had pulled up on the other side of the forklift entry doors.

The fugitive gave another hyena-like laugh and made her move – but not to come aggressively forward. Instead, she leaped down from the other side of the platform, and ran across the loading depot at speed, dodging nimbly around obstacles as she headed towards her getaway vehicle. Lucy tried to follow, but turned dizzy again, tilted over and landed on her hands and knees.

As she knelt there, a pair of feet thudded up a wooden ramp, a door opened and closed, and with a noisy crunching of gears the green vehicle revved away into the night.

Chapter 26

'Fuck!' the girl spat as she loosened the Velcro at her sweaty throat and yanked down the zip on her combat jacket. 'Damn Maggie bitch put up more of a fight than I expected.'

The other girl drove the van steadily as they joined the traffic on the main road. 'I told you she wouldn't be run-of-the-mill.'

'Maybe, but if that fucking cop hadn't intervened . . .'

The driver, whose name was Ivana, frowned. 'That guy on the bike was a cop?'

'It was a woman.'

There was a brief, contemplative silence, and then Ivana cracked an amused smile. 'A biker-chick cop? I've heard it all now.'

'Yeah . . . well, I took care of her too.'

'What did you do?'

'Just busted her helmet open. Didn't actually kill her.' The passenger, whose name was Alyssa, scowled. 'Fucking would have done if you hadn't showed up.'

'I drove round the back in case the nun came out. Is *she* dead?'

'No. Like I say, that fucking cop . . .'

'Doesn't matter.' Oddly, Ivana seemed relieved. 'It's a good thing actually.'

Alyssa glanced around. 'What're you talking about?'

'That cop saw you *and* the vehicle. If she'd also found a dead body, the whole pig pantomime would show up. We'd be in trouble. But if they think it was just a mugging, they won't be too worried. The van'll need to be sprayed again, of course.'

Alyssa acknowledged this with a grunt. It would mean a lot of work, but they changed the van's colour almost as frequently as they changed its plates. It would have been highly unprofessional to keep on using it in the same unaltered condition. And professionalism was the name of this game.

They drove in silence for a minute.

Ivana and Alyssa were nineteen-year-old twins and they resembled each other closely, though Ivana was slightly more severe-looking, with her spiky, red-tinted hair and athletic aura. In contrast, Alyssa had a softer air, though not by much. Shapelier than her sister, she was still obviously an athlete. She wore her fair hair shoulder-length, though at present it was damp and hanging in strings. Ordinarily, she had similar good looks to Ivana, though they were rounder and smoother, but thanks to her foul-up with Lorna Cunningham she was currently battered and bruised, her left eye black and swollen and only partially open.

'How badly did you hurt the cop?' Ivana asked.

'She got up again,' Alyssa responded.

'Fair enough. That works.'

Alyssa was amazed that her sister was being so conciliatory. They'd been looking for the dingbat in the habit and veil for days now, Alyssa hating her more and more because she'd somehow proved so elusive. Ivana, though she was calmer and cooler as a rule, had seemed equally angry.

'I can't believe you don't mind that we've fucked this up,'

Alyssa said. 'You reckoned she was with that old duffer down St Clement's just before we nabbed him. You said you thought she might have clocked us. If the cops are looking into that one, won't they link it to this? It was virtually in the same place.'

Ivana shrugged. 'And who's their only witness to that other grab? A smackhead scrote who dresses like a nun and sells her cooch to get gear. You think they'll listen to her . . . *if* she's able to tell them anything sensible? Yeah, there's a vague possibility they'll connect the two. But none of our plates are traceable, and like I say, we do another respray and we're sorted.'

Alyssa wondered if this was a bit of bravado. The last time they'd been down St Clement's and had grabbed the old guy, Ivana had actually been concerned enough that the fake nun might have seen the vehicle to stipulate that from that point on they'd stop using dummy plates bearing registration numbers that were non-existent, and start using copies – plates mocked up to look like genuine ones belonging to legitimate vans owned by real firms. That way, routine police camera checks wouldn't throw up anything suspicious.

For her own part, Alyssa was just glad that they hadn't mentioned to his lordship that the other grab had been witnessed. He'd have gone hopping mad, and would have had them back on Category Cs again.

'We'll have to tell him, of course,' Ivana said, as though she'd been reading her sister's mind. 'That we went for a Category B tonight but blew it.'

Alyssa's jaw dropped. 'Are you kidding?'

'Lyssa . . . you did all right. The plan worked. I never thought the nun'd be dumb enough to go back to the same place where we grabbed the other one, but you were right . . . she did, eventually. Plus, you'd have got her into the back of the van easy if that cloak thing she was wearing hadn't ripped off. Okay, she was lighter on her toes than Category Bs usually are, but you still caught up with her in a few yards.'

Alyssa snorted. 'And then look what happened.'

'Fucking hell, doll. Even you can't be blamed for a patrolling copper turning up. How often does that happen these days? When was the last time you even *saw* a patrolling police officer? Even the old fella'll be on board with that. Anyway, like I say . . . it doesn't matter. We'll get her at some point.' She had to suppress an excited grin. 'For the moment, something else has come up.'

'What?'

Ivana glanced at her chunky military-style watch, and then nodded at the phone lying on the dash. 'Look at that text. It arrived just under five minutes ago.'

Alyssa grabbed the device and checked the last message.

Recall. Right away. No buts. Drop everything. Urgent job.

'Job?' Alyssa said, mystified. 'Does he mean like . . . the real thing?'

Ivana shrugged. 'He said it's urgent, didn't he? Told us to drop everything.'

'But we haven't even done a successful Category A yet.'

'So what was last night?'

Alyssa was puzzled. 'That meathead from the gym? I was told when we got home that he didn't count. That you'd spiked his drink, so he was Category B at best.'

Ivana snorted. 'That's because his lordship's still pissed off with you about Cunningham.'

'I don't know why,' Alyssa grumbled. 'We got her off the streets, we still completed the job.'

'Yeah, and it was all looking great – our first Category

A, done and dusted. But then you insisted on going toe-to-toe with her. And look at the outcome. You letting your face get messed up could've set us back weeks. No wonder we got put back on Category B. But last night he was well pleased, trust me. After you'd gone up to bed, he said we'd made a chance out of nothing, thought on our feet, improvised . . .'

Alyssa couldn't help feeling miffed about that as well. Okay, it had mainly been Ivana's improvisation – she herself had only been called in by phone at the last minute. But they'd still pulled it off together. *She* was the one who'd struck the fatal blow. *She* was the one who'd come up with the idea to lift one of those eroded stone lids in the Victorian section of the churchyard and lay the meathead and his kit-bag to rest on the bones of some granny from the 1870s. *She* was the one who'd thought to use the fire-extinguisher from the church porch to wash the blood off the steps and path. And yet *she* was the one who'd been sent to bed while the old fella called Ivana in to offer his congratulations.

This was often the way of it, though. The two sisters were the same age, their births separated by a single hour, and had shared exactly the same life experience, and yet somehow Ivana had fallen into the role of leader and Alyssa into that of follower. She didn't like it, but she accepted it because it seemed to be the natural order of things. Plus, Ivana was near enough everything Alyssa wanted to be. The younger-girl-by-one-hour loved her older sibling greatly and admired her even more.

'And you know what he's like,' Ivana continued. 'He's especially happy when a plan comes together. And I mean a *real* plan. Not just brute force and ignorance. He didn't like the Cunningham cock-up, but last night he reckoned we thought on our feet and basically snatched victory from the jaws of defeat.'

Alyssa pondered this again, the realisation of what it

meant, and the subsequent excitement, only dawning on her with gradual, painful slowness. 'Seriously, Vana? That's it . . . we're done on these practice runs, we're actually going *live*?'

Ivana nodded again, still excited. 'I think we *are*, doll!'

'Tonight?'

'Why else get us back in now?'

'He can't wait to retire . . . that's all it is.'

'And does that bother you?'

'Does it bloody hell!' Alyssa punched the dashboard. 'I've been waiting for this ever since we left school.'

Chapter 27

Dusty and tired, Lucy wheeled her Ducati back through the tunnels underneath the warehouse. Even with her broken helmet removed and hooked over one of the handlebars, this was a far from straightforward exercise. Her right hip ached abominably from where she'd crash-landed on it – by morning, she'd be bruised the entire length of that side of her body – and the bike was heavy. It hadn't suffered anything more than superficial damage, and could easily be ridden, but she didn't feel in a fit state. On top of all that, the route back wasn't particularly easy to trace.

She'd hurtled through the network of passages so quickly that she'd barely had time to register landmarks. A couple of times she went the wrong way and had to double back, which was even more exhausting because it often meant manoeuvring the bike in a three-point turn halfway along corridors so cramped that there was minimal room.

It was a good fifteen minutes before she returned to the main undercroft. This place itself would have been difficult to identify, if it hadn't been for the fresh air flowing in through the garage-sized entrance at the top of the concrete ramp. There was no longer any sign of Sister Cassie.

Frustrated, Lucy climbed onto her bike, kicked it into life and rode it up and over the rubble barricade before mounting the ramp. When she reached the top and emerged onto Canning Crescent, she braked.

The ex-nun was seated on a nearby kerb. She'd replaced her wimple, veil and cloak, and was patiently rearranging the various bits of rubbish that had fallen out of her satchel.

'There you are, child,' she said, as Lucy trudged over. 'Thank Heaven. I thought something bad might have happened to you. If only I had a phone, I could have alerted some of your colleagues.'

Lucy regarded her wearily. The ex-nun seemed to be unhurt. At least, no blows had left visible marks on her head or face. 'Sister . . . don't you think something like this was always likely to happen? The places you go, the people you interact with . . .'

Sister Cassie shrugged as she knotted the ends of the satchel's broken strap. 'On the mission, one must take the rough with the smooth, child. Besides, what am I, if not an addict myself, an outcast?' She sighed. 'It *does* happen. More than you might imagine. So long as we are alive at the end, all is well.'

'How'd the bag get broken? Did they try to pinch it?'

'Heavens, no. It was . . . well, it was *me* they tried to pinch.'

'What exactly happened?

Sister Cassie frowned. 'One of them was pretending to be one of us. A disgusting trick, in my view.' She described how she'd seen the pathetic figure huddled and crying under the dirty piece of carpet, and how when she went over to offer succour, the child – who was clearly not a child, at least 'not a child in its head' – leaped up and tried to snatch her. At the same time, she said, a vehicle, a green van, emerged at speed from the entrance to the undercroft and pulled up alongside them.

'A *green* van this time?'

'I know what I saw, child.'

'Don't worry, I saw it too. Or glimpsed it.' Lucy glanced around. 'I don't see any carpet.'

'No.' The ex-nun looked for herself. 'Perhaps the van driver took it?'

Very likely, Lucy thought. *Which means that they're forensically savvy.*

'I actually hit my assailant with the bag,' Sister Cassie added. 'Which is why it broke and spilled its contents. But it's not a major problem. As you see, I can easily make repairs. But it bought me sufficient time to flee down into the basement . . . alas, I wasn't swift enough to make a complete getaway.'

'I thought the van came from down there?'

'It was lurking down there, yes. Just like the one that took Fred Holborn.' The ex-nun eyed Lucy carefully. 'I know that's what you're thinking, child. But this one was a different colour. That one was blue, this one green.'

'Colours can be changed, Sister.'

'Whatever, I'd just struck my attacker with the bag when this vehicle arrived. And that was when I ran. Briefly, the underground passage was the only route open to me.'

'Sister . . .' Lucy crouched alongside her. 'What's going on here? I mean . . . what do these abductions mean? If there's something you're not telling us, you really need to reconsider.'

'My dear child . . .' The ex-nun put her bloodstained hand on Lucy's shoulder. 'You know as much as I. But as I say, here on the outskirts of society, we get attacked.' She sighed again. 'Sometimes, it seems like our role . . . that we are destined to be naught but punchbags for the less than charitable.'

'I'm sorry to say this, but I strongly doubt this was a routine mugging.' Lucy stood up and helped her to her feet.

'I know it might be comforting to think that, in a bizarre kind of way. But I'm not buying it. I saw the girl who attacked you. She was wearing military-style clothing.'

'I see.' Though Sister Cassie clearly didn't see, from her puzzled expression.

'She was also fit – extremely fit.'

The meaning of this was still lost on the ex-nun, who merely shook her head with disapproval.

Lucy didn't bother elaborating on how all this, along with the organised nature of the ambush – the teamwork it had clearly involved, and the fact that the victim was being targeted for kidnap rather than a simple assault – put it way beyond common-or-garden street violence. Instead, she asked: 'I don't suppose the girl said anything to you?'

'Hissed a few foul-mouthed things, that's all.'

'Anything you recognised?'

'I suppose I recognised the words, even if I didn't quite understand them.'

Lucy shrugged. 'Any you'd care to share?'

'Well . . . I dislike the language of course. But I suppose you'll need to hear everything?'

'Unfortunately, it's essential.'

Sister Cassie nodded sadly. 'She called me a "stiff-assed virgin bitch" and said something equally uncouth about "taking me back to fucking Maggies".'

'And did that mean anything to you?'

'I assure you not. Such a foul mouth on one so young. But then it's all we seem to hear these days, is it not?'

'Sometimes feels that way,' Lucy agreed.

'At least I clouted her a good one.' Sister Cassie's face coloured a little. 'My old mother, a devout Christian woman despite her own occasional use of inappropriate words, always used to say that turning the other cheek was only good so long as no fella came up and striped it with his razor blade. She grew up on Sheriff Street, of course, an unforgiving neighbourhood in her day. But alas –' she held up her injured right hand '– though I followed her instruction and tried to stand up to this young bully, I fear I've paid a price.'

'Let me look at that,' Lucy said.

The ex-nun obliged. Her hand was now sticky with blood, most of it from the top of the stick-like middle finger, where the entire nail had been torn away.

'I think this happened when I struck the girl,' the ex-nun said.

Lucy glanced up at her. 'Really?'

'My fingernails are not exactly manicured, as you can see. So, I must have hooked her in some way when I slapped her. But this is a minor thing. I am more than used to—'

'Sister, can you follow me down the slope?'

'Go back below?'

'Just for a minute. Please. I promise you it's important.'

The ex-nun acquiesced, buckling up her satchel, while Lucy went over to her Ducati. She rode it back down the ramp, angling it up on top of the rubble barricade again and parking it just over the apex, so that her headlight flooded the floorway beyond. She climbed off and waited for Sister Cassie to join her, then the two of them scrambled down the rest of the way on foot.

'In case you're wondering, we're looking for your missing fingernail,' Lucy said.

'Dear child . . . I hardly need that back.'

'You misunderstand me. If you managed to rake some exposed flesh with that nail, and we find it, it'll be the first piece of physical evidence we actually have.'

The floor was already strewn with trash, and they weren't sure where the main altercation had occurred. Lucy finally resorted to what she told Sister Cassie was a 'pattern search', whereby they divided the space up into an imaginary grid and worked their way from one section of it to the next, scrutinising each ultra-carefully – and it was this that paid the dividend.

'Ah-ha!' Triumphantly, Sister Cassie indicted a minuscule object at her feet.

It was indeed a human fingernail, blackened and chewed, but slimy and red on its concave side, particularly around the root, which had clearly been torn out.

Lucy ran up to her bike, took a pair of tweezers and a small plastic envelope from the under-seat storage and hurried back down. Once the nail was in the envelope, she sealed it. They held it up for a closer look. At the business end of the nail, which was jagged, dangled a single tiny thread of skin-like fibre.

'This is going to our lab tonight,' Lucy said. 'And you need to come back to the station too.'

Sister Cassie thought about this. 'I can meet you there at a time when it's convenient . . .'

'No, Sister – it's convenient now.' Lucy was firm. 'I need a full statement from you, okay? Not just about this attack tonight, but about everything else that's happened.'

The ex-nun looked doubtful. 'It's rather a long walk. And I was hoping to sleep . . .'

'I'll saddle you on my bike, don't worry. You need to come back with me, anyway. So we can get that hand fixed up.'

For the first time all evening, the ex-nun looked genuinely horror-stricken.

'Me! Ride a motorcycle? I doubt I'd have the courage.'

'Sister, you've just fought off a violent attacker, who could be responsible for several abductions. Plus, you live *here*.' Lucy made an exasperated gesture. 'I'm pretty sure that if you look deep inside yourself, you'll find the necessary courage.'

261

Sister Cassie looked unsure but accompanied Lucy up the ramp, the latter pushing her bike. As they reached the outside, the mobile buzzed in Lucy's pocket. She was puzzled to see that the call was from her mother even though it was after one in the morning.

'Yeah, Mum?' She leaned the bike on its stand.

'Lucy . . . are you at the hospital?' Cora sounded tense and upset, which made the question all the more worrying.

'No, I'm not,' Lucy replied. 'Mum, what's—'

'Then I'll see you there. I'm guessing you know what's happened?'

'I don't know anything. Look . . . are you okay?'

There was a brief, breathy silence. Lucy pictured her mother sitting in her little car, about to set off, possibly surprised by her daughter's ignorance.

'Mum . . . what's going on? Seriously, I've not heard anything.'

'Frank's been shot.'

At first, Lucy was too stunned to coherently respond. She edged away from Sister Cassie, lowering her voice. 'How . . . I mean, hold on a sec . . .'

'I was just about to go to bed, but then it was all over the late evening news. I suppose someone at the hospital talked. Notorious Manchester criminal Frank McCracken . . . found dying from a gunshot wound at the entrance of St Winifred's Hospital. I don't know how badly hurt he is, or how he got there, but –' Cora's voice threatened to break '– but . . . that blonde trollop's with him. I'm sure it's her. They say he had a female companion, who's also been shot . . .'

'Okay, Mum . . . listen . . .' Lucy's panicky thoughts tumbled over each other. At first, no possible solution suggested itself, let alone made sense to her. But there was a question at least. 'Mum . . . why are *you* going there?'

'Why on earth do you think?' Cora sounded shocked.

'What good can you do?'

'I can't do any good. But I'm not just sitting around at home.'

'They don't even know you're connected to him.'

'I don't care about that, Lucy. Like I say, I'm not sitting around at home. It's not like anyone would call me with an update.'

'Mum, listen . . .' Lucy felt a growing sense of alarm. 'Frank McCracken is not *your* concern any more. He's not your husband. He's not even your boyfriend.'

'But he's *your father*, Lucy. So, as I say, I'll expect to see you there. As soon as possible.'

Chapter 28

As Lucy rode back towards Robber's Row police station, there was plenty to occupy her mind. One might assume she would mainly be thinking about the new lead. Or perhaps might be feeling self-conscious about the nun riding pillion, clinging on for dear life, her voluminous skirts and cloak tucked carefully underneath her, her veil billowing out behind the spare helmet.

But it wasn't either of these.

Yet again, it was the Frank McCracken situation.

In purely practical terms, her mother's phone-call had changed Lucy's plans for the remainder of that night. She still needed to get back to the nick to book the forensic evidence in and request a fast-track analysis. But that was a mere matter of filling a form. However, it was no longer possible for her to sit down and interview her new star witness. That would take far too long, and so would need to be rearranged. She still had Sister Cassie with her, though – because now the woman was Lucy's excuse for going to the hospital. On pulling up in the Robber's Row personnel car park, she told the ex-nun to wait by the bike, entered the building through its personnel door and headed straight for the CID office. But her mind was still awhirl with this new development in their lives.

Frank McCracken didn't mean anything to her.

She told herself this repeatedly.

He shared her blood, yes, but he was still an enemy of society. There was no denying that she'd seen things in him a person could like. He had a smoothness about him, and a charm, and, for some reason Lucy couldn't pin down, she felt sure that his affection towards her mother was genuine. But at the same time he was violent, slept with whores and headed up a major department inside the Northwest's pre-eminent crime syndicate.

And yet the news that he'd been shot had hit her like a punch.

The possibility that he was dying blew an icy breath down her neck. As she booked in the evidence, Lucy realised that she was desperate to know more about what had happened.

'Bloody ridiculous,' she muttered.

It was like he mattered to her, like he was a real relative. *I don't feel anything for him. I hate him . . . or at least I hate everything he stands for.*

But he *was* her father. The only one she'd ever known – albeit for a short amount of time.

How often, when she was little, when she'd believed her mum's white lie that her dad was a happy-go-lucky bus driver who'd ditched them both at the first opportunity, had she yearned for more information about him. Anything would have done – a faded photograph, a letter he'd written. She still had an overpoweringly emotional memory of how, when she was about seven, she ran away from home and used her Christmas money to travel the bus routes of Greater Manchester for two whole days, looking for any driver whose facial features she might vaguely recognise. Her mum was beside herself with worry, and apparently fainted with relief when Lucy was found safe and well, fast asleep in a bus shelter in Rochdale on the other side of the city.

Afterwards, Lucy solemnly promised herself that she would never go looking for her father again. But that wasn't just because she regretted upsetting her mother. It was also because her previous knowledge of her father, such as it was, had always been tinged with the excited belief that he was out there somewhere; only now she knew that if he *was* out there, he wasn't hers any more. She could have met him on any one of those buses she'd ridden, and it wouldn't have made any difference. He'd have looked straight through her, much as she'd have looked straight through him. There was nothing left between them; they had no connection at all.

And so she'd gone on with her life, happier, accepting that she had only one parent, which, after all, didn't make her much different from lots of other British kids at the end of the twentieth century.

Until now.

'Sister, I'm going to take you to St Winifred's,' Lucy said, coming back out into the personnel yard.

'The hospital?' The ex-nun was puzzled. 'Why?'

'Your hand needs looking at.'

'My child, it's only a cut.'

'It's not only a cut. You've lost the whole fingernail, and that was a dirty place – the wound could easily have got infected, so I'm taking you to A&E.'

'Don't you have a first-aid kit here?'

'We do,' Lucy said, 'but I haven't got time for that. Likewise, I haven't got time to take a statement from you. So, once I've dropped you off at hospital, I'm going to have to ask you to come back here tomorrow morning. Can we say ten o'clock sharp?'

Sister Cassie sighed. 'Well . . . if you really think it's important.'

'I really and honestly do.'

'Very well. But do we have to ride over there on that awful bike again? I was terrified. I almost fell off three times.'

Lucy held up a key. 'No worries. We'll take one of the CID cars.'

She didn't bother to add that this time it was only likely to be dangerous when they actually got there.

'It's very kind of you to be doing all this,' Sister Cassie said from the back of the battered old Ford Mondeo. 'I always knew you were a good soul.'

'You've got to promise you'll get that finger seen to,' Lucy said over her shoulder. 'I won't have time to sit with you and make sure you do.'

'Do you think I'll be waiting a long time?'

'I don't know.' Lucy glanced at the dashboard clock. 'It's a Wednesday, so I doubt there'll be as many in now as you'd get at this time on a weekend.'

'I sincerely hope not. I have places to go and people to see.'

Lucy again wondered about the wisdom of making such a person a key witness, not that she had much choice. Though it would be less of an issue if the DNA came through.

For the moment she had other things to think about.

She dropped her passenger at the entrance to A&E and looked for a parking space. As she'd surmised, St Winifred's wasn't bustling, and there was lots of room.

Her suspicion was that, if Frank McCracken was still here and not in the mortuary, he'd likely have been operated on and so would be in Intensive Care. A minute later, this suspicion was all but confirmed when she rounded the corner beyond which lay the entrance to the ICU and saw a patrol car parked by the door with a couple of uniforms standing next to it.

She thought about going straight up to them and asking what was happening; she'd already devised herself a cover-story for being here, so it wouldn't look too odd. But a higher priority than finding out what state Frank McCracken was in was discovering where her mother was. She scanned the car park and eventually located Cora's yellow Honda Civic about sixty yards away. That settled it; Lucy had to go in, and she had to do it now.

She strolled nonchalantly forward, heading for the IC entrance, trying to ignore the two officers, whom she recognised as PCs Tooley and Brentwood, divisional lads from Crowley.

It occurred to her, somewhat belatedly, that she perhaps ought to be more nervous about this than she was. She wouldn't have expected a couple of beat cops to know who her mother was; Lucy had only had occasional contact with them herself. But that didn't mean there weren't others around here who *would* recognise Cora Clayburn, and maybe engage her in conversation. Priya Nehwal, for example. Lucy could only hope that if Serious Crimes were here, and if they weren't it would only be a matter of time, they'd send someone other than their bolshy DSU.

She reached the entrance and glanced around. Tooley and Brentwood were too engrossed in conversation to even notice her, their chatter punctuated by bouts of raucous laughter. It was a good night for the cops when a high-end scrote like Frank McCracken got taken out of commission.

She walked inside and was confronted by a waiting room area, more of a corridor really, running twenty yards to the next door, its walls adorned with NHS posters, padded seating arranged down either side.

Her mother was sitting there alone, zipped tight into a blue anorak, hair mussed, white-faced with weariness, one hand clutching a tissue.

Lucy walked quickly towards her. By the look of it, the next door, which was glazed and closed, was the unit's actual entry point. Presumably it was locked at this time of night, and if you wanted access you had to use the bell-push on its left to attract the night nurse behind the desk at the other side. That night nurse, a young black woman with braided hair, who was writing some kind of report, glanced up as Lucy entered the waiting area, but when Lucy sat down, her eyes flickered back to her work.

'Apparently, they dumped him outside,' Cora said, her voice weak, strained. 'Just like that. Like he was a sack of rubbish or something.'

'Who did?' Lucy asked tensely, not knowing which door to keep an eye on most, the locked inner glass door or the open outer door.

'Whoever they were. I've not asked anyone, obviously . . . but I heard two policemen talking. It was someone driving a van.'

'Mum . . . you have to come away from here right now.'

Cora looked slowly round at her. 'What on earth are you talking about?'

'Look!' Lucy whispered. 'You know the situation. You can't hang around. There are police everywhere. If someone sees you—'

'For Heaven's sake!' Cora made no effort to lower her voice. 'I've told you before: no one knows I'm your mother.'

'You'd be surprised. I know most of our lot give the impression they know nothing at all but trust me, that isn't the case.'

'I don't care. I'm not going anywhere. Not till I find out how bad he is.'

Lucy leaned towards her, one hand tight on her mother's wrist, eyes constantly straying to the entry door. 'Mum, why on earth do you care? You didn't see the guy for thirty years.

You've only seen him recently because his criminal activities have brought him into contact with us.'

Cora still made no effort to lower her voice. 'Are you telling me *you* don't care, Lucy?'

'That's irrelevant.'

'Really? Because that's not what your body language is telling me. You're coiled like a spring.'

'Yes, because if someone sees us . . . *oh, God!*' Lucy lowered her head and covered her face with a hand, because a short, squarish figure with familiar white hair and a scruffy tweed jacket had appeared on the other side of the glass door, talking to a doctor wearing scrubs. 'That's DI Beardmore. I'm telling you, Mum, if he sees us—'

'Would you get your hand off me!' Cora raised her voice. 'I'm not going anywhere.'

Lucy released her; she had no choice. At the same time, she risked another glance at the glass door, but Beardmore had moved out of sight again.

'Mum, if you don't care about my career, that's fine,' Lucy hissed. 'But maybe you care about Dad's. Because I'm telling you now, you won't be doing him any favours if you get spotted here.'

Cora stared defiantly at the opposite wall. 'I need to know how bad he is.'

'I can't ask questions like that. I'm not even supposed to be here.'

'And yet you came.'

Lucy had no immediate answer for that. It was true that she'd mainly rushed over here to try and lead her mother away, but at the same time, she too had wanted to know.

'No need to try and hide it, Lucy. I know things have started changing between you and Frank.'

'Erm, excuse me. Nothing's started changing—'

'You've accepted that he's your father. You just called him

"Dad", for God's sake. On top of that you're well aware that he's done favours for both of us in recent times.'

'They weren't really favours, Mum. He was acting to help himself. *Christ . . .*' Beardmore had reappeared, still in conversation with someone. She dropped her head again.

'I've told you,' Cora said, 'I'm not leaving until I know Frank's condition.'

'They're not going to let you see him. Even if you shout from the rooftops that he's the father of your child, they still won't let you in.'

'We always do things *your* way, Lucy!' Cora glared at her. 'It's always *your* viewpoint that carries, *your* decision that counts. Well, not this time. Not till I know how Frank is.'

Lucy stole another glance at the glass door. Beardmore was still chatting to the doctor in scrubs, but now DS Dave Baker, who was currently working Night Crime, had appeared alongside him. Neither had noticed Lucy as yet, but clearly they were about to come through. Lucy had no options left.

'Okay . . . all right.' She stood up. 'I'll ask. Can you at least wait outside?'

Cora shook her head. 'I do that and the next thing you'll be bundling me into your car.'

'Stay here then. But keep your head down.' Lucy moved towards the glass door. 'You know . . . his girlfriend's probably lying in the next room. His *real* girlfriend. The woman he shares his life with. The woman he has sex with every night.'

'She's a jumped-up little madam. Frank'll realise that in due course.'

'I don't believe this,' Lucy said – as Beardmore finally spotted her through the glass.

He hit a button, the door opened and he came through, though Dave Baker lingered behind, still in conversation with medical staff.

271

'Lucy?' Beardmore said.

'Stan,' she replied with a stiff smile.

He glanced behind her, registering Cora's presence. He didn't know her and hadn't noticed that Lucy had been with her, but he lowered his voice anyway. 'What's going on?'

She shrugged. 'Just got a sniff of something. I hear there's been a shooting.'

'That's correct. Do you have an interest in it?'

'Not really.' Now that she was face to face with him, she struggled to think of anything to say. Just claiming that she'd been dropping an assault victim off at A&E didn't feel remotely strong enough. 'But, I hear, erm . . . oh, I heard there was a van involved. That it was an attempted abduction by van.'

Beardmore shook his head. 'No. Who told you that?'

'Just gabbled messages on the radio.'

Rather unexpectedly, though perhaps because he was tired – he'd almost certainly been called in and he looked haggard – he seemed to accept this. 'Well . . . there *was* a van involved. But there was no attempt at abduction. It was a double shooting in the car park at Crowley Old Hall.'

'Fatal?' she asked, attempting a casual air.

'Not yet.' He scratched his bristly chin. 'One of them could turn fatal. The girl.'

'Anyone we know?'

He arched an eyebrow. 'I thought you didn't have an interest in this?'

'Like I say, I heard about the van . . . I was over here anyway, dropping a mugging victim at A&E.'

'We haven't traced the van yet,' Dave Baker said, joining them. He was a big, heavily-built bloke in his mid-forties, though his thick hair and bushy beard were running to grey. He too spotted Cora, who was tactfully absorbed in her phone. He didn't know her either and had no reason to assume that she was earwigging but spoke more quietly anyway. 'It brought the two casualties here. Dumped them on the hospital car park, rocketed off again.'

'Wasn't a black or blue transit anyway,' Beardmore put in. 'As far as we know, it was brown. We've got the VRM, but it was stolen months ago. We're going through footage from the surrounding streets to see if we can pick up its trail.'

'Did the CCTV catch sight of anyone in particular?' Lucy asked.

'No.' Beardmore shrugged. 'Whoever it was, they knew where the cameras were and where they weren't. They chose a blind spot to dump the wounded.'

'No way to treat celebrity crims, to be honest,' Baker said. 'Frank McCracken, would you believe?'

'No?' Lucy replied. 'That nutter from the Crew?'

'And his girlfriend, Carlotta Powell,' Beardmore added. 'Think you've had dealings with both of them, haven't you?'

Lucy nodded. 'Powell was briefly a suspect in the Jill the Ripper case.'

'Well, the boot's firmly on the other foot tonight. She's being operated on as we speak. Sounds like it's touch and go . . . the slug went through her left lung.'

'What about McCracken?' Lucy asked.

'Not as bad in his case,' Baker replied. 'He's already come out of surgery. Sounds like the bullet bounced off the top of his left shoulder. Soft tissue damage and a broken collar-bone, but that's about it. He's going to be okay . . . which is hard lines for us, because it most likely means we're going to have to look after him while he's in here.'

'You mean in case the shooter comes back?' she said.

Baker shrugged. 'It's a possibility. We've scrambled a Trojan, but they're not here yet. The nearest available unit was at the airport.'

Before they could say more, the doctor reappeared in the doorway behind them and called Beardmore back in. Baker shuffled after him, and Lucy took the opportunity to head for the main entrance. Cora got up and scuttled after her.

They strode across the car park, bypassing the two uniforms, who again didn't seem to notice them.

'Well?' Cora asked.

'Just keep walking,' Lucy said tightly.

'I overheard some of that, but I need to know the rest.'

'I'll tell you when we get away from here.'

Cora fell silent until they were alongside her Honda.

'Sounds like he's going to be okay,' Lucy said.

'Thank God.'

'*Look!* For Christ's sake, Mum . . . you've got to get a grip on this! Dad is not your husband, he's not your boyfriend, you're nothing to him.'

Cora blinked in surprise but held her ground. 'Did *he* tell you that? You lie to me, and I'll know.'

'He's a hoodlum . . . okay? He's on every police watch-list there is.'

'That's not what I asked you.'

'Even if he didn't say you're nothing to him, all these things . . .' Lucy made a strenuous effort to calm herself down. 'All these terrible things he does for a living are relevant, because they display a total absence of morality, a vileness of spirit . . .'

'Lucy . . . you know that's not the whole man.'

'Even if it wasn't . . . his partner's lying at death's door. If she dies, or is left in a coma, or survives but is crippled, what happens then? Do you think he's just going to push her aside and get someone else?'

'He'll need to find comfort somewhere.'

'Oh, you can't be serious.' Lucy felt like ripping her hair out, not to mention her mother's. 'Look, I know you're lonely, Mum. I know there hasn't been any kind of romance in your life for a long time. But this path you're walking is fraught with danger for both you and him.'

'I don't think Frank's the sort who worries too much about danger, Lucy.'

'And what about me?' Lucy asked.

'You?' Cora shook her head. She took her keys from her anorak pocket and opened the driver's door. 'You need to learn to live with the fact that your father's a criminal. For the last two years, you've been running from that.' She climbed in behind the wheel. 'For all our sakes, Lucy, why don't you just put it right?'

The door slammed, and the Honda rumbled to life. Lucy stepped back as it swung around and accelerated across the car park towards the exit gate.

As she walked back to the CID car, the whole thing seemed utterly surreal. It was impossible to imagine that something so improbable had emerged in her life. Like she didn't have enough to concern herself with. It wasn't purely about Frank McCracken getting shot and neither her nor her mum wanting him to die – Lucy couldn't help but admit that she'd been somewhat relieved to learn that he'd live – it was the ongoing problem of conflicting interests. How many times was she going to have to be evasive and deceitful with her colleagues? How long could she keep ducking and diving? How much damage was being done all the time this went on and she continually refused to admit the truth?

She'd rounded the corner and was away from the ICU and the cops standing guard there, when from out of nowhere a huge vehicle screeched to a halt in front of her. It was a black Bentley Continental saloon.

Its driver leaned over and pushed open the front passenger door.

'Lucy!' Mick Shallicker said, looking tired and unkempt. 'Get in. We've got to talk.'

Chapter 29

Ivana and Alyssa took the same route home they always did, driving first to the Cranleigh industrial park, just north of the town centre. Here they drove into their father's lock-up on the narrow side-street that was Batley Lane, though in fact it was two lock-ups standing back to back, the other opening onto a parallel side-street called Crimea Terrace.

In the first lock-up they checked the doors were secure, stripped and bundled their combat gear and underclothes into a washing machine. Ordinarily, at this stage, they would clean their 'appointments', as they called them – boots, belts, harnesses, gloves and so on, buffing them with various of the chemicals stacked on the wall of shelves alongside the double-locked medical cabinet where they kept the drugs and syringes. But this was often a lengthy procedure, and at present they were under orders to get home quickly, so they opted to return later and attend to it then.

They padded naked through the adjoining doorway that, unbeknown to the building's owners, their father had installed between the two lock-ups – both units were registered to different, non-existent people, so if anyone ever discovered

277

this by accident, it wouldn't matter greatly – and took a shower, thoroughly soaping themselves and shampooing their hair. After this, they blew dry, put on jewellery and makeup and got dressed again, now in slinky, clingy tops, miniskirts and tall, strappy shoes.

If they got stopped for any reason on the way home now – which was unlikely because the car they kept in the second lock-up was a respectable silver-coloured Volvo V90 estate, fully documented and in mint condition – they were nothing but a pair of ditzy party-girls returning from a cracking night out. And no, officer, they didn't mind providing specimens of breath for breath-tests, because they never drank and drove; their strict, law-abiding father wouldn't hear of it. If anyone queried the marks on Alyssa's face, meanwhile, it would be a tale of woe about a violent ex-boyfriend who now, thankfully, was history.

They returned to Cotely Barn shortly after 2.15am, parking on the drive alongside their father's Merc. The address was 27, Cedar Lane, and it was the essence of suburban respectability, the house once an ivy-covered four-bed detached, surrounded by lawns and flowerbeds, though their father had extended it several years ago, constructing a fifth bedroom above the formerly free-standing garage, which had also now been connected to the main house. The value of the property had increased dramatically, but the real advantage lay in the fact that prisoners could now be brought indoors, in the Volvo's boot, without anyone noticing, and taken away again in the same manner.

The girls let themselves in by the front door, tittering and giggling, again as if they'd just had a great night – normality was so important – and entered a wood-panelled downstairs area, neatly carpeted and tastefully furnished, dotted with original paintings and other ornaments, and now lying in midweek darkness.

To the average outsider, the master of this pleasant-looking house led an entirely conventional, inoffensive life, coming and going unobtrusively, pruning his roses at the weekend and attending neighbourhood barbecues. If his neighbours ever enquired, and they often did because he was affable and approachable, he'd tell them that he ran a bunch of small businesses but that he was now thinking about retiring – all of which was true. He would be vague if the nature of his main expertise came up, talking in airy terms about 'trouble-shooting' and 'consultation', though again this was at least partly true. He spoke rarely about his wife, who most people assumed must have died rather than left, because he had a pair of college-age twin daughters who were beautiful, intelligent and chatty, and seemed very content with their lot.

They were less chatty now, as they ascended the staircase and moved side by side along the landing to the fifth bedroom, which was their father's study. If anything, they were nervous, but this time it was a pleasing kind of nervousness because it was tinged with anticipation.

The light filtering around his partly open door indicated that he was waiting for them. Even if he hadn't been, and if this had been an ordinary night and they genuinely had come in late from a party, he would probably have still been awake. Of late, he'd taken to writing his memoirs, a pastime he'd quickly realised needed to be his main priority in life, not just because it was a labour of love and a huge under-taking, but because when the manuscript was completed and bound, it would be the most valuable item he could bequeath to his offspring. *The Life and Times of Martin Torgau Esq* would not just detail the whole of his own strange, complex and terrible existence, but would name and shame various others whom he'd been involved with over the years and would clear up a phenomenal number of unsolved crimes, as well as several the police did not even know about. There were many highly placed men in the Northwest underworld who would kill quickly and ruthlessly to get their hands on such a prize. But that wouldn't even be an option for them. When Martin Torgau was no longer here, knowledge of the memoir's location would reside solely with his daughters, for whom it was intended to be a shield against the Crew.

The life they were embarking on would naturally entail many risks, but at least, with this memoir in their possession, they'd be insured against the region's deadliest syndicate ever turning on them. At the first intimation that the two girls might for any reason be in their employers' crosshairs, the memoir's existence would be announced, with the threat that, should anything untoward happen to them, their legal rep would forward it straight to the authorities.

They tapped on the study door and entered.

It wasn't as grand a room as the word 'study' might have implied. Originally a bedroom, it still had some of that appearance: a fitted carpet, a smallish window with a Venetian blind, and a wall of wardrobes – though these stood open to reveal a bank of TV monitors displaying live video feeds, not just from the exterior of the property and the cells downstairs, but from the back-to-back lock-ups as well. Instead of a bed there was a large desk, rather ornate, topped with smooth leather and spacious enough to accommodate not only an Anglepoise lamp and desktop computer but a mountain of foolscap sheets, on which Torgau was writing his memoirs in longhand.

He turned in his swivel chair to face them.

He was in his late fifties and shortish, no more than five-foot-nine, and these days rather plump, and was wearing his usual round-the-house ensemble of jersey, tracksuit trousers and white tennis shoes. He had a mop of chalk-grey hair and a drooping chalk-grey moustache. Along with his dark-brown, strangely mournful eyes, this gave him the most unthreatening demeanour possible.

'You missed a target tonight,' he said, in the low, modulated tone he reserved for business discussions, the dark jewels of his eyes fixed on them. This was one thing about Martin Torgau: his gaze. He almost never blinked, which was an unnerving experience when he was watching you, as if there was nothing you were thinking or feeling that he wouldn't detect. On this occasion, though, he didn't seem angry or even particularly inquisitive.

Ivana, who'd already admitted their error by phone, nodded. 'A police officer intervened.'

'So you said.'

'We thought it best just to get out of there.'

He nodded. He'd heard this too, and if he had any concern that a plain-clothes cop on a motorbike was something a little different from the norm, he didn't let it trouble him for now. There was a more important matter at hand.

'We had a private delivery shortly before midnight,' he said.

In Torgau-speak, a 'private delivery' was exactly what it sounded like. A private delivery vehicle would have stopped in front of the house, and a man wearing a legitimate uniform would have pushed a package through the mail box.

That package now lay open at the edge of the desk. As usual, it contained photographs of a certain person, taken from various angles to ensure there'd be no mistake, and printed details: that person's name, address, workplace, the vehicles they had access to, the hours they kept, and any other essential information. At no point in the document were any terms of contract offered; these had been agreed long before. Nor was any reason given as to why the contract had been taken out; all of that was on a need-to-know basis.

It was a question Torgau never asked, in any case, primarily because he didn't care.

The two girls shot glances at the tantalising heap of paperwork. They didn't reach for it yet. They hoped it was for them, but they couldn't be certain.

'I should tell you both that I don't consider your training complete,' Torgau said. 'Not yet. Not quite. However, here's a chance for you to resolve that in one fell swoop.'

He picked up the main sheet and indicated a row of letters printed along the bottom, grouped in threes. To any ordinary person it would be nothing, a typical array of meaningless computer-generated gobbledegook, but again, that was deceptive. The first three letters were 'd', 's' and 'U', standing for 'in due course', 'soon' and 'urgent'. The u being upper-case was self-explanatory.

'It's a rush job,' Torgau said. 'And as you two are still out and about and haven't had a score yet tonight – for which reason you must be hungry – it seems too good an opportunity to miss. Now listen . . . as far as I'm concerned, the Lorna Cunningham incident was a one-off. You underestimated her, Alyssa. Killing at close quarters is a skill that needs to be mastered but going one-on-one is always a risk. That's why I send you out together. Anyway, nothing was really lost, and the snatch itself worked. In addition to which, a cock-up like that went against the grain of your general training, which up until last Sunday has been a story of achievement. The successful hit at the gym was proof that you're back on track – especially as you plucked it out of thin air. It wasn't planned, and I wasn't there to observe, so it's difficult for me to heap you with unmitigated praise as I don't know exactly how it went. But it was a good move: you saw a chance and went for it. And now you have another chance . . . a chance to *completely* redeem yourselves.'

The two girls swapped glances.

'But listen to me,' he said gravely. 'Be under no illusions, girls . . . if you let me down on this, it'll be more than just a case of relegating you back to Category B or even Category C. Do you understand? From this moment, your training is technically over. This is the real thing, and there'll be real consequences, maybe for all of us, if you let this go belly-up.'

'We won't let you down . . . we're ready,' Ivana said.

Torgau glanced at Alyssa, who was bright-eyed with excitement.

'I can't wait to get back out there,' she said, to which he raised a warning finger.

'Don't approach it like that. This is the big league, Alyssa. You need to be professional at all times. Approach this thing coolly and analytically. Because this contract will test you at various levels.' Again, his finger roved along the line of digits at the bottom. 'All these scenarios I've prepared you for. So it's vital that you remember your training.'

The next group of three letters referred to the perceived quality of the target, consisting of 's' for 'soft', 'r' for 'potential risk' and 'C', which was upper-case, for 'carrying', in other words, 'armed'. Though the actual method was always up to the contractor, the next group of three requested the specific type of job required: 'q' for 'quick', 's' for 'slow', and 'T', upper-case, for 'torturous'. The final group was not unconnected to the previous one, specifying the manner of disposal: 'v' for 'make him/her completely vanish', 'n' for 'no particular preference' and lastly 'E', upper-case, for 'make an example'; in other words, the body had to be found and in a manner that would create horror.

'This kind of job,' Torgau told his daughters, 'disposing of someone in a way that sends out an unforgettable message, may seem like the most fun, but it's the rarest kind of contract we undertake – most often the target must vanish – which

makes it the biggest challenge. Enjoy yourselves, of course
. . . that's what this kind of work is all about . . .'

They beamed at him.

'But don't take it lightly. We're not playing games any more.'

'That's okay,' Alyssa said. 'One thing we definitely won't be doing, Dad, is playing.'

In truth, Martin Torgau was not one hundred per cent certain that his daughters were ready for this. As he stood on the landing outside his study and listened to their preparation downstairs, he mulled over several concerns.

He had no doubt that they were physically very fit and strong, and highly skilled with weapons and in hand-to-hand combat. All of this he had seen to personally over many years. They were also committed to the cause. He'd raised them in the family tradition; they knew no other way and were eager to commence their new, high-paying careers.

But were they possibly *too* eager?

Alyssa in particular was very excitable and sometimes overconfident, as the incident with the Cunningham woman had proved.

Torgau had made it a prerequisite of their training that they successfully complete at least one highly challenging assignment, 'Category A' as he termed them, before he'd allow them to take on an actual contract. Though well planned and, for the most part, well executed, and though ultimately the target had been disposed of, the Cunningham hit had nearly gone so catastrophically wrong that it could easily have blown the roof off everything. He'd had no option but to classify it a fail. They'd made up for it since then, admittedly, with the hit at the gymnasium. It had been an on-the-spot thing, Ivana literally taking a chance that came at her out of nowhere, and from the photographic evidence he'd seen and the written report his daughters had given him, it had gone smoothly. He particularly liked it that the so-called meathead was apparently suspected by regulars at the gym of acquiring and selling illegal steroids. So there'd be plenty of blind alleys for the police to follow.

It sounded like a bang-up job, but it still bothered Torgau a little that he hadn't been there to see it for himself.

Up until now, he'd nearly always gone out with them. Mainly as an observer, but also, if required, to provide back-up. He'd go out with them again tonight – to watch and, if necessary, to intervene. But was the fact that they wanted to do it tonight, so soon after the package had arrived, a little worrying in itself?

Was it another indication of over-enthusiasm?

As Torgau stood on the landing and listened to their happy chatter, he wondered if he had too much of a blind spot where his girls were concerned. All his life, he'd been the coldest of professionals, and even at home a stern disciplinarian, though he was sure that both Ivana and Alyssa would counter that argument by saying that yes, he'd been hard sometimes, but that also he'd been fair.

But was he giving them too much leeway here?

Was it a mistake letting them react to this new development so spontaneously, without thinking it through thoroughly?

On one hand, it felt as if a lot more planning was required. But on the other, Ivana had already proved that she could think on the hoof. And on yet another, this particular job was marked 'Urgent', so it had to be done in the next day or so anyway.

If Torgau pressed himself, he'd have to admit that any reservations he held were only slight. The girls had done all he'd asked; they'd successfully performed numerous Category C assignments, which was mainly household pets, several

Category Bs, non-threatening human specimens, such as pensioners, tramps and the like, and now a Category A, which spoke for itself. In addition to that, there'd been a specific instruction attached to the main file tonight, which he had *not* revealed to his daughters. Partly, this was because he didn't like the idea of them learning that he too received orders, but also because this one had come from the very top – and orders from the top even Martin Torgau disobeyed at his peril.

'You know, urgent doesn't necessarily mean tonight . . . not if we're too tired to do it,' Alyssa said, on the far side of the kitchen, where she was scanning the documentation relating to their first official target.

Ivana, who was busy spooning coffee into a pair of mugs, was amused to hear her sister's attempted cool-headed approach. Alyssa was perfect for this line of work, her enthusiasm bubbling over constantly – but that had led her to make mistakes. The Lorna Cunningham thing, for example. Alyssa had insisted that she was past doing Category Bs – indeed, the previous one they'd brought in, that old Hopkins guy, she'd refused to touch, saying Ivana could take care of him herself, with her neck-wire. Alyssa had wanted a *real* challenge. And then, of course, she'd tried to finish the athlete off alone . . .

Even then, though, Ivana felt a special kind of warmth towards Alyssa, not just because they were twins, but because Alyssa was so in awe of her slightly older other half.

In Alyssa's mind, Ivana wasn't just the prudent planner, she could do amazing things at the drop of a hat. Like the meathead. She'd known they'd needed another Category A to impress the old man. And though that would normally take some careful prep, this opportunity had come from nowhere, and she'd planned it all in a matter of minutes. The

10mg of haloperidol they'd hit Cunningham with had needed to be carefully sourced, but ever-ready Ivana always carried lesser drugs around with her – like diazepam, for example. Even then, she'd winged it, instructing Alyssa to bring the van and meet her in the church's car park rather than at the gym, because she was guessing it would have fewer cameras (in fact, it had turned out to have none). She'd also gambled that they'd be able to lure their target round to the back of the holy building. And yet again, because it was Ivana's gig, things seemed to have fallen for them. They hadn't expected to find the pitchfork, or that the church's rear porch would be open, and it was pure fluke that Alyssa's voluminous old cagoule had doubled in the darkness for a monkish habit.

Fluke maybe, fortuitous even . . . but then fortune often favoured the bold. That was something else about Ivana – at least in Alyssa's eyes: she was bold, daring. Little wonder the younger girl was so happily led by her – which was why it wasn't just amusing to see Alyssa adopting the cautious approach now, it was also charming. Because she wasn't trying to impress her older sister by displaying restraint, she was trying to emulate her.

'So, what do you think?' Alyssa glanced up. 'We don't need to do this one straight away, if you don't want to. It's very late and we won't be at our best.'

Ivana shook her head as she poured the kettle. 'Nah . . . we're dressed, we're awake. We'll go out again tonight. Even if it's just to sus the lay of the land. You never know, an opportunity might arise there and then.'

Alyssa looked unsure. 'That might have worked at the gym for the meathead, but this one –' she waved a fistful of photos '– this one's different.'

Ivana smiled as she sipped her coffee. 'I don't know, doll. A lot of these guys . . . they all turn out to be meatheads in the end.'

Alyssa glanced back through the documentation, pursing her lips in thoughtful, grown-up fashion. Ivana smiled again and placed her coffee on the worktop alongside a folded newspaper. It was that day's edition of the *Manchester Evening News*.

Immediately, something on its front page caught her attention.

She stiffened where she stood, and then grabbed it up.

'What's wrong?' Alyssa asked.

Ivana blew out long and slow, mightily relieved that their father tended to have the paper delivered out of habit these days, rather than because he was always in a rush to read it. The story she'd noticed was contained in a box and inset into the bottom left-hand corner of the front page, which explained why he probably hadn't seen it yet.

Whatever happened now, he couldn't be allowed to. Ever.

'Vana, I said, what's—'

Ivana offered the paper, one finger indicating the story in question. 'We *have* to go out tonight, Lyssa, whatever the circs. Even if we only scope out the target and do nothing else there, we must take care of *this*.'

Alyssa read the inset story and shrugged. 'We can look. But it's probably nothing.'

'Probably. But we don't take chances, do we?'

'Suppose not.'

Ivana turned back to the kettle. 'Make sure you drink all that coffee, while I make us another one. It's going to be a long night.'

Alyssa grinned. 'No rest for the wicked, eh?'

Chapter 30

'So . . . what's the prognosis?' Shallicker asked, taking random turns down empty Crowley streets. They'd been driving this way for what seemed like several minutes now, crazily, haphazardly, and this was the first time he'd spoken.

'Why are you asking me?' Lucy said. 'I'm not a doctor.'

'Don't bullshit me, Lucy! I just saw you and Cora coming out. I was waiting for you.'

Her eyes remained locked on the residential roads spooling out in front of them. 'I've been delivering an assault victim to A&E. I don't know what you're talking about.'

'Look . . .' He'd been chomping a huge wad of peppermint-scented gum, and now bared it, along with several teeth, his massive neck muscles standing out, his sweaty, shovel-like hands gripped on the wheel so tightly that his tendons showed like white bands. 'Look . . .' Apparently, it required an immense, nut-busting effort just to put voice to whatever it was he was trying to say. 'Look . . . I might be a scumbag criminal to you, but Frank's my mate, okay? I'm not just his lackey. We've been together for the last twenty-five years. We've been through thick and thin . . . we've had each other's backs in every kind of scrape. Even if you

289

hate me because of my profession, at least fucking respect me as a human being. I'll ask you one more time . . . how is he?'

Ultimately, Lucy didn't see any value in saying nothing. It was nice to see a bastard like Mick Shallicker squirming, but he was the kind of huge fish, who, when he squirmed could do some serious damage – she knew because she'd seen it for herself.

'He'll be okay,' she said. 'Looks like the bullet bounced off his collar-bone. That's broken, obviously. But otherwise he's unhurt.'

Shallicker almost sagged where he sat. His relief was clearly sincere.

'I'm less sure about Charlie,' Lucy added. 'She was undergoing emergency surgery when I left. Whoever it was, they shot her in the left lung.'

'Fuck . . .' he breathed.

'It didn't help that you dumped them on the hospital forecourt like sacks of empties!'

'What the fuck else was I supposed to do?' He swerved left with shrieking tyres, to avoid sitting at a red light. 'Call an ambulance? Give a statement? You think Wild Bill would be happy with that?'

'I'm not sure he'll be happy that you took them to the hospital at all. Don't you have your own doctors for this kind of thing?'

Shallicker grimaced, as if this was something he'd been wondering about. 'Yeah . . . sure. But that's not something you can arrange on the hoof. And the way Frank and Blondie were bleeding so badly . . .' He shook his head in disbelief. 'Panicked, didn't I! Felt sure they were both goners. Only just had time to get them into a disposable vehicle. After that, well . . . St Winifred's was only around the corner. Even then, I didn't think they were going to make it. To answer your question . . . I'll still get a bollocking.' He licked his dry lips. 'It may be worse than that.'

'Well, that's the price you pay, Michael. For selling yourself body and soul to an organisation that really doesn't give a shit about anyone.'

'Mouthy cow you are at times.'

'Yeah, well, I wonder why!' She rounded on him. 'Could it be anything to do with the fact that what you've just told me amounts to another load of underworld secrets I'm now obliged to keep from my superiors? You think I enjoy doing that? You think I'm happy being some kind of unofficial repository of gangland knowledge . . . a helpless spectator while you and the rest of your pathetic brood rape and pillage the whole fucking world!'

He glanced sidelong at her, surprised by the anger in her voice.

'I'm *not* onside!' she shouted. 'Okay, Mick? *I'm not one of you!* I've got one interest only in what's just happened to Frank McCracken, and that's in who shot him.'

'You don't need to worry about that.' He gave a sneering smile. '*That's* already being taken care of.'

'Oh, yeah?'

He made no reply.

'And that's all I get?' she said. 'Nothing? After telling you everything?'

'You should be happy, shouldn't you? Proves that I still think of you as a cop.'

'I need to get back to the hospital . . . my car's there.'

'That's where we're headed,' he said, though at present he looked nonplussed. Having barely seemed to know where he was driving prior to learning that McCracken was going to be all right, it seemed he'd steered them onto a maze-like housing estate and now was having trouble finding his way off it again.

291

'Just as long as you know, Mick . . . you and your bloody mates turn this thing into Buffalo Bill's Wild West Show and I won't help you.'

'Like we need *your* help.'

'I'm telling you, pal. The Crew gets involved in a shooting war in Crowley, and November Division will come after you with everything they've got. Me too.'

'Shouldn't you be doing that anyway?'

She couldn't reply to that.

How could she?

It was true.

Chapter 31

Miles O'Grady would probably have been the first to admit that he hadn't been thinking straight. On reflection, the obvious thing would have been to accept Frank McCracken's offer, a 50 per cent split between himself and the Crew. But he doubted he could ever have lived with that easily. It just wasn't his thing to be an underling. How would he ever get rich when he was basically working for someone else? How could he ever rub those GMP fuckers' noses in it if he just became another gangster? But as he parked the Golf outside Dashwood House and clambered hurriedly out, hair sweat-soaked, clothes clammy and dishevelled, a briefcase clenched under his arm, it still occurred to him that he might have handled this thing better.

He tucked the Taurus into his belt and pivoted 180 degrees, scanning the full length of Long Acre. It was deserted, as it should be at this time of night, but only one streetlight was in operation, so that meant there were lots of hidden crannies. He backed towards the building, fumbling for his keys. There wasn't much of value in the office, but what there was he had to take with him, and he had to do it quickly.

He closed the door behind him, locked it and hurried up the darkened stairs.

The problem was that, though he'd hit McCracken and the dolly bird, he'd missed the bodyguard. In fact, as soon as the bodyguard had pulled a gun of his own, O'Grady had flown. He'd been in such a blind rage, so infuriated to see his schemes come crashing down so quickly and easily that it had briefly overwhelmed all common sense. He'd had one aim only; to teach the bastards a lesson, to show them that he wasn't someone to be screwed with. *You threaten my business, I take you out of the game altogether – that's the O'Grady way.* But the plan had never involved suffering bullet wounds himself. In fact, it had been a very nasty surprise to see that gun. It had never occurred to him that they might be packing heat on their way to a restaurant. To a restaurant, for God's sake!

Either way, he'd run. Of course he'd run.

And now he was back here, still not entirely sure what he was going to do next.

Even when he'd been absolutely certain that punching McCracken's ticket was the only way forward, he hadn't thought this far ahead. Not that it was possible now to sit down and think things through carefully. Because that gigantic bodyguard had seen him, and if he didn't already know who O'Grady was, he'd doubtless be able to put two and two together and come up with his employer's most recent target, Walderstone Enquiries Ltd.

So the only thing that mattered at this moment was getting out.

He drew the blind on the window, turned the office light on and threw the briefcase onto the desk. Opening the bottom drawer, he took out his laptop and stowed it in the case, then lifted the carpet in the corner, moved the boards aside and tapped his combination into the electronic panel on the circular steel door beneath. Usually, he kept nothing in the under-floor safe except petty cash, but the last couple of days had been such a whirlwind of fury and fear that he hadn't really had time to figure out the best way to feed the sixty grand that was his cut from the Dean Chesham job into his normal day-to-day finances, and so had stuck it down here. It was currently taped into six ten-grand rolls. The petty cash was down there too, in a small plastic bag, probably about five grand's worth. He took it all, fishing it out item by item, and throwing it into the briefcase.

When that was done, he stood up and turned around, wondering if there was anything else he needed. Nothing came to mind, because the truth was that he didn't even know where he was going yet. There were one or two hotels in different parts of the country where he could probably hole up. If he could pay cash on arrival, no one would even need to know his real name. How long that could realistically go on for, he didn't know. But he had to get away from here, at least for a few days.

Would he be able to negotiate with the Crew? He didn't know that either. But neither did he think it would be out of the question. With one of their key players dead, they'd now be scrambling to fill that void, no doubt feeding on each other as their type always did. But there was no reason why O'Grady couldn't pitch his own hat into the ring – from a place of safety, of course. As the executioner of the Crew's chief taxman, he could make a case that McCracken had been fucking him over. Maybe had been trying to fuck the Crew over too. That he'd been into O'Grady for huge amounts of money which he didn't intend to share with his bosses. Maybe that he'd been O'Grady's secret partner, and they'd been doing a number on the Crew leadership for months now, with O'Grady suddenly deciding that enough was enough. That O'Grady wanted to make things straight with the house, and that McCracken wouldn't go along with it.

Who would there be to say any different?

A lump-of-meat bodyguard so brainless that he hadn't even been able to protect his employer from an assassin's bullet?

O'Grady switched the light off, grabbed the briefcase and hurried back down the stair.

It still seemed like a long shot, of course, but he was certain he could pull it off. He'd be offering them a regular and lucrative scam. This gig he had going, blackmailing the city's playboys, could be worth millions in the long run. Surely, even the Crew wouldn't turn their noses up at that. Of course, if they got fully involved, it would mean there'd be no place for Roper and Stone. But O'Grady wasn't sure that worried him any more.

At the bottom of the stair, he halted behind the closed door, opened it a crack and peeked out. Long Acre was still deserted. As before, only about half of it was visible, the rest lying in shadow, but there was no sound. It was so late now that even the usual hum of night traffic was absent.

Roper and Stone were likely dead anyway. Even if they hadn't said they were ditching him, any efforts O'Grady might make to protect them would be useless. He couldn't offer any kind of deal to the Crew for a few days at least, maybe for a few weeks. In the meantime, they'd be looking for him, and as they wouldn't be able to find him, they'd settle for going to his ex-partners. God alone knew what would happen then. McCracken's personal team would doubtless want full-on revenge, but if they took that out on Roper and Stone, rather than on O'Grady himself . . . well, he wasn't complaining.

There was one other loose end, of course – and this only struck him as he hurried out to his Golf.

Megan.

The realisation almost stopped O'Grady in his tracks.

Bizarrely, all through this intense little melodrama, he hadn't once considered his wretched wife. But he had no choice but to think about her now.

Possibly, there was nothing to worry about. He could simply call her from whichever hotel he found and tell her he was away on business for a few days. She'd think it odd, sure; that he hadn't taken a change of clothes or any toiletries, and that he hadn't mentioned anything about this beforehand. But she had at least some idea that he got embroiled in nefarious activities from time to time; and if she followed form, she wouldn't ask any real questions so long as he could guarantee there'd be a pay-off at the end.

The other alternative was to swing by Broadgate Green now, on his way out of Manchester, and try to persuade her to come with him – but that just wouldn't happen in the time he had available. She'd have too many queries, too many objections.

He switched the engine on, the car rumbling to life.

If he left Megan at home, of course, the Crew would do something. They wouldn't just leave her alone because she was a woman. But hopefully they wouldn't go for the jugular straight away, and it would only be a quick Q&A before they realised that she didn't know anything. If nothing else, it meant that he'd have to get back to them quickly, to explain his situation and to make his offer.

Despite the narrow confines of the Acre, he pulled a three-point turn and drove towards the entrance. Only to find himself hitting the brake much harder than he needed to, given that he was only doing about ten miles an hour.

An HGV had appeared from nowhere and was now parked there. It was a huge thing, its trailer laden with goods covered in green tarpaulins. Its nearside wheels were on the pavement;

it wasn't blocking the entrance entirely – there was room to get past in a car like a Golf. The problem was that it hadn't been there before.

O'Grady sat stiffly, trying to detect any sign of movement, and initially seeing nothing.

It was entirely possible that someone had legitimately left it. But in the last hour or so? When it was nearly three o'clock in the morning? Beyond Long Acre, an access road followed a circular route around Crowley Bus Station. It wasn't the most obvious place for a long-distance lorry driver to pull up and grab himself forty winks.

O'Grady glanced at the briefcase on the front passenger seat, and then pulled the Taurus from his belt and placed it on top of it.

What? some inner voice asked. *You're just going to drive on past it? And if someone opens fire as you do, you're going to engage them in gun-play?*

It was ridiculous, of course. There was no sign anyone was there, but the back of the lorry was covered. And if he edged past it, which he'd have to do slowly because it would be a tight fit, there'd be nothing to stop them opening up on him with maybe three or four weapons from near point-blank range. They'd have raked his entire vehicle before he could return a single shot.

'Fuck!' he hissed. 'Shit!'

He threw the Golf into reverse, fresh sweat damp on his brow. There was no real question. That wagon had appeared from nowhere, at the dead of night. And it had parked virtually at his door. There was no point pretending this might be a coincidence.

The Golf juddered backward until he was level with the office again. He stopped, climbed out, walked round to the passenger door, opened it, snatched the Taurus, tucked it back into his belt and grabbed the briefcase.

298

He closed the car door quietly and left it unlocked, concerned that to hit the fob would set the sidelights flashing, which might attract attention.

Unless he was prepared to chance the HGV, there was no way out of the cul-de-sac on wheels. On the face of it, it seemed like madness to attempt a getaway on foot, but they might not be expecting that. Plus, the Crew were central Manchester-based. They wouldn't know every highway and by-way in Crowley. He could still outfox them. He stood close to the side of the building, where he was hidden in shadow, turned and strode in the opposite direction.

There was at least one ginnel leading out of Long Acre. He wasn't sure where it led to. But his local knowledge had to be better than theirs.

He walked increasingly briskly, his confidence growing. Glancing back, he could see the HGV, but still there was no movement there.

The entrance to the ginnel came up on the right. It was nothing more than a gap between overlarge buildings, an archetypical inner-city backstreet, unevenly paved and strewn with litter. He hurried down it anyway, mopping his brow with his sleeve, continually glancing backward. No figures intruded into the receding rectangle of streetlighting behind him.

'This is good,' he muttered, daring to hope that he'd slipped the net.

But then he reached a junction of passages. This was something he'd feared. He was pretty certain that he'd be able to work his way through to one of the main roads eventually, but where to go from here? The route on the right curved out of sight. There were no doors along it. The route on the left, however, was broader and ran straighter. Wheelie bins were ranged along it, which meant that it ran behind shops or industrial units. If he went that way, there'd likely be a cut-through to the main road.

He headed left, still walking quickly – but when he was forty yards along, a set of headlights sprang to life just ahead of him.

O'Grady skidded to a halt.

He couldn't see what the vehicle was, but it was already advancing on him, its engine rumbling. For what seemed like several seconds, he was totally frozen, his back stiff, his feet leaden. It couldn't possibly be *them*. They couldn't have known that he'd try to escape this way. They couldn't have covered this eventuality because they didn't know this place.

But nor do you, Miles, that mocking internal voice now told him.

With a clank, the vehicle changed gear and accelerated. A bin hurtled sideways, its putrid contents exploding; sure proof that this wasn't just some late worker heading home.

Instinctively rather than deliberately, he pulled the Taurus from his belt and opened fire – wildly, blindly. By luck, at least one of the slugs struck the nearside headlamp, putting it out.

That might have been a result, had O'Grady been able to follow through with further shots, but he'd first obtained the Taurus when he'd confiscated it during a raid several years ago. He'd never declared it, opting to keep it for himself, even though it had only contained four rounds. And now he'd fired them all.

But maybe he'd bought himself a little time.

He ran back along the alley.

With a clatter, the vehicle changed gear and accelerated again. He heard another thundering impact as a second bin was knocked out of its way. A small mercy, as the tone of the engine altered, the vehicle shifting down to avoid hitting too many more obstacles.

O'Grady carried on running, galloping along the next passage. He didn't think the car, or whatever it was, would be able to fit down this one, and risked another glance back. The single remaining light had stopped at the junction. As he saw this, the arched entry to another passage came up on his left. He slid to a halt, seeing thirty yards of black tunnel, and at the far end of that unrestricted streetlighting.

He hurried down there, now aware that he was an unsightly mess – sweaty and panicking, with a firearm in his hand. He could discard the gun, of course; just release it. It was no use now anyway. But his fingerprints were all over it. Suppose the police married that one with the gun that had been used to kill Frank McCracken and his girlfriend? Suppose it had been used to kill other people before O'Grady had come into possession of it?

He shoved it into his coat pocket as he staggered out onto the pavement of a main road, which he recognised as Bakerfield Lane. His normally impeccable hair was now a wringing mat, his breath coming in wrenching sobs. But the luck that had saved him from the ambush in the alley was still holding, because a couple of dozen yards to his left, a night bus, a double-decker, idled at one of its stops. Both sets of its doors, front and middle, stood open as it awaited last-minute customers. Walking quickly towards it, straightening his tie and the lapels of his coat, O'Grady climbed on board.

He was the only passenger downstairs, so he found himself a seat easily.

All this was good, in fact excellent – his pounding heartbeat began to slow – except that, no, on second thoughts it wasn't good at all; the bus was well-lit and if someone came around the corner now, he'd easily be spotted.

O'Grady got up again, walked to the spiral staircase, and ascended to the top deck.

301

Up there, he wasn't alone. There was someone seated at the very front. But that was okay. He went to the back and sat down. Someone had slashed the seating, so all the stuffing hung out, but he didn't care. Again, that was normal. Everything had to be normal now . . . ordinary, innocuous. He placed the briefcase on his knee and waited, though fresh sweat seeped from his brow as he wondered how long it would be before the bus set off.

Glancing down through the grubby window, he saw a Bakerfield Lane now bare of traffic and pedestrians. He looked to the front again, feeling tense. They had to make a move soon. What was the point in sitting around? There was no one else here, no one was rushing to catch a bus at this ungodly hour.

With a jolt, the vehicle lurched from the kerb.

At last, O'Grady allowed himself to relax, but only a little. He turned and peered through the back window. Like all the others, it was ingrained with dirt, but he could just about fix on the entrance to the arched passage he'd emerged from. There was no one there. Likewise, he hadn't heard anyone else climbing aboard while he'd been waiting here in his seat. The bus jolted again, vibrating noisily as it ascended through the gears, picking up speed along the empty road. His relief grew. Inevitably, it slowed again as it approached the first set of lights, but he was already several hundred yards from where he'd begun, and anyway, the light changed to green as they drew close, and they rumbled through, picking up more speed.

O'Grady had no clue which direction they were headed in. This was one of the night services, so no doubt its final destination lay in some distant part of Greater Manchester. But he was okay with that. Anything to get away from the centre of Crowley.

The problem was, now that he considered it, what did he do afterwards?

Feeling rested a little, he tried to get his thoughts in order. Grabbing himself a taxi, assuming he could even find one at this late hour, would probably be a no-no. As an ex-copper, he knew that many organised crime groups had their hooks into mini-cab firms, so that would be a trail they could follow. He thought about catching a train, though again that depended whereabouts on the outskirts of town he finished up.

He glanced through the window, unable to identify the route. They were still in the town centre, passing Crowley Little Theatre on the right, and then Telson's Van Hire. He sat back, still trying to think. There'd be no local trains running until six o'clock at the earliest, but that wasn't a disaster. There were plenty of unmanned stations in Manchester's suburbs, and if he ended up near one of those, there'd be nothing to stop him going onto the platform, crashing on a bench and grabbing the first service that came along, riding whichever way it took him and hooking up with a national line later on. He'd be down at the other end of the country by noon.

O'Grady had now earmarked a couple of country hotels where he might lie low. Places down in the Cotswolds and the West Country, where he'd spent time as a boy. Fleeting memories of happy holidays during his youth came back to him – only for the bus to lurch violently as it swung a right-hand turn, almost toppling him into the aisle.

He levered himself upright, grabbing hold of the bar at the top of the seat in front. Glancing through the window on the right again, he saw a spread of playing-fields. He raised himself higher, to look through the windows on the left, and there spied another of those bleak, depressing housing estates for which Crowley was so famous. God, it was a crap-hole, this place. No worse than many other parts of Manchester, if he was truthful, despite its reputation, but so typical a slice of modern urban Britain with its gridlocked traffic, boarded shops and desolate blocks of flats.

They swung around another sharp corner, this time heading left. They were now onto the estate, it seemed, and O'Grady was puzzled. Another sharp left followed, and then a sharp right. He was jarred from side to side as the heavy vehicle negotiated narrow streets rendered even narrower by double parking. A hefty *clunk* echoed up from the lower deck. If O'Grady didn't know better, he'd have fancied they'd clipped a car.

He moved to the window again, seeing medium-rise apartment blocks sailing past at what felt like reckless speed.

What the hell was going on?

Though he'd wanted to keep a low profile, to the point that he'd let the bus take him wherever it needed to go, he now knew that he had to find out where that was. He made his way along the aisle, swaying as the bus again veered around corners. Near the top of the stairway, he halted, glancing outside. A street-sign had just flickered by: Turton Avenue.

If that was the same Turton Avenue O'Grady knew, it meant they were on Hatchwood Green, which was probably the best example of a sink estate in Northwest England, and beyond which lay only the Aggies, a district of post-industrial spoil land once belonging to Darthill Colliery. If memory served, there was a bus terminus over that way, at the bottom of Pimbo Lane, close to the ruins of the old Bleachworks. And if that was where O'Grady would have to get off, he'd be a long way from a railway station. He'd be a long way from anything.

Irritated as well as confused, he continued along the aisle.

'Excuse me,' he said, trying to draw the attention of the guy at the front.

This chap was obviously heading somewhere, so maybe

O'Grady was wrong. Maybe the bus would bypass the Aggies and head on into Bolton. But he had to know. He couldn't just keep making and breaking plans on a whim – not when his life depended on it.

'Hello.' He came up next to the passenger at the front. 'I need to know . . .'

The words died in his throat.

The guy was early middle-aged, with short, spiky, grey hair and a bristle-covered jaw. He wore a brown uniform, but the tunic, which had bus driver identification badges down its left lapel, hung open on a crumpled, spittle-stained shirt. His eyes, reddened with broken capillaries, bugged horribly from their sockets, and his mouth, still coated with bloody froth, yawned at impossible width. As the bus changed direction again, his head lolled, exposing a livid bruise, so purple in parts that it was almost black, completely encircling his neck.

Even though O'Grady had seen death before, he couldn't help screaming. It wasn't so much the horror of what had been done to this guy, it was the horror of what it meant.

He descended the spiral stair in leaps, and at the bottom almost fell over. The bus had now emerged from the housing estate and had already passed the point on Darthill Road where it became Pimbo Lane. They must be doing 50mph, the vehicle rattling and banging and bouncing over dips in the road. O'Grady staggered towards the front, shouting incoherently, where, to his astonishment, he saw that the driver was a young girl, no more than nineteen years old. She wore black military-style apparel, her blonde hair hanging in sweaty ringlets over a face that was puffy and swollen.

'What in God's name?' he shouted, unsure whether he could be heard through the Perspex wall shielding her from the passenger area.

She grinned slyly as she turned the heavy wheel, the bus

screeching around a wide bend. It was all O'Grady could do not to fall full length. He steadied himself and shouted at her again. 'Stop this crate! Stop this damn crate!'

She didn't even look at him, just grinned all the more.

He pulled the Taurus and pointed it at her with both hands. 'Stop this bus now, or I'll kill you.'

She ignored him. She wasn't to know that he lacked bullets, of course, but maybe was taking a chance that the Perspex had been reinforced against robbers and other hoodlums. Only a narrow slot, where money was exchanged, allowed actual access, and that was at waist-level, so he could hardly point a gun through that.

'*Stop the damn bus, you bitch!*'

Again, as often had been the case in O'Grady's life when his blood was up, he made errors. On this occasion, as he raged at her and hammered the butt of the pistol on the Perspex, he didn't notice the drape on the under-stair baggage compartment slither back and a second female slide out from it while at the same time drawing a taut wire from the big, chunky 'KGB watch' that she'd purchased on the Dark Web.

He only realised she was there at all when she looped the high-tensile necklace over his head – and cinched it tight.

Chapter 32

'Lucy, you going home?'

Lucy saw Stan Beardmore crossing the hospital car park towards her. The truth was, she wasn't sure whether she was going home or not. She glanced at the Mondeo she'd taken from the CID car pool earlier. She supposed she'd been about to get into it, but Mick Shallicker had only dropped her off two minutes ago, and she was still in a daze.

'I'm sorry, Stan . . . what?'

'I said, are you going home?'

'Erm . . . maybe.'

'And maybe not.' He seemed uncharacteristically flustered. 'I'm sorry about this, Luce, but none of us are going home yet.'

'Okay . . .'

'You've heard there's been another shooting?'

'Erm . . . no.'

'It's almost certainly a sequel to the one at the restaurant. Gunshots reported in the vicinity of the bus station, no actual details. But the firearms unit who were on their way here have now been diverted there.'

'Okay . . .'

'You all right?'

Lucy was still so fazed by the revelations of the last few hours, and the new round of subterfuge it would plunge her into, that the full gravity of the DI's words hadn't yet struck home.

'Yeah, sure . . . it's just been a long day.'

'Well, like I say, we've no firearms on the plot at present, so I'm getting extra uniforms in to cover the hospital perimeter. I could use you too, so get it together. *Come on then.*'

She hadn't noticed that he was already walking back towards the hospital. She followed him, trying to put everything else out of her mind, though it wasn't easy.

'I thought it'd kick off as soon as I heard it was McCracken who'd been shot,' he said.

'Have you let Mr Mullany know?' Lucy asked. Chief Superintendent Charles Mullany was November Division's overall commander.

'I have,' Beardmore confirmed. 'For all the bloody use he'll be.'

'Should help us get everyone mobilised more quickly.'

'Yeah, when he eventually gets here.'

They rounded the corner of the building. It was vaguely disconcerting, now that Lucy knew what was happening, to see no police presence in front of the Intensive Care entrance.

'Brentwood and Tooley are checking the other doors,' Beardmore said, as though reading her thoughts. 'This place is a sieve in security terms. At least one of them's coming back here at the first opportunity, though, to give you support. In the meantime, go through into ICU. It's got an internal security door, which works. You don't have to let anyone in you don't like the look of.'

'Is there a way through to IC from other parts of the hospital?' Lucy asked.

'Yeah, but, like I say, we're currently making sure everything's locked down.'

They entered by the main door and walked through the waiting area, passing the chairs where Lucy had held her tense conflab with Cora.

'We've still not updated the news outlets on McCracken's progress,' Beardmore said. 'As far as they know, he could be stone dead. That's probably a good thing. Lessens the chances of whoever hit him the first time coming back for another pop. Least, I hope it does.'

The night nurse, whose name badge read 'Janice Reynoldson', was waiting on the other side of the glass door. On seeing Beardmore, she hit a buzzer and the door clicked open. Beardmore passed through, Lucy in tow. He made sure to close the door behind them.

'Janice,' he said, 'this is DC Lucy Clayburn. I'm posting her in here with you till we get additional units. You okay with that?'

Nurse Reynoldson looked wide-eyed and frightened but nodded.

'Like I said before,' Beardmore added, 'the chances of anyone turning up here are highly unlikely. No one even knows that McCracken and his lady friend are being cared for in this unit. So all you guys need to do is make sure they don't find out. Any phone-calls, don't say anything. If there are any, they'll most likely be the press – and they'll be easily dissuaded, because they'll be trying every hospital in Manchester, just to see. If anyone *does* turn up here, anyone you're not sure about . . . in fact anyone at all who *you* don't recognise, Lucy, don't let them in. It's that simple.'

'Suppose, I mean . . .' Nurse Reynoldson's eyes widened even more as she wrestled with the potential problems that might still arise. 'I mean . . . if they've got guns?'

Beardmore turned to the glass door. 'Is this thing shock-proof?'

'Yes,' the nurse said. 'I mean, if someone bangs a trolley into it, or throws a chair. But bullets . . . I don't know.'

'It's very unlikely it'll come to that.' But Beardmore's expression was grave, and he hadn't summoned a police firearms team to the hospital for nothing.

'If someone tries to shoot their way in here, it won't happen quickly,' Lucy cut in. 'We'll easily have time to get on the blower.'

'That's true,' the DI agreed. 'Okay . . . I'm going to find out what everyone else is doing.' He buzzed the door back open and stepped out into the waiting area. 'You've got an alarm button behind your desk, I take it, Janice?'

She nodded again.

'Good . . . don't hesitate if anything bothers you. I know that'll only call your own security personnel, but they can get a message to us quickly.'

'But we won't need to,' Lucy said, attempting reassurance. 'I promise you, Janice . . . no one in the history of Britain has ever tried to shoot their way into a hospital.'

Beardmore nodded again, pleased that Lucy was taking charge, then walked away. Lucy shut the glass door behind him and ensured that it was closed properly.

She turned back to the nurse. 'Any chance of a coffee, or something?'

The nurse regarded her with a strange kind of fascination, as if she couldn't quite believe that Lucy was being so calm.

'Seriously,' Lucy said. 'It's the middle of the night and I've been on all day. I need something to pep me up.'

Still not smiling, the nurse nodded and sidled around her desk, passing through a door into a back room. Lucy turned and scanned the reception area. It wasn't hugely different from other parts of hospitals she'd visited: pale cream-coloured walls, a floor that was tiled in light green, handwash

310

dispensers at every corner. The air was scented with disinfectant, but it wasn't overpowering.

Right of the nurse's station, an archway led into a darkened passage. Signposts above it pointed in various directions, reading *Neonatal*, *Paediatric*, *Coronary*. But to the left, the corridor passed a number of doorways, most of which stood open on well-lit rooms. Lucy strolled to the first one and glanced inside. Even with everything she knew and felt about Frank McCracken, it was a shock to see him propped up on a pillow between banks of machines. His face was pale, his eyes sunken and closed. A breathing tube had been inserted into his nostril, while a drip fed painkillers and antibiotics into his arm.

She advanced a couple of steps. The room was windowless and warm, but blankets had been drawn up to the patient's bare chest, revealing that the top of his left shoulder and the left side of his neck were buried under a mountain of gauze and surgical padding. A slow steady *bleep* from one of the monitors sounded as if it meant that everything was okay so far.

She went back into the reception area. There was no sign of Nurse Reynoldson, though what sounded like a kettle was bubbling. Lucy glanced through the glass door, happy to see the waiting area still deserted.

'Can I help you?' a voice asked.

She spun around, to be confronted by a burly, beefy-faced man with bright red hair, wearing black trousers and a white, open-collared shirt with black epaulettes on the shoulders.

Lucy flashed her warrant card. 'DC Clayburn.'

'Oh.' He didn't look relieved to discover that she was a police officer. No doubt, on hearing that a cop would be posted on this door, he'd been hoping for someone a little more like himself. 'Hawcroft. Hospital security. Bit of a mess, isn't it?'

311

'Could be worse,' Lucy replied. 'We've no fatalities yet.'

'Hmm.' Again, he seemed unimpressed – he was probably struggling to work out how Frank McCracken being dead was a worse scenario than Frank McCracken being alive.

'How many guys have you got on site?' Lucy asked.

'Well . . . there's just me on this wing, while the rest are spread around the whole hospital. I mean, it's nights, plus it's midweek, so we've not got as many staff on as usual. To be honest, this is the least vulnerable area.' He pointed into the unlit section of corridor. 'Our office is about fifty yards around that corner. I only came out to see who you were because I spotted you on one of our surveillance screens.'

'How many patients have we got in ICU at present?'

'Erm . . .' He sounded unsure. 'Four, I think.'

That wasn't as many as it could have been, she thought, which was probably a good thing.

'Just to let you know,' he said. 'There'll be staff coming and going during the night. These patients require regular treatment, medication and so on.'

'It's okay.' Lucy moved back along the passage towards the patients' rooms. 'I'll get in the way as little as possible.'

'Like I say, I'm just around the corner if you need me,' he said.

She nodded, walking slowly, checking each room. All the patients were the same: lost under bandages, facemasks, breathing apparatus and such, each deeply unconscious, their vital signs constantly monitored. There weren't four of them, as it turned out, but three, counting McCracken. It didn't look as if Carlotta Powell had been brought here yet. She might still be in surgery, for all Lucy knew. The last room was empty. Beyond that, at the end of the corridor stood a frosted-glass fire-door, which was locked and alarmed. Everything seemed to be satisfactory so far.

'DC Clayburn!' a panicky voice called. It sounded like Janice Reynoldson. '*DC Clayburn!*'

Lucy hurried back down the passage.

The night nurse had appeared from the back room and now stood rigid behind her desk, a mug of coffee in either hand, staring at the glass door. Lucy sensed the group of figures on the other side of it before she even saw them. Six men, all in suits, all of them brutish and scar-faced, a couple pulling on black leather gloves.

'Hit the alarm,' Lucy said. 'Call Officer Hawcroft back!'

'I don't know any Officer Hawcroft,' the nurse stammered.

'Your security chief.'

The nurse looked appalled. 'We don't have an Officer Hawcroft. Imran's in the security booth tonight.'

'Shit!' Lucy was both furious and astounded that she'd been duped so easily.

She swung back to face the entrance, but the buzzer had already been surreptitiously pressed, and the door was open by a centimetre or so. She lurched forward, but it was now swinging open. Her eyes flickered up to the figures on the other side, and finally fixed on the man standing at the front of them.

Lucy knew him well, even though she'd never met him.

That tall, lean physique; that fuzz of wire-wool hair; those square-framed spectacles over eyes that were more like steel rivets.

'Having a coffee, are we?' Wild Bill Pentecost said in his slow, cold monotone. 'Oh dear . . . and you're supposed to be looking after my friend.'

Chapter 33

'I'm sorry, Mr Pentecost,' Lucy said. 'But you can't come in.'

But all six were already in, the door having closed behind them. They stood in a tight group, as though on hostile ground, eyes circling the reception area for cameras and the like. Their fake security guard, Hawcroft or whatever his real name was, didn't reappear; doubtless he was already threading back through the hospital, intent on leaving the same way he'd come in. Nurse Reynoldson remained behind her desk, each hand still clutching a mug of coffee, rigid with fear.

Having thoroughly surveyed the place, Pentecost switched his attention to Lucy. 'I'm afraid you have the advantage of me, my dear?'

She flipped her wallet open. 'Detective Constable Clayburn. Crowley CID.'

'*Constable* . . .? I see.' He took a step towards her, his men following. 'You sure you're not exceeding your authority here?'

'I doubt it, sir.' Lucy had backed up involuntarily, but now came to a deliberate standstill. 'The patient you've come to visit is under police protection and needs to be kept in complete isolation. On top of that, he's sedated. So, there's not much good you can do in here, assuming that was your intention.'

'My, my . . .' He eyed her closely. 'What a barbed comment.'

'No offence was intended, sir. But I have a job to do, and I'll do it.'

'Just like a good little soldier . . . except there's a problem. If you know who I am, you should also know that I'm much more to Mr McCracken than a mere business partner . . .'

He advanced again, his men coming on behind him. Lucy had no option but to shuffle backward along the corridor. The doorway to her father's room was already only a couple of yards behind her.

'I'm actually a rather close acquaintance,' Pentecost said, treating her to a smile that was transparently fake. 'And I'm sure you'll find, if you bother to make contact with your inner female, that stepping aside here would be perfectly okay. That it couldn't do any harm . . . that it would be nothing more than an act of everyday human kindness.'

A real hospital security guard now showed up from the darkened corridor, no doubt in response to the alarm that Nurse Reynoldson had activated with her foot. He was a young Asian guy, balding on top but with a thick black beard. Doubtless, this was Imran, the guy the night nurse had referred to. He was tall and well-built, but two of Pentecost's accomplices swung around to face him, bringing him to an enforced halt.

'The answer's still no, Mr Pentecost, sir,' Lucy said, hoping the severe mask she wore would conceal the fact that underneath she was shaking like a leaf. 'In fact, you and your friends shouldn't even be in this area. So I'll have to ask you to vacate the Intensive Care suite altogether.' She pointed at the glass door. 'If you'd like to go out the way you came in.'

Pentecost regarded her with genuine, if chilling, interest. 'Clayburn, did you say?'

'That's right, sir.'

'That name sounds familiar.'

'It's possible we've had contact in the past, you being who you are and me being who I am.'

He came forward again with a slow, steady gait. Before Lucy knew it, she'd backed into the very doorway of the room where McCracken lay unconscious. She had to make a stand *here*. Whatever else happened, she couldn't retreat past this point.

'Clearly it wasn't close contact,' Pentecost said. 'Otherwise you'd know that grandstanding like this is very ill-advised.'

'Just doing my duty, sir. Now, if you and your friends would like to leave—'

'Fuck this bitch!' one of Pentecost's thugs snapped.

He looked younger than the others, and had a mop of unruly blond hair, but was hugely built under his tight-fitting suit. He lurched forward with fierce, leonine aggression. Lucy grabbed at the tray of surgical instruments on top of the trolley just inside the room and snatched up a scalpel.

'One more step, pretty boy, and I'll stripe that face till your mum wouldn't know it!'

'*Burke!*' Pentecost snapped, his voice a whip-crack.

The blond guy obeyed immediately, but his attack had faltered anyway, his eyes locked on the blade Lucy hefted at him.

Fleetingly, she'd even surprised herself. Did she really care so much about her father? She tried to deny that possibility, to insist to herself that she was simply following orders here, keeping the witness isolated.

And that involves pulling a knife?

She held her ground, anyway. The chances were slim that they'd try to hurt McCracken in a public place like this, but suddenly, and for whatever reason, she was absolutely damned if these scumbags were going anywhere near him.

'Well, well,' Pentecost said. 'Aren't we the feisty one? And aren't we maybe overstepping the mark a little bit? A group of concerned citizens come to check on the health of an ailing friend and you, a representative of the Greater Manchester Police, threaten them with violence.'

'I imagine you understand other languages, Mr Pentecost,' she replied. 'But I can't be completely sure.'

'Now you're just being impertinent.'

'Mr McCracken is doing well. He's had minor surgery, which apparently was completely successful, and he's expected to make a full recovery.' She lowered the scalpel, but not very far. 'I don't think there's anything else you can do here, do you?'

He remained blank, unemotional. But now there was something else there, an additional iciness as he appraised her. Lucy could tell that she'd finally angered him.

'You know,' he said, 'one of the things that strong, independent women like you haven't bargained for in this age of equal opportunities is that if you're going to behave like men, you must expect to be treated like men . . . Detective Constable Clayburn of Crowley CID.'

'That's right, sir . . .' She drew courage from a flickering blue light suddenly reflecting into the waiting area. 'I told you who I am and where I can be found in the full knowledge you'd remember it very well. Which ought to indicate how much I think your threats are worth.'

'Really?'

'You're not untouchable, yourself, sir. Mr McCracken is the living proof. But I'll tell you something . . . if it was down to me, I *would* step aside. Neither would I bother pursuing the guy who pulled the trigger on your friend. Because to me you're all the same . . .' And now she couldn't

317

help herself, all the pent-up frustration, rage and disappointment at the way both her professional and her emotional lives had gone in the last two years pouring out like bile. 'You people are vermin dressed in three-piece suits. A bunch of rodents fattening yourselves off the backs of those who actually work for a living. I'd like nothing better than to see you tear each other to pieces. I'd *pay* to watch that. But unfortunately, I value my job more than I value your deaths. So as much as it pains me, Mr Pentecost, *sir*, I'm not going to move away from this post, and you are going nowhere –' she gestured with the scalpel '– except back through that door. Right bloody now.'

Before Pentecost or any of his mob could respond, several figures appeared behind the glass door. The one at the front was Stan Beardmore. Nurse Reynoldson, seeing that help was finally here, broke abruptly from her trance, slammed the mugs down onto her desk, coffee shooting everywhere, and hurried around it, crossing the corridor at speed, hitting the buzzer with her fist.

Beardmore burst in, followed by Dave Baker, PCs Tooley and Brentwood, and a couple of other uniforms who'd only just arrived. Even the DI blanched a little at the sight of Bill Pentecost and his heavies, but the balance of power had shifted. The gangster tried to look as if none of this mattered, but visibly tensed as the coppers circled around them.

'Everything all right, DC Clayburn?' Beardmore said, standing alongside Lucy, the rest of the officers lined up behind him in a phalanx.

'Certainly is, sir,' she said. 'Mr Pentecost and his friends were just leaving.'

Pentecost returned Beardmore's gaze with blood-freezing intensity.

'You need to go, Mr Pentecost,' Beardmore said simply.

'This is the Intensive Care Unit. The staff here have got important work to do.'

A brief silent tension followed, during which Lucy fancied it was possible to hear the wheels and gears of Bill Pentecost's slow-grinding rage.

'Well done, DC Clayburn,' he finally said. It was barely a mumble, but they heard it. 'You've certainly earned your pay tonight. You go off now and make sure you enjoy it.'

He turned towards the door, his cronies parting for him and then falling into line behind him. Before he left, the blond one hawked up a wad of phlegm and spat it on the floor.

Only when the door closed behind them, the electronic catch thudding into place, did the police relax. Breaths were exhaled, helmets removed from sweat-soaked heads. Lucy felt like a marionette with its strings cut; she was ready to collapse.

'You okay?' Beardmore asked her.

She nodded but couldn't speak.

'You can put that down now, if you want.' He nodded at the scalpel, which she hadn't realised she was still clutching in her right hand.

'Sorry, Stan,' she stammered. 'I need to sit.'

'I'm not surprised. You did well.' He put an arm around her shoulders and squeezed. 'You did very well indeed. Have a minute in there.' He nodded into McCracken's room, to one of the two armchairs alongside the bed. 'I'll try and find out what happened.'

'There was a phoney security guard,' she said. 'He let them in, but he's probably already gone.'

'We need to make sure he's not still here somewhere. You get yourself sorted. But only for a minute . . . we need to be way sharper than we have been. At least Firearms are en route. Should be here in the next five.'

'What about the shooting in town?'

'Your guess is as good as mine. They couldn't find anything. In the meantime, we've got to lock this place down properly . . .'

While Beardmore strode off along the corridor, shouting orders, Lucy meandered into the room, threw the scalpel on the tray, and all but fell into one of the armchairs. Briefly, she was so physically enfeebled that she didn't know if she could lift a hand in front of her face.

'Well,' a croaky voice said. 'Standing up to the boss of bosses. Life doesn't send many tougher challenges than that.'

Lucy glanced at the bed, where McCracken's eyes were open, though they were dull and watery. He'd barely moved from his previous position and was still cadaverously pale.

'You were awake?' she asked him.

'Only partially,' he said. 'Don't think I'd have been much use to you. Besides, I was enjoying watching you look out for your old man.'

'That wasn't what it was.'

'You sure?' He cracked a pained smile. 'Thought you'd be happy watching us rodents eat each other . . . till it came to your dad, and then it was a different story, wasn't it?'

'I'm a police officer,' she hissed. 'I have a duty to protect.'

'Keep telling yourself that . . .'

'Don't you bloody tell me what I think and believe!'

'Doubt you'd be this upset if there wasn't a grain of truth in it. But if it's any consolation, love . . .' He tried to adjust position, cringing with pain. 'If it's a consolation, Wild Bill was probably only here to do what he said . . . check out the health of a colleague. At a time when the press wouldn't be around. So, if it *was* about doing your duty . . . it was a brave but wasted effort.'

'Yeah, well, I wouldn't get too carried away with how clever you are,' she said. 'It can't go on, this – me keeping my mouth shut, watching my colleagues run around banging their heads on brick walls while I pretend I don't know stuff. The first opportunity I get, I'm going to tell my boss exactly what my and your relationship is. And I'll take any consequences that come my way.'

He seemed too agonised to be overly concerned. 'There won't be much down for you on the promotion front.'

'You think I care? I'm happy being a detective constable . . . or at least I would be, if I wasn't always feeling that I'm playing for the other side.'

'No one asked you to do anything for us, Lucy.'

'Christ's sake, Dad . . . *caring* about you is too much. We should be enemies. I shouldn't give a shit about you.'

'And how will telling your gaffers improve that situation?'

'At least then everyone will know their limits. They'll know what I can and can't be asked to do, and why.'

He rolled his eyes towards her, though even that seemed to hurt him. 'So . . . you're happy to be compromised, to say, "Hey lads, I can't be trusted."'

'Damn it, Dad!' she half-shouted. 'I *can't* be trusted! Not by the people who really matter to me. *You* might be able to live with something like that. But I can't. Not any more.'

'In my case it won't be about whether I can live with it as much as whether I'll be allowed to live. Like you said before, you tell your lot and word will have got to our lot in half a day.'

'I know,' she said. 'And I'm sorry.'

'You understand what that means, Lucy? I'm stuck here for at least another week. I'll be a sitting duck.'

She stood up, torn with frustration. 'They're not going to kill you because of this.'

He forced a chuckle. 'You've just met Wild Bill. Do you want to reconsider that statement?'

321

Suddenly, she was too weary to argue further. 'I don't have to say anything straight away.'

'So I get a head-start? Good, that's something. Question is, will it be sufficient to get your mum to a place of safety?'

'Oh, now . . . don't give me *that*.'

'Don't give you what? If they can't get me, who do you think they'll go after instead?'

'That's bollocks.'

'You reckon? There's no point going after Charlie. From what I've overheard, she'll be in here a lot longer than me. Might as well be the next woman in my life.'

'You're a lying bastard!'

'The truth is, Lucy –' he gave her a frank but hollow stare '– I don't know whether they will or won't. But you've got to consider the possibility.'

'If it comes down to it, *I'll* protect Mum.'

'Yeah. You and that army of lads who suddenly won't trust you any more.'

'I'm not debating it with you.' She stormed from the room.

'There won't be any debate,' he called after her, wincing again. 'There won't be time for that.'

Chapter 34

He hadn't been a bobby for very long, but this was undoubtedly the worst job that Malcolm Peabody had ever been allocated. It wasn't so much the stench of the landfill, cloying though it was – to an extent, he'd acclimatised to that by now. Or the all-pervading darkness – he had the torch that Lucy had brought him. Or even the loneliness; he'd been posted out here now, alongside the dog-pit, for ten hours, and hadn't seen or heard from a living soul – but that was often a copper's lot.

It was the boredom.

Sitting around waiting for something to happen was not exactly unusual in police work. But most officers, if they were on an obbo or stakeout, would try to get on with some paperwork, or study for their next exam. But neither of those options was available at present. He'd tried playing games on his phone but had soon become worried by how quickly it was running the battery down. As his radio battery was already out of juice, if he lost the phone as well he'd be completely cut off out here.

Of course, all this had been exacerbated enormously, because he'd been due to finish at three o'clock, but at five-to had received a phone-call from the night shift duty officer, Inspector Robertson, who'd told him that they couldn't spare anyone for another couple of hours as there'd been major incidents across the division.

'Thanks for this, Lucy,' he muttered as he wandered up and down on trampled garbage, his feet occasionally crunching through into soft, stagnant mulch. 'Now I'm here till five.'

He glanced irritably at his watch. It showed less than a couple of minutes' advance since the last time he'd checked it.

'Christ,' he muttered.

A couple of times, he'd tried to get himself comfortable on one of the old chairs set up yesterday afternoon by Sister Cassie's weird congregation. But most were broken or lopsided, and those that weren't sank into the grime when he applied his weight to them. He couldn't even sit on the ground. God alone knew what he might discover if he did that: broken glass, a nail, a syringe, at the very least slimy filth.

So he had to keep walking, plodding around the outside of the incident tape. But it wasn't a big area they'd cordoned off, forty yards by forty, and he could pull an entire circuit only to find that he'd be back where he'd started in less than half a minute. He tried to figure out how many circuits he'd have to make before his relief showed up, but that was impossible given that he didn't know exactly when his relief was due. It was supposed to be sometime around five o'clock, but it could just as easily be half-past five or half-past six. Everything depended on what these big events taking place on the division actually were.

'They'd better be bloody big,' he mumbled.

Once or twice he thought he heard something and stopped to listen. Usually, it was the screech of a hunting owl, or the distant rattling crash of a night train. But occasionally it was harder to pin down.

The first time, it was a heavy, hollow clatter, like some large metal drum being overturned. It echoed across the desolate ridges of the landfill, but it was loud, indicating that it hadn't originated far away. Peabody stood rigid by the incident tape, wondering who might be so close. It was only to be expected that there'd be scavengers around. There was little here that looked to be of value, but tip-pickers were a breed, and they were more likely to come at night, because technically they were committing theft. The second time, it was slightly more sinister: what sounded like a rasping, snickering laugh. That time, Peabody turned his Maglite on and swept it up and down the slopes of refuse. He saw nothing odd, but there'd been something determined and intentional about that laugh – as if he'd been supposed to hear it, or as if whoever it was hadn't cared whether he'd heard it or not.

A little unnerved, Peabody trudged back up the path. It was now more defined because of Lucy's comings and goings on her Ducati, which had ploughed a visible trail. He followed it back through the canyon between the piles of boxes, all the way to the desiccated tree where the eyeless doll was hanging. He shone his light around again, pausing several times on unidentifiable shapes, though almost always they became recognisable eventually: heaps of rubbish bags, rust patterns on abandoned fridges, twists of thorny weed hung with tatters. He allowed the torch to linger on the track that led back towards the landfill offices, wishing he could simply head over there, though it would take a good fifteen to twenty minutes.

Peabody realised that he was sweating, and he wondered why he'd bothered putting his gloves and anorak on. Still no rain had fallen, and when he gazed up, he saw stars rather than clouds. If anything, the waterproof was making him hotter and damper. He pulled his gloves off, followed by the anorak, scrunching it up so that he could carry it in one fist as he headed back. Just as he reached the top of the depression, there was a crackle behind him, like the snapping of a rotted branch.

He spun around, dropping his torch, and scrabbled frantically for it around his feet. As he did, he glanced up; no immediate cause of the sound was obvious, but he now realised that he could see the full length of the cleft between the heaps of boxes without using his light. He glanced east, to a hummocky horizon previously banded with indigo but now turning pale violet.

It wasn't exactly dawn, but at least things were going the right way.

He glanced at his watch, which told him that it was shortly after four. He'd still be stuck here for the best part of another hour, maybe longer, but if the darkness was gradually receding, that would be an improvement.

Despite this, he stumbled on his way back down the slope, and when he tried to right himself, his left foot slid along a moss-slicked sheet of cardboard, landing him hard on his thigh. It didn't hurt, but it infuriated him.

'Dickhead,' he muttered, as he got up and plodded on down to the bottom.

He was soon back by the tent, which rustled in the breeze. He glanced at it, and then up to the rim of the depression on its eastern side – and started violently.

The figure of a man was silhouetted on the gradually paling sky.

Peabody switched his torch on again, but powerful though the Maglite was, the beam didn't reach far enough. Whoever the guy was, he was about sixty yards away.

'Hello?' Peabody shouted, circling around the taped-off area. 'Who are you, please?' There was no response. The

326

figure remained indistinct and motionless. 'You need to clear this area. This is an official crime scene.'

The figure remained where it was.

Peabody was angry rather than alarmed. Primarily at himself. He'd stayed as sharp as he could, and he'd still let this creep sneak up on him. Not only that, he'd told him to get his arse out, and the guy wasn't moving. Did he carry such little authority?

'PC Peabody!' he said, tromping uphill, his heavy feet crunching the trash.

The figure still didn't move, though now the torch was picking him out. Peabody saw a grey suit, a white shirt, a green tie, dark hair – and a weirdly marked face.

'What the . . .?' he breathed. And then he smiled to himself. This was a wind-up of some sort.

Back when he'd been a probie, he'd been subject to all kinds of mickey-taking, as they all were, of course. There was never a trick too nasty or scary for older coppers to play on younger ones, or that they didn't find hilariously funny afterwards. He'd hoped all that was past him now, but apparently not. Except that he'd be surprised if anyone found this situation amusing, and the higher up the slope he ascended, the less amusing it seemed. Because the thinner and stiffer the watching figure seemed to be, the darker its eyes, the more weirdly streaked its face, and . . . the redder its mouth.

'What the fuck?' Peabody said again, this time aloud.

For half a second, he had the horrific notion that a corpse had been propped up. But over the last two or three yards, he realised the truth.

It was a shop mannequin, its suit ragged and filthy, its white shirt not a shirt at all but the mannequin's own polystyrene flesh, its tie a piece of fuzzy-felt, its hair a ratty wig, its face gruesomely plastered with women's makeup.

Peabody halted a couple of feet below the static figure. He half-expected a sniggering copper to come out from behind it. But no one did. The only sound was the rustling and flapping of the forensics tent down in the dip. Cautiously, almost gingerly, he scrambled up the remaining distance until he was face to face with it. When he looked down, he saw that its feet were embedded amid broken, twisted branches.

Okay, so it hadn't happened by accident; someone hadn't just discarded this thing. No doubt there were dozens of such objects scattered across the landfill, but someone must have set this one up deliberately. And in the last half hour or so, because if there was one thing Peabody was certain about, it had not been here earlier.

He circled around it to check the terrain, his light roving down another tilted moonscape. Rusted bikes, thrown-away prams, more newspapers, more bags of household waste. Nothing unexpected. He circled back to the front, staring at the figure's luridly painted features.

If there was one thing Peabody really didn't like it was anything he couldn't figure out – and this was completely unexplainable. No doubt he'd laugh about it tomorrow, but before then, he'd be wondering, for however long it took for his relief to arrive, where this hideous scarecrow had come from. He stepped back, raised his right foot and struck the mannequin's midriff. It was a lightweight thing and went bouncing and rolling down the slope. Still in one piece, but at least, when he returned to the tent, it would be out of his eyeline.

'Good fucking riddance.' He stumped back down into the depression, trying not to wonder if whoever had set it up there had been the person he'd heard laughing.

The one good thing, of course, was the gradual lightening of the sky in the east. Now it was even having an effect down on this lower ground. Both the tape and the tent were clearly visible. Peabody kept his light on anyway, prowling in no particular direction, zigzagging around the central pit, still trying to work out what had just happened. The tent's material, meanwhile, rattled and rustled in the breeze, until it reached the point where it distracted him. He stopped in his tracks and turned to look at it, wondering how strange it was that he hadn't heard such sounds earlier, and how even stranger that he couldn't feel any breeze.

A very ugly realisation struck him.

'Oh . . . crap,' he breathed.

He went through the entryway in the tape as silently as possible, though inevitably he stepped on twigs, crisp wrappers and other bric-a-brac. It was hardly a real issue. Whoever it was, they already knew that he was here.

'All right, enough's enough!' he said sternly, stabbing his light-beam at the flimsy structure. Nothing happened, except that the rustling of movement inside it continued. He yanked the flap back and went in, blasting his torchlight in front of him. 'What in Christ's name are—'

The sentence died instantly.

What seemed like a thousand pin-prick eyes had turned to face him. From all around the dog-pit, not just on its carnage-strewn edges but halfway down and even in the depths of it. Then, with frantic squeals, the rats evacuated, exploding up and out in a volcanic tide of mouldy fur, bloody whiskers and bared buck-teeth. They bolted every which way, under the sides of the tent or out via the exit flap. Peabody could only stand stock-still as they squirmed over and around his shoes, lashing his legs with their tails.

'God . . .' he breathed, sickened to his core. 'Oh, Jeeesus . . .'

It seemed to take an age for the last of them to leave, and before it did, it stopped in the torchlight, hunched and hissing like a demonic, deformed imp, its eyes glimmering, before scurrying out of sight.

He remained in there, so drenched with the stench of rotting dog-flesh that he doubted he'd ever be able to get it out of his clothes, and yet so horrified by what had just happened that he really didn't want to leave. It was a couple of minutes, at least, before he was able to turn and make his way outside, moving like a man intoxicated, barely able to put one foot in front of another. He swayed through the entrance, still nauseated, and even in fresher air found himself teetering, sweat streaming down his body. He staggered on another two dozen yards before jerking back to reality, wondering where the rats might be and if they could be slinking up again.

There was no sign of them when he glanced around, but that didn't satisfy him. He swung his Maglite wildly, trying to cover every inch of ground, turning in drunken, feverish circles. It was only on the fourth revolution that he saw something that shouldn't be there.

A girl's pretty face, close up to his own. Rendered white in the torchlight. Etched with sadistic glee. Pink lips drawn back on feral teeth.

Peabody's shout came out a shocked, unintelligible croak.

It was the last sound he made before a hefty blow smashed into the back of his skull.

'They don't make coppers like they used to.' Ivana toed the unconscious body. 'Scared of a few rats.'

Alyssa emptied the stone out of the sock. 'It was the dummy that did it. Totally threw him off his guard.'

'Soft bastards. When Dad was a lad, they were all ex-Paras fresh from Northern Ireland. They'd give you a good hiding just for gobbing on the pavement.'

'Think we were in time?' Alyssa wondered, nodding at the tent.

'That thing looks second-hand to me. There's no sign the real CSI mob have been here yet.' Ivana hefted forward two of the four six-gallon petrol canisters. They were so bulky and full that when they touched each other, they clattered loudly. 'I mean, how much have they found out? I reckon they've just stumbled across this site. They're probably not sure what it means, or if it means anything. So they stuck a single sentry on it.'

'Poor sod, eh?' Alyssa grabbed the other two canisters. 'Had no idea what he was getting into.'

'We'll worry about him later.'

Alyssa unscrewed one of the metal caps and tipped fuel over the walls of the forensics tent, walking around it so that she got every side. When she'd done that, they both took their canisters inside, and tilted them over the pit itself, rivers of petrol glugging out, glistening their way down into the ossuary below, drenching the twisted, tangled carcasses.

'Use all of it,' Ivana said. 'Make sure it gets right to the bottom. Make sure there's a lake of it down there. We've got to burn every scrap.'

'You don't think they could have linked this to the other jobs?' Alyssa asked.

'Don't see how they could,' Ivana replied. 'But it's weird, isn't it? . . . and they'll be asking lots of questions. Best to get rid properly.'

'You put a torch to a police tent and it'll look even weirder. They'll know for sure that someone was trying to hide something.'

'Yeah, but they won't know what. Whatever line of enquiry this is, Lyssa, it'll end here. Don't fret, doll. They haven't got enough men to worry for long about things that don't make sense.'

When three and two thirds of the four cans were empty, they backtracked outside, Ivana trailing petrol behind them. As she'd calculated, there was just enough to get them forty or so yards beyond the tape. Alyssa then did the honours, dropping a lighted match onto it.

The fire-snake moved swiftly, winding sinuously away from them. When it touched the tent, the whole thing went up in an explosive cloud of flame whose brilliant glare flooded the tortured landscape. But that was nothing compared to the explosion when the flames ate their way down through the mangled canines and hit the lake of fuel at the bottom.

It was Vesuvius, Stromboli and Krakatoa all in one, a glorious upward torrent of flame and smoke, which seared their faces and frazzled their hair.

'Who-hoa!' Alyssa shouted, backing away further, shielding her eyes.

Just as quickly as it had risen, the inferno receded, but not greatly. The tent had all but vanished, only its blackened, blistered framework remaining, but fierce flames still roared from the charnel pit, feasting on bones and decay, the air greasy with the reek of melting, bubbling fat.

Ivana lowered her own hand and nodded, smiling. 'That ought to do it.'

'Hey . . . almost forgot.' Alyssa edged forward, as close as the surging heat would allow her, and hurled the rolled-up newspaper. It disappeared into the conflagration, along with its small front-page story about police spokesmen refusing to comment on rumoured search activities out on the land-fill site at Fairview.

'Good job we saw that,' Ivana said.

'Doesn't matter now.'

'No.'

'Good night's work all round.'

'Yep.'

'Except . . .' Alyssa indicated Peabody lying alongside them. 'What about this one?'

'You gave him a good whack, didn't you? Won't come around for a few minutes yet.'

'Do we want that? Even in a few minutes?'

Ivana frowned. 'What do you mean?'

'What do you think?' Alyssa laughed her eerie, whinnying laugh. 'You said we need to finish the job properly. And he saw you, after all. So . . . let's feed the flames some more.'

Chapter 35

'Okay, gorgeous, up you get,' someone said. 'It's not like you need any beauty sleep.'

At first, Lucy was too fuddled to make sense of things. She sat up in the armchair, blinking, hair hanging over her eyes. Then she realised that the person standing next to her, the one who'd just shaken her by the shoulder, was Priya Nehwal.

The short but authoritative figure, shabby as ever in anorak, faded military-style trousers and trainers, was carrying a plate of buttered toast in one hand and two large mugs of coffee in the other. She nodded towards the door and set off. Lucy got up from the chair still groggy. When she glanced at her watch, it was shortly after seven, which explained why there was an atmosphere of bustle elsewhere in the nick. The night shift would be going home, and the morning shift replacing them.

Yawning, she walked out into the main part of the rec room, where a cleaner was mopping down table-tops, and a couple of the night lads grabbing a game of snooker before they headed home. A smell of bacon issued from the canteen.

Nehwal found a table that had already been cleared and

plonked herself down, indicating that Lucy should pull up a stool. She pushed the plate of toast into the middle and handed Lucy her coffee.

'White without sugar,' she said.

'Erm, yeah . . . thanks, ma'am.' Lucy took a sip; it was hot and tasted like nectar.

'Get stuck into that.' Nehwal nudged the plate. 'We've got a long day ahead.'

Lucy was famished, and it was all she could do not to fall on the breakfast ravenously. 'What are you doing here, ma'am?' she said, munching. 'Do you mind me asking?'

'Well, first of all –' Nehwal took a bite of toast and a slurp of coffee '– I want to know what you and Wild Bill chatted about at the hospital last night.'

'Ahh, right . . . he wanted to get in to see McCracken. I said no.'

'Why?' Nehwal asked, which took Lucy by surprise.

'Well . . . I didn't know what his purpose was. McCracken had already been shot once.'

'Are you familiar with the Crew?'

Lucy was now wide awake and felt nervous about where this conversation was leading. 'Only inasmuch as we all are.'

'Because McCracken and Pentecost are supposed to be thick as thieves. No pun intended.'

'I've heard that, ma'am. I just wondered if something had happened that could have turned them against each other.'

'Well, if it has, and that's possible, it's highly unlikely that the Chairman of the Crew's board of directors would deliver the death message personally. But I reckon you did the right thing. It's anyone's guess what would have happened in there. It was brave of you. Just out of interest, did you speak to McCracken?'

'Yes,' Lucy admitted, wondering if they were coming to the crux of it. Had someone overheard her conversation with her father, and did they all now know her dirty little secret? 'But he was out of it . . . hadn't really come around from the anaesthetic.'

'Say anything interesting?'

'Not really. Congratulated me on standing up to his boss. Said that he'd probably only turned up to check on an injured friend.'

It was only a partial lie, but again something inside Lucy twisted, left her feeling depressed as well as worried about the strange, intangible world she'd somehow slipped into, this limbo between law and disorder.

Nehwal nodded, seeming to accept this. 'He didn't say anything about who he thought might have shot him?'

'Nothing like that, ma'am. I'd have reported that already.'

The DSU munched more toast. 'I might as well put you in the picture fully. Something happened in the early hours of this morning, which, frankly, only an idiot would not connect to the McCracken shooting. A stolen bus was found burning on wasteland down near the old Bleachworks. You know that place?'

Lucy nodded. 'The bottom end of the Aggies. Where the colliery used to be.'

'That's right. Well, the Fire Brigade managed to put it out, but inside they found two male bodies. The bus driver, and another one whom we've now identified as a former police officer called Miles O'Grady.'

Lucy shook her head. 'Don't know him.'

'He was dismissed several years ago on corruption charges. Been working as a private eye ever since. The main thing is, it seems that he was in possession of an unlicensed firearm, which might very well be the same weapon that fired those shots into McCracken and his girlfriend. It's currently under-going tests. More important, though, Lucy, especially where *you're* concerned, is that, though the post mortems haven't been completed yet, and it'll take a bit of time as the bodies were badly charred, there's a clear indication that both men were garrotted with some kind of neck-wire.'

Lucy sat up sharply, but Nehwal was still talking.

'Now, is it my imagination or did you say something to me on the phone yesterday about one of the dead dogs you found on the landfill having been garrotted with wire?'

'I did say that,' Lucy replied. 'A few of them, in fact. Ma'am, does this mean—'

Nehwal raised her palm. 'Let's not rush ahead of ourselves. It's still tenuous. But it's now looking possible that the abduction of Harry Hopkins and Lorna Cunningham could be connected to a double murder. So, as SIO, the first thing I'm doing is having you and your oppos on the abduction case attached to the murder enquiry. Don't worry, I'll fix it with Stan. In addition, I'm arranging for a full CSI team to examine that dog burial site out on the landfill—'

'You might want to hold your horses on that,' a voice intruded.

They turned and saw Stan Beardmore approaching. He was sallow-faced from lack of sleep and wore a grim expression.

'Okay,' Nehwal said. 'Why?'

The DI looked at Lucy first. 'Apologies that no one told you about this sooner, but I've only just been told myself. It seems that doggie-grave, or whatever it was, has been incinerated.'

Lucy stood up. 'I don't get it.'

'Someone drowned it in petrol and put a match to it.'

'I put a guard on it. It was being watched all night.'

He shook his head. 'Because of the extra security we needed at the hospital, not to mention the extra bodies needed at Crowley Old Hall, the bus station and then down on the Aggies, Nights had no one available.'

'In that case, Malcolm Peabody should have stayed on,' Lucy retorted. 'He had orders to stay there until he was relieved.'

'PC Peabody's on his way to hospital,' Beardmore said. 'Seems the morning shift *did* have someone to spare, and they're the ones who found him.'

'What happened?'

'Sorry, Lucy. You know as much as I do.'

'Mum, it's me,' Lucy said.

'I thought it might be,' came the humourless voice at the other end of the line.

'Look . . .' Lucy glanced around. She was in the personnel car park, waiting by Priya Nehwal's metallic beige Lexus RX. There was no sign of the DSU as yet, so she felt free to talk. 'I want you to stay away from the hospital.'

'Do you indeed.'

'Mum, this really isn't a game.'

'Already, Lucy?' Cora's tone tautened. 'It's not nine o'clock in the morning yet, and I'm already on the end of another of your officious lectures.'

'Mum . . . if you won't listen to me, at least listen to the facts. There was a double murder in Crowley last night. Two men were strangled and burned. Very likely, in fact almost certainly, it was retaliation for what happened to your beloved Frank McCracken. And it might not end there.'

Cora greeted this with shocked silence.

'These are very dangerous people,' Lucy said. 'And Dad's as bad as any of them. I'm terrified that if you get re-involved with this man, you'll end up getting hurt. Maybe worse.'

'Lucy . . .' Cora's voice had changed slightly. There was less annoyance there now. 'I know you don't remember it, but . . . well, I was part of that world once.'

'No, Mum . . . you weren't. You were a stripper in a sleazy

338

nightclub. Everything's got a lot worse since then, especially where Dad's concerned. Back then, his job meant throwing drunks out. It's a thousand million times more violent now.'

Lucy was still stunned that she was having this conversation. The mere thought that Frank McCracken might even be vaguely interested in recommencing a relationship with middle-aged ex-flame Cora seemed surreal, if not downright ludicrous, except that he'd been so ambivalent when Lucy had laid it on the line for him.

'How is he anyway?' Cora asked.

'He had minor surgery last night, but he's okay. He was talking a short time after.'

A faint sigh sounded.

'Can't you just stay away?' Lucy begged her. 'For a couple of days, at least. I mean, St Winifred's is a hive of police officers at present. DSU Nehwal's on the case. She *knows* you're my mother, and if she spots you hanging around, she'll want to know why.'

'I can't help how I feel, Lucy.'

'I know that, but . . . he just isn't the man he was. You were a daft girl then, Mum, and he was a daft lad. Trust me, so much has changed . . . and much, much for the worse.'

Another sigh, this one deeper, more heartfelt. 'I'll stay away.'

Lucy closed her eyes with relief.

'But only for a day or so. He sent me those flowers and birthday wishes, Lucy. He's the only man who's done anything like that for me in the last thirty years. I have to go and check on him at some point.'

'Okay, fair enough.' Lucy didn't like that caveat but supposed she could work with it. 'Just be careful when you do. Make sure there's no one around who knows you.'

'I'll try.'

She'll try. Wonderful . . .

The station's personnel door banged closed. Lucy turned, and saw Nehwal approaching, digging into her capacious pockets, presumably for her car keys.

'I've got to go, Mum. I'll call you as soon as I hear something.'

'Thank you.'

Lucy cut the call.

'Everything all right?' Nehwal asked.

'My mum. She heard about the shootings on the news. Wanted to make sure I'm okay.'

Nehwal nodded and climbed in behind the wheel. Lucy slid into the front passenger seat.

'We've heard from St Winifred's,' the DSU said as she drove them out. 'Your pal Peabody's going to be all right.'

'Thank God for that.'

'Someone clouted him with a blunt object. He's had stitches and he's got concussion, but they're letting him out.'

'We'll need to debrief him.'

'I've already sent that message. He might be on sick leave, but he's only going home via Robber's Row.'

As it happened, Malcolm Peabody was the first person they saw on arrival at the hospital. They were in the car park, climbing from the Lexus, when the tall, lanky figure, still in the suit he'd been wearing yesterday, now muddy and crumpled, emerged from A&E with ashen features. He didn't see them at first and walked unsteadily towards the taxi rank. Lucy noticed that the back of his head now sported a huge plaster, and that streaks of brackish, congealed blood lay all down the back of his jacket.

'Malcolm . . . hey, Mal?' she said, approaching.

He turned dazedly, recognising her straight away, but not bothering with his usual cheeky grin. 'Morning, Lucy. Oh, Ma'am . . . how are you?'

'Better than you, by the looks of it,' Nehwal replied.

Up close, he wasn't just pale and pained, he was dirtied by smoke. He'd clearly tried to wash his face but had missed most of his forehead and chin.

'Do you want to tell us what happened?' Lucy said.

'Got walloped from behind. Sorry, but whoever it was, I didn't even hear them coming.'

'Were you paying attention?' Nehwal asked.

'Excuse me, ma'am?' His words were polite, but his tone hovered on the verge of insolence.

'I mean were you tired or did they get the drop on you by using stealth?'

'Could be the difference between a bunch of yobs with nothing else to do, Mal, and something more sinister,' Lucy said.

'Oh right . . .' Now he understood, his expression turning apologetic. 'I thought I saw someone, but I honestly can't remember. There were weird things going on all night, to be honest.'

'What weird things?' Lucy asked.

'Don't worry about that now,' Nehwal cut in. 'You'll have to put all this in a statement, PC Peabody, you understand?'

'Yes, ma'am. Erm . . . when?'

'Now. While it's fresh in your mind.'

Delicately, he touched his left temple. 'Nothing feels very fresh inside here.'

'That's as maybe, but your recollection at present is as good as it's going to get.' She slid her phone from her pocket. 'I'll make a call, get a patrol to take you back to Robber's Row. Afterwards they can take you home, but before then we're setting up the Incident room on the top floor. Go up to it and speak to Detective Sergeant Brannigan from Serious Crimes. Tell her I sent you and to explain the situation.'

He looked puzzled. 'Incident room . . . for a police assault?'

'Kate Brannigan will fill you in properly, after she's taken your statement.'

He nodded as though all that made sense, even though it patently didn't. Nehwal wheeled away from them, speaking into her phone.

'Sorry, Malcolm,' Lucy said.

'Hardly your fault.'

'I'd say you look rough as a badger's arse, but you usually do on earlies.'

'Cheers.' He grimaced slightly. 'When I woke up, I thought I'd died and gone to hell. Swamped in smoke, heat from the fire. Felt like a steamroller had gone over me. I had no phone or radio to call it in, so I tried to walk back. Collapsed halfway. Next thing, there was a uniform there.'

'Least they've patched you up.'

'Yeah, and shot me full of drugs, thanks to which I'm feeling dizzy as shit. I turn too quickly, and I think I'm going to faint. Sick as a dog too. Must have puked up about three times since they brought me in. It was black – from all the smoke I inhaled.'

'It's tough, I agree . . . but I think you were lucky, Malcolm.'

He looked at her askance. 'Is that a joke?'

'No, seriously. Don't ask me why, but for some reason I think you were very lucky indeed.'

Peabody was still eyeing her sceptically about two minutes later, when a patrol car swung into the hospital car park. Without another word, he climbed in and was taken away.

'Now, the real reason we're here,' Nehwal said.

Lucy looked at her. 'Sorry, ma'am . . . the *real* reason?'

Nehwal set off walking. 'I'm assuming he's still in ICU.'

Lucy followed. 'McCracken?'

'Who else?'

Chapter 36

When they reached the ICU entrance, a single uniform was on duty outside. They flashed their warrant cards and he passed them through. At the interior door, the day nurse, also after checking their IDs, buzzed them in. Two firearms officers in full battle-kit, MP5 carbines held across their chests, were standing outside McCracken's room, talking and chuckling together as they sipped from paper cups. They knew Nehwal on sight and nodded to her as they stepped aside.

Inside the room, the gangster looked in better shape than he had done the night before. He'd regained his complexion and was sitting upright, a rack of pillows behind him, his left arm fixed in a sturdy but comfortable-looking sling. A trolley stood to one side, the remnants of his breakfast on top of it. A newspaper lay on the coverlet.

He gave them his trademark wolfish smile. 'And who might you lovely ladies be?'

'You can save the smarm, McCracken.' Nehwal showed her warrant card and stuck it back into her pocket. 'I'm not lovely and she's not a lady . . . she rides a Ducati and she bangs idiots like you in jail for a hobby.'

He glanced from one to the other, his mouth a perfect O. 'Now you've got me intrigued.'

'Actually, we're the ones who're intrigued. I'm Detective Superintendent Nehwal, Serious Crimes Division. This is Detective Constable Clayburn, who once locked you up, you may recall.'

McCracken arched an eyebrow at Lucy, but no light of recognition came into his eyes. 'Sadly . . . it's happened so often.'

'Hey,' Nehwal said. 'It may happen again.'

He frowned. 'Correct me if I'm wrong, but wasn't it *me* who got shot?'

'Yes, but you weren't the only one who got hurt last night, and that's a problem for us.'

'Ah . . . so, do I need to have my solicitor present?'

'I don't think we need to make any of this official just yet. And I think it's safe to say that, whoever did what we're here to talk to you about . . . it wasn't you.'

He shrugged, wincing slightly. 'In that case I'll endeavour to assist you any way I can.'

'Great. So how well do you know Miles O'Grady?'

Again, he looked blankly from one to the other. 'I don't know him at all. Am I supposed to?'

'He's a former police officer,' Nehwal said. 'An ex-detective chief inspector with the Fraud Squad, no less. Three years ago, he was dismissed on suspicion of corrupt practices.'

'Oh dear. Another one, eh?'

'Though we actually suspect he may have been guilty of a whole lot more.'

McCracken tutted. 'The standard of your recruits has taken a real nosedive in recent years.'

'Either way, it's all irrelevant now. Because he's dead.'

'I see.'

Lucy watched McCracken carefully; he expressed only

344

mild surprise and concern at this, which would be the expected response if the deceased was someone he didn't know. But then her father was an expert at playing this game.

'He died last night,' Nehwal said. 'About five hours after you got shot.'

'Well, Manchester's a rough old city these days.'

'He died rather unpleasantly, I'm afraid.'

'Sorry to hear that.' He still didn't seem overly affected.

'We found him in a burnt-out bus.'

He shook his head. 'Disrespect for private property as well . . .'

'Alongside the body of the bus driver.'

There was no immediate chippy response to that. For the first time, Lucy thought she spotted a flicker of emotion on her father's face, a very slight tightening of his features, as if that last bit of info was something he really hadn't wanted to hear. And this, she now realised, was exactly what Nehwal was aiming for. McCracken was an underworld professional. He'd never hesitate to kill if he deemed it necessary, but he wouldn't like collateral damage, because that was always messy.

'Maybe it was just an accident,' he said in a reasonable voice. 'And this O'Grady guy was the last passenger on the last bus home.'

'If only it was that simple,' Nehwal replied. 'Both bodies were extensively burned, but not to such an extent that we couldn't identify the cause of death fairly quickly.'

'I'm sure you're dying to tell me what that was.'

'Strangulation. With some kind of steel wire. There's no question that they both suffered. This was an exemplary kind of hit, wasn't it, Frank?'

He frowned again. 'A hit?'

'Let's not play silly buggers,' Lucy couldn't resist saying.

He regarded her coolly.

345

'Not only exemplary in that it would teach a lesson to anyone else thinking of taking on the Crew,' Nehwal said. 'But also, unintentionally, as a stand-out example of how *not* to do these things.'

He frowned all the more. 'If you say so.'

'What I mean is, Frank . . . we don't just have the bodies, we also have a weapon.'

He remained bemused. 'The steel wire?'

'No,' Nehwal said. 'There was a gun there too. A Taurus .357. It was badly burned, obviously. We'll not lift any prints off it, but there's enough of it left for our ballistics lab to give it a good going-over. See if it matches up with any recent shootings we might be investigating.'

'Like mine, for example.' He smiled. 'Now wait a minute, don't tell me . . . if that gun is the same gun that fired the shots that downed me and Charlie, you will definitely be coming back to talk to me, and on that occasion, I *will* need my solicitor.'

'You seem very relaxed about that,' Lucy said.

'And why shouldn't I be, DC Clayburn? As you yourself have already admitted, I was lying right *here*. There'd be nothing I'd be able to tell you, under caution or otherwise, that I couldn't tell you right now.'

'After you were dumped outside the hospital last night,' Nehwal said, 'before you were taken into surgery, you made a statement that you had no clue who the shooter was.'

He nodded. 'Pretty sure I was hit by the first round. Charlie and I were just getting into the car when someone called my name. I looked, but there wasn't enough light to see who it was. The next thing though, bang-bang. And we both went down.'

'He called your name?' Nehwal said. 'Not a professional, then?'

'Not much of one, no.'

'Or he wanted you to know who was shooting you?'

'If so, he failed.'

'So you definitely didn't see his face?'

'Do you think I wouldn't tell you?'

Lucy snorted. 'You don't seriously want us to answer that question, do you?'

'A witness inside the restaurant kitchen says that he only caught a glimpse of what happened through the window, but he could have sworn that someone in your party returned fire,' Nehwal said. 'Not a lot. Just a single shot.'

McCracken shrugged. 'I'm sure you'll agree that neither me nor Charlie were in any fit state to do that.'

'You said in your initial statement that you were knocked unconscious instantly, or at least you assume you were, because you weren't aware of anything else for quite some time.'

'If you disbelieve that, I suggest you try taking a pistol shot to the collar-bone yourself, Detective Superintendent Nehwal. See what impact it has on you.'

'I'll pass,' Nehwal said, watching him carefully. 'But the thing is . . . what I have real trouble believing is your assertion that you've got no idea who it was who whisked you away from the restaurant and dropped you off here.'

'Your mysterious kitchen witness can't assist with that?'

'Sadly, he'd gone to get help. When he came back with others, you'd already gone. As had your assailant.'

He made a gesture. 'One of life's good Samaritans, I guess.'

'The vehicle that dropped you off at the hospital was caught on several different surveillance cameras and identified. But it was one that had been stolen several months ago in Burnley. We've found no trace of it since. Likewise, we've found no trace of your rather swish Bentley. It certainly wasn't in the car park, where you supposedly left it.'

McCracken responded with a helpless shrug. 'Perhaps not quite so good a Samaritan then.'

He gave Lucy a brief stare, and she had to avert her eyes. She'd never felt worse as a policewoman, standing here alongside her boss, knowing full well what really happened after the Crowley Old Hall shooting, and not just keeping schtum about it, but allowing her superior to continue the line of questioning, inadvertently making a complete fool of her.

'You've nothing else to add?' Nehwal said.

'I'm afraid not.'

'Well . . . in that case there's nothing else to ask. We'll leave you in peace.'

McCracken nodded and gave them a genial smile.

'But I will send word when we get the result of that ballistics test,' Nehwal said from the doorway. 'I'm sure you're dying to know the outcome.'

It was late morning when Lucy and Nehwal returned to Robber's Row. There was minimal space on the personnel car park, lots of bodies from the Serious Crimes Division having arrived. Nehwal, already gabbling on the phone, went upstairs to the Incident room to brief her team. Lucy would have gone with her, but Tessa Payne accosted her in the corridor outside the DO, waving two sheets of print-out.

'Lucy, you sent a request to the forensics lab last night, concerning an attack on a homeless person?'

'They've done it already?'

'Sounds like they're clearing the decks now there's been a double murder on the patch.'

'Okay, so what've we got?'

'A result . . . of sorts.' Payne handed the paper over. It

comprised two rap-sheets. 'I took the liberty of pulling these off the system for you. The one on top is the one you're looking for. It was her DNA under the assault victim's finger-nail. Very minor form, though.'

Lucy saw an image of a gawky teenage girl with long but messy blonde hair. Her OTT makeup was blotched by tears; she'd clearly been upset at the time of her arrest.

'Alyssa Torgau,' Lucy said, reading the details. 'Fifteen years old . . . shoplifting.'

'Like I say, hardly the villain of villains.'

'This was back in 2014, which would only make her nineteen now.'

'I was wondering about that . . . think they could have made a mistake?'

'No.' Lucy recollected the lithe, blonde-haired figure that had eluded her through the industrial basements. 'But it's a puzzler. I'm just wondering when this silly young cow went and joined the commandos.'

'What?'

'Nothing.' Lucy flipped the papers around. 'Who's the other one?'

'That's her dad, Martin Torgau. I only include him because he's the only known associate she's got.'

This suspect – though 'suspect' was probably too strong a word at this stage – had a little more form. His last and only arrest had been in 2002, in Liverpool, when he'd been imprisoned for a year and a half for illegal possession of a handgun and for carrying a banned knife, though he was released after eight months for good behaviour.

Lucy was intrigued that he'd been jailed at all, but there were plenty of additional notations on his sheet to explain this. It seemed that he'd been arrested after paying a taxi fare, his overcoat falling open and the driver catching a glimpse of what looked like the butt of a pistol hanging in a shoulder-holster. On being taken into custody, the pistol was found to be a loaded Beretta M9, which was heavy stuff. A full body search had then found what was described as a 'Rambo knife' strapped to his lower left leg – which made Lucy think about the cross-guarded fighting knife she'd seen in the possession of her assailant at St Clement's. But more important than any of this, Torgau had refused to explain his possession of these implements during interview. He'd admitted his guilt and apologised but had pointedly said nothing else.

The Merseyside detective on the case had been so concerned by this, because he'd felt that possession of such weapons meant the guy was more than he appeared to be, that he'd made a big issue of Torgau's lack of cooperation, which the CPS later reflected in court, and the trial judge agreed with.

An additional footnote added that Martin Torgau, who'd been a widower at the time, had two young daughters, Alyssa and Ivana, twins, who, as there were no other living relatives, were placed in a Catholic care home for the brief time he was imprisoned.

Lucy wondered if she was going crazy. 'Alyssa Torgau attacked a nun . . . having been held in a Catholic care home when she was a kid. Is that some kind of link?'

'Not following,' Tessa Payne said.

'Sorry, Tess. Thinking aloud. And then that bloody commando knife . . .' Lucy tried to concentrate on the paperwork. 'Home address was 27, Cedar Lane, Cotely Barn. Do they both still live there?'

'Yeah. I checked with the Voters' Roll.'

'Excellent work, Tessa. I mean it . . . this is great.'

Payne beamed in response. 'I'm guessing we've got a new lead?'

'Well . . . we've got a lead on whoever attacked Sister

Cassiopeia. And that's something.' Lucy lowered the documents. 'How are you doing with the CCTV?'

'A bit to go yet. Boring as hell.'

'No hits, though?'

'There's no shortage of transit vans. The trouble is they're all registered to legitimate companies.'

'You're making a list of them anyway?'

'Sure. But there are none running under dummy plates. None that I've spotted. And I've got lots more footage to look through yet.'

'Because now that Malcolm Peabody's off sick, someone's going to have to do the mission halls and shelters as well.'

For all the enthusiasm she wanted to project in the presence of her idol, Payne looked wearied simply by the prospect of this.

'Sorry, babes,' Lucy said. 'But we're all pulled out.'

Payne nodded. 'Least it'll get me out the office.'

'Plus, I'll be able to help you. For the meantime, though, get on with the flicks.' Lucy folded the print-outs. 'I'll check out the Torgau situation.'

Payne wandered back into the DO, while Lucy went out to the car park, jumped onto her bike and hit the streets. She already had more than enough to arrest this Alyssa Torgau, but that would not have been the clever way to do it. Circumstantial evidence, *very* circumstantial, connected the girl – and maybe her father, because someone had been driving that van she escaped in – to the other abductions, and that in its turn connected them – possibly, maybe – to the dog carcasses on the landfill, which – possibly, maybe – connected them to the double strangulation on the Aggies, which – also possibly, maybe – connected them to the shooting of Frank McCracken.

That was an awful lot of possibles and maybes to use as a basis for going crashing in. So the first thing to do was check out the lie of the land at Cedar Lane. She would head over there now, but not on her Ducati, because that would likely attract interest in a quiet neighbourhood. Instead, she went first to her mother's terraced house in Saltbridge, where she'd left her Jimny the previous day.

When she arrived, the Jimny still sat at the front. She rode around to the back, installed her bike in the yard shed, briefly examined the visor on her dented helmet, which still hung loose at one side, and deciding to take it with her to try to get it repaired later, walked through the house. It was empty, her mum being out at work, so she locked up behind her, threw her helmet into the Jimny's rear seat, climbed in and headed back across town towards the much more prosperous suburb of Cotely Barn.

She was there within fifteen minutes, her driver's window down as she cruised, seeing lush front gardens, a few now reddening in the early days of autumn, and pleasant detached houses built in cottage and country styles. The neighbourhood was quiet, as she'd expected, most folk now at work, and the kids at school – which was not necessarily a good thing, as it made her more noticeable. The trick in that case was to keep her visit short and sweet.

On Cedar Lane itself, she spotted No. 27 straight away. It was only different from the others in that it was prettier than most, a large detached in handsome beige brick, with neatly pruned ivy cladding its front. However, the thing that caught Lucy's eye most was an extension on the left side of the house. It looked as if it had been constructed relatively recently, and now connected what had formerly been a free-standing garage to the main building. Ostensibly, of course, this had been to accommodate a fifth bedroom over the top of the garage, but it also meant that if someone was to park inside the garage, any illicit cargo could be transferred indoors without any danger of prying eyes.

Despite that, when Lucy glided to a halt opposite, she wondered if she'd ventured too far into the realms of supposition. The route she'd followed here was tenuous enough without going back to Priya Nehwal and telling her that she'd found the killers because they'd recently added a new room to their house. Nothing about the building stood out otherwise. On first appearances, the whole place was terribly respectable. The car on the drive was a silver Volvo V90 estate, while further up, inside the open garage, Lucy could see what looked like a black Audi A3. Both carried relatively recent registration marks, which meant they'd be expensive – and wealth rarely went hand in hand with violent crime.

Unless it's violent crime of the organised variety, her inner detective told her.

Lucy considered that.

And DNA rarely if ever lied.

She studied the Volvo estate, thinking that you probably couldn't find a better kind of car if you wanted to smuggle bodies or prisoners, or both, into and out of a house in a built-up area. She glanced past it to the Audi, and for the first time noticed that its front nearside light-cluster had been broken and was now covered with cellophane.

Everyone's car got bumped from time to time. Nicks and scratches were commonplace. But was it really too much of a stretch to – possibly, maybe – link this damage to the unresolved shooting incident in central Crowley the previous night?

Then someone stepped in front of her, blotting out her view of the property.

Lucy was so surprised that at first she couldn't react.

Whoever it was, they'd stolen up from behind, and she'd been so absorbed in the house and the two cars that she hadn't realised. She glanced up and saw a girl of about nineteen. She had spiky blonde hair with red highlights, shaved at the sides.

353

She was wearing a large denim jacket over a summery dress, but both hands were deep in her jacket pockets.

'House-hunting, are we?' the girl said.

'Sorry.' Lucy tried a disarming smile. She was in plain clothes, so there was no reason for anyone to assume the worst. 'Yes, actually. I was just checking the area.'

The girl didn't return the smile. Anything but. Her blue eyes literally blazed. 'Had a bump on your bike recently?'

Immediately, with a gut-thumping shock, Lucy realised her error: the helmet in the back seat.

'Out!' the girl hissed, her hands still in their pockets, but the right one pushed forward against the material, the metallic object she clearly held in there aimed directly at Lucy's face.

Instinctively, Lucy's hand strayed towards the pocket where she normally kept her radio – only to remember that, thanks to rushing to respond to the Malcolm Peabody situation that morning, she hadn't yet thought to check one out.

'Quickly and quietly!' the girl instructed her. 'Don't think I won't shoot! There's no one round here during the day . . . I can do what I fucking want!'

Lucy felt like contesting that, asking why, if there were no potential witnesses here, the girl was concealing her gun, but there was something about that crazed expression that brooked no argument. So she complied, turning her engine off, climbing from the car.

'Keys!' the girl said, her left hand coming into view. 'You fucking bitch.'

Hand shaking, Lucy handed the car keys over.

'Across the road . . . up the drive and into the garage.'

This time Lucy resisted, until the girl stepped behind and prodded her in the spine with a cloth-covered muzzle, which indicated that she really *did* have a gun down there. 'You want I should do it *this* way?' she asked. 'Sever your nervous system with a single shot?'

Sever my nervous system . . . Christ.

Lucy started forward across the road, praying that another car would come along, or some friendly neighbour step outside for a chat. Though what would they see if they did? A neighbour's daughter whom they'd known all their lives? A potential house-buyer being shown around? Lucy could shout for help, of course, but her captor seemed to be reading her mind.

'Quickly!' she hissed as they walked up the drive. 'And don't open that pretty trap of yours, or it'll be the last thing you ever do.'

This message was delivered with such harsh intensity, that Lucy had no doubt it was true.

'I mean it, pig,' the girl added, as they entered the garage alongside the Audi. 'You've given us no choice. I'll blow you the fuck away.'

If Lucy had harboured any doubt that she was onto the right team, it ended there.

You've given us no choice, the girl had said. *Us*. She and whoever else she was involved with really were playing for high stakes, and were so alert, so paranoid, that they'd immediately fingered a casual observer as law enforcement.

Lucy heard a click. With a slow, grating sound, the garage door levered downward behind them, closing off the daylight.

'You know it was never part of our plan to kill a copper,' the girl said. 'And we could've killed one last night. We nearly did. We thought that might be the best way to cover our backs. But then we said, "Nah . . . they're good lads. They work hard, they have families. We don't want to hurt decent chaps like that."'

With a resounding thud, the garage door closed.

The girl chuckled loudly. 'Actually, no.' Her voice became hard, scornful. 'We didn't even *think* anything like that. We just didn't want you coming after us with everything you've

355

got. But seeing as you've done that anyway, maybe we *should've* put a match to him, hey?' She chuckled again. 'I'll tell you one thing, doll . . . we'll certainly be putting a match to you.'

Chapter 37

Mick Shallicker found Frank McCracken on a bench on a lawn outside an open fire-exit at the rear of St Winifred's. It wasn't a particularly relaxing place; there were a few straggly flowerbeds, and then a car park, from which vehicles came and went constantly. And McCracken didn't look particularly relaxed, perched stiffly with ruffled hair and a grizzled jaw, wearing only slippers, pyjama bottoms and an NHS-issue dressing gown draped over his bare shoulders to accommodate the sling and bandages.

'I wondered when *you* were going to show up,' he said sourly.

Shallicker stood there awkwardly. 'Seems the Old Bill don't consider you worth guarding any more.'

'I suspect because I'm not actually giving them anything.'

'You okay to be outside?'

'They've moved me to a recovery ward. If I'm good for that, I'm good for the fresh air . . . at least, there's no chance of concealed microphones out here.'

Shallicker nodded thoughtfully. 'How's Charlie?'

'Apparently, she's going to be all right.'

The big guy looked relieved. 'That's good.'

'But she's had major surgery, so it's going to be a long one. Six months, maybe.'

'Shit.'

McCracken looked up at him. His voice grated as he spoke. 'I'm more concerned about what the blue fuck's been going on elsewhere!'

Shallicker raised his hands. 'First of all, I had no choice . . . I *had* to bring you here. I thought you were going to kick it.'

'I'm not concerned about that. I mean O'Grady.'

'Well . . . it was *him*, Frank. We both saw him.'

'We're never likely to see him again, are we! Just tell me it wasn't *you*, Mick.'

'Course it wasn't.'

'Because I'd expect schoolboys to do a better fucking job than that.'

'Yeah, well . . .' Shallicker gestured that he would sit if that was okay. McCracken moved up and he plonked himself down. 'You're more right about *that* than you realise.'

'In what way?'

'First of all . . .' Fleetingly, Shallicker seemed tongue-tied. It was a new experience for McCracken to see his gigantic minder so uneasy, and he wasn't enjoying it. 'First of all . . . I shat myself after I'd brought you here. I knew I should've gone looking for one of our own sawbones, but like I say, I thought you'd had it, Charlie especially. Anyway, I didn't want to hang around waiting for Wild Bill to come to me. So, I went to him . . . well, I rang him. Told him what had happened. He ripped me a fucking new one, as I thought he would. But he was less pissed off when I told him the shooter was O'Grady, and that it was retaliation for you putting the muscle on him over an earner. He told me to leave it to him.'

McCracken shrugged. 'There's nothing wrong with this

picture so far . . . and yet we've still ended up with a situ
where I might get nicked.'

'They've nothing on you, Frank—'

'Fuck's sake, Mick!' McCracken would have gesticulated
angrily had he been able to raise his arm. 'That bus job was
cowboy stuff. They've got the bodies, they've got the gun
that was used against me . . . which puts us straight in the
frame for conspiracy. They've even got the body of an innocent bystander. A bus driver, for God's sake! What did *he*
do wrong?'

'Think he was just there . . . just inconvenient.'

'*Inconvenient?* This is the kind of amateur shit these
eighteen-year-old pushers round Longsight and Moss Side
are always pulling. I'm amazed no dozy twat filmed the
whole thing on his mobile and then lost it outside a fucking
cop shop.'

'You've got it right about the age, at least.'

McCracken glanced round at him. 'I'm not following.'

'Wild Bill wanted a big lesson taught. So he sent the
Ripsaw Man.'

'The Ripsaw Man,' McCracken said with slow disbelief.
'The same guy who's carried out a hundred clean hits in the
last ten years? Who's been so clean, in fact, that most people
on our network don't even know he exists, let alone the
fucking coppers? *That* Ripsaw Man?'

Shallicker shrugged apologetically. 'It was Bill's idea. He
said O'Grady had overstepped the mark big time, and that
it had to be special.'

'It was special all right! What went wrong?'

'What went wrong is it wasn't the Ripsaw Man who filled
the contract. From what I've heard, he's looking to retire.'

'So, who did it then?'

'Seems he's been training up his daughters.' Shallicker
shrugged again. 'Wild Bill knew about it, liked the idea – said

it was cute, two pretty slips of lasses carrying out nasty hits for him. But previously, he'd said only when they knew their stuff. Anyway, when he sent the contract through last night, there was a note on it: "The kids are all right."'

McCracken's astonishment was growing steadily. 'And is he aware they were nowhere near all right . . . that it was a total fuck-up?'

'All I know is that they've been practising, and Bill had been told they were almost good to go – and he wanted to see if that was true.'

McCracken pondered this, not believing for a second that Wild Bill would take such a chance without having an ulterior motive, and now thinking it far more likely that he himself was being served up, maybe as a punishment for letting one of his own victims get the better of him.

'Look, Frank . . .' Shallicker attempted some consolation. 'If that gun's any use to the cozzers – it's been burned, remember, probably inside and out – it wasn't like *you* fired it. It'll bring a bit of heat down, but not very much . . .'

'Any heat is too much,' McCracken retorted. 'And the fact an innocent guy got chopped as well means that it won't be minor heat. Like it or not, the gun will link it to *us* . . . and to these stupid young bitches. And if they're so pathetic as to have left it there in the first place, they could have left other stuff too . . . which the forensics teams will find. Christ, if this isn't a fuck-up enough! I mean, how do we know they won't talk? GMP have brought the Serious Crimes Division in. You know how good they are when it comes to asking questions. These two stupid kids'll be meat and drink to 'em.'

'Come on, Frank . . .' Shallicker still tried to lighten it. 'We don't *know* they'll talk.'

'And we don't know they won't. And we can't afford that.'

McCracken's good fist clenched till his knuckles cracked. 'Think about it, Mick. It's not just this incident. It's all of them . . . every job Ripsaw's ever done for us. Think how many that is. And these two bitches aren't just his daughters, they're his students, his protégées. They'll likely know everything.'

Shallicker looked uncertain how to respond, but the penny was slowly dropping. 'Shit,' he said. 'You don't really think . . .?'

'They've got to go.'

'What?'

'You heard me,' McCracken said. 'They've got to go.'

The minder dug out his mobile. 'You want to get on the blower to Wild Bill?'

'He'll say no. He'll have to. Because if he doesn't he'll lose face . . . it'd be admitting that he made a mistake.'

'But if it's this serious . . .'

'Wild Bill's losing it too, Mick.' McCracken's face was pale and tense. 'I've been saying that for a while. He was always a nutter, let's be honest. But now it's getting serious. Look at those three lunatics he sent after our Lucy last year. They levelled half the town and didn't hit a single target.'

Shallicker thought this through, and as usual, it was a lengthy process.

And this time he's so bent on trying to bring me down, that he's endangered the entire organisation, McCracken almost added. *He doesn't like someone who tells him stuff he doesn't want to hear, especially when it's right.*

But he withheld those charges in case it made him sound a touch too paranoid.

Shallicker shrugged. 'So they've got to go? Seriously? Without the board okaying it?'

'Wild Bill owns the board . . . so how else?'

The big guy looked even more discomfited. Small-time wipe-outs were no real issue and were nearly always left to the discretion of Crew underbosses. But names, associates, coppers, judges and the like were a different story.

'What about Ripsaw?' he asked.

McCracken stared at him. 'Well . . . work it out. Anyone who's so blinded by the amazingness of his two kids that he can't see how fucking stupid they are is never going to give permission to have 'em topped, is he?'

'So?'

'So, *he* goes too.'

Shallicker looked incredulous. 'Ripsaw and Wild Bill go right back . . .'

'That's why we don't cough to it. Perhaps we can make it look like O'Grady's crew.'

'No one'd believe that. They're small time.'

But from McCracken's expression, he wasn't worried what anyone else might think.

'Listen. Frank.' Shallicker dropped to one knee so that he could lean close. 'Ripsaw may look like a fat retiree who mows his lawn all day, but he's well organised. This won't be easy.'

'That's why I want *you* to handle it. Pick a team who won't fold under Bill's questioning afterwards. Tell 'em they'll all be on quadruple time.'

Shallicker stood back up. He looked troubled, but less so than before. Ultimately, it was Frank McCracken he owed everything to. 'You absolutely sure about this?'

'We're in the frame for a double homicide, Mick. *You* maybe more than me. At least, I can argue I was in the operating theatre. Where were you . . . the guy who dumped me at the hospital, the guy who'd already engaged in a gunfight with one of the blokes who later got murdered?'

'Okay.' When Shallicker pondered it in those terms, it made perfect sense. 'When?'

'The sooner the bloody better. Just get it done. And like I say, take a team who know what they're doing.'

Chapter 38

With the main door to the garage firmly closed, Lucy's captor whipped the firearm out of her coat pocket. It was the real deal, a Browning BDA, and Lucy was now marched at gunpoint through a connecting passage into the main body of the house. It was only dimly lit, most of its Venetian blinds closed. However, the rooms were spacious and well appointed, and, from what she could see, they'd been furnished tastefully, laid with wooden block flooring, with rich drapes on the windows and handsome paintings on the walls. She was poked through into the largest and plushest of these, which seemingly was the lounge. A right-angled leather sofa faced an enormous flat-screen TV, while a thick rug lay in front of a huge granite hearth with an ornate real-flame gas fire. Another girl was waiting in here, standing behind a carved wooden chair, which looked as if it had been brought in from the dining room. Years had passed since the custody shot had been taken, but Lucy immediately recognised her as Alyssa Torgau.

'Searched her yet?' she said.

'Nope,' the girl with the gun replied, lobbing Lucy's car keys onto the couch. 'You're about to do that now.' She stepped to the side, aiming her Browning at Lucy's head with both hands.

Alyssa Torgau came around the chair. She was wearing trainers, running shorts and a sports bra, her exposed flesh glinting with a sheen of sweat as though she'd been in mid-workout. Lucy noted that her face was swollen and bruised, and that there were dried cuts on it. Quite clearly, this was the same girl who'd attacked Sister Cassie.

'Think you two have met before, haven't you?' Lucy's captor said.

Alyssa eyed Lucy curiously, particularly her leather jacket. 'Well . . . if it isn't the biker chick who helped that Maggie slut.'

'She was sitting outside in a car.' The other girl came back into Lucy's line of vision, though she still kept the weapon trained on her head. 'Not very observant, I have to say. Didn't see me coming up from behind. Your handiwork was sitting on her back seat. Question is . . . is *that* incident the only reason she's here?'

Alyssa rummaged through Lucy's jacket pockets, pulling out her phone, which she placed on the mantel, then her handcuffs, and then the wallet containing her warrant card. 'Detective Constable Lucy Clayburn,' she read aloud. 'Crowley CID.'

'No radio?' the other one said.

'Not on her.'

'Go and check the car.'

Alyssa took Lucy's keys, and sauntered out into the hall. While she did, the other one grabbed Lucy's phone.

'What's the security code?' she asked, keeping the gun level.

With no option, Lucy gave it to her. The girl used one thumb to access the list of recent calls.

'You got any mates out there who think they're about to

storm this place,' she finally said, throwing the phone at the stone fireplace, where it shattered, 'guess who dies first.'

Lucy didn't answer, because she wasn't sure what the right answer might be. If they thought she was only here to investigate an assault, that was good – it was less serious. But they'd now abducted her, of course, so they might still need to take drastic action. On the other hand, if they thought she was part of a larger operation, they might consider it sensible to keep her alive as a hostage. But with dangerous criminals you simply never knew.

In light of which, the best plan was surely to keep them guessing by saying as little as she could get away with.

Alyssa returned, closing the front door behind her and tossing the keys back onto the couch.

'No radio in the car,' she said. 'No sign of anyone else out there, either. Think this one was just being nosy, Ivana.'

Ivana, Lucy thought. *Alyssa and Ivana.*

The Torgau twins.

They wore their hair in different styles and dressed differently, and one had marks on her face, but they still resembled each other. That said, the one with the gun, Ivana, had more of an air of authority. She gestured with the Browning at the dining room chair. Lucy did as she was told, sitting down in it. Alyssa slid around to the rear, twisting Lucy's hands behind her back, pulling them through the spindles in the chair's backrest, and locking them together with her own handcuffs. While this was happening, Lucy heard heavy feet descending the staircase, thudding impacts that resounded throughout the house.

'Watch her,' Ivana said. 'I'll go and speak to him.'

Alyssa nodded and moved to a corner of the room, near the front window, where she picked something up that Lucy hadn't noticed previously. It was another gun, a battle-rifle with a large magazine attached. Despite everything, this shocked her. Originally, she'd wondered if they were dealing with some kind of ultra-dysfunctional family here, a bunch of sexual sadists and thrill-killers. Okay, the murder of Miles O'Grady, and the gangland connection that suggested, put it into a slightly different league, but she hadn't expected heavy firepower like this. Ivana, meanwhile, moved out into the hall, half-closing the lounge door behind her. A muffled conversation followed. Alyssa approached slowly, clutching the rifle in both hands but, as per the manual, keeping it dressed down.

'You ride a mean bike, I have to say,' she said.

'And yet you outran it,' Lucy replied. 'You must be fit as a fiddle.'

'We train a lot.'

Ivana came back into the lounge, still talking. 'She's made no calls to anyone but her mum since this morning. Plus, she's got no radio. She's only local fuzz too. She's not Murder Squad . . .'

A man entered the room behind her.

'The route's clear, by the way,' Ivana added. 'Alyssa checked it first thing, as usual.'

The man said nothing. From the sound of his footfalls, Lucy had been expecting someone larger and heavier, but as it turned out, the biggest thing about him was the travel bag he was carrying. He dropped it, and it struck the floor a reverberating blow. She eyed it quickly. Police grab-bags tended to be a lot lighter, but then detectives only usually needed overnight stuff, because they'd be home again soon. For hoodlums on the run, the future was less certain. Not that Martin Torgau – because this was the same guy she'd seen in the custody shot from 2002 – looked much like a hoodlum. He was about five-foot-nine, with a slightly portly build, which wasn't enhanced by his chosen attire of jersey and tracksuit trousers. She put him somewhere in his late fifties.

'Seems we may have panicked over nothing,' Alyssa said.

'No one's panicking,' he replied, not looking at her. 'Go upstairs. Watch the road.'

She hurried from the room with rifle in hand, scampering upstairs.

Torgau took Lucy's warrant card from Ivana, studied it and placed it on the mantel. He regarded his captive with eyes that were deep, brown and strangely soulful. 'I congratulate you, DC Clayburn. You're the very first police officer ever to encroach on this sanctuary. I'm not sure that bringing you inside so quickly was the wisest course –' he threw a quick glance at Ivana, who reddened slightly '– but I understand it was a taut moment, which required some sort of immediate response. It wasn't totally unreasonable that Ivana, on learning who you were, took the action she did.'

Lucy said nothing.

'Just getting close to us, though, is impressive,' he added. 'Either you're remarkably adept at your job. Or you've been incredibly lucky. Or unlucky, depending on your viewpoint.'

He possessed a Manchester accent, but it was refined, as if he'd spent much of his life working to modify it. He also spoke in leisurely, casual fashion, as if he had plenty of time on his hands. He might not be panicking, but she'd have expected greater urgency than this.

'Naturally, my curiosity is piqued,' he said. 'Which means that I want to know all about you.'

Ivana left the room and returned with another dining chair, which she handed to him. He placed it in front of Lucy and sat down. Again, there was no air of haste.

'You already know everything there is,' Lucy replied. 'I'm DC Clayburn from Crowley CID.'

He ignored that. 'Such as how you came to be here . . . at my house.'

'I obviously can't tell you that.'

'How unfortunate.'

'Mr Torgau, you do realise that abducting a police officer means hefty prison time?'

'Oh, I'm in no doubt.' He seemed saddened by that prospect. 'Which is why you should be in no doubt that when I ask you questions, I'm serious about wanting answers.'

'Then you're going to be seriously disappointed.'

He sighed and looked at his daughter, who approached the hearth, bent down and, throwing a switch, brought the real-flame gas fire to life. Lucy felt a gush of heat. The girl took a blackened fire poker from a hook and inserted it into the flames.

'You look worried, DC Clayburn,' Torgau said.

Lucy glared at him. 'You're getting yourself into so much trouble here.'

He seemed intrigued. 'Is it possible, I wonder, that you really don't know who you're talking to? That you really have no idea what you've stumbled across?' He paused. 'I'll tell you what, I'm going to play a little game with you. I tell you a bit about myself, and then you tell me a bit about yourself. Yes?'

Lucy glanced at the poker again, its blackened tip still resting in the flames. Sweat was gathering on her brow.

'It *is* going to get hot in here, I'm sorry to say,' Torgau said. 'But it doesn't need to get *terribly* hot . . . so long as you play the game.'

'For God's sake!' she hissed. 'You've unlawfully imprisoned a police officer. How do you think this is going to end?'

'That's entirely up to you.' He sat back with arms folded, as though contemplating the best way to start his game. 'I'm what you might call a professional problem-solver. I mean, I operate a number of ordinary, legitimate businesses. But none of them make any money. My real gig is . . . well, let me tell you how it began. I was a child at the time, growing

369

up on the same Moston estate as the legendary Bill Pentecost.'

Lucy was unsurprised to hear it confirmed that this thing was connected to the Crew.

'I didn't associate with Wild Bill back in those days,' Torgau said. 'I knew who he was, he knew who I was . . . but we had our own rackets. Me and my lot, we burgled, stole car radios, rolled drunks. But for all that, we were just punks, hustlers really. Bill had more of a plan. He was loansharking, ringing motors, running a whole stable of working girls before he was twenty. Then, one day, we learned about this gun shop down Alderley Edge way. It was off our normal patch, but we went over there, got inside, helped ourselves to . . . oh, forty or fifty shotguns. Hundreds of boxes of cartridges. Afterwards, we spent three months selling them out of the back of a van, all over the Northwest. Word had got around. Anyone planning a job, we were the armourers. This brought us to Wild Bill's attention. He was setting up a real network by then, which meant that we were around at just the right time. We armed his desperadoes, and at a good price. The upshot, me and Bill . . . we became solid.'

'Why are you telling me all this?' Lucy asked, genuinely puzzled.

Torgau pondered. 'It's a good question, DC Clayburn. Most of my life, I've flown under the police radar. You can call it skill, you can call it luck, you can call it the Devil looking after his own. But after a lifetime dedicated to breaking the law – I mean, I've barely ever done an honest job and look at the life I lead – I have the smallest criminal record imaginable. So maybe, just maybe . . . this is an opportunity to show at least one of you what you've been missing. Cosy in the knowledge that it won't mean a damn thing.'

'Dad hasn't told you what he was really good at yet,' Ivana chipped in.

Lucy saw that she'd lifted the poker from the flames and

was blowing gently on its tip, which had started to glow.

This was Torgau's cue to talk a little more about himself.

'Wild Bill was impressed no end by the gun thing,' he said. 'But what he really liked about me was how I excelled at violence. You may not believe that, because I'm not a big man. And back in Moston in the bad old days, when I was *very* young, that made me a target for every kind of bully. It began with my father, who hammered me regularly for the most minuscule things. But mainly it was this big kid in the neighbourhood – Arun Swaraj. He gave me a kicking every single day. Until my father saw it happen and refused to let me in the house afterwards. He put an empty milk bottle in my hand and said that I couldn't come home until I'd smashed it over this guy's head. I knew he meant it. So that was what I did. Arun went down like the pathetic sack of shit he was. But the really amazing thing was the way his wingmen ran away. My father taught me an important lesson that day, DC Clayburn. Violence works. Especially the nasty kind. The kind from which there is no coming back. That kind of violence doesn't just earn you respect, it can actually earn you a living.'

Lucy was stunned, not just by how unconcernedly he was revealing his criminal past to her, but by how long he was taking to do it. It was a dead cert that they wouldn't be telling her all this if they intended to let her live. But shouldn't there be an air of urgency by now? She was a police officer who'd vanished from the grid. She'd be missed.

Unless that was the purpose of the delay.

Were they waiting to see what would happen?

They were clearly ready to run – the weighty travel-bag for example – but perhaps they weren't sure whether that was a good option. Were there other cops out there, covertly watching them? Would they be followed if they ran? All of these had to be considerations. Or would it be safer to assume that any surveillance team should have reacted by now? Lucy was 'local fuzz' after all, not 'Murder Squad'. So, might it indeed be the case that she wasn't here as part of a larger operation? Might it be that the Torgaus didn't need to flee at all?

Martin Torgau was still talking, shedding more light on his villainous life. Describing the street-gang he put together, and how it came to enjoy unparalleled success because of his ruthless leadership. How various enemies sought to tear him down. How he and his cronies responded savagely: shooting them, stabbing them, clubbing them, the bodies disposed of down derelict mine-shafts or thrown into lakes and reservoirs with concrete chained to their feet. And how, in due course, Wild Bill had persuaded Torgau that his real vocation lay not in petty crime, like selling guns, but in real problem-solving.

'We'd just done a one-off job for Bill,' Torgau said. 'A Stockport gangster called Jerry Coonan was cutting in on Bill's action. Bill didn't want the problem solving publicly. Nevertheless, he wanted to know that Coonan had been properly punished. Me and a couple of lads, we nabbed Coonan when he came out of his local and took him to this derelict workshop. We'd already got a workbench laid out, with clamps and vices. And we had a camera set up – we had to film it, you see. Bill wanted to watch it for himself.'

Torgau half-smiled, as though it was a fond recollection.

'We did a real number on him. Pliers, nutcrackers. Then I got this ripsaw, and I cut him up while he was still alive. Piece after piece. After it was over, we bagged him, laid him down under some new cement. He's holding up an office block these days. Anyway, Bill watched the video, and he was so happy afterwards that he said: "Martin, you can be my personal problem-solver." And he's certainly kept me busy since then. Too busy really. Which is why I've been training up the girls.'

'Training?' Lucy said, trying not to show how sickened she felt.

'In the end I did away with all my other sidekicks because I wanted it purely to be a family business. And now someone must take that business over. Anyway, *your* turn, detective.' His mournful face split into an unexpected smile. 'The game . . . remember.'

It was difficult for Lucy to know how she should respond. She glanced at the fire again, where the poker lay white-hot.

'Pretty green eyes you've got, DC Clayburn,' Ivana said. 'Would be such a shame.'

My eyes . . . God almighty!

Lucy still didn't know how to respond.

Quite clearly, she had to give them something. But what?

Lie that the rest of the police knew everything, and even now were circling the neighbourhood, mustering their forces – and that might convince them that it was better to keep her alive. Though it might also mean that they'd adopt a scorched-earth policy, destroying all evidence, warning their contacts in the Crew that they'd been rumbled. A better option perhaps was to play things down. If they didn't know anything about the connection she'd made between the van and the strangled dogs and the double murder on the Aggies, they might stay here and try to brazen it out. They'd still have to do away with Lucy – they wouldn't be able to argue their way out of having abducted a copper – but there were ways to allay that too.

'I'm investigating an assault on a homeless person,' she said.

'Indeed?' If this was something Torgau had been hoping to hear, he didn't sound a whole lot happier.

'I came across the incident by accident, while working undercover to buy drugs in the St Clement's ward.' That sounded plausible, she thought. 'I overheard the sound of the attack and intervened. I pursued the assailant on my motorbike, but she got away.'

'You knew already that it was a *she*?' Torgau sounded less than satisfied, but not necessarily with Lucy.

'I *saw* that it was a she,' she replied. 'I saw her face during the attack. And this was confirmed later on by forensic examination of organic material found under the fingernail of the victim.'

'That's impossible!' Ivana snapped, stepping forward with the brightly glowing poker.

Torgau warned her off with a raised hand.

'It was your sister,' Lucy said to her. 'Alyssa.'

'Alyssa would've known if she'd been clawed,' Ivana said.

'I sometimes wonder if Alyssa even knows what day it is,' Torgau rumbled.

'Alyssa already had facial injuries when the victim struck her in the face,' Lucy said, wondering why she was making excuses for the girl. 'It's probably no surprise that she didn't realise blood had been drawn.'

He still looked unimpressed.

'After that, the DNA brought me here,' Lucy added. 'Alyssa has a criminal record, after all. I asked around the neighbourhood, to be sure, and two or three different people were able to direct me to your house. If it's any consolation, Mr Torgau, they think you're all very nice people who wouldn't say boo to a goose.'

I'm sure it'll be no consolation, though, to now think that several different witnesses can place me right here, she added to herself. *So checkmate, you bastard!*

Before Torgau could reply, there was a scuttling of feet overhead, as if Alyssa was running from one side of the house to the other.

Ivana went rigid. Her father leaped to his feet.

'Assault team, coming in by twos!' Alyssa yelled down the stairs. 'Front and back!'

Lucy was as startled as the rest of them but was still handcuffed to the chair and could only watch as Torgau lurched out into the hall. Ivana, meanwhile, advanced with the poker raised over her head. Lucy tried to duck away, the chair falling sideways. But when the poker came down, which it did several times, it was on the chair's backrest, smashing and burning it. This proved to be a lengthy process, Torgau returning while it was still going on, unzipping his travel-bag and taking something out of it; to Lucy's bewilderment it was a cardboard cylinder, about three feet long, with an old image of a bulldog wearing a Union Jack waistcoat imprinted on it. Possibly it contained a weapon of some sort, because he immediately took it back out into the hall.

Ivana, meanwhile, threw the poker into the hearth, wrestled what remained of the chair's woodwork apart, and dragged the hostage to her feet. The next thing Lucy knew, she was being hustled out into the hall, the muzzle of the Browning pressed into her neck.

Torgau had braced the front door with some furniture and was now shouting upstairs. 'How many?'

'Four, so far,' Alyssa's voice shouted back.

'How are they dressed?'

'Body-armour and balaclavas.'

'Shit!' Ivana swore. 'SWAT.'

But her father shook his head. His expression was uncertain, confused. 'Police would have spoken to us first, tried to resolve it peacefully.'

'Shotguns!' Alyssa shouted.

'Does it matter?' Ivana asked, bewildered.

Alyssa came hurtling downstairs, still clutching the battle-rifle. 'I didn't see any back-up or support vehicles!'

'Give me that HK!' her father replied.

She threw the rifle to him. He caught it, passed the cardboard cylinder to Ivana, and swung around to face the front door.

'Do that slag, Vana!' Alyssa shouted. 'Do her now!'

'*No!*' her father roared, glaring at them both, red-faced. 'What do you not understand about bargaining chips?'

'But if they're coming in anyway!' Alyssa protested.

'*You goddamn idiot bitch!*' Froth flew from his mouth. '*These are not cops!*'

Chapter 39

'Get out of here, the pair of you!' Torgau roared. 'Use the route. And take her with you!'

The front door shuddered at a massive impact. Torgau shouldered the rifle and fired three deafening rounds, a trio of fist-sized holes exploding through the woodwork at chest height.

His girls might be under orders not to kill Lucy, but they weren't gentle with her. A stinging blow to the side of the face, delivered with the butt of the Browning, knocked her senseless, and she found herself stumbling across the hall between them, a hand hooked under either armpit. Meanwhile, a gunshot sounded somewhere to the rear of the house. Followed by another, and another. Lucy had heard something about shotguns. Presumably they were now being used to blow the hinges off the house's back door.

As if realising the same thing, Torgau dashed past them along the hall. He opened fire again with the battle-rifle before he'd even entered the kitchen. The noise was cacophonous in the suburban house, the air already thick with cordite.

'Down here, you bitch!' Ivana hissed.

A triangular doorway had opened underneath the stairs,

377

and Lucy was shoved towards it. Still dazed, she wondered why they were thrusting her into a closet, but then spotted the top of a staircase. A foot planted itself on her backside and propelled her forward. She tripped as she went, falling headfirst into darkness, turning over and over down the steep, stone flight. With hands cuffed behind her back, she was unable to protect herself, banging her head repeatedly, along with her spine, hips and knees. At the bottom she lay in total blackness, swooning with pain, only for a hand to slam a switch and a glaring white halogen light to come on overhead.

Despite what sounded like continuous shooting, she heard two pairs of feet thumping down the cellar stairs after her. As she came to, they lugged her upright again. A corridor of whitewashed brick, with a white-tiled floor, lay ahead. They hurried her along it, cursing and hissing at her, passing doors on the left, all partly open but all made from heavy sheet-steel. On the right, meanwhile, stood a recessed wardrobe. Its front had been disguised with fake white polystyrene brickwork, but now stood open, revealing two steel racks inside, each filled with firearms. The upper contained automatic rifles, submachine guns and pump-action shotguns, the lower pistols and revolvers. As they scrambled past, Alyssa grabbed a handgun and a couple of boxes of ammunition. Yet more gunfire thundered upstairs. It sounded like a shooting gallery rather than a family home.

'We should be up there!' Alyssa said, her voice cracking with emotion.

'No,' Ivana replied. 'He's not buying us time so that we can just waste it.'

Lucy, meanwhile, was now coming around properly and starting to figure things out. Torgau was right; it clearly wasn't the police who'd arrived – they'd have given these lunatics a chance to surrender before attacking. There was likely no help to be had up there. But allowing herself to be dragged ever deeper into this stronghold of the insane made no sense at all. They were midway along the corridor, another half-open steel door awaiting them at the far end, but though the Torgau girls were fit, they were still teenagers, while Lucy worked out as well, and at thirty-two, was stronger than them anyway. She dug her feet in and brought them to an unexpected halt.

'You bitch!' Ivana hit her with the Browning again, smacking it across her left cheek.

Lucy responded with a head-butt, delivered right to the middle of Ivana's nose.

Cartilage cracked, and the girl squawked. But Alyssa dug a right hook into Lucy's lower back, specifically her kidneys, knocking her physically sick. With legs like water, Lucy sagged forward, a karate chop clobbering the back of her neck. She was so stunned for the next few seconds that she hadn't even realised she was being dragged forward again, this time on her knees. With a *clang*, they crashed into the metal door at the end, which swung open, revealing a small but empty brick room. Like everything else in this extensive cellar area, it had been whitewashed, but in the centre of the floor lay what looked like a circular metal lid with a dial-type handle in the middle of it.

A manhole? Even as her senses swam back, Lucy was nonplussed. They dropped her to the floor alongside it, where she lay still, feigning semi-consciousness.

Ivana, bleeding freely from the bridge of her nose, squatted and turned the handle left and right in a sequence she'd evidently memorised. She then tried to lift the thing, but this wasn't easy; it was more like a circular slab of steel than a regular lid. Alyssa helped, all the time keeping the muzzle of her pistol jammed into Lucy's neck. Together, they got it upright, a stale reek wafting free. Lucy glimpsed the hole underneath. At first, she was perplexed. It was about two feet across; perhaps half a foot down there was a polished crossbar of tubular steel, and below that a similar tubular bar, this second one descending into pitch darkness like a fireman's pole. But only when Ivana put the cardboard cylinder down, letting it drop into the blackness, did Lucy realise what she was seeing.

This was it. The route.

Though how she was supposed to get down there with her hands cuffed behind her back, she didn't know.

'Just drop her,' Ivana told her sister, wiping at her nose with her sleeve, smearing red all over her once pretty face. 'So what if she breaks her fucking legs?'

Alyssa snickered, tucking the gun into the waistband of her shorts so that she could grab the hostage with both hands. Lucy knew that this was the sole opportunity she would get, and so, with the sort of Herculean effort only the truly desperate can muster, she swung her torso upward, slamming the flat of her left foot on the floor, and levering herself upright on one leg.

'Fuck!' Alyssa shouted, trying to grapple with her.

Lucy kneed her in the groin. It was a better tactic against male opponents, but it still had the desired effect, Alyssa doubling forward, gasping. Ivana, hunkered alongside the hole, tried to grab her legs, but Lucy kicked at her, knocking her sideways, and then turned and, still with hands cuffed, bolted out into the corridor.

She ran down it pell-mell.

Ivana shrieked incoherently, coming out behind her.

Lucy could sense the gun levelled on her back. But before they could fire, a figure came stumping down the stairs ahead of her. She slid to a halt, blinking through her sweat. It was the unmistakeable form of Martin Torgau. He stood as though barely seeing her, the battle-rifle hanging by his side. He was swaying, she realised, face milk-white, eyelids fluttering.

She looked down at his chest, where blood seeped from eight or nine minor puncture wounds. When he pitched heavily forward, smacking the tiled floor with his face, the jagged meat and bone of the exit wound in the middle of his back was the size of a dinner plate.

More heavy feet came clumping down the stair behind him. Blocking her escape.

Bone-weary, still dazed from the blows she'd taken, Lucy sank to her knees and slumped against the whitewashed bricks at the side of the passage. As she did, she glanced behind her. Ivana and Alyssa were both at the far end, framed in the doorway to the manhole room. They'd levelled their pistols at her but hadn't opened fire. Instead they stood stock-still, faces blanched, mouths agape.

Their father had just died in front of them.

Then another shot was fired, this time from the direction of the stairs. An almighty shotgun blast. Lucy felt the pellets whistle over her head and saw them rip their way along the wall, exposing streaks of red brick beneath the white.

The Torgau girls darted backward, slamming the steel door. A second load of shot hammered into it, denting it, punching multiple holes. A bulky figure, clad all over in black, wearing black gloves and a black balaclava, strode past Lucy, a pump-action levelled in his fists. He'd clearly seen her, but for the moment was more focused on his official targets, the Torgau twins. The third shot he fired slammed the steel door open, buckling it in its frame, but the room behind it was empty, the lid still upright on the manhole.

As though in a dream, Lucy looked the other way again, towards the foot of the stair, where a second figure, similarly clad to the first, had also come down. He'd seen her as well, but at present was ignoring her. However, he too carried a pump and, as he walked past Torgau's body, he casually unloaded a round into the back of its head, which from that range blew it apart like a water melon, blood and brains splurging across the white-tiled floor. He halted just in front of her. She sensed the first one coming back, and all she could do now was lower her head and screw her eyes shut.

'Fucking thing leads down to the sewers,' the first one said. 'Sodding maze down there. They'll be well away.'

'All right. We got the main target.'

'Yeah, but here's another for the fucking pot.'

Lucy tensed, as the first one worked the slide on his weapon – clack/clunk – and she sensed him squinting down the barrel at her head.

'Please . . . please . . .' she whimpered. 'I'm not, I'm not one of—'

'*Wait!*' a third voice bellowed. 'Not that one.'

Slowly, hardly daring to believe it, Lucy opened her eyes.

Again, sweat blurred her vision, but she was still able to focus on this third person, who had also come down to the bottom of the cellar stair. He too was armed with a shotgun, and clad in black from head to toe, but he was distinct from the others because while they were average-sized, he was a giant, towering almost to the ceiling.

There was no argument. The two gunmen ignored Lucy, sauntered back along the passage with weapons by their sides and tromped upstairs. The giant stood to one side, watching her as she knelt amid the smoke and blood. Lucy couldn't make eye-contact with him. There was too much distance between them, and she was too tired and hurt to scrabble any closer. But she knew Mick Shallicker when she saw him.

All her police life, she'd never thought she'd be so relieved at the sight of that towering, ruthless maniac.

Her head sank down for a second, her neck too weary to hold it upright.

When she finally managed to look again, he'd gone.

*

Cedar Lane was filled end to end with police and CSI vehicles – aside from the area immediately in front of No. 27. That and the house itself, including the drive, garage and front garden, were doubly taped off.

Curtains twitched continually as neighbours regarded every coming and going with utter astonishment. Lucy Clayburn, though, was less captivated. She watched it with dull, tired eyes, barely registering the Tyvek-covered examiners on the other side of the tape, some in conflab with Serious Crimes officers, others taking photographs, others on hands and knees as they examined the ground. Only when Detective Superintendent Nehwal emerged from the entry tent, having stripped off her own Tvyek and thrown it into the dirty-box, did Lucy straighten up.

She'd been leaning against her car, which remained where she'd parked it earlier. A sheet of survival-foil hung from her shoulders, where a medic had previously placed it. He'd wanted to take her away in the ambulance because he felt that she was going into shock, but Lucy had replied that she was fine, and rather snappily, had told him to stop fussing. It wasn't her normal style, but her inner turmoil was becoming too much, overwhelming all sensibilities, all inhibitions. Beyond this point there lay nothing but serious damage.

'One hell of a strange house,' Nehwal said, handing Lucy her car keys. 'Looks as if Torgau completely refitted the cellar area, but . . . I mean . . .' It was a rare occasion indeed when Priya Nehwal wrestled to find the adequate words. 'We've got gym equipment in some of the rooms, torture devices in others. We've got medical texts detailing human anatomy, stockpiled CDs, which on first glimpse seem to comprise military training techniques . . . SAS, Navy Seals. On which subject, there's a whole arsenal of illegal weapons. One room's like a prison cell . . . I hate to see what we'll find in there when we get the luminol out. There's even a Tannoy system and video links connecting it all together.'

'So the teacher could watch as they practised,' Lucy said, half to herself. 'And offer guidance.'

Nehwal regarded her carefully. 'You say this lunatic had been training his two children to murder?'

'To be Bill Pentecost's personal murderers,' Lucy replied tiredly. 'And torturers. And believe me, ma'am, they've got the energy for it if not the skills. Which is why, until we snag them both, we've still got a major problem on our hands.'

'Two nineteen-year-olds?' The DSU sounded unconvinced.

'You've every right to be doubtful, ma'am,' Lucy said. 'But it looked to me as if Martin Torgau taught them almost everything he knew. Or was in the process of that.'

Nehwal appraised the cosy-looking house. 'Still waters running deep, eh? Whoever attacked the place . . . that was clearly a professional hit. You say you thought there were three of them?'

Lucy tightened inside. Because this was it. Whatever this moment brought, there was no way around it – and maybe no way forward afterwards.

'I saw three, yes. And I think I recognised one of them.'

Nehwal looked slowly around. 'You recognised one of them? Who was it?'

Lucy knuckled her eyes. In normal circumstances she'd be furious to find tears there. Hardened coppers didn't cry, not in public. But this situation was beyond abnormal.

'I know you've just been through an ordeal,' Nehwal said, 'but try and think clearly. If you can identify one of these killers . . .'

'Ma'am, there's something I have to tell you.' Lucy swallowed bitter saliva. 'It's very serious.'

'Okay.'

'Two years ago, during the Jill the Ripper investigation, I

discovered something. It's very personal, but I *have* to tell you.'

Nehwal nodded slowly. After thirty-plus years as a cop at the sharp end, she knew when she was on the verge of something momentous. She tapped the bonnet of Lucy's Jimny. 'Get in the car. Tell me everything.'

Chapter 40

This was it. They'd reached critical mass. Lucy was simply fed up with the duplicity, with the lying, with the ongoing pretence, with her stomach knotting each time she played dumb about her father's firm's involvement in serious violent crime.

It was only a matter of time before the truth came out, anyway; of that she was certain – especially the way her mother was behaving.

But she couldn't allow more situations like that at the hospital to arise, where she'd known full well what had happened the night before and yet had said nothing while the man responsible feigned innocence with the SIO. Let alone an incident like this – an armed home-invasion and mass shooting – and she again keeping her mouth shut, even though she had a very good idea who'd ordered it.

It wasn't just that things were getting complicated, or more tangled, or more likely to catch her out. It wasn't simply that Lucy was now tortured by fear and doubt whenever her father's name was mentioned, and that this was spoiling her quality of life. It was the sheer, unadulterated immorality of it. She wasn't actually in limbo, as she'd so often told herself, in some kind of midway place between the law-enforcers and the law-breakers. It was much, much worse than that. She was supposed to be a police officer, so her failure to act, her refusal to shop the underworld on the various occasions when she could have done, was the most bare-faced kind of treachery. For all her protestations to Mick Shallicker, it absolutely made her one of the villains.

And that couldn't go on.

Lucy had joined the police as one of the good guys. That had been her sole motivation, and now it was time to ensure that she left them the same way.

'I never knew my father,' she said, slumped behind the steering wheel.

Priya Nehwal, in the front passenger seat, looked nonplussed. 'Nothing to be embarrassed about these days . . .'

'Until I met him a couple of years ago . . .' Lucy swallowed; fresh tears stung her eyes. 'And found that it was Frank McCracken.'

Over the years, Priya Nehwal had earned a reputation for being the toughest woman in the job but despite that, the first lady of hardcore policing still looked utterly shell-shocked by what Lucy Clayburn had just told her.

'Lucy . . .' She could barely get the words out. 'Lucy, you're a police detective.' Even then it was a whisper.

Lucy nodded. Again dumbly.

'And Frank McCracken's an underboss for the Crew.'

'I know.'

'We suspect him of authorising –' Nehwal shook her head, dumbfounded '– God knows how many murders, woundings, beatings . . . he may well have carried out a number of those crimes himself.'

'Ma'am, I know.' Lucy struggled to halt the tears.

'And you've been sitting on this for two whole years?'

'I can't sit on it any more. Not after today.'

Nehwal gazed through the windscreen, speechless. Lucy did the same. For a minute at least, the figures moving about outside were a blur to both of them.

'You're saying this was a Crew hit?' Nehwal finally said.

'I'm pretty sure, yes.'

'Because you recognised one of the assassins.'

Lucy didn't answer straight away, her loyalties once again tearing her down the middle. Mick Shallicker was another scummy hooligan who'd killed people to order, but today hadn't been the first time he'd saved her life.

'I . . . that bit, ma'am, I'm not so sure about.'

Nehwal's eyes narrowed. 'Just how deep in with them are you?'

Lucy jerked upright. 'I'm not in with them. I'm not. *God, no!* I've barely spoken to McCracken during those two years.'

'Which means that you actually *have* spoken to him?'

'We've occasionally encountered each other.'

'Lucy . . . this is serious stuff, but it's only going to get worse if you lie to me.'

'I'm not lying!' Lucy's voice became strained, heated. 'Ma'am, I arrested him once, remember? Doesn't that prove something?'

Nehwal shook her head as if this was irrelevant. 'You made a very brave stand when Wild Bill tried to bully his way into the IC suite . . . where your *father* was being treated. You were so determined to keep him out that you pulled a scalpel on him.'

'I was doing my job,' Lucy pleaded.

'With extras.' Nehwal's eyebrows lifted. 'I mean . . . a scalpel. I was impressed when I heard you'd done that, but I also thought it seemed a little extreme. Now I know why.'

'I don't have a relationship with Frank McCracken. I barely know the guy.'

'This has to be looked into. You understand that? I mean this whole thing . . . it has to be done formally.'

Lucy turned away. She felt mildly dizzy. She hadn't gone into shock during or after the shootout in Torgau's house, but she wondered if she was about to now.

'Look at me,' Nehwal said. 'Lucy . . . *look at me*.'

Lucy did so, sniffling.

The DSU peered at her with soul-searching intensity. 'Do you solemnly promise me . . . do you give me your word of honour as a police officer that you've been completely passive in this relationship, that you've not made any kind of deal with Frank McCracken, no matter how beneficial to law enforcement, that you've not fed him any kind of information that could be useful to him or his underworld associates?'

'Ma'am, I promise all that!' Lucy blurted.

The truth was that her dealings with her father had often been so convoluted and had so frequently involved life-threatening situations that she couldn't remember exactly what kind of deals she'd made with him, but she knew that none of them had been official; he'd never been her informant, nor she his. She'd always tried to keep him at arm's length, had continually tried to dissuade him from even thinking about her as his daughter. So that much was true.

Nehwal seemed to relax a little, though she was hardly satisfied.

'So what now?' Lucy asked.

'You have to go home.'

Even though Lucy had known this would end badly for her, for some reason – some ridiculous reason – she hadn't been expecting *this*.

'Home? You mean now?'

'Of course, now. And you stay at home until you're sent for.'

'I'm being suspended?'

Nehwal struggled. 'Call it sick leave. No one will question it after today. I'll speak to Stan, tell him I sent you home because you were in a bad way. But we'll have to bring in Chief Superintendent Mullany, and it may end up becoming a formal suspension. You understand that?'

'Ma'am, please . . .'

'Lucy, listen to me! You're no use here till this has been cleared up. No one will even look at you the same way unless we sort this thing out.'

Lucy's heart was sinking. This was so much everything she'd feared. 'They won't look at me the same way even *after* that.'

'It will show that you've got nothing to hide. That you've been completely open . . . albeit belatedly.' Another thought occurred to the DSU, which clearly pained her. 'You've been involved in a number of high-level investigations since you uncovered this information, haven't you?'

'Yes, ma'am.'

'Then your role in those cases will need to be reviewed by Professional Standards.'

Lucy felt a new sense of despair. 'How long's that going to take?'

'I don't know.' Nehwal shook her head. 'I doubt there are any precedents for this.'

'I don't want people thinking I'm on the other side. Because I'm not . . . I'm really not.'

'I believe you. But it's not me you're going to have to convince.'

'So I'm going home?'

Nehwal opened the passenger door. 'You're going home. But be available. At the very least we're going to need a statement off you for what's happened here. On top of that, they'll want to give you a medical, a hearing test and such . . .'

'Yeah . . . shit!' Lucy snapped. 'More excuses to can me!'

'That's the way it is in the job today. Would you rather they didn't care?'

390

'Who's going to take over the missing persons enquiry?'

Nehwal gave her a look. 'I've not exactly had time to think about *that*.'

'No one else is on top of it the way I am.'

'Lucy! I don't want you involved in operational policework for the time being.' Nehwal pushed the door open properly. 'I'm getting out now. And the first thing you're going to do after that is drive yourself home. Home, do you understand? Straight home.'

When Cora Clayburn arrived at St Winifred's Hospital, having been informed that Frank McCracken had been moved to the Brockhole Ward, she felt very relieved. It didn't just mean that he was responding well to treatment, but that the difficulty of getting in to see him no longer existed – because it was now six o'clock and officially visiting time.

But even as she approached the entrance to the hospital block where the recovery wards were located, she was stunned by the sight of McCracken emerging in front of her, in company with several of his heavies, including Mick Shallicker. McCracken was dressed in the trousers and shoes he'd been wearing when they'd first taken him in, his suit jacket draped over his shoulders to protect his bare but bandaged torso from the evening chill, but was walking briskly and discussing something with his men. When he saw her, he fleetingly stopped in his tracks, but then cut left, crossing the car park towards his Bentley.

'Frank . . . Frank!' she called, hurrying after him.

He stopped, shoulders sagging, before asking the rest of his team to give him some space.

Obediently, they moved off, halting by the car about twenty yards away, watching with interest. Only Shallicker hung close.

'What're you doing?' she asked, in a voice of genuine concern.

McCracken shrugged. 'What does it look like? I've discharged myself.'

'Frank . . . you only got shot yesterday!'

'Cora, you should *not* be here. Hasn't Lucy told you?'

'I don't take orders from Lucy.'

'Well, you should on this occasion.'

'Look . . . it's Lucy I want to talk to you about.'

'There's a surprise.' He walked on.

'She's told her bosses.'

He stopped again and turned. Shallicker came forward too.

'She's just rung me,' Cora said, pale-faced. 'Told me to come and see you. I couldn't believe it. But she wanted me to give you *that* message. Apparently, it's for your own safety.'

'When you say she's told her bosses,' he said, 'told them what exactly?'

'That you're her father.'

McCracken exchanged a glance with Shallicker. He shrugged again. 'It doesn't matter.'

Cora was baffled. 'Won't it change your situation?'

'My situation, as you call it, has already changed. But like I say, that doesn't matter now. What matters is that you get right away from here.'

'I don't understand . . .?'

'Away from *me*. Do you understand that, at least?'

'I see.' Cora couldn't conceal how upset this made her.

'It's for your own good.'

She nodded but said nothing.

'Tell Lucy I appreciated the heads-up.'

He walked on, veering towards the rest of his men.

'That's it, then?' Shallicker said.

'That's it,' McCracken replied. 'We haven't got a bloody choice now.'

Chapter 41

As Lucy pulled onto the drive of her bungalow on Cuthbertson Court, she heard the landline ringing inside. She hurried indoors, just in time to catch it.

It was Tessa Payne at the other end. 'Lucy . . . glad I caught you. I've been trying your mobile, but—'

'Don't worry, it's kaput,' Lucy said.

'Well . . . at least it's not you, eh?' Once again, the trainee detective sounded breathless and excited. Doubtless, this fast-moving enquiry, with its potential enormous pay-off, was just the sort of thing she'd joined CID to get involved in. Evidently, she hadn't yet learned that Lucy was *persona non grata*.

'I suppose I agree with that,' Lucy replied, too emotionally exhausted even to make it sound like the sarcasm she'd intended. 'Sorry, Tessa. Yeah . . . least I'm alive.'

'I'm so sorry . . . I mean, sorry you had to go through all that alone.'

'Two of us being nabbed wouldn't have improved things, Tess. Thanks for the thought, though. How's it going?'

'What do you mean?'

'The search for the Torgau girls.'

'Oh . . . well, the house is getting turned over. Their escape route led through an old sewer and came up again in a derelict garage about three streets away. We've located a lock-up near the town centre too. Think that's where they were keeping the van. There's a respraying kit in there, goggles, paint-stained overalls, a load of fake registration plates and spare clothes. The van's not there though, obviously.'

'No indication where they might have taken it?' Lucy asked.

'Not yet. But I heard some of the Serious crowd talking. They don't reckon they'll get very far. I mean, they can travel as far as the petrol takes them, obviously, but we've put an all-points out, so it won't be easy getting a refill. On top of that, what are they going to do in the middle of the night? Park in a layby and sleep? Maybe one night, maybe two, but that can't go on indefinitely, can it? Even if they change vehicles, that situation won't improve.'

'Unless they've got somewhere else to lay low,' Lucy said. 'Somewhere more secure.'

Payne thought about that. 'You mean if they've got more accomplices?'

'It's hardly going to be the Crew. But the Torgau girls are bound to know other folk. They've not been living like nuns . . . hang on, *whoa!*'

'What's up?' Payne asked.

'Nuns,' Lucy said, mainly to herself.

'What do you mean, "nuns"?' Payne wondered. 'You said something about that before.'

'Nothing, it's all right.' A compelling new thought had just occurred to Lucy, and it was already taking a deep, fast root. 'Just let me know if you hear anything, yeah?'

'Aren't you off sick?'

'Yeah, but this was my case, I want to know how it pans out.'

394

But Payne now sounded intrigued. 'What did you mean, "nuns"?'

'Tessa, I've got to go. Stick with the footage.'

Lucy cut the call and stood thinking.

Nuns . . .

She dashed back outside, jumped into the Jimny, threw it into reverse and swung it onto the road.

The Torgau girls could be anywhere. They could have another vehicle, another lock-up, not to mention all kinds of well-resourced associates that no one in the police knew about. But most likely the latter did *not* apply. Martin Torgau had been successful for so long because he'd kept everything in-house. He'd flown under the law enforcement radar, shielded by a façade of decorum. By playing the good neighbour, socialising only with respectable people, he'd done nothing whatsoever to draw police attention to him – which also meant that he'd kept his fraternising with fellow criminals to a minimum. Even if that hadn't been the case, the Crew had tried to wipe both him and his daughters out. So how many hoodlums would seriously be willing to offer them refuge? And yet those two girls had taken off like bats out of Hell, like girls with a real purpose.

And that purpose wasn't just to ride the roads until they ran out of fuel. They were headed somewhere they could hole up, somewhere they could lie low and reorganise, somewhere no one outside themselves and their father knew about.

With one possible exception.

Lucy turned her vehicle in the direction of St Clement's.

This enquiry had seen her gamble on some genuine longshots, and yet this would be the longest shot of all. It was tenuous as a strand of chewing gum, but just at present, as her entire career was hanging by it, she'd take any chance that came her way.

*

'Oh dear, look what I've found,' Lucy said, after kicking open the door to the only cubicle in the row that had a door attached.

It was obscenely filthy in there, the walls covered with brown smears and scrawls of vile graffiti, the stench thick enough to knock a person down. But unlike all the others, this toilet had a seat and a lid on it, though the lid was currently closed, Sister Cassie's satchel lying on top, and on top of that her a slim metal box lying open on several key items: a foil wrap, a cigarette lighter, a blackened spoon and a small plastic syringe cap.

The ex-nun herself was on the floor, crammed into the niche alongside the porcelain throne, her left sleeve unfastened and rolled back, and a cord tied around her upper arm. In her right hand, a syringe filled with clear fluid hovered over one of several ugly bruises.

'If it isn't someone in possession of controlled drugs!' Lucy declared.

Sister Cassie's face looked pinched and pale. Now it turned peevish. 'My child, let's not be foolish. You know that I'm purely a user. I never distribute this material.'

Lucy pulled one of her leather motorcycle gloves on and flexed her fingers. The ex-nun watched, helpless, as the cop reached down and took the syringe away, fitting its cap in place and sliding it into one of her jacket pockets. After that, she took the wrap of heroin.

'You're still in contravention of the law, Sister.'

'And are you really going to arrest me?'

Lucy backed out of the cubicle, beckoning. 'Come on, on your feet.'

Sister Cassie stayed where she was. 'It wasn't my fault about this morning. I came to the police station, like you said, but you weren't there.'

Lucy was briefly regretful. It was correct that she'd

arranged for the ex-nun to come in and give her statement, but in the fury-ride of overtaking events, she'd forgotten all about it. Not that it made any difference now.

She beckoned again. 'Come on, Sister. Move it.'

Whimpering with frustration, the ex-nun released the cord and put what remained of her bits and pieces back into the flat tin, which she carefully lidded. 'Lucy Clayburn, I am very disappointed in you. I thought you were different from the others.'

She got to her feet, shivering as she tightened her cloak against a chill that Lucy didn't feel. She was sweaty too, her nose running, all of which implied that she was strung-out, which wouldn't help. But it could have been worse. She could have been high.

Shouldering the satchel, she emerged into the main body of the toilet block. It was the one Lucy had been told about, on the end of the row of derelict shops near Penrose Mill, and it was a dank, dingy hole, filled with litter and broken glass, and strewn with old syringes.

'I thought you were different too,' Lucy said. 'You might not be a dealer, but you keep the dealers in business, don't you? And what about this place? It's supposed to be a public convenience, not a dump site for dirty needles.'

'Those are not my needles,' the nun protested. 'I always take mine to the Exchange.'

'Unless you're too stoned to remember.'

Sister Cassie looked shocked at the suggestion. 'That's never happened.'

'How would you know? Uh? When you're walking down the street like the living dead, throwing away that wonderful education you gained at the taxpayer's expense? Do you ever wonder about the generations of kids you didn't inspire after you became an addict?'

'What's all this about?' The ex-nun looked puzzled, at

least partly because she'd offered her hands to be cuffed, and it hadn't happened yet. 'You've never moralised like this before.'

'I'll tell you what this is, Sister . . . I'm about to do the world a favour. I'm going to throw you in the slammer. They'll break you of the habit in there. They'll *make* you get clean.'

'And what about my regulars? Who will look after them?'

Lucy shrugged. 'They chose this bed to lie on, so that's their problem. Unless . . .' She raised a cautionary finger. 'Unless there's a way we can help them too.' She paused. 'What does "Maggie" mean?'

Sister Cassie looked bemused. 'Isn't it a name? Short for Margaret?'

'Yeah, but it's a name I've heard used twice in the last couple of days . . . on both occasions in reference to *you*.' Lucy paused again, but the ex-nun merely shrugged. 'The girl who attacked you yesterday night. You said she called you a "stiff-arsed virgin bitch" and said that she would "take you back to fucking Maggies". And then, not four or five hours ago, the same girl referred to you as a "Maggie slut".'

Sister Cassie looked even more baffled. 'I honestly have no clue. Obviously, a disturbed individual, who—'

'None of this "disturbed characters who don't know what they're doing" crap.' Lucy grabbed her by her wrists. 'Listen to me, Sister . . . it's vital that you help me. Otherwise, your regulars are going to find there'll be no one to tuck them up at night for quite a few months. What does "Maggie slut" mean?'

'How could I possibly know?'

'Because I had a thought earlier on. It's got to be in reference to what you *are*, or what you once *were*. That girl I spoke about, she and her sister spent some time in a Catholic care home . . . when their father was in prison.'

'But that had nothing to do with me. My students were O Level and above. There were no special needs, no children with any kinds of problems that I . . . *oh!*' Her expression changed, as if something remarkable had just occurred to her. 'Oh, my word . . . Maggies.'

'Yes?' Lucy prompted her.

'Bless my soul. I'd never have . . . oh, but it can't be that.'

'Can't be what?'

Sister Cassie's eyes, previously clouded with pain and misery, had suddenly cleared. 'The term Maggies might refer to Santa Magdalena.'

'Santa . . .?'

'Santa Magdalena.'

Now, it was Lucy's turn to look bewildered. 'I've never heard of it.'

'It was a childcare community operated by the archdiocese. On the outskirts of Crowley. If memory serves, the children used to refer to it as St Maggies.'

'Take you back to Maggies,' Lucy said slowly.

'I only visited occasionally, but it was run by my own order,' Sister Cassie added. 'The Carmelite Sisters.' She looked sad. 'Rather a pejorative term for some very hard-working women . . . but *they* would most likely have been the "stiff-arsed virgins" that this ungrateful girl referred to.'

'You say the kids *used* to call it St Maggies?'

'That's my point. It's been closed for ten years at least. It's no longer used for anything, but the buildings are still there. Some kind of dispute is raging about who owns them—'

'Where is it?'

'I don't know the address, but it's over towards Glazebury.'

'Could you find it if we got in the car?' Lucy asked.

'We aren't going to the police station?'

'If you can direct me there, Sister . . . we'll call it time served.'

Chapter 42

Frank McCracken's official residence was 17, Yellowbrook Close, Didsbury, in South Manchester. The house, a five-bedroom detached, surrounded by extensive gardens, was located on a swish but secluded housing estate, where the average property price could be anything between £700,000 and £1,000,000.

At present, though, there was no one home. It was nearly eight o'clock in the evening, and Mrs Hepplethwaite, McCracken's housekeeper, finished no later than six. Most of the neighbours were indoors, their children along with them because it was a school night. Overhead, the evening sky turned from lilac to indigo, while down below, the dim orange bulbs of streetlights flickered to life one by one.

Slowly, unusually cautiously, Mick Shallicker drove along the empty street, parking the Bentley in front of McCracken's house rather than using the fob on the key-ring to open the electronically operated gates. Yellowbrook Close was a cul-de-sac, which always made him feel hemmed in, even in normal circumstances, so to go onto the drive now would seem like sheer folly. He climbed from the car and loitered on the pavement, scanning the surrounding gardens, paying particular attention to other parked vehicles, seeing if there were any that he didn't recognise. No one would think it strange to see him here, for all that his size made him an eye-catching individual. He was known locally as an employee of McCracken's, a security man who often lived on site, though this behaviour might have appeared a little strange.

At present, of course, he had too many other things on his mind to be worried by that.

He finally used the fob on the pedestrian gate, which stood to one side. It swung open, and he walked up the drive, unlocking a side-door to the house. Inside, he deactivated the alarm and stood for a second, listening. The palatial interior was perfectly still and smelled clean and fresh.

Satisfied, Shallicker trotted upstairs to the third bedroom, which was reserved for guests. In an upper section of its wardrobe, he found a series of matching tan suitcases of decreasing size, each one placed inside the next like the parts of a Russian doll. He selected one of the smaller ones, though not the smallest, and took it through to the main bedroom. Opening the wardrobe in there, he yanked out various clothes and threw them all into the case. He then moved through to the bathroom, which was all gold and chrome and crystal, the tub large enough to accommodate several people at once – and that had happened at least a couple of times to Shallicker's memory, his employer frolicking two and even three at a time with some of his favourite ladies.

In the mirrored cupboard, he found a zipped toiletries kit, containing everything for the man on the move. He tossed that into the case too, and then hovered, trying to ensure there was nothing else he'd missed. McCracken already had his wallet and his laptop, and any data files he might need on the pen-drive he always kept on his person. Shallicker then remembered the other thing – in some ways, it was the most important item of all. He could have slapped himself on the head. Hunkering down alongside McCracken's four-poster bed, he pulled out a drawer. Inside it, there was a shoebox, and inside the shoebox a Walther P22, with six full magazines. Shallicker threw those into the case as well, compressed everything down and tugged the zip closed.

He glanced at his watch. It was now after eight. What daylight remained was diminishing fast. He descended the staircase, humping the heavy bag alongside him. At the bottom, he stopped to think one final time, dying sunlight lying in crimson stripes across the whole of the downstairs. It would be dark by the time he hit the M60, which while it didn't give him any kind of decisive advantage, would be more useful to him than broad daylight.

He left the house the same way he'd come in, reactivating the alarm and then closing and locking the side-door behind him. As he walked down the drive, Yellowbrook Close still looked deserted. He retreated backward through the pedestrian gate, pushing the suitcase onto the pavement with his foot, while turning and using both hands to ensure that the gate closed and locked behind him.

'Going on holiday, Mick?' someone asked.

Shallicker twirled around and found Benny B a couple of yards away, with three of his black-suited goons at his back. Further movement drew his attention down to the end of the street, where two of the Crew's security chief's trademark black Audi A6s trundled into view.

Shallicker shrugged. 'Getting Frank a change of togs. He's been discharged.'

'Already?' Benny B wasn't clever enough to affect mock-surprise. He sounded *genuinely* surprised, but two of the trio behind him were visibly wielding handguns inside their jacket pockets, while the other one wore a raincoat over his shoulders, mainly to screen the Uzi submachine gun he was carrying. So Shallicker had no doubt that this wasn't a courtesy call.

'Frank's walking around,' he ventured. 'No point him staying in hospital.'

'Well . . . he's certainly walking around,' Benny B agreed, the two Audis now gliding into place and braking, blocking the Bentley in. 'That much is truthful. That's why he discharged himself earlier on. So, where you really going, Mick? And where you taking that gear?'

'Look, Ben . . . I just do what I'm told.'

'Don't we all?' Benny nodded towards the nearest Audi, the front passenger door to which had clunked open. 'After you, pal.'

More nervous than he'd ever been in his life, Shallicker picked the case up.

'Leave that,' Benny B said. 'Frank may not know it yet, but he's actually going nowhere.'

'Can't leave it on the street, Ben . . . there's a piece inside.'

'Speaking of which . . . arms up.'

Shallicker leaned against the Audi, hands outspread. One of Benny's goons made a quick search of his upper body, extricating the Colt Cobra from his shoulder-holster, and then searching his pockets, taking charge of the keys to the Bentley. Another one picked up the suitcase.

'Okay,' Benny said. 'You're good to go.'

Shallicker climbed into the front passenger seat, back and shoulders tense as hardboard, especially when he sensed Benny and two of his men climb in behind. Doors slammed.

'Don't be too worried,' Benny said. 'We just want to know what's going on.'

Shallicker shrugged again. 'Frank discharged himself and he's going away for a few days to recover. What's the big deal?'

'The big deal,' Bill Pentecost's voice sounded from the dash, 'is that first he ordered a hit on a high-level affiliate of ours without running it by the board!'

Shallicker initially jumped on hearing the voice, but then realised that Wild Bill was at the other end of a phone somewhere.

'Don't tell me *you* were involved in that, Michael?' the Chairman said, in the kind of disappointed tone that indicated he already knew the answer.

'Look, Bill . . .' Shallicker held his hands up as though the guy was there in front of him. 'I've already said . . . I just do what I'm told.'

'In that case do what you're told now,' Pentecost retorted. 'Give us the skinny. What's going on and where's Frank? It may be that he had a perfectly good reason to wipe out the Ripsaw Man. I mean, it's a shame such a talented associate is gone. But if it had to happen, it had to happen. The point is . . . I'd like to know why.'

'I don't know why exactly . . .' Shallicker stiffened as a muzzle jabbed the back of his left shoulder. 'But I think Frank was unimpressed by a job he did for us recently. Caused some collateral damage, left a paper trail for the cops to follow.'

'And that's the reason he's gone into hiding?' The voice sounded unconvinced.

'He's not gone into hiding.'

'So it's just a coincidence that he's done a runner from hospital, that he's not answering his mobile and that his minder is packing his bags for him?'

'Frank's aware that he's breached protocol, Bill.'

'If that's all it is, he's not the man of steel he once was. So, where is he?'

With a click, Benny B cocked the pistol.

'All right, all right,' Shallicker said hurriedly. 'He's got a safehouse. Down in Delamere Forest.'

There was a brief silence before Pentecost spoke again. 'Benny, you know what to do.'

Then he cut the call.

Benny B dug his pistol into Shallicker's back again. 'You know what to do too, Mick.'

Shallicker nodded and started issuing directions. The Audi pulled off the estate and headed south towards the motorway. The second Audi and McCracken's Bentley, now with one of Benny's goons at the wheel, fell into line behind it.

From the M60, they joined the M56, heading west. Gradually the South Manchester conurbation melted away behind them, replaced by the occasional woods and flat, quilt-work fields of rural Cheshire. About forty minutes later, night had fallen completely, and they'd pulled off the main road network and were following rutted back-lanes between deep, dark hedgerows. They finally drew up against the verge at an unmarked crossroads. There were no streetlights now, their headlamp beams illuminating a white-painted fingerpost offering arrows to destinations like Winsford, Weaverham and Cuddington, which remained mostly unknown to Benny B and his crew. What was most noticeable was the mileages involved. They were all in double-figures, which meant that Frank McCracken had chosen this particular safehouse carefully; it was a long way out.

'It's that one.' Shallicker nodded to the lane on their left. It didn't promise much, disappearing beneath a canopy of trees into complete blackness. 'Why don't you let me go in alone, Ben? I can talk to him first. Then there'll be no hassle.'

'There'll be no hassle anyway,' Benny replied. 'How far down there is it?'

'Hundred or so yards. There's a layby about thirty yards along, where we can leave the cars. They'll be okay there. No one else ever uses it.'

Benny instructed the driver to go left. A short distance

along, they pulled into the layby and went the remaining way on foot, the big minder at the front, still being prodded in the back with a pistol. The road, which was so narrow that even a tractor would have trouble negotiating it, curved sharply and an opening appeared on their left. Shallicker went through, the others following silently, now with deep bushes on either side. These only ended another fifty yards on, when a broken-down farm gate on the right revealed a thatched cottage with several dilapidated outbuildings ranged to the left of it in horseshoe formation. Light streamed out onto a courtyard of beaten earth, but everything else lay in darkness.

'Any motion sensors out here?' Benny wondered quietly.

Shallicker shook his head.

'So we're not going to get bathed in a glorious light-show?'

Again, Shallicker shook his head. 'The idea of this place was that it *wouldn't* draw attention to itself.'

Benny jabbed him with the gun again, marching him forward towards the main structure. The other seven followed, fanning out, firearms drawn. One scampered ahead, flattening himself against the cottage's front wall and sidling along it until he reached the window, at which point he risked a quick peek.

'He's in there,' he whispered, chuckling.

'Alone?' Benny asked.

'Yeah.'

'What's he doing?'

Another chuckle. 'Watching telly.'

Benny shook his head in disbelief.

'Overconfidence was always your gaffer's weak spot,' he told Shallicker. 'Was always going to lead to a bad end one day. Sorry, Mick –' and he nodded at the others, one of whom produced a sledgehammer and advanced on the cottage door '– but this fall from grace is well overdue.'

Chapter 43

'You didn't need to threaten me, you know,' Sister Cassie said, as they drove. She still sounded mildly offended; she was also shaky and sweaty, strongly in need of her 'medicine'. 'I'd have helped you. I always help if I can.'

'If you can . . . that's the thing,' Lucy replied, slowing as they approached a red light, though there were few other vehicles on the road. It was now after nine, and they were on the southernmost outskirts of Crowley. 'Sometimes, you're just a bit too addled. Like when you didn't mention that you'd actually witnessed Fred Holborn's abduction until nearly two weeks after.'

The ex-nun harrumphed, as if that was a small and rather silly point.

'At this moment, Sister, I have a burning need to take two very bad people off the street. So I need focus and concentration, not garbled silliness from a head that's been ruined by drugs.'

'And are you sure you've got that now?' Sister Cassie said. 'It's the next left, by the way.'

'You're certain, this time?'

'Yes. I think so, at least.'

'I *hope* I've got it.' Lucy turned down a country lane, with small clutches of new housing built on either side of it.

'Because even if we find this old orphanage . . .' the ex-nun said.

'Which we *have* to,' Lucy asserted, 'because you said you *knew* where it was!'

'Even if we find it, I'm not at all certain that it will be relevant to your investigation. As I say, it's empty. A ruin.'

'We won't know unless we look.'

'It's a big place too. It'll take the two of us all night to search it.'

'There is no two of us. It'll just be me.'

The ex-nun was surprised. 'You alone?'

'You're a civilian. You'll have to stay in the car.'

'Surely you can call other police officers?'

Lucy sighed. 'Not at present.'

'Then you have a task ahead of you which is well-nigh impossible.'

'Tell me about it . . .'

They drove in silence for a few minutes, Lucy doing her best to keep a lid on her vexation. All her fears and frustrations of earlier had been amplified in the last two hours by Sister Cassie's confusing and contradictory directions. Given that the Santa Magdalena care home, though on the edge of the borough, was officially within Crowley, they ought to have located it some time ago, but they'd constantly gone the wrong way and needed to turn back. Several times they'd had to wing it because the ex-nun simply didn't know where they were. Even Lucy's sat-nav was useless as they didn't have an address and, since the care home hadn't existed for well over a decade, it didn't figure in the list of local landmarks. Lucy didn't know where it was herself, because it had closed before she'd started as a cop, and she couldn't just Google it or ring someone to ask because she had no phone with her. On reflection, she ought to have gone home and looked it up on her laptop on first hearing about it, but Sister Cassie had seemed to know where it was and, at the time, letting her direct had seemed like the quickest option.

Lucy now realised that she ought to have known better.

'There's been so much building work since I was last here,' the ex-nun complained. 'I don't recognise half of these housing estates.'

This was true, and much of the extensive redevelopment was still under way. At one point, they'd found themselves meshed in a web of roadworks, their route ahead blocked by a succession of dirt-carrying dumper trucks moving into and out of a fenced-off hardhat area, a bored-looking workman leaning on his 'Stop' sign as if it was the only thing keeping him awake. So irritated had Lucy become that she'd activated the blues and twos for a couple of minutes to clear themselves a passage.

'I can't identify this part of town at all.' Sister Cassie's voice, progressively more querulous, intruded on her thoughts.

'Look,' Lucy said. 'We have to find it soon. This is Lower Green Lane, which means we're not just on our way out of the N Division, we're on our way out of the entire Greater Manchester Police area.'

'Wait! Wait . . . I recognise that!'

A pub had appeared from the darkness on their left. It was boarded up, but the sign over its door was visible if Lucy slowed down, which she did, revealing that it had formerly been the Plough and Harrow.

'You're sure?' Lucy said.

'Yes, *yes*!' The ex-nun's confidence grew. 'It's a little further ahead on the right.'

There were now trees on their right, ranked densely behind a low stone wall. It *did* look as if they were following the boundary to some enclosed area. They passed a bus stop.

'Yes, we're almost there,' Sister Cassie confirmed. 'That's where visitors to the care home used to get off.'

'So . . . the next turn?' Lucy ventured.

'It should be.'

When the next turn came along, it was on the right and it looked promising. Overgrown trees hemmed it in, while two tall brick gateposts stood one to either side of it, though there was no gate suspended between them. Lucy pulled in and stopped. A sign stood on the left, half hidden by leafage, and faded and flaked to illegibility. The surface of the driveway dwindling away into the darkness ahead of them was broken and weedy.

'Doesn't look like many people come here,' she said.

'Why would they?'

'Why indeed?'

Lucy eased her foot down, and they accelerated forward, following a winding route, no more than a single vehicle wide. Deep undergrowth, still lush and tangled from the summer, grew close on either verge, creating a claustrophobic, tunnel-like atmosphere, which seemed to run on and on.

'Talk about cut off from the world,' Lucy said. 'Why did this place close, anyway?' She glanced sidelong. 'Your lot getting up to no good again?'

'Not this time,' Sister Cassie replied. 'It's just that foster care and adoption are the preference now. And recent rationalisation of Church expenditure means there are fewer homes of this sort anyway. Of course, there are still legions of unwanted children, many of whom are actually in the care of *your lot* – the state. Where they've always been safe and sound, haven't they!'

Lucy didn't respond, because they rounded a bend, and suddenly a gate was barring their path. Two gates, to be precise, ten feet tall at least, vertically barred, though on closer inspection it looked as if they were standing ajar by a few inches. More interesting than this, there was a car parked to the left-hand side of them.

Lucy braked, guiding her own vehicle to a halt.

'I thought you said this place wasn't used any more?' she said.

'I didn't think it was.'

'Stay in the car.' Lucy switched the engine off, released her belt and climbed out.

Outside, the night was astoundingly quiet. There was no hum of distant traffic, no mutter of breeze amid the unseen woodlands to her left and right. She walked forward feeling worse than vulnerable, feeling as if she was being watched – she hated that term, but it was always so appropriate – until she reached the parked car, at which point she stopped in her tracks.

Because suddenly she recognised it.

It was a tan Vauxhall Corsa; two or three years old, carrying several dents and minor rust patches. Lucy was certain that it was one of the pool cars from Crowley CID. If so, it was a kind of relief. She wouldn't be here alone, plus someone else had come to the same conclusion she had, which was a sort of vindication.

But the Corsa stood empty and locked.

She walked around it a couple of times, bewildered, before turning to appraise the gates.

Whatever colour they had once been was now undetectable as they were so caked in rust, but as she'd seen before, they were open. A single chain, equally rusty, had once been used to bind them closed, but this hung loose. Lucy lifted it and saw that it had been snipped through, literally sliced, as though with a pair of bolt-croppers. She examined it, only to jump and look sharply around at the sound of skittering undergrowth, as if someone or something had just darted

411

away through the foliage. But there was no visible sign of anything, the leaves and branches hanging still in the glare of her headlights.

She glanced at her own car, and the outline of Sister Cassie behind the windscreen, and then at the chain again. It was difficult to tell whether it had been cut recently, but it was clearly deliberate. The question then was: had whoever'd arrived in the police Corsa done this? If they had, it was drastic action on their part, which made it feel unlikely. Especially as they clearly hadn't come team-handed – there were no spare bodies mooching about, there was no one standing guard on the vehicle, there was no sign at all that this was part of an organised raid.

She pushed at the gate on her right, and it swung back easily; there was no creak or groan from its hinges, suggesting that they'd been oiled recently.

She walked back to the Jimny, opened her driver's door and, rooting in the glove-box, took out her Maglite.

'What's happening?' Sister Cassie asked.

'I wish I knew,' Lucy replied.

She walked back to the Corsa, switching the light on and shining its beam through the various windows as she circled it again. Almost immediately, she spotted a heap of paperwork spilled across the back seat. The majority of it looked like print-out images.

Lucy leaned right to the glass, cupping her eyes to see more clearly.

They *were* print-out images, black and whites depicting what appeared to be vehicles at road-junctions or speeding along highways.

Print-outs from traffic camera footage, she realised.

'Oh, crap!' She strained her eyes to see better. And no ordinary vehicles, by the looks of the few pictures she could actually focus on. Just *one* vehicle in each case. A dark-coloured

412

van. She backed away, shaking her head. '*Tessa* . . . what the hell are you playing at?'

Lucy hurried back to her Jimny and stuck her head through the driver's door. 'How far is it from here?' she asked. 'The main building?'

The ex-nun shrugged. 'We're almost there. Probably just round the next bend.'

'Okay. In that case, I don't want to bring the car any closer.'

'You're actually going in there alone?' Sister Cassie appeared to have got on top of her DTs. She still looked pale but was steadier now and seemed to be concerned for Lucy rather than herself.

'I wasn't going to,' Lucy admitted.

And that was the honest truth. For all her bravado about searching the place solo, she'd only been intending to have a quick poke around the exterior, to see if there was any sign that she was on the right track. The vandalised gate on its own would maybe have sufficed, but all she'd have done then was go looking for a phone to call Priya Nehwal.

Unfortunately, there was no time for that now.

'But it seems that someone else has got here ahead of us,' she said. 'One of our less experienced officers. Looks like she found the cut chain and decided to have a sniff around. So I've got to go in too.'

'Don't you need a warrant for that? The place is in private ownership.'

'Not if I think there's someone in danger here.'

'Your officer is in danger?' If it was possible, the nun paled even more than earlier. 'You think these two horrible people are here now?'

'I don't know, okay?' Lucy said. 'But I *have* to check. Now listen . . . Sister, can you drive?'

'Drive?' Sister Cassie was taken aback. 'Well . . . yes, I

413

used to drive. When I was a teacher, I had access to a car. I haven't done it for years, mind.'

'I'm sure you won't have forgotten everything.'

'What do you want me to do?'

'Nothing. Except get away from here quickly, if you need to. Which is why I'm leaving the key in the ignition. Now listen . . .' Lucy regarded her intently. 'I'm trusting that you're not going to steal my car and go off to try and score some more smack.'

The ex-nun looked exasperated. 'My dear child . . .'

'I mean it, Sister. You do that, and you'll be stealing a police vehicle, as well as obstructing a murder enquiry. It'll be the big house, for sure.'

'My child . . . do you really think I'd maroon you here? I've just said that I don't think you should be going in there alone.'

'And like I've said –' Lucy was already walking '– I've got no choice now.'

'Those buildings are too big!' the nun called after her. 'Plus, they're old and probably dangerous.'

But Lucy had already gone, sidling through the gap between the gates, and pressing into the darkness.

Chapter 44

Lucy sensed the thinning of the trees and the open space just ahead, and so veered off the drive, forging the last twenty yards through deep and heavy rhododendrons, switching her Maglite off. It was so late now that she couldn't imagine anyone seeing her emerge from the woods on the drive, but she was determined to do all she could to minimise the chance. As the undergrowth lightened, she slowed, finally stopping with only a thin wall of greenery in front of her.

Beyond that, moonlight speckled by blots of cloud-shadow lay across a compelling vista.

The drive, still covered in weeds, bent left as it emerged from the woods, swerving past the spot where she now stood, and curving around what looked like an immense ornamental pond, before halting in front of a row of several large buildings. The pond, which was probably large enough to be classified as a mini lake – oval, at least a couple of hundred yards long by a hundred wide and bordered by a low brick wall – was black, flat and, in the parts where it wasn't thick with bulrushes or dotted by lily-pads, glimmering with lunar light. The buildings were visible in great detail, the central and largest one, presumably the care home itself, a towering gothic structure with rows of ecclesiastically arched windows, a central spire and what might be gargoyles leaning down from its parapets.

It boasted a huge pair of central doors, heavily and untidily nailed over with planks, as if some frantic, terror-stricken person had hammered them there in a desperate rush to be done with the place. Above the doors, there was a colossal stone pediment, on which a grimy clockface was visible.

The buildings to left and right were more functional. Admin sections perhaps, or kitchens. One thing was certain, though; the site was still officially disused. It wasn't just the front door. Most windows were boarded too, and there was no sign of any vehicles parked out front.

Despite the urgency of the situation, Lucy hesitated to advance further.

She had never believed in the supernatural, but she wasn't a hard-headed rationalist either, and this was just about the eeriest-looking group of buildings she'd ever seen, particularly the main one. It would be difficult, if not impossible, wandering through the gloomy, web-shrouded halls inside, not to think about the generations of unwanted youngsters who'd passed through there, in who knew what state of sadness and depression. There'd be a lot of melancholy shadows gathered in its dingy corners.

Not that it mattered now. All that mattered at present was locating Tessa Payne.

At which point she saw the light.

Lucy squinted through the leaves.

It was difficult to see exactly where the light was coming from, and at first it appeared to be on the ground floor of the central building. However, as her vision slowly adjusted to the dimness, it looked more and more as if it was issuing from a passage between the central structure and the one on its left.

She waited tensely, at any moment expecting someone to emerge from that passage carrying a torch. Hoping it would be Payne.

But that didn't happen, and the seconds ticked by.

Perhaps that light was nothing to do with the trainee detective? Maybe it had come on inside and was shining out through an aperture of some sort? It wasn't necessarily sinister, of course. If the lights were working, the building was obviously still hooked to the grid, which suggested that whoever was in there had the blessing of the owners. A caretaker or maintenance man possibly. Though if that was the case, wouldn't some kind of vehicle be parked?

And what about the damaged gate?

However, the main mystery was still where Tessa Payne had gone. And that was now a serious conundrum, because though Lucy increasingly felt that she ought to call for some cavalry here, she still lacked the means, and going looking for a pay-phone would only take time, during which Payne could be in all sorts of trouble.

She continued to watch, but still nothing moved.

Finally, as warily as possible, she stepped onto the drive and commenced following it around the lake, walking slowly, all the way hanging close to the wall of vegetation. The night's silence was broken only by the occasional *plop* from the water, most likely frogs. Meanwhile, the great baroque pile that was Santa Magdalena ballooned towards her. The closer she drew, the grimmer and more neglected it looked. Fallen roof tiles scattered the driveway; pipework hung loose; thick tufts of weed grew from its gutters.

As she reached the first building, there was a loud *splash*, this time from the edge of the water. She stopped and stared, but nothing moved out there, not even ripples on the surface. The trees along the far shore were visible but motionless, the spaces beneath them utterly black. She proceeded on, undecided whether to stay close to the building to shield herself from prying eyes, or to keep a safe distance in case someone reached out from a hidden recess. Eventually, she opted to stay close but not too close.

The second building was something like a low-rise office block made from pebble-dashed concrete. It looked very modern compared to everything else, but no less bleak. Lucy didn't pay it much attention, because the main building – the care home itself – was just ahead. Its frontage had been impressive enough, but she could now see that it went back a significant way, a hundred yards or more, and was a huge, dense block of a structure, which, for all its cornicing and traceried stone, must have been a gloomy and austere place to spend your formative years.

Directly in front of her now, the stripe of light lay across the drive from the passage entrance. She slowed, treading as lightly as possible. When she reached the corner, she halted and peeked around it.

The passage was wider than she'd expected. It was more an alley, wide enough to take a vehicle. Where it eventually led, presumably the rear of the property, was hidden in darkness. But about thirty yards along, on the wall of the care home itself, stood a pair of double-doors made from timber, with frosted glass panels in their upper sections. A garage, by the looks of it. The doors stood open about half a yard, and yellow light spilled out.

Lucy walked down there, slowly, tentatively. When she reached the door, she flattened herself against the wall and listened. Still nothing, though she was certain someone was here. She'd seen this light be switched on. More to the point, the garage doors had been forced open, the area around the central lock having splintered outward.

Surely Tessa Payne hadn't done that?

Lucy sidled forward and glanced inside, seeing a large

space where several vehicles could have been installed. Its floor was asphalt, its walls and pillars concrete, its ceiling made from wood, but none of the usual accoutrements of a garage were on show. There were no tools, no spare tyres, no shelves loaded with oily, grubby equipment. There *was* a vehicle, though. Only one, but it told its own story – because it was a green transit van.

Lucy slid inside so that she could look more closely. It was a nondescript vehicle, bearing no distinguishing features. But she was in no doubt that if she picked up a stone and scraped its flank, she'd expose evidence of earlier spray-jobs: blue beneath the green most likely, and beneath that black. She circled it, trying its rear doors, but they were locked. She tried the driver's door and then the passenger door, but they were locked too. On the other side of the van, a portable electric light hung from a hook on a pillar, fed by an insulated cable, which snaked across the floor and vanished through an internal door standing open a couple of inches.

Lucy moved to this second door and listened. Again, silence.

She retreated to the van, wondering if she could disable it in some way, to prevent the bastards making a quick getaway; perhaps get under its front end and rip some wiring out, or maybe just let the air from its tyres, anything that would maroon them here while she nipped off and called for back-up – though she still wasn't prepared to do that until she knew where that wretched Tessa Payne was. She returned to the internal door, ear cocked, again hearing nothing. For several seconds she was torn. On one hand, she ought to keep investigating for the sake of her colleague, even if that meant penetrating deeper into the building. But on the other, it went against the cardinal rule of street-policing, that you never entered a suspicious premises alone.

And then she heard the moan.

Incredulous, she leaned against the internal door.

Another moan sounded. It came distinctly from what sounded like an adult female.

Lucy yanked the door open.

A brick stairway overhung with cobwebs led down into a basement area. There was no light on the stairs, but the door at the bottom stood half open, and a weak, reddish glow shone past it. She hurried down, half tripping on the cable, which descended alongside her.

Another moan sounded, more protracted this time, laden with pain.

She reached the bottom, opened the door and found herself facing a bare corridor with numerous doorways leading off it. Unlike the subterranean passage in the Torgau house, it was dank and filthy, the dull, reddish glow filling it. When she heard the fourth moan, it was louder and led her straight to a turn on the left.

Around it, lying splayed on the passage floor, head resting in a semi-congealed crimson pool, was Tessa Payne.

'Christ!' Lucy slid to her knees alongside her.

The young detective mumbled something inaudible, her eyes not completely closed, their lids fluttering. Lucy flicked her Maglite on and saw that the casualty's crinkly hair was clotted with freshly shed blood.

'Lucy . . .' Payne muttered.

'Lie still, don't try to move.' Lucy laid her torch on the floor alongside them, then dug the last pair of disposable gloves from her pocket, and pulled them on, before carefully working her way along Payne's scalp, foraging gently through the lush but sticky locks.

'Tried to . . . call you back. But, your mobile . . .'

'Yeah, my mobile's knackered,' Lucy said, distracted. 'I told you that. What the hell, Tessa . . . who did this?'

420

'Din' . . . see them.' Payne's voice became a whimper as Lucy probed the wounded flesh, searching for signs of a fracture. 'They came . . . from behind.'

'Tessa, what are you doing here?'

'You said . . . said something . . . about . . . nuns.'

'And?'

'Couple of days back, saw . . . saw van . . . dark-blue . . .'

'You saw a dark-blue van?' Lucy glanced down at her, trying to work out what she meant, but then remembered the screen-grab print-outs in the back of the CID car. She quickly realised what had happened, picturing the diligent young copper working on her CCTV footage over the last few days, latching onto various suspect vehicles as they threaded their way through Crowley, plotting their routes as she followed them from one camera to the next . . . 'And this one led you *here*?'

Payne tried to focus up at her, but her eyes were rolling in their sockets. 'Lost it . . . last junction . . .'

'And so you, being a conscientious copper, checked the area to see where it might have disappeared to. And you found Santa Magdalena?'

'Yeah, but . . .' Payne's eyes fluttered closed again, though she appeared to retain consciousness. 'Didn't think anything . . .'

Now Lucy understood. 'You didn't think anything of it until I mentioned *nuns* earlier this evening? Having already mentioned them to you once before – as well as talking vaguely about a Catholic care home.'

'Thought . . . thought you might need . . . some . . . help . . .'

Lucy resumed picking through the gore-matted hair. 'So why come here alone?'

'Seemed . . . a long shot. Plus . . .' Payne's eyes flickered opened again, her red-tinged gaze strained with agony, '. . . knew you were supposed . . . off sick. Didn't want . . . drop you in it.'

421

Lucy now found what she was looking for: two deep lacerations running side by side through the follicles, inches long each, both still oozing with blood. The results of at least two savage blows with a blunt instrument.

Even at first glance, the wounds were maybe a centimetre deep.

'Sodding hell . . . have you got your priorities wrong, Tessa.'

'Sorry, Lucy . . .'

Lucy knelt back, ripping her bloodied gloves off and tossing them away, before searching the casualty's jacket pockets. She found only a handkerchief, which she wadded into a compress, and then pushed against Payne's scalp. 'Where's your phone?'

'Not there?' Payne sounded vaguely surprised. 'Don't . . . know.'

Lucy grabbed the Maglite with her free hand and shone it along the passage, wondering if the phone had simply fallen from the girl's pocket when she'd been attacked. If it had, there was no sign of it now. Which meant that the assailants had taken it.

There was nothing for it. Under normal circs, she wouldn't want to move a head injury victim without medical supervision, especially when she had no clue how serious the injury was – the girl could be about to die for all Lucy knew – but she had to find a way to call assistance, and there was no possibility she could leave Payne here alone.

'Do you think you can stand?' she asked.

But Payne's eyes had closed again. 'Dunno,' she mumbled.

Lucy placed Payne's own hand on the compress, telling her to hold it in place, and then manoeuvred herself around, thinking to hook the girl under the armpits and lift her from behind. 'What the hell made you come inside on your own,

Tessa? You were three years in uniform, you ought to have known better.'

'Didn't . . . want to.'

Lucy glanced down at her again, puzzled.

'But I heard . . . heard . . .'

Somewhere nearby, in one of the connecting rooms in this dismal basement, a child started crying. A very young child.

Lucy spun around, startled.

'A baby . . .' she breathed. Then, louder, '*Dear God, have they grabbed a baby?*'

She straightened up, still scarcely able to believe what she was hearing. It wasn't especially muffled, and in fact was loud enough for the child, which sounded distressed to the point of hysteria, to be very close by.

She now completely understood why Payne had disregarded her own safety and gone running into the old building alone – because if there was one thing no police officer could ever ignore, it was a child that might be in danger.

Meanwhile, the mite was still crying, loudly, frantically. It was a terrible sound. Even in a public place, like a supermarket or park, you might've felt motivated to go and see what the problem was.

'Just stay here,' Lucy said quietly. 'I've got to check this out.'

Payne muttered something about hardly being in a position to move, while Lucy edged away from her with torch in hand, advancing along the corridor.

Just ahead, the insulated cable from the garage divided into two, one part snaking through a side doorway from which the red light appeared to shine, the other leading off into darkness, from which direction she heard the low rumble of what sounded like a generator.

So much for Santa Magdalena being hooked to the mains, Lucy thought, taking the route that led to the light. It was another short corridor leading to yet another half-open, red-lit doorway. She went forward again and opened the door, the groan of its aged hinges drowned by the bawling of the child. The red light, now much stronger, showed her a traditional old-fashioned cellar divided into various sections by vaulted brick arches, and filled with age-old rubbish: stacks of rickety, worm-eaten furniture swathed in cobwebs, boxes brimming with bric-a-brac so furred with dust that it was impossible to identify.

She switched her torch off, no longer needing it. Because another of those portable bulbs, this one bright scarlet, hung from a hook in the middle of the central arch. At the far side of the cellar, it showed her a further door standing open, and a few yards beyond that what looked like a cradle draped with dirty but semi-transparent cloth; not just down its sides, but over its top too, the material suspended from a kind of peaked framework, making it look like one of those tented cribs in fairy stories. By the increased volume, the crying child was in there.

Lucy advanced, glancing left and right. There were many niches and nooks down here where someone could hide. Frightened as well as bewildered, but focused on the cradle, she pressed on through the open door and immediately was assailed by a grotesque stench, both organic and chemical in its content. Immediately, it got into her nose and throat, and made her want to retch. She resisted, crossing to the cradle, trying not to look at the greasy black soot that caked the brickwork above and around her.

Below the dingy, gauze-like cloth, she saw the outline of a diminutive human form. No bigger than a new-born child, it wailed with anguish – and yet it didn't move. Lucy reached out a trembling hand. As she pulled the cloth away, she thought she sensed someone behind her, but it was too late, and she was too fixated on the child.

With a rustle, the material slid free – and she saw the eyeless, dirt-encrusted doll that had hung in those dead branches out on the landfill. Next to its head, there was an iPhone, and alongside that, as though to keep it snug, a boombox, out of which an unknown child continued to bawl.

Sensing the movement behind her again, Lucy tried to duck away, but not quickly enough.

The wire loop slipped over her head and tightened, encircling her neck. The next thing, it was biting into her, chewing through flesh and sinew as two tight-muscled arms began to twist and twist and twist.

'Benny's back, boss . . . he's on his way up,' Spicer, one of Bill Pentecost's thicker-necked, more bull-headed goons, said from the doorway connecting the Head Office to the boardroom.

The Chairman looked up from the *Manchester Evening News*. 'Is he alone?'

'Nah. Got company.'

Pentecost tossed his newspaper on the desk before turning to his laptop, hitting the keyboard and bringing his screen to life. He hit another key to access the security feeds. There were nine in total, each one a live image delivered by a different camera somewhere inside the Astarte. The one on the top left showed the interior of the express elevator from the private car park. It depicted several men. Four of Benny B's heavies were ranged across the back. Their hands were out of sight, but they were clearly training firearms on the two men in front of them: Frank McCracken and Mick Shallicker. Briefly, the twosome looked ridiculous, the enormous minder standing side-on to his infinitely shorter, leaner employer, who appeared unusually dishevelled. McCracken's left arm was still in a sling, and his jacket was draped over his shoulders; he wore no tie and his collar was open.

In front of those two, almost the same height as McCracken, but the same breadth as McCracken and Shallicker put together, was Benny B, grim-faced and silent as they rode.

Pentecost turned to Spicer. 'You know what to do.'

Spicer nodded and disappeared.

Pentecost got up from his chair and walked slowly into the boardroom, where he stopped and waited – with his own tie loose, his hands in his trouser pockets. It was not *his* normal look, either. But then these were not normal times.

Outside in the penthouse lobby, Spicer and two assistants stood by the lift doors. All non-security staff – barmen, waitresses, chambermaids and the like – had been given a half-day, so the threesome were alone. They waited loose-limbed and with pistols drawn, watching the red light above the doors, as the car ascended from floor to floor. In truth, they weren't expecting that Benny B would need any additional muscle, as he seemed to have things well in hand. But just in case, here they were.

With a *ping*, the lift arrived.

The double doors slid open – and Benny B was in their faces, features white, glasses askew, head crooked to one side by the Walther P22 jammed into his right ear.

'Drop 'em!' McCracken ordered, coming out behind him, pushing Benny's bulk forward as a human shield. 'Do it now or Benny gets it. You know I'm not kidding.'

Spicer and his oppos were stumped. Especially when they saw that Shallicker was carrying an Uzi submachine gun and levelling it at them over the security chief's shoulder. One burst and he'd take them all down. Of the four men left behind in the lift, it seemed that only two, the two in the middle, were Benny B's. The two on the outside, who now that they weren't being viewed through a grainy TV monitor, were clearly McCracken's, clutched pistols against their guts.

'You can live or die, Spicer,' McCracken said in a voice

426

that brooked no discussion. 'Your call. But if it's the latter, Benny dies first.'

Spicer and his sidekicks gazed past the great, quivering lump of uselessness that was Benny Bartholomew into Frank McCracken's cold eye and they didn't need to hear what had happened at the safehouse to know that no further assistance was coming.

Later on, they'd be told how it went down. Namely, that as Benny and his boys, who'd been led to the isolated cottage with remarkable ease by Mick Shallicker, went smashing through its front door, other doors – stable blocks, barns and the like – had opened behind them, and Frank's men had come out blazing. The ones at the back had fallen immediately, leaving those not caught in that first fusillade to unhesitatingly surrender. As for Benny, who'd now entered the cottage, he'd barely had time to react to the shooting behind him when he'd found two pump shotguns levelled on him by a pair of likely lads on the nearby staircase. When McCracken had casually emerged from the living room, he was unarmed. But it didn't matter – it was already over.

'What sickens me to the pit of my stomach,' McCracken now said, as the stand-off in the penthouse continued, 'is that our inner sanctum has been penetrated so easily. What do you think Bill's going to say, Spicer, that we got this far? And it's not just us. There's another seven or eight of my lads waiting to come up.'

As he spoke, the lift doors closed, and the elevator commenced its descent.

Spicer and his men backed away, dumbstruck. Spicer's eyes were drawn constantly to the black hole at the end of the Uzi. In truth, he didn't care about Benny B. The guy was ballast, a makeweight, a passenger from Wild Bill's early days. But that bloody submachine gun would tear all three of them apart, and the bloke on the other end of it, Mick

Shallicker, who was grinning like an overlarge devil, looked like he couldn't wait to pull the trigger.

'But I'm actually prepared to make a deal with you, Spicey, old mate,' McCracken said, now stepping around Benny's bulk, still keeping the pistol in his ear but, perhaps to show trust, presenting himself as a clear target. 'I want to start from scratch. I want to make everything right again with minimum trouble. That's why I've been talking on the phone all the way here from Cheshire. That's why I've called another emergency meeting. That's why the entire board of directors are on their way here as we speak. And I want *you* to be at that meeting too, Spicer.'

Spicer's face registered surprise.

'Yeah, I know,' McCracken said. 'You're just a grunt, aren't you? Your job is to keep your mouth shut and to soldier. Well, not any more . . . maybe. You guys hand your pieces over, and everything won't just be okay, it could actually be *better* than okay.'

It wasn't a difficult decision. One by one, Spicer and his men offered their firearms. McCracken took them, passing them to his own men.

'Now,' he said. 'Where's Bill?'

'In the boardroom,' Spicer replied. 'Waiting for *you*.'

'Excellent.' McCracken slid his Walther back into his shoulder-holster and straightened his jacket. 'All the rest of you . . . go through into the bar. Relax, get yourself a drink, make friends again. Just like me and Wild Bill are going to.'

Chapter 45

'Well, well,' Ivana whispered into Lucy's ear. 'If it isn't the agent of all our misfortunes.'

Unable to draw breath, Lucy clawed at the wire, but couldn't get so much as her little finger underneath it. She was walked backward, so hurriedly that she almost tripped, and then turned roughly around, so that the rest of the room lay before her. It was near enough empty, apart from an old school chair with the cardboard cylinder depicting the bulldog lying on top of it, and in one corner a pair of large and solid plastic drums. These latter were streaked down their sides with a gummy brown residue and had a pair of heavy stone slabs, clearly pried up from the floor, laid over the tops of them as improvised lids. The stink was still unbearable, the walls and ceiling coated with a foul, slimy clag.

With a weird, whickering giggle, Alyssa Torgau emerged from the shadows. She was pale-faced, with sweat-soaked hair and cheeks streaked by mascara, but her eyes glinted with a new, crazy kind of glee. She reached into the cradle and switched off the iPhone, finally silencing the wailing child.

'Like the baby trick? That's how we lured that raggedy old slut with the cats.'

Lucy still couldn't breathe, let alone speak. The strength was seeping out of her, her knees threatening to buckle as her hands dropped to her sides. But the pressure of the ligature, though intense, had slackened a little. They weren't trying to kill her – not yet.

'We didn't lure her down to this very room, you understand.' Alyssa walked towards the two drums, pulling on a pair of heavy-duty plastic gauntlets. 'Just caved her bonce in with a brick and left her in a derelict house. She'll get found eventually, but no one'll care. Just like they never cared about all the homeless ones Dad practised on when *he* was young. We have to have a bit of variation, you see. Like the meathead from the gym. They'll never find him, but if they ever do, it won't be connected. You see, there are lots of reasons for disposing of people, and lots of reasons for doing them all differently. That said –' she patted the nearest of the stone lids '– most of them need to disappear . . . which is why *most* of them end up down here.'

With a big effort, she pushed the lid away, dropping it to the floor, where it landed with a crash. The stink intensified. Lucy gagged, her eyes watering.

'I know . . . horrible, isn't it?' Alyssa said. 'You want to get a whiff of it when it's fresh . . . and unpolluted.'

'Enough gabble,' Ivana said. 'I take it she's alone?'

'Seems to be,' Alyssa replied. 'There's no one else outside.'

Ivana tut-tutted. 'Flying solo again, DC Clayburn? Something tells me you lot do a lot of work off the clock. Very unwise tonight.'

'Just about the biggest mistake you ever made.' Alyssa produced something from behind her back. Through Lucy's blurred vision, it looked like a thick plastic pint-glass, the sort supplied at outdoor wedding events. Grinning, the girl dipped it into the open drum and, when she lifted it out again, it was filled with a brown, soup-like liquor, which fizzled and hissed as she carried it over, holding it at arm's length.

'You've heard it said that whatever doesn't kill you only makes you stronger,' she said. 'Well, this stuff's a bit different. In this case, whatever doesn't kill you . . . turns you into an unrecognisable monstrosity. Not that you'll see it. Those pretty green eyes won't last a second.' She raised the beaker to Lucy's face. 'They'll melt like sugar cubes . . .'

'Hang on, no,' Ivana said, jerking Lucy backward. 'We can't just waste this stuff.'

Alyssa pulled a face. 'We can get more.'

'Yeah, but not straight away. Dad arranged all that. But even then, it was expensive. That's why he didn't let us use it on the dogs. Don't worry, we'll get some more, but until then we conserve what we've got.'

'But she needs to suffer!' Alyssa said this with feeling; she all but spat it.

'She'll suffer.' Ivana twisted the tourniquet, not once but twice, cutting off Lucy's air supply again. Lucy clawed at the wire, barely able to gag.

'Wait!' Alyssa shouted. 'Memento first.'

She moved to a shoulder-high stone shelf, which already looked to be cluttered with bits and pieces: among numerous other items, Lucy saw false teeth, a medal with a faded ribbon, an old-fashioned hearing aid. Alyssa carefully placed the beaker down among them, and then returned and violently searched Lucy's jacket pockets. Almost immediately, she found the wallet containing her warrant card. She flipped it open and showed it to her sister. 'Her pig ID.'

'That'll do nicely,' Ivana said.

Alyssa went back to the shelf and made room among the other oddments. The fumes were visibly affecting her: she coughed, her face gleaming with sweat, her eyes running, though it mainly served to make her triumphant grin seem all the more deranged.

'What do you think of this stuff, DC Clayburn?' She held things up one by one. 'An old guy's hearing aid. The Cat Lady's false teeth.' There was even a pair of colourful running shoes. 'Don't need to tell you who these belonged to. UltraBoost, too. Would've been a shocking waste putting those in the acid.' She folded Lucy's wallet backwards, so that it would stand open on the warrant card, and then placed it directly alongside another that was very similar to it. 'Matching pair, eh? You and that young rookie you sent ahead of you. Looks like we got ourselves a couple of Category As tonight . . . without getting a kicking in the process.'

'We're doing you a favour, showing you all this,' Ivana whispered into Lucy's ear. 'We're letting you know that at least there'll be something left to remember you both by.'

Lucy struggled, only for her captor to twist and tighten the tourniquet. Lucy's eyes goggled, her tongue lolling.

'No – you – don't,' Ivana chuckled. 'I know it hurts, but that's the whole point.'

Alyssa, meanwhile, had moved to the nearest of the two drums and, holding a cloth to her mouth with one hand, now held a thick plastic rod in the other and was using it to stir the contents.

'This stuff's viscous,' she complained. 'It's more like sludge.'

'It's ready for pouring,' Ivana replied. 'Try the other one.'

Alyssa moved to the second drum and, with a huge effort, dislodged its stone lid. Again, the chemical reek filling the air intensified. Lucy felt her eyes stinging.

Alyssa coughed all the more. 'Yeah, this is better . . .'

With Ivana distracted, her grip on the tourniquet lessened slightly, and Lucy could drag some air into her lungs. Revived, she didn't try to yank the ligature loose now, but rent at her own clothes, searching for anything she could.

'If you don't quit that, we'll put you in there while you're still alive!' Ivana snarled, lugging her backward and twisting the wire several times, forcing Lucy down into a painful squat, and bracing her there by jamming a knee into her spine. 'You little bitch! We should do that anyway!'

Over by the second drum, Alyssa tittered as she stirred the brew, though her proximity to a much fresher supply of fluorosulfuric acid was having a real effect on her now. She was blinking repeatedly and coughing hard despite the cloth she'd clamped to her mouth.

'How would you like that, detective?' Ivana hissed. 'A chemical grave . . . *ouch!*'

She hadn't noticed that Lucy had sneaked something from her jacket pocket, flipped off its lid and jammed it backward into the fleshy part of her thigh.

Ivana jumped back from her victim, allowing the ligature to loosen, peering in disbelief at the syringe hanging from just above her knee. Lucy, though groggy with pain and asphyxiation, stuck her fingers under the wire and tore it over her head, before falling forward on hands and knees and scampering away like an exhausted animal.

Behind her, Ivana's cry of shock and outrage became a roar of bestial anger.

'Fucking bitch! What've you stuck me with?'

Lucy swayed to her feet. A few yards away in the corner, Alyssa hadn't yet realised what had happened. She was too busy coughing and spluttering and dabbing her eyes with the cloth. But Ivana was coming fast from behind, so Lucy tottered sideways, blundering against the shelf where the trophies were kept. She spun around to fend off an attack. And just in time, because Ivana, having yanked a brutal-looking knife from her webbing, now charged, howling. The girl didn't know that she'd been shot full of heroin, but it was taking effect rapidly. She stumbled suddenly, losing balance. Lucy threw herself aside and Ivana crashed chin-first onto the shelf – just where the beaker of acid was balanced.

It flew against the wall, bounced back and drenched her face and hair.

Lucy could only back away in morbid fascination. She was still unsteady, her throat aching abominably, but for a couple of seconds the fate of Ivana Torgau was the whole of her world. She'd dropped to the floor instantly, and now writhed and screamed, flopping over and over. Was this due to the heroin overdose, or the corrosive substance by which her features were already dissolving into a gluey red/green mask?

'Vana?' a confused voice said.

Lucy backed away all the more, as Alyssa, eyes streaming, mouth covered in phlegm, came staggering across the room.

'*Ivana!*' Her confusion gave way to utter horror as Ivana, or what remained of her, came to rest on her back, jerking spasmodically, ragged breaths wheezing from a mouth that was little more now than a melting, frothing hole.

Lucy had seen enough. She lurched for the nearest door. Instinctively, Alyssa whirled after her, snarling as she pulled something from her harness. As Lucy closed the door behind her, there was a monstrous detonation and a massive hole punched through the middle of it. The strength of desperation flooded her limbs as she threw herself blindly along a dark, brick passage. She had no idea where she was going. She turned a corner, just as the door behind her crashed open and Alyssa stood silhouetted in the crimson light, aiming the gun with both hands. With a *boom* and a flash, a fountain of dirt and brick-dust exploded from the wall close to the point where Lucy had just been.

'*You cop bitch!*' the crazed girl shrieked.

Huffing for breath, sweat whipping off her, Lucy mounted a steep flight of stone stairs. Ten treads up, she rounded a switchback corner and mounted another flight, and at the top of that another flight, and then another.

'Oh God,' she whimpered, weary beyond belief.

Alyssa came racing up after her. She fired a third shot, and a fourth. They were wild, uncoordinated, the heavy slugs careening from wall to wall in the tight stairwell. Lucy could only keep going. But she was hurt and her energy flagging, and her nemesis was pursuing with the strength of the insane.

Just over two hundred yards off, Sister Cassie jolted awake in the front passenger seat of a small car. It was not a happy waking. She had the shakes again and was damp with the sweat of withdrawal, and at first, she was too stupefied to realise where she was or why.

But then she recognised the interior of the vehicle, and saw the tall iron gates ajar just in front. Then, the noise that had woken her sounded again – a distant booming of gunfire.

'Oh, my goodness!' she breathed.

Reluctantly, because it was always so much easier when you were tired and strung out to simply sit there and vegetate, she opened the passenger door and slithered through. Once she was outside, she had to lean against the car.

Gradually, the memories of that day came back to her.

Yes, it was easier to do nothing, but there was one thing Sister Cassie had never divested herself of, even through all these years of hardship and sadness, and that was a sense of duty to her fellow men.

She heard it again: the booming reports of a gun.

'Get help,' she said, working her way around the front of the Jimny to the driving door. 'That's it. Go and get help.'

She clambered in behind the wheel. The key still hung from the ignition. She turned it, and the car came to life.

'Go and get help . . .'

But from where? Who would listen to her? And how long would it take?

More shots thundered.

She tried to make sense of the controls in front of her. Could she even drive this car? She hadn't driven for years, and it looked very different from the vehicle she'd learned in.

She placed her hands on the wheel and depressed the clutch, pushing it into gear.

What had Lucy done when driving?

Sister Cassie threw her mind back, and she remembered. She'd seen everything.

But what would Lucy do *now*?

One thing was sure, the ex-nun knew. She wouldn't run away.

Chapter 46

There was a door at the top of the stairs, but it was locked. Only by a single bolt, but this was stiff. Lucy struggled with it frantically as feet clattered up the penultimate flight behind her. The bolt came free, she yanked the door open and hurled herself out – and with a thunderous *bang*, another round was discharged, the top left corner of the door exploding.

She ran forward, panting, a fresh breeze relieving her nose and throat and her stinging eyes. The sky, a blaze of moon and stars after the red-tinged darkness below, dizzied her, but she tottered on, feet drumming on what felt like tarmac laid over wooden boards. She realised that a tall, tapering structure standing fifty yards to her left was the steeple. That was a shock, but it only really struck her that she was on the care home's roof when she half-tripped over a curved aluminium hood capping the top of a ventilation shaft.

How safe it was to be up here, she didn't know. It felt flimsy, the pitch-covered boards cracking and groaning under her feet – and then suddenly ending in three rows of bricks rendered greasy with moss, and beyond those a sheer drop. Lucy only just stopped in time, teetering on the edge, the vast moonlit spread of the ornamental lake lying in front of her. Directly below, some eighty feet down, was the driveway. About ten yards to her left, a couple of feet beneath the parapet, a stone gryphon-like creature, with a curved back and beaked head, jutted menacingly out, its upper portions caked in bird droppings. Some ten yards further on, there was a Tolkienesque goblin, and beyond that, maybe thirty feet down, she saw the top of the stone pediment on which the care home clock was displayed.

'You bitch!' came a voice strained with exhaustion.

Lucy turned and found Alyssa Torgau limping towards her from the shattered door.

Before Lucy could speak, Alyssa pointed her pistol one-handed and pumped its trigger. A succession of metallic clicks followed. The girl's swollen, sweat-soaked face twisted with fury and disgust, but she threw the empty gun away and came on regardless, this time reaching into the combat webbing at her back and pulling out a huge knife. It was the same type of weapon that Ivana had wielded, the same type of weapon Alyssa herself had produced in the cellars at St Clement's, with a medieval-style cross-guard and a heavy blade serrated down one edge. Alyssa raised it in her right hand as she approached, holding it upright, a gesture designed to show that she knew how to use it.

Lucy had been considering fighting the teenager, trying to overpower her physically. But she had no doubt that Alyssa's father had trained her well. Plus, there was this knife.

'I'm going to enjoy this,' the girl drooled. 'I'm so going to enjoy this.'

Lucy darted right, trying to run along the narrow band of bricks edging the rooftop, but her feet slipped, and she almost pitched into the abyss, only preventing it by sliding to a stop and windmilling her arms. Alyssa continued her pursuit at a walking pace but snickered. 'You are so out of your depth . . .'

438

Lucy was starting to think this was true. It was impossible to describe how tired she felt. She had no weapons with which to resist. All she could do was turn and back away, veering across the tar-coated planking, hoping to God that it wouldn't simply collapse and drop her down into some empty, dust-filled dormitory.

When it didn't, she ran again, heading across the roof towards the other side. Who knew, she might find the top of a fire-escape stair. Or perhaps there'd be ivy she could clamber down.

Yeah, right.

She came to the next parapet more quickly than she'd expected, finding herself high above a central courtyard, where vegetation grew wild and jungle-like from a central quadrangle surrounded by paved walkways and benches. Again, it was an eighty-foot drop, and there was no means of descent. The nearest window ledge was a good twenty feet down, and no more than a couple of inches wide.

'Why don't you do it?' Alyssa taunted her, advancing across the roof in slow pursuit, breathing more easily now, clearly regaining her stamina, and still holding her blade aloft. 'It'd be quicker than what I've got planned for you.'

Lucy ran again, awkwardly, with weary, clumping footsteps, in no real direction. The structure of the steeple lay dead ahead, but before she could even reach it, she spied another level of roof, made from sloping slate-work atop a brick wall at least twelve feet high, which completely barred her path. Again, she changed direction, hobbling alongside the wall, slapping her hand on the bricks to steady herself. Glancing right, she saw Alyssa moving parallel to her some twenty yards away.

'Alyssa,' Lucy stammered. 'You have to be mad to keep doing this. What do you think you've got to gain?'

'It's simple,' the girl replied. 'We carry on where the old man left off.'

'There is no *we* any more. Can't you see?'

'You'll pay for *that* too, you prize bitch!'

'For God's sake,' Lucy said. 'You're still young enough to wriggle out of this. You're only . . . what, nineteen? It'll be easy to sell the story that you were led, that you were influenced by an evil man.'

'You dare talk about him like that!'

Lucy stopped trying. She needed to save her breath anyway. Plus, it was all lies. Alyssa was so deeply embedded in this horror, and so far into the age of adult responsibility, that it was difficult to envisage her drawing anything other than a full-life sentence – and at nineteen that was a long time. So, the options were still fight or flight. Since she was unarmed, the first was out of the question, so she ran again. But this time forward instead of away, heading straight for her tormentor – who halted, confused, swapping the blade around to wield it dagger-like – but then swerving left, putting all her strength into one final dash, hoping to arc around the girl and make it to the steps leading back down to that hellish vault.

Alyssa needed only to run sideways to intercept, but with a crunching *crack*, the girl's right foot broke through the tarred planking, dropping her down past her ankle.

Unable to believe her fortune, Lucy ran on, straightening up for the open doorway, which beckoned only fifty yards away. And then, incredibly, she too lost her footing, tripping over a flap of dried tar. She went sprawling, landing on her hands, face and chest, the blow so brutal that it knocked the wind out of her.

Fateful seconds passed before she could lever herself up and look around. Alyssa had already hacked herself free with the blade and was only a few yards away, coming more slowly, more prudently, but still smiling, still hefting the knife.

'Sweet Jesus . . .' Lucy breathed.

'Don't blaspheme,' Alyssa cackled. 'You'll be meeting him in a minute.' She held the blade higher, the moon catching it, flashing silver. 'Well . . . maybe a bit longer than that.'

And then a police siren sounded.

Not in the distance, but very close by.

Not only that, there was a light-show. A blue radiance was suddenly swirling on the lake in a repeating pattern.

Alyssa dashed past Lucy towards the parapet, which creaked loudly when she halted on it.

Lucy glanced up and around, startled.

'No!' Alyssa screeched, her shoulders hunched with disbelieving rage. 'No! I don't believe it! I don't . . .'

The aged bricks beneath her feet creaked again. Then one of them noisily cracked.

'Alyssa!' Lucy shouted.

The bricks gave way.

With a squawk of terror, Alyssa tottered where she stood, half turning as mortar and masonry visibly crumbled under her – and then fell from sight.

Amazement lending her extra strength, Lucy sat bolt upright. Breathing hard, she scrambled towards the roof's edge on all fours. The first thing she saw when she reached it and gazed down, was her own Jimny – halted about thirty yards along from the main building. Its blue lights still swirled, but its siren had ceased.

'Sister.' She almost laughed. 'Oh, my lovely Sister Cassie.'

'You cow . . .' came a choked rasp.

Lucy glanced downward, and to her astonishment, saw the Torgau girl hanging one-handed from the head of a gargoyle. Even as Lucy watched, the clenching fingers slid through bird-filth, losing their grasp.

'Quickly . . . *here*!' Lucy flattened her body against the roof and thrust her own right hand down. 'Grab hold.'

Alyssa reached up, and struck at the extended arm with her

knife, slashing a deep wound across the back of the hand. Lucy yanked it back with a yelp both of pain and astonishment.

'You slag!' the deranged girl snarled, her face a mass of sweat and straining muscle. 'You cop slag!'

She slipped loose, but even as she descended, at incredible speed, she flung the knife upward. It twirled past Lucy's head, missing it only by inches.

A split second later, there was a crunch of bone and flesh.

More numb and exhausted than she'd ever been, Lucy rose slowly to her feet. She couldn't take her eyes off the gory spectacle down on the drive.

'Like you said, love,' she muttered, 'quicker than what we'd have planned for you.'

When Frank McCracken sat down at one end of the board-room table, the room itself was empty, aside from Wild Bill Pentecost, who was already seated at the opposite end. The Chairman was even greyer-faced than usual, and unchar-acteristically ruffled.

'All this over a breach of protocol, Frank?' he said.

Gingerly, McCracken adjusted his sling. 'If only it were, Bill . . . I reckon we could shake hands and walk away again.'

Pentecost pondered that, but not for long. 'Just tell me what's really going on.'

'You obviously haven't heard yet. But you will soon.' McCracken regarded him long and hard. 'Detective Constable Lucy Clayburn. You know her?'

Pentecost frowned. 'She gave me some grief at the hospital.'

'And you put a contract out on her last year.'

'Ahhh.' Now, the Chairman seemed to recall. 'I thought the name was familiar.'

'You ought to have remembered it, Bill . . . that trio of numbnut freelancers you sent blew it totally.'

'In retrospect, I should have sent the Ripsaw Man.'

'From what I'm seeing this year, his operation wasn't much better.'

'I'm losing my touch, then? Is that what this is? I'm putting my trust in people I shouldn't, Frank?'

'Yes. But that's not what this is.'

'Now, wait a minute . . . wait a minute.' Pentecost looked thoughtful; he even raised a forefinger. 'Clayburn? You tried to get me to call that contract off, if I remember rightly. In this very room, you tried to persuade me otherwise.'

'I tried to appeal to your common sense. Yeah.'

'She was connected to that Red-Headed League investigation, wasn't she?'

McCracken nodded. 'That's right.'

'And then, when those idiots missed the target, you negotiated a deal with the Robbery Squad . . . made it all go away.'

McCracken nodded again.

Pentecost gave one of his rare cold smiles. 'You were a busy boy on our behalf, back then, weren't you, Frank?'

'Maybe I'm a better team-player than you've always thought, Bill.'

'And especially on behalf of this DC Clayburn.'

'Maybe I'm a better father than *I* always thought.'

Pentecost stared at him confusedly. Then he looked amused again, as if everything was now explained. 'You've got a daughter, Frank? In the filth?'

'Shocking, isn't it?'

'What's shocking is how you managed to sit on it for so long.'

'It's not been as long as you think.' McCracken adjusted his posture again. 'I only found out myself a couple of years ago. But it's been difficult, I'll admit.'

'Do her gaffers know about this?'

'They do now . . . as of today.'

'Which is why *you've* also decided to break the news?'

'She left me with no choice.'

'And this is something you think we couldn't have worked out?'

McCracken smiled grimly. 'Let's not pretend, Bill. You'd never have trusted me again. And I'd never have trusted you . . . especially when my back was turned. I mean, I'd have struggled to trust you anyway, purely on the grounds that you green-lit Torgau to send his dipshit daughters to do O'Grady. You think I wouldn't twig it . . . that a pair of newbies would leave evidence linking the hit to me? Not conclusively maybe, but putting me under police surveillance for years to come, paralysing me as a contributor. Making me completely expendable.'

Pentecost shrugged, half-smiled again. 'At this level of command, Frank, it's the prudent ones you've got to be wary of. The sensible ones, the good advice-givers. Because blokes with brains are rarely content to be servants for long. Though I'm not sure that even your big brain is going to do you much good from now on. You having a copper for a daughter . . . who'd a' thought it, eh? That's the kind of problem that won't be resolved simply by me disappearing, you know.'

'That depends on the rest of the guys,' McCracken said. 'They're all on their way here now. Some may already be here. We'll need to see how they respond to the new, typed-out deal that Mick Shallicker will shortly be circulating among them.'

'So . . . this is a complete change of management?'

'Certainly is. And under the new administration, contributions to central funds will be far less onerous.'

Pentecost looked scornful. 'You really think it's that simple?'

'We're talking the likes of Benny B and Nick Merryweather, Bill . . . yes, it'll be that simple.'

444

'Just out of interest, how much?'

'Prior to today, we each paid seventy-five per cent. You then raised it to eighty-five. I'm only looking for fifty.'

Pentecost snorted. 'You enrich those cretins, Frank, and you empower them. They'll end up building their own princedoms again. Suddenly, we'll be back in a twelve-way war.'

'Not *we*, Bill.'

There was a lengthy silence.

'And that's your final word?' the Chairman said.

McCracken nodded.

'I'm sorry to hear that.' Pentecost took the grip of the sawn-off double-barrelled shotgun that he always kept screwed to the underside of the boardroom table, swivelled it lengthways and pulled the trigger twice.

Nothing happened.

Until McCracken slapped his good hand on the table, leaving two cartridges there.

The men gazed at each other, faces graven in rock. Pentecost finally cracked another half-smile. This time he seemed genuinely amused. 'I should have wondered why you were waiting in here alone after last Thursday's meeting.'

'Yes, you should.' McCracken drew the Walther from inside his jacket. 'Of all your recent errors, Bill – and there've been plenty – that was the worst.'

Outside in the lobby, Mick Shallicker waited. Some of the other underbosses were still to arrive, and those already here he'd ushered into the lounge. He was standing there alone when a single pistol-shot echoed from the boardroom.

A second passed, and then its door opened a few inches.

'Mick,' came Frank McCracken's voice. 'We need a clean-up crew. Meanwhile, start sending my fellow directors through to the office. One at a time.'

445

Chapter 47

By the early hours of the morning, the whole of Santa Magdalena had become a crime scene. The dilapidated structure of the care home glimmered blue as innumerable beacons swirled lazily along its drive, maybe a dozen police vehicles intermingled with CSI vans. The main building had already been cordoned off with incident tape, while an outer cordon had been deployed around the perimeter of the grounds, including the lake. Nobody moved in the inner circle unless they were clad neck-to-toe in Tyvek. A few yards to the right of the building's main doors, a couple of detectives and medical personnel stood in discussion alongside the unmoving shape of Alyssa Torgau. Near to them, but outside the inner cordon, seemingly oblivious to the presence of the corpse, DSU Nehwal and a couple of her oppos from Serious pored over a collapsible trestle-table, on top of which a number of foolscap sheets had been spread out, all now encased in protective plastic. The cardboard cylinder bearing the bulldog logo, from which they'd been carefully extricated, was propped alongside them, also inside an evidence sack.

'We've just heard from the hospital,' someone said.

Lucy glanced up from where she'd been sitting glassy-eyed

on the low wall at the edge of the water. Beardmore stood there. He'd removed his Tyvek coveralls and was now straightening his lapels and the knot of his tie.

'Tessa's going to be okay,' he said. 'Severe concussion, that's all.'

'I hope she's not going to get into any trouble, sir?'

He shrugged. 'She shouldn't have come up here alone.'

'Yeah, but from what I've heard, the van that led her out here was running under a duplicated plate rather than a dummy one. There was an actual vehicle of that make and model, with that same registration mark, owned by a legit firm. She had no cause to assume she was tracking a wrong un.'

He pondered this.

'She was just following her nose,' Lucy added. 'Having a bit of a snoop. Isn't that what good detectives do?'

'She could've called it in when she heard the baby.'

'Come on, sir. Moment of panic. She probably would've done anyway, but they clobbered her as soon as she ran inside.' She shook her head grimly. 'It fooled *me* too, I'll be honest.'

'Yeah, well, to tell the truth, Lucy . . . it's *you* that's giving me the headache. Not Tessa.'

She glanced up at him.

'Aren't you supposed to be on sick leave?' he said.

'Oh,' she sighed. 'It's a long story, sir.'

'And what's all this "sir" business?'

'Sorry, Stan. I'm not quite with it.'

'You don't believe in making my life easy, do you?' he said. 'How can I put you forward for a commendation when you weren't even supposed to be here?'

Even in her current state of mind, Lucy was surprised by that. 'A commendation?'

'You may have closed a significant number of cases. That

trophy-shelf alone links these guys to quite a few deaths and disappearances.'

'We'll never know how many, though, will we?' she retorted, too weary to feel real anger, but disgruntled with just about everyone, including herself. 'That shelf'll help us a bit. I've already seen the relics of Harry Hopkins and Lorna Cunningham . . . that's sick enough, but at least it provides proof of who they were and what happened to them. But that was because they had families who were concerned. What about the homeless those two nutcases practised on? How many of *them* were there? How many were even missed?'

'Lucy—' he tried to interrupt.

'By the sound of it, Torgau preyed on them in exactly the same way, for practice, God knows how many decades ago—'

'Lucy!'

'And they didn't always melt down the evidence. According to Alyssa Torgau, there were others they killed who they just dumped, or hid in ruined buildings. More randomers, Stan, targets of total convenience . . .'

'*And it's over!*' he said firmly. 'Because of you . . . yeah?'

'Because of me . . .?' Momentarily, the words meant nothing to her.

'Who else?'

Lucy glanced towards the twisted body of Alyssa Torgau. Several streams of blood had trickled across the gravel before congealing. 'If it's such a win, why do I feel so lousy?'

'Probably because you're a decent person,' Beardmore said. 'Carnage is a never a cause for celebration. But that doesn't mean this isn't a result. How's the hand, anyway?'

Lucy examined her thickly bandaged paw, still baffled that it had happened at all. 'Eighteen stitches . . . but I've still got to go to Casualty. They want to give me some shots.'

'Sensible precaution.'

From somewhere to their right, a pair of female voices intruded. They looked round and saw Sister Cassie being ushered into a CID car by Kirsty Banks. At long last, they'd pinned her down for an official interview.

'Our nun friend again,' Beardmore commented.

'She *is* a friend,' Lucy replied. 'And an observant one. She saw me operate the blues and twos at some roadworks on the way in here. And thank God she did.'

'She doesn't seem any the worse for wear, I must say.'

'She's a tough one, that's for sure. I didn't let her go down into the cellar, though.' Lucy swallowed in revulsion. 'That place would have tested even *her* faith in God.'

'This girl who got the acid in her face . . . I don't know whether she'll ever be fit for interview.'

Lucy shrugged. 'I'm amazed she's even alive.'

'You can probably thank the heroin for that. Knocked her out cold, while that stuff burned her almost to the bone.'

Lucy brooded on the human stew in the plastic drums. 'She got off easily.'

'DI Beardmore!' someone called, and he made his apologies to Lucy, heading across the drive to speak with the FMO.

Briefly, Lucy lowered her head, trying to shut out the lights and noise. She felt nauseous but put that down to shock rather than the chemical fumes she'd been exposed to, though the ambulance crew had wanted her to get that checked out at hospital too. They'd told her that the ultra-concentrated acid in the cellar had likely been weakened by the pollutants – in other words the multiple organic remains that now clotted it. If it had been fresh and uncontaminated, just being in that room would probably have blinded and poisoned her.

'Well, miss . . .' someone else said.

Lucy got tiredly to her feet. 'Ma'am?'

Priya Nehwal's stony expression was as merciless as ever. 'You've got some explaining to do,' she said.

449

'I'm terribly sorry, ma'am.' Lucy didn't see what she could do other than apologise. She doubted that even one of Nehwal's infamous bollockings would make her feel any worse at present. 'I had to keep going . . . I had to prove that I'm still onside.'

'That admission itself, after I had specifically ordered you to go off duty, could be sackable.'

'Then . . . fuck it. Yeah, that's it.' Lucy couldn't keep the charade going. She plonked herself back on the wall. 'Fuck it. Give me the heave-ho, why don't you? Christ . . . you'd be doing me a favour. You think I'm enjoying this bloody abattoir—'

'Enough!' Nehwal said firmly. 'Don't make things worse for yourself.'

'Well, I'm sorry, ma'am, but I'm a bit dizzy at present. I mean, on one hand you want to kick me out—'

'I didn't say that.'

'And on the other, DI Beardmore wants to commend me.'

'And you deserve a commendation.'

Lucy regarded her uncertainly.

The DSU still seemed unimpressed, but perhaps had softened a little. 'If you'd given me a chance to speak, I'd have told you that myself.'

'Look, ma'am . . . I'm sorry,' was all Lucy could say, again. 'I know you won't send me packing. I know you wouldn't do that even if I hadn't made this score. But to be frank, I'm not sure I care any more. I mean, some future I've got in the job, eh . . . related to a major player in the Northwest underworld? I might be estranged from him, I might hate the ground he walks on . . . but that shadow of suspicion will follow me around throughout my career, won't it?'

Nehwal glanced back towards the trestle-table and its heap of plastic-wrapped paperwork. 'Less so after tonight,

450

possibly. That cardboard tube you directed us to. The one with the bulldog on it. You saw me inspecting the contents?'

Lucy nodded glumly. 'I hope it was useful.'

'It appears to be a kind of hand-written memoir . . . an account of Martin Torgau's entire career as an assassin working exclusively for the Crew.'

Lucy looked up slowly.

'It details almost every murder he's ever committed, those he could remember . . . going way back to his earliest days.'

Initially, Lucy couldn't respond. This was too good to be true. 'Why would he create such a record?'

Nehwal shrugged. 'Your guess is as good as mine. Maybe as a form of insurance against the Crew ever turning on him. Perhaps as a training guide for his daughters. There's some grisly detail in there. And making his daughters au fait with every aspect of the family trade seems to have been his focus these last few years.'

'Does it name and shame the bastards who hired him?'

'Well . . .' Nehwal was careful how she replied to this. 'We've not gone through it closely yet, but some players are mentioned by name. Not that it will necessarily be useful against them. Don't get me wrong, it's a treasure trove in terms of new leads appertaining to a number of open cases dating back several decades. We've already dispatched search teams to look for key missing remains. But in terms of convictions, well . . . when you've only got the written word of a dead man, who was also a psychopath and mass murderer in his own right. Plus, you know what top-level mobsters are like. They've got the best legal representation, they've got fake witnesses coming out of their ears, foolproof alibis, the lot.' She shrugged again. 'We can certainly bring in a few Crew underbosses for questioning, but whether it'll go further than that . . . who can say?'

Lucy nodded.

451

'Of course –' Nehwal looked sternly down at her '– the question you really want answering is whether Frank McCracken is mentioned?'

Lucy glanced up at her. She didn't deny it.

'Not, as I've seen so far,' Nehwal said. 'Though, as I say, I haven't gone through it with a fine-tooth comb. Your father must have been a smart guy to reach the level he has, Lucy. If he ever did use Torgau, all the contacts were likely made by underlings, all fees paid in cash so there'd be no electronic trails to follow. On which subject, the death of Martin Torgau himself still needs investigating.' She arched an eyebrow. 'Didn't you say you thought you recognised one of the team that hit him?'

Lucy pondered this. She hadn't seen Mick Shallicker's face, of course, but had clearly recognised him by his voice and height. Even so, she replied: 'I didn't see anyone well enough to identify them, ma'am.'

Nehwal's face turned stony again.

'I'm sorry,' Lucy said. 'They were all masked, so how could I have recognised anyone?'

'Only yesterday, you told me—'

'I was wrong. Probably because I was so shaken up.'

Lucy was adamant about that, at least. If the Greater Manchester Police were going to make life difficult for her now, and they would in some shape or form, she was damned if she was going to make it easy for them. Besides, she owed Shallicker. Twice now, he'd saved her life. That wouldn't always give him a pass – he was a brute criminal, a murderer – but on this occasion, his target had been the Ripsaw Man. She could hardly judge him for that.

'I must take you at your word, of course,' Nehwal said coolly. 'But if it ever comes to light that your father was involved . . .'

'Do you seriously think he would be?' Lucy interrupted.

452

'He's a top dog, isn't he? Haven't you just said that he's virtually immune from prosecution? Is he then going to endanger all that by killing someone right in front of a police officer's eyes?'

Nehwal considered this long and hard. She still didn't seem happy. 'I know you're not supposed to be on duty at present. But you're not going anywhere, okay.'

It wasn't a question.

'I need to go to the hospital,' Lucy said.

'The medics have patched you up, so it can wait.' Nehwal edged away. 'Given that you've already, very inconveniently, started forgetting things, I want everything that's happened this last couple of days written down quickly . . . before you forget that too.'

Lucy nodded resignedly as the DSU stalked off.

With Sister Cassie still making statements, Lucy drove back towards the nick alone, swinging by her bungalow at Cuthbertson Court first, just to freshen up a little. A shower and a quick change of clothes later, she was heading out again, when her landline began to ring.

One glance at the clock showed that it was almost three in the morning. Clearly, this wasn't the kind of call she could just ignore.

'Sorry about the hour,' Frank McCracken said. 'But I've been trying you on your mobile, and I was getting worried.'

'You don't need to worry about me,' Lucy replied. 'Though I must admit, I'm surprised to hear that *you're* still alive.'

McCracken was on the penthouse suite balcony at the Astarte Hotel, a large malt whisky and soda in his hand. The entire city centre was spread below him, its glittering streets and ritzy premises, the shops, bars, nightclubs, the temples of finance, the trendy boutiques, the high-class restaurants. It was quiet now, but the traffic would soon be thronging again, the commercial life of Manchester throbbing to its own tireless, ever-prosperous beat. It was a heady moment to look down on it from such a height; it almost made him giddy.

'Yes, I'm alive,' he replied. 'And likely to stay that way for some time. You see, I've handled things at my end, Lucy. I'm just wondering how you're doing?'

'I'm not flavour of the month,' her voice replied sulkily. 'But I don't think I've lost my job. At least, not yet.'

'If you ever do, you can come and work for me.'

Rather to his surprise, she chuckled.

'You think that's funny?' he said.

'No. I'm just amused that you're being so nice about it when my own side are likely to give me the cold shoulder for the next ten years.'

'They say blood's thicker than water.'

'And that's the only reason for your attitude, is it?'

'Not quite. I'll be honest, Lucy . . . I reckon you've helped out with a real knotty problem. You see, your reckless action has provoked me into doing something that has needed doing for some considerable time.'

'I'm not sure I want to know what that is.'

'No, best if you don't.' He sipped his malt. 'But you've got some rewards coming, my love.'

There was a brief pause. 'What are you talking about?'

'No doubt we've got some heat coming our way, thanks to the Ripsaw Man,' McCracken said. 'But internally at least, I'm in what you might call an unassailable position. So I don't think anyone will object if I drop a few names your way.'

Another pause. 'What do you mean, exactly?'

He smiled, as though she was right in front of him. 'You'll need the arrests, won't you? Make sure your lot understand that you're still one of the good guys.'

454

'Oh, I see. So, anyone you want off the streets, anyone who doesn't get with the programme . . . I get to lock them up, and the problem goes away?'

'And we'll both be happy. What's not to love, eh?'

'You don't think the rest of your people will see it differently, Dad?'

'Maybe that was part of the package I sold them. How useful it can be, me having a copper for a daughter, rather than how risky.'

'Well my people won't be so forgiving.' Her voice thickened with anger. 'Not when they twig where it's all coming from.'

'Will it matter what the grunts say if you're Manchester's top thief-taker, if you've put more villains away than the average chief constable's had three-course lunches?'

A silence followed. McCracken wished he could believe that she'd be mulling it over, working out the pros and cons, and ultimately, inevitably, figuring that the advantages outweighed the disadvantages. But he knew that wouldn't be the case, because, in the end, his daughter was actually very like him. She was a battler, and she had pride and ambition, and her own code of ethics. The fact that she'd be jailing criminals purely because other criminals didn't want them on the street was hardly the crime-fighting career she'd dreamed of.

'You've not had that crusader spirit knocked out of you yet, Lucy?' he wondered.

'It's not about being a crusader, Dad. It's about being able to live with myself.'

'Having overly high expectations of yourself is often the route to failure.'

'We'll see.'

'So, we're still at daggers drawn?'

'There can't be any other way,' she replied. 'Look, you do your thing and I'll do mine, and sometimes our paths will cross, and sometimes it may even suit us to scratch each other's backs . . . I've had *that* much of the crusader spirit knocked out of me. But let's not pretend we're a real family, eh? Because I find that very objectionable.'

'In times of crisis who else can you rely on?'

Another silence followed. She was a realist too, his daughter. She ought to know that she'd need all the help she could get in the months ahead, and who else was offering her a hand of friendship?

'I'm sorry, Dad,' she said, and she actually sounded as if she meant that. 'But if we cross swords when we're about our business, I'll have to take you down. It may even be that that's the *only* outcome possible for me . . . if I want to have a genuine police career.'

'As I say, Lucy, those are some high expectations. Don't be surprised if you crash and burn.'

'That's the other possible outcome,' she replied, and she cut the call.

A Stranger is just a killer you haven't met . . .

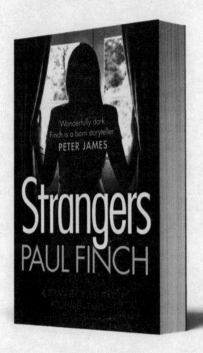

Love PC Lucy Clayburn? Then why not head back to where it all began with the first book in the series.

Do you know who's watching you?

PC Lucy Clayburn faces one of the toughest
cases of her life – and one which will prove
once and for all whether blood really is
thicker than water . . .

Love Paul Finch? Then why not try his Detective Mark Heckenburg series?

Dark, terrifying and unforgettable. *Stalkers* will keep fans of Stuart MacBride and M.J. Arlidge looking over their shoulder.

A vicious serial killer is holding the country
to ransom, publicly – and gruesomely –
murdering his victims.

The next Detective Mark Heckenburg thriller
from bestseller Paul Finch.

**DS Mark 'Heck' Heckenburg is used
to bloodbaths. But nothing will
prepare him for this.**

Brace yourself as you turn the pages
of a living nightmare.

Welcome to The Killing Club.

As a brutal winter takes hold of the
Lake District, a prolific serial killer stalks
the fells. And for Heck, the signs are
all too familiar . . .

The fourth unputdownable book in the DS
Mark Heckenburg series. A killer thriller for
fans of Stuart MacBride and *Luther*.

Heck needs to watch his back.
Because someone's watching him . . .

Get hooked on Heck: the maverick cop who
knows no boundaries. A grisly whodunit,
perfect for fans of Stuart MacBride
and *Luther*.

Is your home safe?

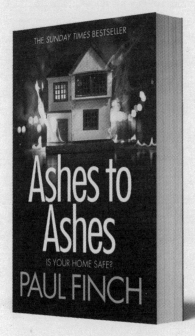

Heck is back in an unforgettable crime thriller, perfect for fans of M.J. Arlidge and Stuart MacBride. Read the *Sunday Times* bestseller now.